UNTITLED FOR NOW

This is a work of fiction. Any characters and events, aside from the portrayal of Billy Ray and the loss of my daughter, in this novel are fictitious based on real life events.

UNTITLED FOR NOW

Copyright © 2023 by Desiree Moore

All rights reserved.

No part of this book may be reproduced in any form or by any electronic or mechanical means, including information storage and retrieval systems, without written permission from the author, except for the use of brief quotations in a book review.

A Desiree Moore Books publication

ISBN 979-8-9880206-0-8

To my beloveds, my muses, my daughters,
I tried to break them all — the curses that plague our family, but I couldn't.
My hope is that I broke enough for you to finish the job.
I love you,
Mom

CONTENT WARNINGS

This book addresses the following topics: animal cruelty (the cats make it out okay), domestic violence, child loss, murder, suicide/suicide ideation, an explicit sexual scene, trivializing mental illness, child abuse, and drug use/addiction. These themes are portrayed to shed light on the complexities of human experiences. However, if you feel these themes may negatively impact your well-being, choosing not to continue reading is perfectly valid.

UNTITLED FOR NOW

DESIREE MOORE

FOREWORD

As you delve into the pages of this book, I want to address some important truths that lie within the narrative. While the suffering, grief, and guilt that permeate these pages are genuine reflections of my journey through life, it is crucial to understand that this is a work of fiction based on real-life events.

Within the narrative, you will encounter characters and events that may have been inspired by people I know and my life story. These characters and events were altered or fictionalized to serve artistic and dramatic purposes. I have taken creative liberties to heighten the narrative, simplify parts of my journey, and safeguard the privacy of those involved. Any similarities to actual persons should be considered coincidental and not a reflection of any authentic person. It is essential to regard this book as a work of fiction rather than an exact representation of my life or the lives of others.

However, there are several specific elements of this story I want to call attention to as being reflective of the reality I have lived. First, the heartbreaking truth is the chapters detailing my daughter's death very closely resemble my honest recollection. The pain of losing her is a wound that will forever linger in my heart. It is a truth I grapple with every day.

In addition, I would like to pay tribute to Billy Ray, the taxi driver who saved my life. While many characters in this book have been altered or created for storytelling purposes, Billy Ray is an actual person who played a crucial role during a pivotal moment in my life. His mentorship and selflessness are a testament to the compassion found in unexpected places.

While these specific events are true, it is essential to remember that the overall narrative of this book is a work of fiction. By blending elements of fact and fiction, I strive to convey the depth of my emotions and experiences while respecting the privacy of the individuals involved and maintaining the artistic integrity of the story.

Authoring this book has been a profound and deeply personal journey for me. I intended to share my subjective truth, explore the complexities of grief and guilt, and craft a compelling narrative that resonates with readers.

With love and care,

Desiree Moore

Chapter 1

Before Helen Lost Her Memory

Dirt cascaded from a sun-bleached toy shovel. I poured the soft earth over my small, pudgy toes. Each scoop of the loose soil cooled the tops of my feet, beaten red by the North Carolina summer heat. The wind chimes hanging from our small wooden porch swayed to their song. I inhaled a deep breath of freshly cut grass and dandelion weeds. I was supposed to start kindergarten soon, or so Daddy said. Until then, we had to soak up as much summer as we could.

The impact between the screen door and the metal frame made me turn to see Daddy emerge from our small trailer house. Set among a bed of overgrown weeds, our metal-sided home was where the sun shone the brightest, leaving its paint-chipped sides exposed. Daddy wore cut-off jean shorts and a blue cotton tank with a white stripe across the middle. He had a dark brown mustache that matched his thick, wild hair. Two glasses of lemonade sat in each of his palms, and beads of condensation covered the frosted glass like dewdrops on the morning leaves.

Taking a seat next to me, Daddy handed me a glass, and we braced our backs against the thick trunk of a pear tree. We sipped the sweet, tart juice, both of us silently enjoying the early afternoon breeze. A bit of the liquid ran down the corner of my mouth. Daddy smiled and wiped it away with the collar of my shirt. I rested my legs over a root growing out of the ground. Between the trees and Daddy's house was what I liked to call my secret garden, like in the book Daddy sometimes read to me before bedtime. It was our very special and very secret place.

Spots of sunlight showed through the swaying leaves and danced on the ground where we sat. I watched them, mesmerized by their movements.

Then a crash of thunder erupted from above. The small white clouds that decorated the sky became large and dark. A crack of lightning shone in the distance. The jagged bolt lit up an area where the clouds had obscured the sun's rays from penetrating the earth. Daddy and I scrambled from the ground, running out from underneath the tree. I tilted my chin up and welcomed the fat, warm raindrops. The world spun around me as I teetered from foot to foot—around and around I went. My hands splayed wide from my sides until Daddy's hand caught one of my arms. His touch was intentional, and I trusted him enough to stop and listen. His voice carried over the thunder as he yelled about how we didn't want to be too near a tree in case lightning struck. We moved into a clearing, out of danger's way, and together, we twirled, letting the water dampen our clothes and leach the summer heat from our skin.

Present Day

The day Daddy and I twirled in a rainstorm is the last memory I can hold on to. I know I'm Helen Joy Birch, a thirty-six-year-old woman, but everything else I should know is, well … unknown.

But I don't mind. My body is burdened with overpowering exhaustion, which suggests that the inability to recall the past thirty years of my life is a good thing.

I am spinning—hands splayed wide—when the nurse knocks on the door. She makes her way in after three taps. With each rotation, I catch glimpses of her. She is a beautiful Black woman with hair pressed into a shoulder-length style that frames her round face. Her smile is like the North Carolina rain, warm and soothing.

"Now careful you don't make yourself sick with all that spinning," she tells me. "It's time to take your vitals."

I stop, but the room continues to move around me.

Pulling a cart behind her, we meet at my bed. She attaches a soft plastic clamp to my fingertip to measure my oxygen before securing a blood pressure cuff around my arm. With a couple of quick squeezes of the little bag, the cuff inflates and then releases pressure as the nurse watches the dial. Taking a pen from the breast pocket of her scrubs, she writes her findings on a paper attached to a clipboard and declares, "Near perfect!"

A variety of clear tubes labeled with my name already sit on the cart. My nurse is gentle as she finds a vein in the crook of my left arm and pokes me. I count to ten on repeat to ward off the nausea that follows a blood draw. When she is done, she replaces the needle with a cotton swab and uses a bright pink bandage to secure it in place.

"It's time for breakfast, but make sure you weigh in first." She lets out a small giggle at the end of her sentence. I wonder what is so funny, but I don't dare ask.

In the hallway, patients wait to step on the scale before another nurse. My fingers caress my forearms. My skin is dry, but somehow the raindrops from my memory still linger, as if I had just come in from the storm.

I follow the others to the cafeteria, where each person routinely grabs a tray and moves down the line one by one. I meld into the activity and scoop eggs, a sausage, and hash browns onto my plate. Holding my tray, I turn and scan the room for a friendly face. When I came to this place last night, it was so quiet. Most patients were asleep in their rooms, and the low murmur of staff at the nurses' station was barely audible. The contrast of the current noisy cafeteria is striking. An empty table sits at the edge of the room, welcoming me.

I sit to eat, and it isn't until I swallow my first bite of egg that I recognize the soreness in my stomach and throat. Each swallow is laborious, but my stomach wins out, and I eat every morsel of food. When was the last time I ate? I can't remember.

During breakfast, a nurse stands next to a cart and calls names. Each time a patient gets up and goes to the cart, the nurse hands them two small paper cups. The patient tilts their head back and, one after another, swallows the contents. Then they open their mouths for the nurse before discarding their cups in a waste bin nearby.

The activity transports me to the night before. During my intake, a nurse gave me these same cups. One held the medication that would help me sleep, and the other held a small amount of water. A psychiatrist met with me and asked so many questions, most of which I didn't have the answer to. At first, the questions were straightforward, but they quickly became more difficult to answer.

What is your name?
Helen Joy Birch.
What is your age?

Thirty-six

What is your occupation?

I don't know.

Do you have an emergency contact?

I don't.

Do you use tobacco?

I don't think so.

Have you ever tried illicit drugs?

Probably not.

Have you ever received outpatient mental health treatment?

I don't remember.

Question after question. If it was a test, I was failing—horribly. My head pounded, and the room twisted. I didn't know the answers to any of these questions.

In the last six months, have you fainted?

No, but I think I might right now. My head hurts.

I leaned forward, my head in my hands, trying to keep the room still for a moment. All I needed was a moment. Despite my distress, the psychiatrist's questions persisted, and my head throbbed harder. Surely, the doctor was becoming frustrated with me. However, the more questions I responded to, the more self-assured he seemed. By the end of the interview, my stomach was in knots, and it was all I could do not to vomit on the clean linoleum floor.

"Wait right here," he said. "The nurse will be in shortly to show you to your room."

Wait right here. Wait right here. I repeated this about a million times. Each time, the phrase would become a little more distorted until it sounded foreign when I said it aloud. *Wait right here.*

When the nurse finally arrived, I was no longer sitting on the exam table but lying in a fetal position. Chills wreaked havoc on my body, and I couldn't seem to get warm.

"Are you cold?" the nurse asked.

I nodded. I knew the answer to that question.

She came back a moment later with a blanket and a single paper cup. The nurse helped me into a sitting position, draping the blanket over my shoulders. She handed me the cup, and I saw two oblong white pills inside. Taking another cup from a stack on the counter, she filled it with water from the faucet and handed it to me.

"This should help with your headache. After you take it, we'll go find your room."

Using her badge, she led me through the hospital, unlocking doors until we reached a hallway decorated with detailed paintings. My room was small and plain. It had two twin beds, each paired with a small nightstand, and a bathroom with a stand-up shower.

"Lucky for you, both of the patients who were last in this room were discharged today, so you get the whole place to yourself tonight," the nurse told me.

In the cafeteria, the sound of my name brings me back to the present. I swivel my head to find the source. The nurse handing out medication is calling for me.

At the nurses' station, I ask, "What's this for?"

Without looking up, the nurse says, "Lexapro. It will help with your anxiety and depression."

"I have anxiety and depression?" I ask.

"You'll have to talk to the doctor about that," she says. Her face is expressionless. I don't know how she feels or what she thinks of me. "Take it quick. I don't want to be here all day handing out meds."

And based on that remark, I know she's annoyed.

"Sorry," I mumble.

The medication is bitter when it hits my tongue, so I rush to wash it down with the small cup of water, causing myself to choke. With each abrupt cough, my body heaves, and I think I might lose my breakfast. Another patient pats me on the back while the nurse hands me a second cup of water, rolling her eyes. I catch my breath and sip slowly.

After I take the meds, I follow the other patients into a rec room. There is a ping-pong table without a net, a short bookcase filled with board games and puzzles, and a small television mounted to the wall. The other patients seem so sure of themselves. They all know exactly where to go, what to do, and who to sit with.

I pick an empty table that is partially covered with a half-finished jigsaw puzzle and have a seat. I feel so ... uh ... what is the word? Cutting through the fog to find this one word is nearly hopeless. I search the edges of my mind and almost give up when it appears. It's so obvious. The word is *blank*. I feel blank.

CHAPTER 2

Before Helen Lost Her Memory

The valley was vast with sand that decorated rolling hills for miles. My eyes ached from the sun's reflection on the endless landscape. It was all so new and foreign that I didn't dare close my eyes. The air smelled of showers, and the road ahead looked wet. But when we approached, the water was gone.

Momma sat in the front seat of our red sedan, lighting her next cigarette off the one she had just smoked to the filter. Circles of smoke traveled to the back seat, where Lucy and I sat among all our earthly possessions. A song played on repeat. "Heads Carolina, Tails California." Momma sang along, her thick blonde curls swaying side to side as she bobbed along to the music.

Momma was a beautiful woman — probably the most beautiful woman I'd ever seen. People noticed her when we went places. They told her she looked like Farrah Fawcett because of her blue eyes, slender nose, and square jawline. She even wore her hair in the same style as Farrah, her ash blonde locks feathered and curled away from her face.

I looked nothing like Momma. My hair was dark and frizzy, my eyes were a deep amber, and I had a small round nose. Momma said I looked like fall, but I wished I looked more like her—like summer. Momma knew she was beautiful, too. When we'd go to town, she'd always hold her head high, pulling her shoulders back and walking with all the confidence in the world. Sometimes men would whistle at Momma, and she would respond with a show. She'd sway her hips back and forth and give the men this half smile, half smirk that kept their attention.

I admired how she moved through the world, so much so that I would sometimes practice walking the same way. With one hand on my hip, my lips pursed, and my eyes narrowed in a sultry manner like Momma, I would saunter through our house.

But, at home, away from outside eyes, Momma was different. The moment she crossed the threshold of our house, her shoulders would drop, and she'd begin her daily ritual of peeling the layers of fabricated confidence from herself. I would watch her wipe away her makeup, remove her jewelry, and strip off her clothes. The process transformed her. She was no longer self-assured and bright. Instead, she was somber and sad. By watching Momma, I learned confidence isn't a thing you have but a thing you fake.

Yet, in the car that sunny day, driving through the deserts of Southern California, she was happy—singing and smiling. There was no faking it.

Only two days before and less than a week after kindergarten ended for the year, we had left Hubert, North Carolina. Momma crawled into bed with Lucy and me in the early hours of the day and said, "Girls, we are going on an adventure."

Momma bounced around the house, packing our things with enormous energy and enthusiasm. We filled liquor boxes and grocery sacks with our most treasured items and made sure the car still had enough space for Momma, Lucy, and me.

When I asked Momma why we were going on an adventure, she said, "I asked God what to do, and then my quarter landed on tails."

"Will Daddy come too?" I asked. My Daddy lived in a different house than Momma. We were used to going places without Daddy, but we'd never gone this far before.

"Later, baby. He will catch up with us later."

And that's how we ended up in the car, driving through the desert on our way to my grandpa's house in Thousand Palms, California. Momma said we would meet her sister, brother, my cousin Tyler, and Grandpa.

I stared out the window and examined the funny-looking trees that decorated the sides of the road. These trees were called palm trees, and their leaves fanned out wide, so the large surface of each leaf could drink in the sun. I'd seen these trees before on a postcard from Grandpa David, but it felt so special to see them in real life. I still had the postcard, which I hid with a photo of my dad in one of my socks.

In the car, Lucy was asleep. Her head dipped each time there was a bump or dip in the road, causing her dark curls to bounce. Her mouth hung open, and a bit of drool glinted from the corner of her mouth. I wanted to wake her to show her the palm trees, but Momma said I couldn't.

As we drove through miles of desert, sweat trickled down the hollow of my back. My legs were stiff and restless.

"Momma, how much longer?" I asked. I lost count of how many times I had already asked this question.

"Almost there, baby." She turned up the music to prevent me from asking again.

I dropped my head back on the seat and crossed my arms. I didn't know what *almost* meant.

Within several hours, the landscape transitioned as houses and shops broke up the endless sand. The buildings were so different from those back home, and I couldn't seem to take them all in before they disappeared in our rearview mirror.

Our car turned the corner onto a street of adobo-style houses and pulled into the driveway of the first house on the left. The house was small and beige with a gravel driveway. It had no porch. Instead, a slab of concrete protruded several feet from the front door. Yellow and pink metal flowers lined the sides of the driveway, their petals spinning in the wind. I woke Lucy, and groggy, she wiped the sleep from her eyes. She looked around, dazed.

"Are we here?" Lucy asked, but Momma answered before I could. "Yes, we are, darling! We are home!"

Our new home was in one of the three bedrooms in Grandpa David's house. Aunt Joy, Momma's sister, lived in the second bedroom. Uncle Pete, Momma's brother, lived down the street from Grandpa's house with his son, Tyler. And although we had never been a part of this family before, it wasn't long before we felt at home with them.

We learned about our family through the lens of how Momma saw them. She loved them but was quick to point out their faults.

"Joy needs to get her shit together. You coddle her, and she takes advantage of you."

I overheard Momma talking to Grandpa while they drank caramel-colored coffee at the kitchen table. I didn't agree with Momma's assessment of Aunt Joy. Aunt Joy was fun, and even though we'd only lived here for about a month, I already loved her.

"What do you want me to do? Kick her out? Also, that's rich coming from someone who is also living here rent-free."

I was glad to see Grandpa defend Aunt Joy. Momma was too critical.

"It's different. I'm getting a job." Momma paused before continuing. "Look, Dad, I'm not trying to tell you what to do, but Joy and Pete take advantage of you."

Grandpa snorted at her remark.

"Pete? He doesn't live here!"

"I know that. But Tyler might as well. He's always here. Breakfast, lunch, and dinner."

"That's different. Pete's hard on the boy, and I kind of like having my grandson with me," Grandpa said.

"Whatever," Momma replied, rolling her eyes.

I couldn't grasp why Momma disliked Tyler's constant presence, but I was all too aware of Uncle Pete's character. He was the sort of person who enjoyed scaring kids. He'd fashion his belt so that when it was pulled tight, it produced a sharp snap. He also liked to make fun of us, and his hurtful words always lingered a little too long. I wanted to know why he was so mean. So later that day, I asked Momma about it.

"Momma?" I said as she sat engrossed in her book featuring a long-haired man with an unbuttoned shirt and a woman who wore a flowy lavender dress on the cover.

"Yeah?" she said without looking up.

"Why is Uncle Pete kind of ..." I couldn't decide on the word to use. Mean? A jerk? I didn't want to get in trouble.

"An asshole?" Momma said, finishing my sentence.

My eyes widened. I wasn't allowed to say that word.

Without looking up, Momma said, "He just is."

I waited for her to tell me more. Her shoulders dropped when she looked up from her book. She set the book in her lap.

"Our real dad, not your grandpa, was a bad man, and your uncle struggled. Kids picked on him a lot when he was younger."

"Why?" I asked.

Her shoulders dropped further. This was the last question I was going to be able to ask before she told me to go play.

"He talked funny, and he was fat and freckled. After a while, it put a chip on his shoulder. Now, go outside and play with your sister."

I didn't know what having a chip on your shoulder meant. I imagined Uncle Pete missing literal chunks of his flesh. It must have been painful because Uncle Pete was an asshole. The only person he didn't mess with was Grandpa.

Grandpa was also gruff, but unlike Uncle Pete, when you stripped away his hard exterior, you could always see a twinkle of mischief behind his eyes. A zany Filipino man, his voice rolled through the house like an earthquake. He teased us girls endlessly, telling jokes we didn't understand the punchline to and laughing heartily at our confusion. His enormous belly, accentuated by the white t-shirt that stretched over his skin, shook as he roared.

If we misbehaved, he would threaten to hang us by our toenails. Something Lucy and I knew could never happen. Aunt Joy liked to play along with Grandpa and would tease him back on our account. Sometimes she would feed me witty rebuttals I could arm myself with, combating Grandpa's teasing.

"You better stop messing around at the dinner table, or I'm going to beat you with a wooden spoon," he would say when Lucy and I squirmed too much or played with our food.

"Not if I beat you first," I retorted.

I had slowly grown more brazen in the presence of Grandpa and tested the limits of how much I could dish out without consequence. Grandpa would chuckle and shake his head, a sign that he felt defeated.

Grandpa was Momma's stepfather, but he was the only dad she and her siblings claimed. After Grandma died, long before I was born, the three siblings became the only family Grandpa had. I was curious about Grandma and how she passed, but in our family, we left the past where it belonged—behind us.

I learned this from Momma one rare morning when the house was empty except for me, Lucy, and Momma. From the back of a storage closet, Momma reached the shelf where an old banker box sat, collecting dust among other forgotten artifacts. She brought the box to the table and carefully lifted the cardboard top. Inside were old photographs, many of which depicted my grandmother at various stages of life.

Momma's sadness sloughed from her in waves, and I tried to capture it and hold it for her but didn't know how.

Lucy picked up a photo of our grandma laughing. Momma peered over her shoulder. "Her light shined too bright. No wonder it burned out so quickly," Momma said, shaking her head and hastily scooping the photos back into the box.

I gently placed a photo of Grandpa and Grandma on their wedding day back in the box. Two little girls and a grumpy boy stood at Grandma's feet.

"Why doesn't Grandpa keep any of these pictures out?"

Momma looked at me, studying my face for a moment. She measured me with her eyes. "Sometimes the past is too painful, darling. It's better to look ahead."

Shortly after we settled into our new home, Momma got a job at a nearby diner, and we spent our days with Aunt Joy and Tyler while Momma and Grandpa were at work. Aunt Joy either had too much energy or none, and on the days Aunt Joy slept, we usually went outside. On days she was awake, she helped us craft Barbie furniture from old fast-food containers, cereal boxes, and egg cartons. Along with bits of paper, paint, and toothpicks, we furnished a Barbie house crafted from a large cardboard box that once held a microwave.

We had two Barbies. One of them was always naked because we didn't have any clothes for her, and the other had no hair. Someone had cut it all off. I preferred the one with the hair because I liked to use rubber bands to create inventive updos that reminded me of movie stars on television. I desperately wanted to recreate the hairstyle Julia Roberts wore for her wedding in *Steel Magnolias*, but I could never get it right. My bouffant was always flat. Lucy opted for the Barbie that wore a colorful striped mini dress, and Tyler played along with his G.I. Joe.

Tyler was unlike the rest of our boisterous family. He reminded me of the boy, Colin, from *The Secret Garden*. Rather slim and lanky, with nearly transparent skin, he had white hair that forever fell in his eyes. His constant swiping at his bangs became so much a part of him that even after he got his hair cut, he would swipe at his forehead, pushing away the imaginary hair. But, unlike Colin, Tyler was not rude, bossy, or mean. Instead, he was soft-spoken, kind, and sensitive.

One afternoon, Lucy and I argued about what game we should play with our Barbies. Tyler wasn't there to break the tie.

"I hate playing school!" Lucy said. School was my favorite game. "I want to play an adventure game. Our Barbies should be pirates!" Lucy picked up a little plastic toy chest from a recently lost baby tooth. She thought it would be fun to hide it and make me look. I hated hiding games.

"It's only fair! You always pick," I said.

"No, I don't," Lucy argued.

"Yes, you do!"

Momma came out of the bathroom wrapped in a towel, her hair dripping wet. Soapsuds sat on her shoulder, and her nostrils flared out as they always did when she had enough of our bickering.

"I swear on all that is holy, if you girls don't find a way to get along, I'm going to beat both of your asses until they're black and blue."

"But, Momma," I began to say.

"Don't you *but* me, Helen Joy. You are the bigger sister here. Act like it!"

I clamped my mouth shut.

"Now, quiet down. Joy is sleeping."

Momma returned to the bathroom, and Lucy and I wordlessly fiddled with our Barbies on the living room floor.

A loud knock at the door brought us to attention. Lucy and I raised our heads and made eye contact. No one ever knocked. They only came in. Grandpa had been in the backyard and came through the house to answer the door. When he opened the door, he saw two police officers. Grandpa's posture sank, and he walked outside. Before the front door shut behind him, I heard him say, "Which one is it this time?"

We silently waited for the door to open again, anticipating what was to come.

"You girls are quiet," Momma said from behind us.

"The cops are here," Lucy said without taking her eyes off the front door.

Momma walked to the door, but right before she got there, it swung open, and Grandpa stepped inside, followed by the police officers. Grandpa's arm extended, pointing toward the door that belonged to Aunt Joy's room.

"Dad, what's going on?" Momma said.

Grandpa didn't respond. His face was stone, and even though I hadn't seen that expression before, I knew it meant to stay out of the way.

We watched as the officers approached the door, methodical in their movements. They tried to turn the knob, but it was locked. Stepping back, one officer raised a leg and kicked the door.

Crack! With one single blow, the door separated from the frame. Wood splintered around the metal faceplate where the lock had been. Adrenaline coursed through my veins as I watched, and at some point during the action, I stood and walked closer to see better.

I peeked inside Aunt Joy's room, only to see her bottom half hanging from the tiny open window. It appeared she had tried to dive out the window headfirst but had gotten stuck in the process. Her bare legs kicked into the air as she struggled to escape. Within minutes, both officers pulled her back into her bedroom. She did not fight or try to flee again. Instead, she willingly turned her back as they fastened handcuffs to her wrists and guided her out the front door.

Shock held me in place until the police drove away. Momma put her hand to her forehead and gave Grandpa a look of disbelief.

"Really?" she hissed.

"What? Before, I was letting her take advantage of me, and now you're mad I didn't harbor a fugitive?" he snapped, throwing up his hands as he walked away.

Lucy turned to Momma to ask the question that had been burning inside me since it began.

Why was Aunt Joy arrested?

Before Lucy could get the words out, Momma simply said, "I don't want to hear a word out of the two of you. It's best you learn to mind your own."

CHAPTER 3

Momma hated it when we asked questions, especially when we asked about Daddy. He never followed us like Momma said he would.

When we asked, Momma said, "Child, it is not my responsibility to keep tabs on your father."

I tried asking Grandpa, too, but he said, "That's your mom's business. Not mine."

Eventually, Lucy and I learned to stop asking.

I kept a picture of him, my only one, rolled and tucked into a pair of socks along with the palm tree postcard from Grandpa. Every day, I would take out the photo and give myself one minute to look at it before tucking it back away. I don't know why or how this habit developed, but the postcard and photo comforted me when I needed it most. The urgency with which I pulled them out grew when Momma met Matt.

Matt was a friend of Uncle Pete's and was always present at barbecues, where dozens of hamburgers and bowls of macaroni salad warmed in the sun. Flies swarmed the food while flocks of neighborhood kids ran barefoot through sprinklers in a neighbor's yard. Uncle Pete, Matt, and several other friends sat in lawn chairs, making their way to the bottom of a twelve-pack of beer. They wore matching white ribbed tank tops, plaid button-ups, and khaki Dickies shorts. Classic rock and mariachi music from a neighboring house competed for airspace.

One day, Matt wasn't sitting with the men but stood leaning into Momma while she sipped a wine cooler, her back against a shady side of the house. She fluttered her eyes at him, laughing sporadically as he talked.

I couldn't understand what made her so giddy. Was it how he dressed and slicked his dirty blonde hair back? I thought it looked stupid, but Momma disagreed.

Grandpa called Matt a pretty boy, and eventually, that pretty boy became a staple of everyday living at Grandpa's house. With Matt staying over most nights, our small room that barely fit three people had to become big enough for four.

With every hug or gift from Matt, I reminded myself that he wasn't Daddy. Even more, I let him know whenever he tried to act like it. Matt would sit with us at the kitchen table, coloring. When he was done with his page, he'd hold it up to show me. I would have the satisfaction of saying, "My daddy is a lot better color-er than you are."

One day, Momma announced we were moving out of Grandpa's house and in with Matt.

"I don't want to live with Matt," I told Momma.

"I don't either," Lucy said.

She was always copying me, but this time I was grateful for it.

"Too damn bad because that's what we are doing. Plus, it's just down the street. You can walk here and see your grandpa every day for all I care."

Grandpa wasn't too sure it was a good idea, either. "I'm glad you aren't going too far with that ruffian," Grandpa said to Momma the day before we moved. Lucy and I listened as we inhaled pancakes and bacon at the kitchen table.

"Oh, stop it, Dad. He's not a ruffian, and you know it. We should be grateful for all he has done for this family," Momma told him as she applied a thin coat of peach lipstick in the living room mirror.

"What's a ruffian?" Lucy asked.

"Oh, don't mind that nonsense. Grandpa is being senile. Now hurry and finish your breakfast, or you'll be late for school."

Matt tried to buy his way into our hearts, but it didn't work. Sometimes, he would tuck a couple of dollars in my pocket and give me a small smile. I liked the money, but I didn't like him. Also, I didn't know how he had so much money, given that he had no job. While Momma was at work, he spent his days drinking beer and killing time. I asked Momma where he got all his money without a job, but she told me it was none of my business.

"You would be wise to mind your own, Helen Joy."

I had to know, so one day, while Matt and I were alone grilling burgers in our new backyard, I asked him how he made money. He responded, "There is always someone looking for a good time or looking to forget a bad time." I had no idea what that meant, but it was enough to let my imagination take over.

The next day, I told Tyler, "Did you know Matt is a hypnotist?"

"No, he is not!" The news made Tyler laugh wildly.

"Yes, he is. He told me so." I made sure my face was stone-cold sober, so Tyler would believe me.

"Oh yeah, why haven't I ever seen him hypnotize anybody? I've known him longer than you have."

"You can't hypnotize kids. It's illegal!" I told him. I made that part up but wasn't about to let Tyler know. "But you can't tell anyone I told you," I warned Tyler. "He performs under a stage name to protect his identity. If you tell, I'll get in BIG trouble."

"Okay, fine. I won't say anything."

"You gotta pinky promise," I said, stretching my hand to meet his.

After that, Tyler would hold a red Yoyo when we played. In a low voice, he'd say, "You are getting sleepy. Very, very sleepy." I regretted my lie.

I heard the grownups discussing a wedding only a few months after moving in with Matt. Alarm bells rang in my head.

Are they getting married? Already?

I liked it better when it was only Momma, and marriage seemed permanent.

To my relief, it wasn't Momma and Matt but Uncle Pete and his girlfriend. I didn't know his girlfriend that well, but Tyler said she was okay. He said they fought a lot and thought she looked like a skeleton. He wasn't wrong. She was skinny and had little scabs all over her arms. She creeped me out, but I would never say so.

On Uncle Pete's wedding day, sometime in the middle of February, I stood before the mirrored closet door in my bedroom and ran my fingers over the shiny pink fabric draped gracefully around my knobby knees. The dress gathered tightly at my waist, creating satin folds of cloth that glinted when I swished the skirt from side to side. I also wore white socks trimmed with lace that rose from glossy black Mary Janes. A pin adorned with faux pearls intertwined with my dark brown curls, which were piled high and glossy from heat and hairspray. I practiced my face in the mirror, trying to smile the right amount. I wanted to be pretty when I sprinkled satin rose petals down the aisle later that day.

I left the bedroom and walked into Momma and Lucy's bickering in the kitchen. Momma fussed over Lucy as she tried desperately to detangle Lucy's matted head of hair.

"Ow!" Lucy screamed as Momma caught another large tangle with the brush.

"If you would brush your hair every now and again, it wouldn't hurt."

"I don't want my hair done," she whined.

"Too bad. You can't go to a wedding with this bird's nest."

Lucy glowered while Momma continued to yank on her poor head.

"I don't want to be a flower girl! It's stupid!" Lucy screamed.

"Lucy! Being a flower girl is an honor. Now fix your attitude, or I'll fix it for you."

Lucy crossed her arms and shut her mouth.

Matt came in from outside and looked at me.

"Look at you! Don't you clean up nice!" Matt exclaimed.

I giggled and asked, "Do you think I'm pretty?"

"The prettiest!"

Recently, I had started to let my guard down around Matt. Lucy mocked me, mouthing the words, *do you think I'm pretty?*

"Momma! Lucy is being mean!" I yelled.

"Oh, stop it, Helen. Lucy is not doing anything."

I rolled my eyes. Momma never believed me, no matter how rotten Lucy acted.

Behind me, Matt told Momma, "I have a few more stops to make today, but I'll be back in time."

Momma gave him a pointed stare.

Matt lifted his hands in the air. "I know. I promise."

Spinning back around, I asked, "What do you promise?"

"How many times, Helen, do I gotta tell you to mind your own?" Momma scolded. I was never allowed to ask any questions.

After getting ready, we walked down to Grandpa's house, which doubled as the wedding venue. Lucy tugged on her dress the whole way and complained it was itchy.

"I'm wearing the same dress, and I don't think it's itchy," I said. It wasn't that hard to behave, but Lucy never could.

"Of course you don't," Momma responded, rolling her eyes at me. Her eye roll made my chest feel tight. I was trying to help, but she never saw it that way.

A long white cloth stretched down Grandpa's gravel driveway, flanked by two rows of folding chairs and a white metal arch decorated with lavender and deep purple flowers.

The yard was empty, but the house was abuzz. Inside, everyone gathered in different areas, talking enthusiastically and sipping bubbling liquid from clear fancy glasses. Momma's mood turned from annoyed to furious when she saw Aunt Joy.

Making her first appearance since being arrested months ago, Aunt Joy stood unassuming in the kitchen, pulling at the ribbon on a bundle of candy-coated almonds wrapped in tulle. She looked fatter than when she went away. Her face had filled out, and her belly, nonexistent before the arrest, pooched out over a pair of blue jeans.

I followed behind just close enough to hear Momma say, "What on god's earth do you think you are doing here?"

Aunt Joy did not seem bothered as she popped a pink almond into her mouth. "Got out last night." She cocked an eyebrow. "It's a shame not a single member of this family bothered to answer the phone. I guess you were too busy planning a wedding to worry about little old me. And guess what?" She waited for a few beats before talking again. "I had no money, so I had to walk home."

"That's not my problem," Momma said. Her lips formed a thin line under a scowl.

"Well, next time you need something from me, it won't be my problem either." Aunt Joy turned away from the conversation.

Momma's shoulders sank. "Look, we can talk about this tomorrow, but I need you to go," she pleaded. "It is Pete's wedding day."

Aunt Joy gave a slow shake of her head and smiled. "Fine. I'll go, but I will be back. I have just as much right to be here as anyone else."

When Aunt Joy left, I asked what was happening, but Momma dodged the question. "Helen, I swear if I have to ask you one more time to mind your own, your behind will be too sore to make it down that aisle today. Do you understand me?"

I did understand her, so I kept my mouth shut.

A little while later, we migrated next door, where the bride and her bridesmaids finished getting ready. Like Momma, these women wore matching plum-colored dresses. A bottle with a label that read Boone's Farm was passed around, and each woman drank directly from the opening before passing it along.

One bridesmaid used a playing card to sort a little mountain of powder into clean lines atop a mirror the size of a floor tile. I wanted to know what she was doing but knew better than to ask. I didn't want to get scolded again. Momma relegated Lucy and me to the den, where half a dozen other kids, some barely old enough to walk, played and watched TV. Unfortunately, Tyler was with the men.

By the time the wedding started, most of the women were too drunk to walk in a straight line. The herd of disorderly women stumbled to Grandpa's house in a zig-zag pattern in their strappy high-heeled shoes.

The men, including Matt and Grandpa David, stood in a row at the edge of the driveway, waiting to accompany each of the bridesmaids and the bride. Instrumental music played from a boombox on the porch. Then in pairs, the bridesmaids and groomsmen joined Uncle Pete at the arch.

It was our turn to sprinkle the petals. While I was careful to disperse them evenly down the aisle, Lucy took big handfuls and plopped piles of petals every couple of steps. Although I was doing it right, all the grownups laughed and fawned over Lucy. No one ever noticed how hard I tried to be perfect, but I kept trying. Tyler was last to walk before the bride, carrying a small pillow with rings tied to the top.

Finally, Uncle Pete's soon-to-be-wife came down the aisle. As she walked, the audience made sounds of approval, gasping, and oohing. But halfway down, something bonkers happened.

All at once, a disheveled woman jumped onto the bride's back and grabbed fistfuls of her hair. That woman was Aunt Joy. People rose from their seats, and Uncle Pete ran to intervene. He tried to rescue his soon-to-be wife from Aunt Joy, but Aunt Joy's limbs moved wildly through the air, making it difficult for Uncle Pete to get close. Grandpa pushed Uncle Pete away and tried to break up the fight. Too many people came to help, creating chaos, and soon everyone was throwing punches and pushing.

In no time, the wedding party and guests became embroiled in a brawl. Two bridesmaids spun in circles, their foreheads touching as they yanked on each other's hair. Momma grabbed hold of Aunt Joy and tried to push her toward the house, but as they reached the front door, Aunt Joy wrapped her arm around Momma's neck and put her in a headlock. The screen at the front door gave way with a resounding rip as Aunt Joy pushed Momma's head through it. Tyler and Lucy stared. Tyler was ashen-faced while Lucy bounced on her toes, her voice adding to the chaos of the mob.

I took Lucy's hand, and Tyler followed behind. I had to get us out of there. We navigated through the pockets of grownups and into the house. I didn't plan on doing what I did next, but there was no better time to do it.

A cake decorated with white buttercream roses sat among scattered lavender and silver confetti. I climbed onto a dining room chair and sat on the table. The silver cake knife caught the light as I pushed it through the top tier, carving out a large slice. Tyler went to the kitchen and gathered three cans of root beer from a cooler on the floor. Together, we hid in the backyard behind a rusty tool shed. In the dirt, we sat, our legs crossed, filled our bellies with the sweet, bubbly liquid and rich white cake, and listened as the sounds of sirens came into earshot.

CHAPTER 4

It was hot enough that if you cracked an egg on a car's hood, it would pop and sizzle—cooking in just moments. Yet, despite the blistering heat, we somehow learned to survive it. Flip flops, tank tops, and shorts—our uniform. In the sun, our blood felt like it might boil. Sweat became steam that rose from our pores, salty and pungent. A water hose provided us with a temporary reprieve from the harsh conditions. We were left with a film of sweat and hard water residue on our skin.

The street we lived on was paved, but there were no sidewalks. The asphalt crumbled into the dirt, and we would tightrope walk the line where the asphalt ended and the earth began.

At the end of our cul-de-sac was a large desert lot. The desert was our purgatory and our playground. We tromped among the rolling hills and sand dunes, pretending we had superhuman powers or were adventurers on a quest to find a hidden tomb in the ancient ruins.

One summer day, sometime after second grade, I was hunting for seashells with Tyler in the desert.

"Helen!" Lucy yelled from somewhere in the distance. I rolled my eyes and pretended not to hear her.

"Helen!" Lucy yelled again. Her voice grew louder.

I felt irritated. She always followed me around.

I moaned. "What does she want?"

Tyler shrugged and brushed the hair out of his eyes.

"I think we should hide," I whispered.

Tyler cocked an eyebrow. "I wouldn't do that. Last time you did, Lucy told your mom, well, you know …"

I did know. I usually didn't get spanked because I was a good kid. I followed the rules, tried to mind my manners, and kept Lucy, who was wild, in check. Momma rarely spanked us, but Matt never hesitated to pull out the belt. I thought about the last time the belt snapped across my bare skin.

"Fine!" I groaned, pushing the few seashells I'd collected into Tyler's chest, and marched, huffing and puffing, toward Lucy's voice.

Before leaving the desert, I looked back at Tyler. He stood there, clutching the shells, his jaw clenched, chest puffed, and eyes wet because of me. It was clear I had hurt his feelings. A wave of guilt hit me. I'd seen that expression many times, but usually, it was Uncle Pete who put it there.

Uncle Pete believed Tyler to be too sensitive, and even though he wasn't wrong, Uncle Pete used Tyler's delicate nature against him.

One time, Tyler received a new remote-controlled car for his birthday. It was a squatty black and neon green machine with tires larger than the car's body. Tyler and I were outside, taking turns driving it through an obstacle course we made out of rocks. Uncle Pete appeared and watched us for a minute before asking if he could try it. Reluctantly, Tyler walked over, and his gaze fell as he handed him the controller.

"What's the problem? You gonna cry because I want a turn with your new toy?" Uncle Pete taunted.

Tyler didn't respond. I knew Uncle Pete saw Tyler's lack of response as a gesture of disrespect. In an instant, Uncle Pete reached into the bed of his pickup and grabbed a wooden baseball bat. He strode over to the tiny car with a confident swagger, holding the bat aloft. The bat's barrel bobbed up and down as he flexed his hand and wrist, brimming with satisfaction. Tyler stood there, silent, holding his breath to keep the tears at bay. I said a silent prayer, asking God to intervene for Tyler's sake.

"If you can't share your toys, what makes you think you deserve them? Selfish boys don't get nice things."

"Uncle Pete …" I tried to protest.

"Shut your fucking mouth, Helen."

The silence was loud and only let up when Tyler sucked in another breath, holding it tight in his chest. His eyes misted, but he was determined not to let a tear form.

"Are you going to cry like a little bitch over a piece of fucking plastic?"

"Please don't," Tyler whispered.

That was all Uncle Pete needed to hear. Shards of lime green plastic bounced from the impact, exposing the wires within. Tyler lost control, and a single tear slid down his face.

Wiping his brow with the back of his hand, Uncle Pete muttered, "I knew you would cry, you little bitch."

The bat swung in his hand as he walked back into their house, leaving Tyler to pick up the broken pieces of plastic and hardware.

"Your dad is the worst," I told Tyler as I helped collect the bits of plastic strewn across the ground.

Tyler shrugged. "He doesn't want me to be weak."

The memory made me remorseful. I never wanted to make Tyler sad like Uncle Pete did.

I turned around. "Sorry, Tyler!" I yelled, but he wouldn't acknowledge me. He might be sensitive, but boy, he could hold a grudge.

"Helen!" Lucy called again, more urgently.

When I made my way onto our street, Lucy was running toward me. Bare feet pounded the asphalt, and small dust clouds rose with each step.

"What?" I yelled, a tinge of annoyance coloring my tone. Then I saw her face.

Pink skin was visible where her tears washed away the dirt and grime of the desert. Lucy never cried, or at least she rarely did. She was hard as nails for a girl only seven years old.

"I need your help!"

I didn't wait for her to explain. I just started running. Realizing this, Lucy turned and ran ahead. She stopped before an old blue pickup truck with a mismatched white truck cab nestled in a small dirt lot between houses. Squatting, Lucy ducked her head to look underneath the truck. Then I heard soft meows and whimpers coming from inside the hood.

"I can't figure out where they are!" Lucy said, dropping to her knees to get a better look at the undercarriage.

Lucy had a habit of rescuing animals whenever she could. In most cases, they didn't need rescuing, but to her, every animal needed a home—our home.

I sighed and frowned. "I'll see if Grandpa's home."

"No! I'll get in trouble!"

"What are you going to do with them? Bring them home?"

"I want to."

"You can't."

She stood and let out a frustrated sigh.

It wouldn't be her first time bringing an animal into the house. Last time, Lucy brought a lizard home, and Momma was the one to find it. Momma stood terrified on the couch, screaming until Lucy and I could trap the small reptile with a broom and a cup. Momma was so mad.

Lucy stood there, staring at me, a plea in her eyes. Guilt got me for the second time that day.

"What do you want me to do? We don't even know whose truck this is."

"I want you to help me get them out," she pleaded. Her eyes, amber like mine, welled with tears, and I fought the urge to help her.

I sighed. "I'm not doing that."

"Please, Helen, they're all trapped in there, and it sounds like they're hungry. I can't leave them to die! It's so hot out! They're cooking in there. You wouldn't want them to die, would you?"

The urge to help her wins.

"Fine, but we got to be careful. If anyone sees us messing with this truck, it will be both our butts." I pointed to the edge of the lot. "Go be my lookout."

The driver's door was unlocked. Inside the truck's cab, I looked for a lever or something that would open the hood. I had seen Momma do this when her car wouldn't start. I felt around, unable to find it, and was about to give up when I felt a small plastic handle under the dash. Pulling hard on the lever, the hood unlocked.

When I looked up, Lucy was jumping for joy—making more noise than necessary. Vexed, I pointed to the street, reminding her she was on lookout. Realizing her mistake, she spun back to watch the road. Moving to the front of the truck, I slid my hand under the truck's hood, feeling for the latch. The metal was warm in my hand, so I tried to work quickly. Finally, I felt a thin, curved metal rod. Pulling on it, the hood released, but I was too short to push it up. I climbed onto the front truck tire and, with all my strength, pushed the hood into the air. Inside, next to what might have been the engine, were seven kittens, each the size of my hand, all black and huddled together. Lucy ran over, stood on her tiptoes, and peered inside.

"Lucy!" I yelled.

She was a lousy lookout.

"You take lookout, so I can get them out."

I jumped from the truck tire and walked over to where Lucy had stood a moment before. At least this way, I would spot anyone coming. Behind me, I could hear Lucy cooing at the kittens as she moved them one by one to the seat inside the truck's cab.

"Helen, can you shut the hood? I can't reach," Lucy asked when she was done.

When the truck's hood was closed and the kittens were safe, I turned to Lucy. "What are you going to do now?"

"I'm going to take care of them. I think their momma left them."

"I'm sure their momma will be back."

"You don't know that. Daddy never came back."

"We left Daddy!" Lucy tilted her chin up.

"Whatever," she said.

She knew how to get to me. This would be the last time I helped her rescue some dumb animals.

"Momma better not find out," I warned her as I started back for the desert. From behind me, Lucy hollered, "She would have to pay attention to find out."

CHAPTER 5

Present Day

Each day is the same—wake up, vital check, weight check, breakfast, and meds. Afterward, I'm allowed to go into the rec room or shower. I always shower if given the opportunity. It is the only time when I feel alone. Fifteen minutes twice a day. I don't even bother with soap or shampoo. Instead, I stand motionless, allowing the warm water to caress my face until my time is up.

After I shower, I'm expected to attend group therapy, where we sit through guided exercises on coping or goal setting. This all seems pointless because, after nearly three full days, I still don't know why I'm here. I get the same answer whenever I ask. "You will have to talk to the doctor about that."

I assume it is an issue with my memory, but I want to confirm.

Then I have lunch and go to group therapy again. After the second group, many of the patients return to the cafeteria for visiting hours. They corral patients without visitors to the rec room to watch TV. No one has come to see me.

Maybe I should be concerned, but I'm not. It's peculiar when uncertainty is serene. Because although this place is quite awful, and I would like to know how or why I arrived here or when I'll go home, wherever that might be, I'm perfectly content. Sometimes in the morning, my head spins, and I feel like the force may dislodge me, but it only lasts a moment.

Once visiting hours are over, we are all made to take part in physical activity, whether it's a walk outside in the courtyard or yoga. There are very few opportunities to go outside, so it's a simple choice. The sun on my skin and the sound of the birds are the only things that make me feel alive in this place.

I'm not alive, but I'm also not dead. I'm simply stuck in the middle, in this purgatory that is a psychiatric hospital. By dinner time, I am done with the day. The simple act of moving between each activity is draining. I skip art therapy and group reflection and go to bed, despite the warnings given to me by the staff. What are they going to do to me? Lock me up?

I have a roommate now. Her name is … shit. I forgot her name. Doesn't matter, anyway. The day my roommate arrived, I reached out my hand to shake hers, but instead of shaking my hand, she yelled, "Don't touch me!"

Since then, I have pretended she doesn't exist, and in return, she has done the same. I'm thankful.

It has only been three days, and the constant routine already makes my skin crawl. Only the dichotomy of this place makes the monotony interesting. For example, although I am never alone, I am never in the company of anyone. No one besides the nurses talks to me, and most of them don't say more than is required. It's strange because I want to be alone but also feel hungry for connection, and despite the constant sounds, it is noiseless. Someone is always talking, crying, or screaming, yet I can go through nearly an entire day without speaking. When I do speak, my voice fades and cracks. I imagine my voice as a little old man emerging from a long slumber. He needs to stretch and move his limbs so his body warms.

The same nurse checks on me each morning, and she is quickly becoming my best friend. At least, as close to a best friend as you can get in a place like this. She must find me amusing because, after each sentence, she invariably giggles. It's a short chortle of sorts, and I'm fond of it.

"Ms. Birch, it looks like you haven't been eating like you should. You've already lost a couple of pounds. Any thoughts on how we can fix that?"

"Get better food," I tell her. She laughs with intention, and I smile. A joke between two friends. It is my first genuine connection since the last time she took my vitals.

She tells me I have an appointment after breakfast. So, after I take my meds, I am saved from the repetitiveness of the daily routine as we walk out of the ward and down the hall.

Upon opening an office door, she gives me an encouraging glance. I hope to hear her giggle, but she doesn't, and our interaction feels incomplete. The unfinished contact makes my stomach ache.

"Please come in," says a voice from inside the office.

I slowly enter and make my way toward an overstuffed yellow chair, waiting for the woman before me to look up from a manilla file folder lying across her lap. She is a thin woman, probably in her early fifties, with long, wispy strawberry-blonde hair. Highlights of silver make it shine. It's hard to be certain of her age, given she has yet to make eye contact.

I wait, drumming my fingers on the arm of the chair. Another source of dichotomy. Despite the rigid schedules and constant activity, being here is like sitting in a never-ending waiting room. We move from activity to activity just to sit and wait. It's dreadful, and I don't have the patience for it.

I don't know how I know this, but I feel like I was always in motion before this place. Sitting is difficult, but I'm also too tired to keep moving.

The woman adjusts herself in her seat, pulling at her cream-colored linen poncho so it loosely lays over her form. She is stylish—another contrast to the scrubs and pajamas worn by everyone else in this place.

She sets the folder on a table beside her and picks up a notebook. When she finally looks at me, I'm struck by her eyes. They appear to be translucent and seem to drill right through me. Unfortunately for her, I am empty. There is nothing to find.

"Helen, I am Dr. Faneli, but you can call me Jaqueline. I specialize in dissociative disorders, which is why I am here. Can you tell me the last thing you remember?"

"I remember my first night here," I tell her.

"Yes, but tell me what happened right before you arrived."

"I don't know."

I have fought the urge to mentally inventory what I know. It may be irrational, but I'm afraid of what I will remember. If someone asked me to describe my memory, I would say it is almost like someone wrote my life down on a single piece of paper. The center of which caught fire, burning a gaping hole. I am left only with the memories that remain around the edges. Everything in the center objectively existed at one time but no longer does.

"Does it matter?" I ask.

Jacqueline chews on my words for a moment.

"I guess that is for you to decide."

How am I to know if it matters?

Jacqueline continues, "Tell me, Helen, why are you here?"

The need for connection pulls at me. I don't know her, but I want to make her happy. I want her to like me, so I try to remember. I try to fashion some sort of recollection I can present her with—an olive branch. But the more I try, the denser the fog becomes.

My gaze falls to the floor. "I don't remember anything," I mumble.

"I am only asking you to try. Just give it a go. See what happens," she says.

If it were that simple, I wouldn't be here, right? I surmised I must have amnesia, as it is the only logical explanation for the hole at the center of my existence. I assumed that having amnesia would land you in a hospital because what else does society do with a person with no memory?

I'm already tired. I want to leave but don't want to disappoint this woman, this stranger, so I try again. I run my hands through my hair and push my fingers into my scalp, creating varying points of pressure. Even if I'm unsuccessful, maybe this show of effort will cause her to fold and tell me I don't have to try. I strain my mind trying to make sense of this place and how I got here.

Think, think, think.

Closing my eyes tight, I bite my bottom lip to force concentration. Where was I last? What is the last thing I remember? I see a face, and my heart quickly picks up the pace. The face is of a girl with doe-like brown eyes. She is hurting. I try to understand what is before me and why it has this impact.

I can't. I can't. I can't.

As soon as the face comes, it is gone. She fades like a photograph left in the sun. In its wake lingers a throbbing ache, obliterating any trace of the fleeting vision.

I touch my face to find tears have graced my cheeks. Jacqueline sits there, still staring. The lines around her mouth show concern, but she says nothing. She is waiting. Her blue eyes knowing. This all seems so familiar to her. I wonder what she knows.

"Can I ask you a question?"

Jaqueline nods.

"Do you know why I am here?"

She nods again. If she knows, why not tell me?

"Then why am I here?"

She brushes past my question and asks her own.

"Did you remember something?"

I pick at the cuticle on my thumb until the skin breaks. It stings—a welcome distraction from the present.

"I don't know."

It is becoming my favorite phrase. Maybe it will be the sound bite for which I am known, I think, amusing myself.

"When you try to remember, what happens?" Jacqueline asks.

"My head hurts, and I feel sick. The more I try to remember, the fuzzier the details become."

She picks up the file folder again and opens it. The pain behind my eye worsens, and the ground below me tilts. I need to anchor myself. I concentrate on taking in my surroundings.

Behind Jacqueline are floor-to-ceiling windows overlooking what seems to be a grassy field backed by a thick row of trees. The white office walls reflect the sun's rays coming in through the window, which worsens my discomfort.

I shut my eyes to block out the light, the questions, and the headache. I let my mind rest. Maybe I will never open my eyes again. Then, only then, I will have control of the thoughts in my head. I relax, and my breathing becomes shallow. Maybe I will fall asleep. Wouldn't that be so blissful? I could fall asleep and never have to wake up again.

Glowing dots flood my mind. They dance through a tree's branches and leaves, and the smell of the earth calms me. A cloud above, puffy and white, darkens. The screen door on our trailer slams, and I twist to see Daddy. I'm in my secret garden.

"Where are you right now?"

I startle. I forgot she was there.

I almost lie and say I am nowhere. I struggle against my need for acceptance. I want to answer her question, but not at the risk of remembering more. That memory is all I need.

"You don't have to tell me, but if you remember something, I can help you know more," she promises.

I think about that. The thought of remembering sends waves of panic through me, and I search the room, trying to process what I'm feeling. I need to leave.

"I don't want to know more. Can I leave? Leave this hospital?" I ask.

She judges me for a moment. "You cannot."

Chapter 6

Before Helen Lost Her Memory

Kittens soared through the air, one after another. The evening sun cast a glow on the edges of their soft fur. Little cat arms and legs flailed as they reached for something to grab onto. When their tiny claws finally sunk into the bark of a palm tree, they held on tight before making a slow and deliberate climb down the tree's trunk. On the ground below was a tattered cardboard box and a small blanket.

Over the last several weeks, Lucy had woken early each morning before the world came to life to take pilfered milk and odd bits to the kittens. She had cared for them as if they were her babies, and now they were much larger than when we first found them.

Uncle Pete held one of the small black cats in his hand and laughed as he tossed the poor creature to the treetop, delighted by its shrill meows and nonsensical movements. Tyler stood nearby watching, silent and paralyzed by disbelief. I gawked as each kitten flew higher than the one before, soaring over the horizon's line in the distance. The kitten then dropped. Its tiny body dragged back to Earth by gravity's force. I held my breath, unsure if the cat would make it, but it grabbed a hold of the tree just in time, extending its claws and arching its back.

My front door slammed, and Lucy emerged from our house. She wobbled where she stood, taking in the scene before her. The heartbreak on her face swelled inside me like a balloon, threatening to pop.

"Stop!" she cried. She grimaced at the scene but didn't move. She knew better than to intervene. Uncle Pete ignored her and bent to grab another kitten from the box. Suddenly, I forgot how afraid I was.

I ran.

My legs pumped as hard as they could toward where my uncle stood. His eyes, lined with wrinkles, met mine just before I slammed my small, nine-year-old body into him. He stood firm as I bounced back, dazed and disoriented. My heart was racing, but a new sense of determination shrouded me.

I wouldn't let him hurt those kittens. Not if I could help it.

In one swift move, Uncle Pete extended his elbow quickly. His forearm crashed against my face. Lucy let out a scream, and I hit the asphalt. Sitting up slowly, I tried to make sense of how I ended up on the ground. The white-hot heat of blood from a cut above my right eye trickled down my cheek and made me dizzy. His wristwatch had cut me.

He stood above me, seemingly a giant from that vantage point. I might have saved the kittens, but no one could save me.

"What the fuck do you think you are doing?" Uncle Pete chuckled.

He swung his foot back, and I braced myself for the impact, squeezing my eyes tight. Stupid, stupid girl. This was how I would die. Saving cats for Lucy. My muscles tensed. I waited for his foot to make contact with my soft belly.

"Pete, take a step back before I make you," Matt said, suddenly appearing. Still clenching my muscles, I waited for Uncle Pete to kick me. But too many moments passed without impact, so I opened my eyes.

Uncle Pete had stepped back, his hands held up in a gesture of surrender. I watched him warily, still trembling from the impact of his blow. Matt kept his eyes on my assailant as he lifted me from the ground, cradling me like a newborn. I hated his touch, but I leaned into it. I needed comfort.

"You okay?" asked Matt.

I didn't answer. My head throbbed, and my throat was tight.

"Let's go inside and get you cleaned up."

"The cats," I croaked. Even though I didn't like them, I couldn't leave them to be tortured. Matt looked up at the tree where three kittens were gingerly making their way back down the trunk.

"I'll take care of it," he said.

Inside the house, I lay where Matt had left me on the couch, holding a dirty t-shirt to the cut above my eye. I almost died today—well, maybe I was being dramatic. Everyone always told me I was too dramatic. I kind of wished I would have died. Just a little. It would have been easier. Wouldn't it? But then, who would take care of Lucy? The answer was no one.

It wasn't always this way.

UNTITLED FOR NOW

In North Carolina, when I was in kindergarten, on the days we were with Momma, she would take me to the bar after school. Momma and Daddy broke up a long time ago, so bouncing between houses was normal. At Daddy's, I had my secret garden, and with Momma, I had the bar. I loved that bar with its dark wood paneling and the hum of conversation.

I would sit at the bar, sipping tall glasses of Coca-Cola and munching on ham and cheese sandwiches while Momma set up for the night. I was only in kindergarten, but I felt grown-up and sophisticated, surrounded by interesting people with stories to tell.

When Momma took her break, she would pick up Lucy from daycare, and we would head back to our cramped two-bedroom apartment. We didn't have much, but we made do. Lucy and I spent our evenings watching old VHS tapes and eating cans of pasta.

Long after Lucy and I turned in for the night, Momma would come home and crawl into bed with us. She'd gently rub our backs until we woke. We then gathered heaps of pillows and blankets in our small skinny arms and crawled into Momma's bed to snuggle up. Light from the small bubble television that sat atop an old wooden dresser would paint her room blue, and we'd watch a movie until our eyes could no longer fight sleep. It was our ritual.

We didn't have rituals anymore unless you counted listening to Momma cry and Matt yell every week. Now Momma used makeup to hide the color on her face rather than add more of it. It was confusing because Matt wasn't always mean. He spoiled us, took care of us, and loved us. But he also got angry a lot. I found myself drawn to him on his most cheerful days, as the reprieve from the bad days was hard not to appreciate.

The afternoon we saved the cats, Momma came home from work, and Matt told her about what happened.

"He has no right to put his hands on my kid," Matt said.

I wasn't his kid, but I wasn't about to say that.

"I'll talk to Pete, but what else can I do? He's your business partner and my brother. Helen did tackle him," Momma said.

Only because he was throwing those cats in the air. I couldn't believe Momma was making excuses for Uncle Pete.

When Momma and Matt finished talking, they got ready to take the cats to a nearby shelter as Lucy sobbed.

"Can we keep one? I'll take really good care of it!"

But Momma said since we couldn't even care for ourselves, we definitely couldn't care for a cat—a poor excuse. Lucy and I took care of ourselves just fine.

But something must have changed her mind because an hour later, they came home with litter, a bag of cat food, and one black kitten.

Lucy was beside herself with joy, jumping and hugging everyone in the house. The new kitten, a tiny fur ball with wide green eyes, captured her heart. She named him Shadow, a fitting name for a cat who followed her every move.

I liked to pretend that I didn't care for the furball, but even as I grumbled and complained, I couldn't help but love the stupid cat. His playful antics and soft purrs were like a balm for Lucy's soul, and I loved that.

And in those quiet moments, when Shadow curled up beside Lucy and me and purred himself to sleep, I knew everything would be okay for at least a little while.

CHAPTER 7

Momma was right. We weren't particularly good at caring for Shadow, but Momma and Matt weren't particularly good at caring for us.

Gone more than they were home, Lucy and I had to fend for ourselves. It started slowly. Momma and Matt would only leave us for a night at a time, but eventually, those nights turned into weeks.

I couldn't decide if I liked it better when they were here or gone. When they were gone, there was no fighting, and we couldn't get in trouble. But, when they were home, there was food.

We were not strangers to the feeling of hunger. Our cupboards were often bare, and Lucy and I did what we could to soothe our empty stomachs. We learned to make do with whatever we had, mixing garlic powder and seasoning salt into bowls of microwaved water to create a makeshift soup that filled our bellies quickly but only satiated us temporarily.

On the weekends, when there was no school lunch, reading became a refuge, a way to forget about my hunger for a little while. I taught Lucy to do the same, sharing my love of books and showing her how to lose herself in a story. We devoured books, feverishly turning the pages and trying to forget the gnawing ache in our bellies. I preferred books based on reality, but Lucy was enamored by anything with magic and imagined creatures.

"No offense, but your books are kind of boring," Lucy would say. I didn't care that she thought my books were boring. I was only grateful we shared this escape.

Tyler was in nearly the same boat, but not as bad. Together, we would raid Grandpa's house anytime he was home. He always remarked on how we had bottomless stomachs. Grandpa wasn't stupid, though. He knew that something was wrong, that our constant hunger was a symptom of a larger problem, and he tried to reason with Momma.

One Sunday afternoon, Momma and Grandpa stood in Grandpa's kitchen talking while Lucy and I watched television in the living room.

"Amy, I'm worried," Grandpa said.

"Worried about what?" Momma already sounded annoyed.

"These kids. They come over here acting like they've never eaten before. Tyler too."

"You don't know what you are talking about."

I lowered the volume on the TV and moved to a spot on the couch closer to the kitchen to hear better.

"Helen!" Lucy whined, looking at the TV.

I put my finger to my lips and pointed to the kitchen. She understood.

"I know these kids are starved for food and attention, and you're too high to notice," Grandpa said.

"Don't you dare try to tell me how to raise my kids."

"I'm not. All I am saying is that you need help. You're sick, Amy, and your kids are suffering."

Was Momma sick? Those words stuck out more than the rest, but Momma started yelling before I could process the new information. She was unwilling to hear what Grandpa had to say.

"You know what? Fuck you! You and Joy think you are so much better than everyone else."

"Joy?"

"Yeah, Joy. She thinks she is all high and mighty now that she's sober. Fuck her."

"Amy, do you hear yourself?"

"Do you hear yourself?" Momma mocked.

"Seriously?" Grandpa said, shaking his head as Momma stormed out of the kitchen and into the living room, waving her arms at us.

"Girls, come on. We're going home."

We scrambled from the couch and followed her to the front door. Grandpa was close behind us.

"Amy!"

Momma whipped around and glared at Grandpa. "Fuck you. FUCK YOU! FUCK YOU!" she growled.

When we left the house, Momma turned to face the front door and yelled one more time, loud enough for the entire city of Thousand Palms to hear.

"FUCK YOU!"

That argument between Momma and Grandpa fractured the little family we did have. Momma stopped talking to Grandpa altogether, and her siblings took sides. Aunt Joy took Grandpa's side. Uncle Pete thought Grandpa and Aunt Joy needed to mind their business.

"If you keep your nose out of it, you'll keep your nose clean," Uncle Pete said.

But us kids desperately needed someone to put their nose in.

Sometime in October, during third grade, I sat on the living room floor, eating the last of our saltine crackers and reading. Shadow lay next to me, softly purring in his sleep. It was a lazy Saturday morning.

Lucy had already ventured out to play. A new family recently moved in two doors down and had kids close to our age, José and Claudia. Their parents took pity on Lucy. Sometimes Lucy brought home clothes that Claudia had outgrown, little bottles of soap, or small Mexican candies.

Momma and Matt had come home late the night before and were sleeping in their room. A steady snore traveled through the otherwise quiet house.

Our front door flew open, disrupting the quiet. Tyler chased Lucy inside, which was quite unlike him. What had Lucy done to get him so worked up? Wiry and fast, Lucy easily dodged his advances.

"I thought you were playing with Claudia and Jose?" I called to Lucy.

"They can't play," Lucy yelled back as she ran.

Lucy let out a high-pitched scream as Tyler tackled her. With every ounce of her strength, Lucy wiggled out from underneath him. Her yellow-orange feral eyes glimmered as she dipped her finger in her mouth and pulled it out, along with a string of saliva. Her finger landed in Tyler's ear, and he lurched backward, away from Lucy. Tyler screamed and laughed all at the same time, and Lucy took off running again.

It was then I realized, a split second too late, their mistake.

I rushed after my sister and cousin, trying to quiet them, but the bedroom door flew open and hit the wall, signaling I was too late. Matt's footsteps shook the house as he set off for the living room. He marched over to Lucy and grabbed her arm, forcing her small lanky body against the wall.

"I'm sorry. I'm sorry. I'm sorry," Lucy repeated, but it was no use.

He pulled down her loose cotton shorts and underwear and hit her. Lucy tried to cover herself with her loose hand.

"No! Stop!" she screamed.

Matt grabbed the flailing arm and pinned it too. The screams that accompanied her laughter just moments before were now met with tears as Lucy's face contorted.

Lucy let out a blood-curdling shriek with every blow while I just sat there with my hands over my ears and my knees pulled to my chest, waiting for it to end. I felt sick. I wished I wasn't so scared.

Tyler made himself as small as possible, backing into the kitchen and standing behind the counter. Sometimes our best defense was to make ourselves invisible.

Matt landed the final blow and bellowed, "Shut the fuck up! Your mother is sleeping!"

He didn't care about Momma. All he cared about was himself. Lucy and I were the only ones who cared about Momma.

When he returned to his bedroom, Tyler and I dared to look at Lucy, who had crumpled to the floor, her hands clutching her bottom. Tyler lifted Lucy from the ground, and I helped her pull up her shorts. Together, we carried her to our bedroom.

In our bed, Lucy's breathing was sporadic, and her sobs were violent.

"Why is it always like this?" Tyler asked. He gently ran his fingers through Lucy's hair.

I didn't know, but I felt it wasn't supposed to be this way. I remembered Grandpa's words. Momma was sick, and maybe if she got better, so would life?

"It won't always be like this. I'll make sure it gets better," I promised. But my promise was empty because it got worse, and Momma got sicker.

Chaos and upheaval followed the weeks alone at home as Momma and Matt's partying spiraled out of control. Strangers came and went, fights broke out in the middle of the night, and arrests became a regular occurrence. Momma lost her job, and Matt, who had always had money before, soon had none. So much was outside our control, but I tried to hold on to a sense of normalcy. I cared for Lucy and managed all the household tasks, albeit not well. I thought maybe if I worked hard enough, Momma would get better. Her illness became our suffering, and our house was where we survived rather than lived.

CHAPTER 8

As much as we needed help, I knew it was important to stay invisible. The risk of people outside our family noticing the turmoil in our home was greater than the danger we lived in. But despite my best efforts, people eventually took notice. At school, the teachers noticed the holes in our shoes, our tattered and dirty clothes, and the smell of urine that clung to us from the cat and Lucy's bedwetting. They saw how hungry we were for affection, how we clung to every hug like a lifeline.

For more than a year, they took notice of our bumps and bruises. They watched us closely as we tried to explain away the marks, sensing that something was deeply wrong but not knowing what to do about it.

They had noticed enough that one day, while on Christmas vacation in the fourth grade, two people emerged from a blue sedan and made their way to our front door. The man and woman both wore button-up shirts and black trousers. ID badges hung from their necks, displaying proof of their position, and I immediately knew who they were. CPS had arrived.

Lucy heard the knock and swiftly jumped off our bed to answer the door, but I stopped her.

"No, don't!" I whispered.

She resisted, "Stop! You always tell me what to do!"

I blocked the door.

"Move!" Lucy said, trying to push me out of the way.

"Lucy! Those are social workers," I said, struggling to stand my ground.

Her eyes bulged. She knew the meaning behind those words. We'd been warned plenty of times.

These people take kids away, separate them from their siblings, and put them in foster homes. Children are abused in foster homes. "They treat you like animals," Momma had once said. "I should know."

Lucy's muscles were visibly tense. "What do we do?" she asked.

It was my fault they were here. I couldn't protect Lucy or help Momma if I was in foster care.

I thought back to a week ago when Lucy refused to shower before school. We had a bad fight. Lucy's nails were always long, like daggers, and when I tried to physically put her in the shower, she dug those little knives into my arm until I bled. Mad, I hit her in the face and gave her a bloody nose. We struggled on the bathroom floor, pulling the shower curtain down on us in the process. For at least ten minutes, we pulled each other's hair and hit each other until we were out of breath and lay side by side, cut and bloody, on the bathroom floor.

That day at school, we got more looks and questions than usual. I told them the truth, but they didn't seem to hear it. My job was to prevent something like that from happening, and I failed.

I tried to think.

What do we do?

The knock got louder, and I heard footsteps on the living room floor. Momma or Matt were awake. The front door opened.

"Can I help you?" I heard Matt say. The voices that followed his question were too low to hear.

I turned my attention to Lucy. "We will refuse to go with them. They can't take us if we don't let them. Okay?"

We would say nothing and do nothing, making it impossible for them to take us.

So, we waited. We sat still as statues on the bed. Our bodies became heavy and immovable.

Momma had gone outside, shouting at the social workers and creating a scene. They wanted to come in, but she wouldn't let them. She cussed, screamed, and cussed some more, trying to protect us, but no one else raised their voice in response.

I'm sorry, Momma. I did this.

From my position on the bed, I looked out our bedroom window and saw two police cars pull up behind the blue sedan. Momma stopped yelling and cursing, and we could hear Matt come back into the house. He knocked around in their bedroom, making a ruckus, but I could not discern what he was doing. One of the police officers held a walkie-talkie to his mouth as he approached Momma, who was standing with the social workers just beyond the window's vantage point. The other cop retrieved a big tan dog with pointy ears from his car. I held Lucy's hand tight. Things had escalated rather quickly.

"It's going to be okay," I whispered. When Lucy didn't reply, I repeated it three or four times so she knew I meant it.

Lucy and I continued to strain our ears but couldn't make out any words. We could only hear hushed voices and Matt throwing things in the bedroom. The front door opened, and his noisemaking stopped. Then a door slammed into a wall, and the house shook as footsteps pounded the floor. The noise evaporated just after we heard the back door slam. My heart was racing.

A light knock at our bedroom door made me jump. The doorknob twisted, and a female social worker slowly pushed the door open and stepped into the room. We simply stared, saying nothing, just as planned.

"Can I come in?" she asked.

I released Lucy's hand and got off the bed. Then walking over to the open door, I placed my hand on the knob and shut the door right in the social worker's face. I walked over to the window and looked outside again. The police and Matt came back into view. One had their hand on Matt's elbow, leading him to the patrol car while the other officer followed, speaking into his radio. They had handcuffed Matt's wrists behind his back. With his hand on top of Matt's head, the officer opened the door and guided him inside.

I was glad they arrested him, but my heart ached for Momma. She ran outside, still cussing and screaming. Her voice rolled into the house, but she talked so fast that her words made no sense. An officer tried to reason with her, and eventually, she fell like a slinky to the ground. She had given up.

Lucy started to weep, but I ordered her to stop. Crawling back into bed, I stared into her amber eyes.

"Shhh. We can't cry. Stop crying."

She sniffled and wiped her eyes. We had to stay strong. We couldn't let them see us cry.

There was another knock on our bedroom door. This time, both social workers came into our room. I stayed with Lucy this time. They looked at us with such pity. I swore I could hear their eyes say, "You poor children."

The woman held her hand out as if we were rabid animals.

"I know you are scared. And it is completely natural to be. This is scary. All we want to do is ask you some questions. Is that okay?" She looked from me to Lucy.

"No." My face was deadpan.

"Lucy?" the social worker prodded. Lucy shook her head. *Good job, Lucy.*

The woman stepped further into the room. Her nose twitched as her nostrils picked up the scent of urine.

She was pretty. Her black hair was pulled tight into a perfectly round bun, and she had full lips painted red-brown. She looked too pretty to be in this room, where piles of trash, dirty laundry, and broken toys littered the floor. The once beige carpet was stained and dirty, and a streaked mirror reflected two small girls huddled on a bare mattress surrounded by dingy blankets and flat pillows without pillowcases.

The social worker moved slowly toward us. Her male counterpart remained just outside the door, watching. When she got close enough to the bed to touch us, I pulled Lucy's arm, and we scooted away, our feet kicking at the yellowing mattress until our backs hit the wall.

"I'm only here to help," she breathed.

"We don't need your help," I told her.

"I understand." She held out her hand again. "You might not need my help, but I think your mom does."

Help and Momma. Those words changed things. Momma needed help, and as much as I tried, I couldn't help her. The woman took our silence as an invitation and sat on the edge of our bed.

"I don't want to take you away from your mom," the woman said. "I want to help her be the kind of mom you girls deserve. I talked to your mom already, and she said you have a grandpa down the street. You can stay with him while we help your mom."

I sat with her words for a moment.

"What about Matt?" I asked.

"The police arrested him," the woman said. "It will just depend on what the courts have to say. I don't have any control over his situation. All I can do is help your mom and you."

After Lucy and I agreed, the social workers sat with Momma in the living room while we gathered some things. Momma quietly whimpered, wiping her eyes and nodding as they spoke. They talked her through what they called the *next steps* and *a plan for reunification.*

We filled our school bags and stuffed the things that wouldn't fit into a black trash bag. Shadow was now an outside cat most of the time and survived on mice and other small desert creatures, so we knew he would be fine.

When we finished packing, we hugged Momma while the social workers hovered close by. We would be back together again soon. I knew it.

Bags in tow, we followed CPS to their car. Before fully exiting the house, I dared to look over my shoulder to steal one last glance at Momma. She sat slumped on the sofa. Her once-beautiful blonde hair was matted and tangled, and bruises and sores covered her arms and hands. She looked lost and defeated, a shell of the woman she once was.

CHAPTER 9

The sun peeked through the living room curtains, casting rays of light on my face. Half-sleeping, I rolled over on the dark blue sofa sectional, trying to shield my face from the light.

"Hey Rugrat, you ever going to wake up?"

Realizing what day it was, I rolled over quickly and opened my eyes. It was the New Year and my tenth birthday. Grandpa sat on the coffee table facing me. Tyler and Lucy were still asleep, sprawled out across the living room floor.

The night before, we all stayed up until midnight to watch the ball drop. We sipped sparkling cider from fluted glasses and obnoxiously blew black and gold party horns, all compliments of Aunt Joy. Tyler and Lucy pretended to be drunk, and Aunt Joy laughed as they stumbled around the house, making a fool of themselves. For a moment, it was easy to forget about all the pain and struggle that had brought us to this point. We were together, celebrating a new beginning and the promise of a better future.

"Happy birthday, Rugrat!" Grandpa said, holding a small, slender gift wrapped in Christmas paper. I always liked that my birthday was on the New Year. It felt like everyone in the world was celebrating the day I was born. I sat up and reached for the gift, but Grandpa yanked it back before I could grasp it.

"Nah-ah! What do you say?"

"Thank you? Please? You're welcome?"

He laughed, and his belly shook. "I guess one of those will have to do."

I took the small paper parcel from his hands and slowly opened it, careful not to tear the paper.

"Come on. We don't have all day!" Grandpa teased.

Beneath the wrapping paper was an oblong metal tin with a vintage Mickey Mouse face on the front. I smiled at Grandpa, and he motioned for me to hurry and open it.

Inside was a watch. A spotted brown leather band extended from each side of the watch's gold case, which held the face. Mickey Mouse stood in the center. His outstretched arms moved with the hours and minutes. I gasped, surprised and delighted.

"Wow!" I said, taking the watch out of the tin. "This is so cool, Grandpa!"

"Now, I know you wanted to go to Disneyland, but this was the best I could do."

I had asked Grandpa to go to Disneyland for Christmas, but he let me know Disney was out of his budget. As I unwrapped a hardcover copy of *Little Women* on Christmas morning, I could sense Grandpa's hesitation, worried I might be disappointed. But when I held the book in my hands, I felt the familiar sense of anticipation that always came with a new book.

And now, I have a watch, which, once again, I'm grateful for.

Grandpa flipped the tin to show me the watch was made exclusively for Disney theme parks.

"This means that you can only buy this watch at Disneyland. Nowhere else."

"How did you get it?" I slid my fingers over the engraving on the back.

"I know people." He winked at me.

I loved it. I had never had a watch before and couldn't wait to wear it to school. I couldn't stop smiling as I imagined my classmates saying, "Cool watch, Helen!" This was the best birthday, and it had just started. But there was one thing missing—Momma.

After CPS had taken us from our home, we went to a government building where we sat in a room with the social workers and answered questions. My goal was to protect Momma and ensure Matt would never return. So, when they asked about our home, I painted the picture I wanted them to see. Lucy didn't challenge my lies, and for that, I was thankful. Shortly after the interview, Grandpa arrived, and we were allowed to go with him. The social worker promised I would see my Momma again soon, and I prayed that unlike me, she was telling the truth.

According to Grandpa, Momma was in rehab. Grandpa told us rehab would be good for her. I knew he was right, but I still missed her.

"Joy is cooking breakfast. Why don't you go help her, and I will set your watch after I wake up the rest of these Rugrats," he said, gesturing at Lucy and Tyler asleep on the dark green carpet. A flowered crocheted blanket in various muted colored sat bunched up between them.

I bounced up and hurried to the kitchen. Aunt Joy stood at the counter reading a recipe from an old cookbook. The plastic on the cover had turned yellow with age. She held a cigarette with one hand while the other rested on the pages.

"What are you cooking?" I asked.

Aunt Joy jumped back from the counter, and a bit of ash fell to the ground.

"Oh Jesus, you scared me." She held her hand to her chest and looked me up and down.

"Wow! Look at you! I swear you grew overnight! What happened?" she asked.

I giggled. "I'm double digits now! That's what happened." I put a dramatic emphasis on *double digits*.

"In that case, you are old enough to help me with breakfast while I read the recipe for your birthday cake. Waffles are in the freezer. I'm sure you can figure out how to toast them."

We spent the day making my birthday cake and playing board games. When it was time to decorate the cake, Aunt Joy and I used hard multi-colored candies in the shape of letters to spell out *Happy Birthday*.

After dinner, we gathered around the kitchen table, the soft glow of candlelight flickering across our faces. They sang "Happy Birthday" to me in unison, their voices blending into a single melody. I closed my eyes and made a wish. A wish for Momma to get better.

A week after my birthday wish, they enrolled us in a children's program at the Betty Ford Rehab Center. The Betty Ford Rehab Center was a place where grownups went to work on recovery, and we were here to learn about it. At the end of the program, we would get to see Momma.

Holding Lucy's hand, I marveled at the large building with all its glass and clean lines. Grandpa opened the door for us, tapping his foot to let us know we were walking too slowly.

"Come on, Rugrats. We are already late."

Pulling Lucy behind me, I increased my pace, but she met me with resistance.

"Stop it, Helen, you're hurting me."

I turned back to her. "No, I'm not. I barely pulled your arm!"

"Yes, you did!" she cried.

Little sisters were the worst sometimes. "Stop being such a baby!"

The door to the building clattered shut, and Grandpa was right next to us. He bent at the hips so he could look us in the eyes.

"Listen, Rugrats. I need both of you to be on your best behavior today. Do you understand? I don't want to hang you by your toenails when we get home."

I rolled my eyes, and although he saw me do it, he said nothing. Instead, he straightened and led the way into the building.

Yesterday, Aunt Joy helped me use bits of embroidery floss to make Momma a bracelet. Aunt Joy called it a friendship bracelet, but I renamed it a recovery bracelet. She could look at this bracelet and remember Lucy and me if she ever felt sad or lonely. I checked my pockets for the one-hundredth time to make sure the bracelet was still there.

After checking in, we made our way to a classroom across campus. In the classroom, tables were pushed against a wall, and the chairs formed a circle in the center. A teacher and a dozen other kids occupied the seats. Lucy and I took two of the remaining empty seats.

"You'll see here. We have a backpack. Now I must warn you, the backpack is very heavy," the teacher said, motioning to the center of the circle. Her eyes swept across the room as she spoke, intentionally making eye contact with each of us. "You will all take a turn picking up this backpack and carrying it from one side of the room to the other. Who wants to go first?"

Every kid raised a hand except for me. I was apprehensive. But when I saw I was the only one with my hand down, I put it up so I wouldn't stick out.

The first kid to go was a tall, gangly boy, probably thirteen-years-old. He lifted the backpack, and a small grunting noise escaped his lips when he realized how heavy it was. With a great amount of effort, he carried it across the room. His lanky body pulled to one side.

After each turn, the group applauded and cheered. Lucy's performance was probably the most comical of them all. She got the backpack a few inches off the ground and bent her knees, crab-walking it across the room. The classroom laughed wildly in response. Lucy glowed at the attention. After we all had a turn, the teacher shared the significance of the exercise.

"You see, your moms and dads have been carrying around a heavy bag like this on the inside." She touched her heart. "Sometimes life isn't easy, and with that comes a lot of big emotions like fear, anger, or hurt. So, each time something happens, and your parents feel those things, they put a rock in their bag." The teacher opened the backpack and revealed a blue rock with the word *loneliness* written on it. She passed the rock to a kid on her left and reached in to grab another. The kids passed around rocks one by one until each of us held one. "If we collect too many rocks, it's very difficult to walk through life. Our bags are just too heavy. That is why parents may turn to drugs or alcohol. It provides them with temporary relief from all the heartache they feel."

I thought about Momma and where her pain came from. I thought of Matt and all the times he would yell at her, break something, and hit her. He caused her pain, and I was glad he was gone.

But then, I remembered how Momma used to be before Matt. When we lived in North Carolina, she would sometimes lay in bed and cry. I would go into her room and hold her as she trembled with sadness. Momma was carrying rocks long before she met Matt. But where did they come from?

I raised my hand.

"Yes?"

"Do kids sometimes ... Never mind." I didn't want to ask my question. It was stupid, and I didn't want to know the answer.

"Go ahead. All questions are welcome and encouraged. What were you going to ask?"

I chewed on my lip for a minute, trying to decide whether to continue, and almost didn't, but then it came out.

"I wondered if sometimes kids are the reason their parents have rocks?"

The other kids mumbled, and the teacher's expression changed.

"What is your name again, sweetie?"

"Helen."

I stared at my hands in my lap, waiting for her answer.

"When our parents struggle with addiction, it's very common for us to blame ourselves. However, you all need to know it is not your fault. We will talk a lot about that throughout this program, and I hope by the end, you all understand that your parents' addictions have nothing to do with you."

The teacher continued with her lesson. She asked us all if we recognized the emotion on our rock. Mine said *helplessness*. I recognized it and felt it all the time. She then instructed us to describe the emotion. The teacher said that by recognizing and describing the emotions, we begin to process them. This was also the work our parents will do throughout their recovery.

When it was my turn to describe my word, I said, "Helplessness is like when bad things are happening, and you have no power to stop them." I knew I was right and had no power to stop anything, but it still felt like my responsibility.

On the second day, we learned about treatment and recovery—how Momma would overcome addiction. The teacher provided us with lined paper and pencils and directed us to write a letter to our parents. We could say anything we wanted to, but the objective was to share our feelings—to release our rocks. At the end of the day, she escorted us to an area on campus with individual rooms where we would take turns meeting with our parents to read our letters. When I saw Momma, I threw myself into her, buried my face in her chest, and wrapped my arms tight around her. She kissed the top of my head, and I was reminded of what her love felt like. It had been so long since I felt it.

"Oh baby, I missed you so much," she whispered.

"I missed you too, Momma."

Sitting across from her, I read my letter aloud. I told her I was so sorry about all the rocks she had to carry around for so long, and I promised to help her let go of those rocks so she could walk through life without pain and suffering. I told her I would love her no matter what happened. Momma didn't cry or speak. She only sat and listened.

When I was done, I reached into my pocket, pulled out the recovery bracelet, and handed it to her.

"This is a recovery bracelet. I made it for you. To help you."

Momma took it in her hand and examined the colorful threads woven together.

Finally, she looked up and said, "Helen, I swear to you, I will change. I will be better for you."

CHAPTER 10

Present Day

Jacqueline's words echo in my mind. "You cannot."

I am stuck here, in this place that is suffocating and monotonous. She says I have to remember, but I don't want to.

"This seems unfair. What if forgetting is a gift?" I ask.

"Why don't you want to remember?" She narrows her eyes. "Most people would be alarmed by such a large gap in their memory."

She's perplexed, so I try to explain it to her.

"I'm curious, sure, but I also don't mind not knowing. The more I accept it, the better I feel, which makes this an impossible situation."

"Impossible?"

"I am stuck here because I can't remember, but I have no desire to change that. Impossible."

"That is not exactly why you are here," Jacqueline says. "The reason you are here is a little more complicated than that. You may recall me mentioning I specialize in dissociative disorders?"

I nod.

"The events that occurred before you were admitted make treating you more complicated. I have served many individuals through outpatient care, even those with memory loss as significant as yours. However, I can't help you until you remember because of how you came to be here."

"If I am not here because of my memory loss, then why am I here?" I ask.

"While your type of dissociative disorder isn't common, sometimes when an individual experiences trauma, they drive away or suppress memories associated with it. We refer to this as dissociative amnesia. It only affects about 2.6 percent of women and even fewer men." Jacqueline explains.

"Dissociative amnesia," I repeat the words, forcing myself to meet her gaze. "You have yet to tell me why I'm here."

She ignores my statement and continues. "When Dr. Jacobs, the psychiatrist you saw, did your intake, he did an assessment and concluded that you have dissociative amnesia, so he called me. Lucky for you, although I don't normally practice in this hospital, Dr. Jacobs is a friend."

"Okay. So, why am I here?" I want her to stop talking around things and just answer my questions.

"It appears you may have forgotten rather large chunks of your life if not most of it. This aligns with generalized amnesia, but I'll be certain once we spend more time evaluating your existing memory. That is why I asked you to tell me what you can remember. I need to understand just how much there is to uncover."

The more she talks, the more annoyed I feel. I want to leave.

"I don't care about my diagnosis. I want to know what event landed me in a psychiatric hospital."

Jacqueline reaches for the file folder and leans forward, stretching her arm to hand it to me. I open the file, and I recognize my handwriting immediately. The title of the first page is *Mental Health Intake Form*. I see the words *I am tired* scribbled across the page repeatedly. It is clearly my handwriting, but I have no memory of writing this. Each word looks more hurried than the one before until it is nearly illegible. The prompt above the hasty chicken scratch says, *What are the problem(s) for which you are seeking help?* A sensation of déjà vu envelopes me, and I have to physically shake it off.

"Did I write this?" I ask although I know the answer.

Jacqueline nods her head slowly.

"Did I admit myself?"

"No." She gestures for me to keep reading.

I scan the rest of the first page. I read each question and corresponding answer twice to make sense of it all.

Have you ever had feelings or thoughts that you didn't want to live?
- Yes
Do you currently feel that you don't want to live?
- Yes
How often do you have these thoughts?
- All the time
When was the last time you had thoughts of dying?

- Right now
Has anything happened recently to make you feel this way?
- I am my mother.

I stare up at Jacqueline, my eyes pleading for answers.

"Most likely, the gaps in your memory are tied to either one or more events your brain feels the need to protect yourself from," Jacqueline explains. "Your case is unique. You attempted suicide before you came here, but the hospital staff admitted they were unaware of your amnesia. That may be because it didn't manifest until after you filled out these forms. Do you remember the hospital?"

I stare at Jacqueline, stunned. I attempted suicide? No wonder they won't let me leave. Why would I kill myself? Or, I guess, why would I try to?

"No. I don't remember the hospital. You said events. What events? My suicide? Is that what my brain is protecting me from?" I ask.

"It makes sense to assume so. A suicide attempt is traumatic, but we can't say for sure, given the severity of memory loss. Typically, your brain blocks the traumatic memory rather than decades of life. Your case is unusual."

"Well then, how do we know which events caused this? If I can't remember anything, is there someone who does? A friend or a family member?" I ask.

"Unfortunately, we can't tell anyone you are here because of privacy laws, and no one has come looking for you yet. Even if they did, we could only tell them you were here once we got your written consent. Usually, if there was someone you would want to be informed, you would tell us, but that's not possible in this case."

No one has come for me? I assumed I was alone in this world, but to hear it confirmed is heartbreaking. I really don't have anyone. No wonder I tried to kill myself.

"If there is no one to ask, then what? Do I just stay here until I miraculously remember?" I laugh at the absurdity of all this. A woman, thirty six years old, with almost no memory, walks into a psych ward. What is the punchline?

"I won't know what is causing your amnesia until we can uncover the trauma of your past."

"How do we do that?"

Jacqueline adjusts herself in her seat, straightening her spine. "We talk. You tell me what you remember, and hopefully, the things you have forgotten seep in from the edges of those memories. If that doesn't work, we can always try hypnotherapy, but I prefer talk therapy."

I huff. This is stupid. Jacqueline waits for me to say something. I'm simply going to talk myself into remembering? Sure. That sounds plausible. I don't want to be here anymore.

"Since I don't remember why I attempted suicide, technically, I'm no longer suicidal. What if I promise to not try to kill myself again? Can I leave?"

"No," Jacqueline says. "There is a chance your memories could come flooding back suddenly, and without the support of your care team here, that would be very bad for you."

I swallow and look at my hands. They are shaking, but only slightly. I feel backed into a corner and want nothing more than to run away. I take a deep breath. I'll have to trudge through if I can't find a way around it.

"Fine. Let's talk. I was in my secret garden."

"I'm sorry?" She looks confused.

"You asked me where I was earlier and what I remember. I was in my secret garden."

"Oh," she begins to write in her notebook. "That sounds interesting."

"Not really. It was just a bunch of overgrown weeds and fruit trees in my dad's yard when I was a kid." I bring my knees to my chest and wrap my arms around them. The position brings me comfort. "It's the last thing I remember, and it was my favorite place to be. My dad would read me that book, *The Secret Garden*. You know it?"

Jacqueline nods.

"Every night at bedtime on the nights I stayed with him, he read it to me. It was my favorite book. He said it was the only way he could get me to sleep after he and my mom broke up. They were never married, so they're not really divorced."

"So, you're close to your father?"

"I was. At least I remember being close to him."

I bring my hands to the front of my knees and intertwine my fingers reflectively, rubbing one thumb over the other.

"When was the last time you spoke to your dad?" Her watery eyes have transformed once again. They are red-rimmed, and the translucent blue is now a seafoam color.

"When I was seven?" My voice is a wisp as I try to capture the details of my past as the memories swim around in my head. Struggling to grab one, I reach out as the current sweeps it away.

"What happened?" she probed.

I seize a faint memory of my dad and hold it in my mind. He is doing my hair. We are getting ready to go to town for the day. Together we walk the streets, my hand in his.

"I'm not sure. All I know is one day, he was there, and the next, he wasn't. I don't know why. We were close, though. I remember that."

I think of my dad. His fingers are in my hair as he twists strands into a loose braid. I'm standing in front of the mirror, admiring his work. His brows furrow, his eyes fixed in intense concentration. He is gentle as he braids.

I smile at the memory, forgetting, for a moment, where I am.

Chapter 11

Before Helen Lost Her Memory

Inside the brick community center, an audience of recovering addicts listened to the testimonies of others. When they called Momma's name, smiling faces watched as she stood from her seat. They all applauded in unison as she accepted her one-year chip. The whole family cheered until our collective voices were hoarse.

"You did it," I said to her when she came back to her seat.

"Only because you girls were here to help me."

Pride blossomed in my chest. I had helped Momma get better.

After Momma left rehab, she got a job doing secretarial work for a lawyer and moved into a triplex apartment across town. Within three weeks, we were with her again. Shadow couldn't come with us, but he preferred roaming the desert, searching for mice and small lizards to eat. He would be okay.

In our new home, we settled into a routine, a comforting rhythm that brought a sense of stability and normalcy to our lives. I never knew how much I needed routine until I had it. Each evening, we gathered around the table for dinner. With our mouths full of Hamburger Helper, we shared the events of our days.

After dinner, we washed the dishes and set out on our nightly walk. We strolled the quiet streets as the world slowly settled into a peaceful hush. Our destination was the community building a couple of blocks away, where Momma attended her Narcotics Anonymous meetings several times a week.

I liked these meetings. People told stories about how they fell into addiction. They were fascinating and heartbreaking. So many people. So many rocks.

Aunt Joy often came to the meetings as she was working on her recovery, too. Her sobriety was more important than ever, as she was seven months pregnant with my soon-to-be cousin, Nathan. No one knew who the dad was except Aunt Joy, and Momma said we better not ask.

I recognized a pattern. Grandpa wasn't Momma's real dad. Uncle Pete was Tyler's dad, but he wasn't a good one, and my dad, well, he never did follow us to California. You couldn't count on dads.

Momma became obsessed with recovery and talked about it with anyone who would listen. She carried her most recent chip everywhere we went, and when she got nervous, she'd rub the chip between her thumb and forefinger. It was her sobriety rosary.

"I am worthy of recovery," she would say.

Lucy made friends, and sometimes Momma would let one of them come over after school. Our clothes were regularly laundered. We had real birthday parties with invitations, balloons, and goodie bags. I entered the gifted and talented program at school, and Momma got me a computer. Aunt Joy said if I wanted to make something of myself, school was the way to do it. I wanted that—to make something of myself. I wanted to do something that mattered.

A couple of weeks after Momma accepted her one-year chip, she came out of her room in a slinky red dress and black high heels. She had painted her face so her eyes were smoky and her lips matched her dress.

"Are you wearing that to the meeting?" I asked Momma as my eyebrows arched.

I was sitting at the table, adding the finishing touches to my diorama of the rainforest ecosystem.

"No ..."

She tittered.

"Then where are you going? On a date?"

"Just meeting someone for a drink," she said, grabbing her purse off the hook by the door.

"But you're not supposed to drink?" Panic rose in my chest, and my gaze followed her to the door.

"Oh, Helen, I don't have a drinking problem." She rolled her eyes at me. "If I did, I would go to Alcoholics Anonymous, not Narcotics Anonymous. I shouldn't be gone long. Will you tell Lucy when she gets out of the shower?"

"I guess," I said. I had a bad feeling.

It was way past our bedtime by the time Momma got home, but I couldn't sleep. I lay in bed, staring at the rails underneath Lucy's top bunk. She asked me about five million questions after Momma left, and I was glad she was finally asleep, so she couldn't ask anymore.

When the front door opened, I could hear two people whispering. Their hushed voices moved through the living room and into Momma's room. Anxiety rose in my chest as I tried to remain calm. I lay there as long as I could, but eventually, I got up. I needed to know who the second person was.

Momma's door was slightly ajar. I quietly pushed it open, careful not to make a sound. Momma sat on her bed beside a man I had never seen before.

Between them on the bed was a small mirror with two perfect lines of white powder.

"I know I have a dollar in here somewhere," Momma said as she dug around in her bag.

"Got it." Her hand shot out of the bag, holding a single dollar bill.

I felt sick. I knew she was about to make an enormous mistake. I tried to speak. I wanted to warn her, but my throat closed, and I couldn't form the word that played on repeat in my head—*Stop!*

Momma sensed my presence, and her eyes found mine through the crack in the door. Her mouth formed a perfect O, but before she could react, I stepped back from the doorway.

I swallowed hard. My throat was still tight with shock. I was unable to speak, so I ran. I ran through the front door and out into the night. I ran until my lungs felt like they would explode, and my legs felt like jelly.

How could she?

My mind raced in circles. The edges of my vision blurred. I braced my hands on my knees, gagging as I emptied the contents of my stomach onto the sidewalk.

As I looked around, I realized I was lost, but I didn't care. I wasn't going back. I couldn't. The sky was dark. Not even the moon was visible tonight. And although the streetlamps and neon signs from nearby businesses made the ground glow, the air felt sinister.

Run away—that's what I would do. It was the only thing I could do. I couldn't go back to the way it was before. We wouldn't survive it.

A car approached at a crawl. The driver was curious about a girl, only eleven years old, wandering alone at night. I shivered, and the hair on the back of my neck lifted.

I sucked in a deep breath, knowing I had to go back. My chest caved in on itself, squeezing out the air. I didn't want to return home, but I had no choice. Needing time to think, I decided I would go back tomorrow when I had a plan to get Lucy and me out.

I walked for what seemed like hours with no destination in mind. Sometime later, another car pulled up next to me, and I picked up my pace.

"Helen!" Aunt Joy called from the driver's seat. Momma must have called her.

I ignored her. She wouldn't be on my side. She was an addict, too. I couldn't trust her either.

"Helen Joy!" she yelled again.

I started running, crossing a large grass field so she couldn't follow me.

Behind me, she shouted, "Helen! I'm pregnant. Do you really expect me to run after you?"

No, I expected her to leave me alone. Regardless, she pulled over, got out of the car, and ran. But I was faster, and she couldn't keep up. When I believed I had finally lost her, a wail penetrated the dark.

"Ohhh shit!" I heard Aunt Joy cry.

I stopped in my tracks, listening. The heaviness of my breath made it difficult. She sounded like she was in a lot of pain.

What if she was faking it? Using her pregnancy to trick me?

I rocked on my bare feet and clenched my jaw. I couldn't leave her. Finally, on the third cry, I ran back to Aunt Joy.

When I got to her, she was buckled over, holding her bulbous belly in her arms.

"Are you in labor?" I asked.

"Dammit, Helen. What do you think? Shit!"

"But how?" I stammered, my voice trembling with fear. Nathan wasn't to be born for another month.

"He's early," she said through gritted teeth.

"Is that bad?" My voice shot up several octaves.

"Yes, it's bad! Help me to the car!"

"I'm sorry."

She groaned again. I hooked my arm through hers but wasn't strong enough to pull her up. She continued to writhe on the ground for several more moments. Then her whole body collapsed. My eyes widened as she relaxed into the grass. *Oh, this is bad. This is bad.*

"Helen, I need you to help me to the car before the next contraction," she said between labored breaths.

She could support herself this time, but I had led Aunt Joy fairly far from her car. We walked until another contraction took hold of her, and I waited, terrified, until it was over. Again, we moved toward the vehicle.

We were both panting as we finally approached the car. I opened the door and helped her inside, but she was in too much pain to drive.

"I don't know what to do!" I told her.

"Get help," she said as she bent forward in pain.

So, I left her there and ran to a nearby convenience store. As I ran, the world moved past me in a blur, but each step seemed too slow. I had to fix this. Fix what I had done.

"My aunt is in labor! Can you call 911?" I shouted to the attendant before the doors had a chance to swing shut again.

I could just imagine what they thought as a young girl stood barefoot and winded in a convenience store after midnight, yelling for an emergency call.

The attendant and I told the dispatch where we needed an ambulance, and I ran back to Aunt Joy, who was still struggling against the pain of labor.

Kneeling before the open driver's door, I asked, "What do I do?"

She grabbed my hand and held it to her chest.

"I'm sorry," I whispered.

As I watched her and waited for the ambulance, I felt helpless. I didn't know how to help her or me. Helpless. The word I had to describe. But this time, it was different because I wasn't the victim. I was the cause.

When the ambulance came, EMTs put my aunt on a gurney and loaded her into the ambulance as I climbed inside after her. On the drive, the ambulance jostled, and the EMTs instructed Aunt Joy to breathe.

"That's right. Deep breaths, in and out," an EMT repeated.

"I can't fucking breathe!" Aunt Joy snapped back.

If Nathan wasn't okay, it would be my fault. I fought to hold back tears as the guilt ate away at me.

At the hospital, Aunt Joy labored, and I stood by her, petrified by the consequences of my actions. She squeezed my hand and yelled obscenities.

"I'm sorry," I said. And when she didn't seem to hear me, I repeated it.

"Stop fucking apologizing, Helen."

Nathan finally made his way into the world, and Aunt Joy cried tears of happiness and relief. He was okay.

Besides Aunt Joy and the medical staff, I had the honor of being the first person to hold Nathan. I cradled his tiny body and silently vowed to love and protect him.

As the sun rose, welcoming a new day, our family filled the hospital room where Aunt Joy and Nathan recovered. Still in her red dress from the night before, Momma looked haggard, and Lucy still had sleep in her eyes. Momma didn't mention what had happened, and the guilt from what I had done made me hesitant to confront her. Like we always did, we left the past where it belonged.

CHAPTER 12

Aunt Joy's light faded to black after becoming a mother. I convinced myself it was because Nathan came early, and he came early because of me.

"It's called postpartum depression," Momma said on the way home from Aunt Joy's house one day.

"Does it go away?" Lucy asked.

"Eventually."

I thought maybe I could help Aunt Joy like I had helped Momma.

Lucy and I took the bus to Aunt Joy's house after school. As we walked through the front door, the first thing that hit us was the overpowering smell of stale fast food, curdled formula, and dirty diapers. Sadness and frustration simmered as I looked around Aunt Joy's room. She had always been such a bright light, someone who, despite their addiction, consistently showed kindness and love. But now, she was lost and adrift, unable to do anything beyond the bare minimum.

Lucy and I got to work, one of us holding Nathan while the other cleaned the house. Momma showed up just after five, when she got off work, to cook dinner for everyone. I was certain Momma's relapse was a one-time thing, and although we didn't go to meetings as often, she seemed to be doing good. At least, I hoped so.

As Aunt Joy's depression lifted, she began to go out with friends, and leave me at her apartment with Nathan. Before long, Aunt Joy declared me Nathan's official babysitter, a responsibility I took very seriously. I'd stay at her house on weekends, caring for Nathan while she was out. Sometimes

Lucy would come, but most of the time, it was only me. I didn't mind. I loved Nathan, and it was good to see Aunt Joy smile again.

One evening, I sat on the toilet in Aunt Joy's bathroom with Nathan on my lap as she prepared for a night out. I couldn't help but admire her. She was bold.

"One of my girlfriends always wears her lips like this," Aunt Joy said as she applied a thin line of brown lip liner and finished it with gloss. "Do you like it?"

"It looks super pretty," I said.

She turned and smiled at me. "You want some?"

I sat still while she worked on my lips, and when she was done, she modeled how I should rub them together to create a similar effect. I did as instructed and stood to look in the mirror.

"Wow," I mumbled. Although the makeup wasn't much, it transformed my face, adding a maturity I hadn't seen before.

As if reading my mind, Aunt Joy said, "You look so grown up!"

I felt grown up.

Momma became concerned when babysitting extended beyond weekends to the occasional school night.

"I don't know why she needs you over there all the time. You are not that baby's mother. She is," Momma said as I waited for Aunt Joy to pick me up to babysit.

"It's okay. I like babysitting," I replied.

One morning, early in May, the phone rang as I got ready for school. Momma answered it in the kitchen.

"Hello? Joy? What's wrong? Joy? I can't understand what you are saying. Nathan? What? Joy, I'll be right there. I'm coming."

Momma hung up the phone and hollered for us to hurry.

"Girls, we gotta get going. Hurry and load up."

"What's going on?" I asked Momma as we piled into the car.

"I don't know." Her voice cracked as she pulled out of the driveway.

Lucy and I exchanged worried glances as Momma dropped us off at school and sped away. A pit formed at the bottom of my stomach and remained there all day. Something was wrong.

We came home on the bus that day, and a thick cloud of cigarette smoke met us as we walked into our triplex apartment. Momma sat at the kitchen table in front of an ashtray that was overstuffed with orange butts. Momma's eyes were bloodshot, and her face was ashen.

"Girls, sit down." Her voice wavered as her gaze fell to the floor.

Lucy slowly sat across from Momma, but I remained standing. I needed to prepare myself for whatever was coming.

"Nathan passed away last night. He's dead."

An audible gasp ran through the room, but I wasn't sure if it was me or Lucy who made the noise.

"How?" Lucy asked.

"We don't know."

Momma cried without remorse, and we followed suit.

I couldn't make sense of him being gone. It didn't feel real. It had to be a trick. At any moment, someone would jump out from around a corner and yell, "Surprise! Got you!" while holding Nathan in their arms. It just didn't make sense. I had played peek-a-boo with him only two days before while he babbled and slobbered on his fist. Only two days before.

But it wasn't a trick. He was gone. And it seemed to me there was a sinister reason behind it all. The grownups conversed conspiratorially from afar, trying to keep their conversations out of earshot of the children. And when they weren't whispering, they were sad. I hated seeing their pain. I was also sad, but I thought my sadness should come second. Like maybe I didn't have a right to be as sad as everyone else, so I tried not to be.

Instead, I tried to be more like Momma, the only one who seemed okay. She kept herself busy by taking care of arrangements, coordinating fundraising activities, cooking, and forcing others to eat. Momma had not shed a tear since the day she told us he was gone. She was holding it all together. She was strong. My Momma wasn't perfect, but I felt compelled to emulate her as we managed our grief.

On the other hand, Aunt Joy was unhinged and switched rapidly between laughing hysterically, crying, and yelling. Seeing her like this was unbearable.

"She's going to be okay. Just not today," Momma said.

Our family gathered at Grandpa's house the night before Nathan's funeral. It had been nearly two weeks of watching them whisper to one another, and I needed to know what they weren't telling us. I tried all evening to listen in, but they always sensed my presence. So, when the adults sent us to bed, I convinced Tyler and Lucy to follow me to the backyard and over the fence to hear their conversation.

Outside, the world was mostly silent, except for a whisper of noise so faint the origin was indistinguishable. We crept along the side of Grandpa's house, careful not to make a sound.

We sat on gravel, our backs against the outside of the house, while the adults talked near an open window.

I heard Momma say, "I know you don't want to, but the police can help you, Joy."

"No, they can't. You don't understand, Amy. These are not the kind of people you fuck over. They will kill you all. They'll kill every last one of you and your children, too. Look at what they did to me. To Nathan," Aunt Joy sobbed.

"They will not fuck with me," Uncle Pete said, trying to sound tough, and I could imagine Momma glaring in response.

"Can't they issue a restraining order or put you in witness protection or something? It just doesn't seem fair that you could go to prison." Momma's voice sounded desperate.

Grandpa joined the conversation. "Amy, listen to me. These men have killed cops. Regardless of what Pete thinks, we can't take any chances."

"What the fuck?" Momma yelled. "I can't do this anymore. I can't sit by while they prosecute my sister for what those assholes did to my nephew. And the fact that you can just stand by and let Joy ruin the rest of her life like this. I can't even look at you."

"Amy, please," Grandpa sighed.

Footsteps signaled that Momma had walked out of the room. I turned to Lucy and Tyler. My heart pounded in my chest. As I looked at them, I couldn't help but notice their identical expressions of shock—jaws hung open, mouths agape, and eyebrows raised high in disbelief. I was acutely aware of the fact that my expression likely mirrored theirs.

"Let her go," said Uncle Pete. "She just needs to cool off."

"I should go to prison. I let those men into my house. I let them near my son. That's on me," wailed Aunt Joy.

"You did not kill your son," Uncle Pete said.

"I might as well have. I knew what they were capable of, and I never should have gotten myself mixed up in their business."

Just then, we spotted headlights in the distance. Not sure who it was, we panicked and made a run for it, but instead of going back to the house, we ran down the back alleyway behind the houses. Our hearts thudded in our chests as we ran, gasping for air. Adrenaline surged through our veins, spurring us onward. We headed toward the barren expanse of the desert, determined to put as much distance between us and what we had learned.

When we reached the edge of the desert, we skidded to a halt, panting and heaving, our nerves shot. I looked at my sister and cousin. Their faces held all the horrors we had heard.

"Someone killed Nathan?" Lucy's voice trembled with uncertainty as she struggled to process the news. Her face became a canvas of conflicted emotions, flickering between fear, shock, and devastation, each fleeting expression etched with pain and disbelief.

Tyler and I nodded, unable to form words. This was all too much. Too big to process.

Together, the three of us sunk to our knees in the desert, none of us able to break the silence. Nathan was dead. Someone dangerous killed him. Aunt Joy might go to prison.

Tyler shook the hair out of his eyes and looked out into the desert. "So, what do we do now?"

He brought his eyes back to me, searching for answers, but I couldn't give him any. There was nothing we could do. We were helpless.

"What if they come for us too?" Lucy asked, referencing the men who killed our baby cousin.

"I won't let them," I said. Tyler's brows shot up. He knew I couldn't keep such a promise, but he didn't argue. He let me make it. The weight of the situation pressed down on me like a bag of rocks, and I knew I couldn't stand idly by. Life was about to change, and I had a sinking feeling that we would need each other more than ever. I had to do something.

Reaching into my back pocket, my fingers closed around the postcard that had comforted me over the years. The one with the palm trees Grandpa had sent me so long ago.

"Grandpa sent this to me a long time ago, and I've kept it for good luck. Maybe this is dumb, but I think we need it. So, here." I tore the postcard into three equal pieces and handed one to Tyler and Lucy. They each reached out and took their portion of the thinning cardstock, examining it closely. With the pieces of postcard resting on our chests, we lay under the stars and linked our hands to form a human chain amidst the rolling hills of sand. I couldn't tell if Tyler or Lucy had drifted off to sleep, but I remained wide awake. A question spun endlessly in my head like a perpetual record. Would Nathan still be alive if I had been there to babysit? Had I broken my promise to always protect him? And was I doomed to break the promise I made to Lucy?

The next day, at Nathan's funeral, Momma bustled around while everyone else sat with their grief. I took note. During times of grief, this was what you did. You worked. I jumped in to help Momma and found that the more I worked, the less guilty I felt for failing to protect my cousin. Also, as I busied myself, it was easier to forget my fear. So as people cried and exchanged watery glances, Momma and I set up chairs, refilled pitchers with water and tea, and welcomed guests.

The funeral felt performative and scripted. I couldn't connect with the words, prayers, and songs offered by others. I distanced myself from it all, as it was the only way I could manage such an incredible loss.

At Grandpa's house, after the funeral, we sat together, eating cheap pizza under a blue canopy in the backyard. We were out of words and out of tears. Even Aunt Joy was quiet. The silence was only marred by chewing as everyone filled their bellies.

Abruptly, a guttural sound rose like a geyser, forceful and without inhibition. Everyone looked up at the same time. Momma had dropped her pizza into the dirt, and her shoulders sank as unbridled sobs shook her body.

The weight of Momma's grief shattered my heart. It was my fault she was hurting. It was my fault everyone was hurting. I should have been there. I should have protected Nathan. I didn't know how to manage the emotions that expanded in my chest, so as Momma sobbed and the others watched teary-eyed, I stood to clean up our dinner.

Chapter 13

I was so tired of trying to save cats.

After Nathan died, it was like we had played the Uno reverse card. Momma shattered, and her frequent depressive spells spiraled out of control. Although she would never admit it, sobriety was no longer a priority. We hadn't attended a meeting in two years, and Momma's sponsor gave up trying to get in touch.

The day Aunt Joy was sentenced, Momma stood in the kitchen swaying from side to side as she screamed at no one.

"Those motherfuckers murdered my nephew, and no one cares. Not the police, not your grandfather, no one!"

Momma had stopped trying to protect us from the truth. Since Nathan died, I learned that the men who killed him were drug dealers. They had put drugs in Nathan's bottle, which killed him. Aunt Joy was asleep when it happened because they also put drugs in her drink. The one thing I didn't understand was why. And although no one had come for us yet, I was always worried that they would come one day.

"I want them to pay for what they did!" Momma continued. I walked toward Momma. My hands were held out as if she was a wild animal.

"I think it's time to go to bed, Momma," I said.

"Don't fucking tell me what to do!" she screamed, and I watched the tequila bottle she was holding drop and shatter on the tile floor. Momma stepped back to avoid the glass shards and walked out the front door. She left me alone with the remnants of her rage.

Eventually, Grandpa, Uncle Pete, and Tyler seemed like people in a dream. Although misplaced, Momma blamed them for our misfortunes. She was angry that they encouraged Aunt Joy to take a plea deal. And because of that, they left Lucy and me alone on an island of destruction.

Mornings before school were either spent picking up beer cans and dumping ashtrays full of cigarette butts from the night before or coaxing Momma to leave the bathroom floor so Lucy or I could use the toilet.

"Come on, Momma," I said to her one morning. She whimpered as I lifted her off the beige linoleum.

"Lucy, can you get her some water?"

"Got it," Lucy said, and the kitchen sink turned on.

"I'm sorry, Helen. I'm so sorry," Momma mumbled on our way to her room.

"It's okay, Momma. It's okay."

I tried to convince myself that if I helped her, she would get better again. I struggled between feelings of love and anger. After two years of this, she only seemed to be getting worse.

After we got Momma to bed, Lucy and I stood in the kitchen, staring at each other. She looked as tired as I felt. I searched for words, but Lucy spoke before I could.

"We can't keep doing this, Helen."

Tears welled, and I nodded. "You're right."

Our family's collective tragedy ruined Momma, and we were collateral damage. Momma was hurting because Nathan and Aunt Joy were gone, but we also missed Nathan and Aunt Joy. We were hurting, too. I tried to save Momma, but I couldn't anymore. This rock was too big, and the weight was crushing me.

We had to find a way out.

One afternoon, I came home from school, and Momma was gone. I didn't wonder where she went. It was normal. She was either sick and sad or gone. Unopened mail, empty food cartons, and random junk littered the kitchen table. I began to sort the items, trying to make space to do my homework. As I stacked the pieces, I noticed a standard white envelope that once held a check for child support, now torn open and empty. My heart stopped, and an idea formed when I saw the name and address in the top left corner.

The city—Rock Springs, Wyoming. I read my dad's name—Sam Birch. My answer had been here the whole time. There was a way out, but I hadn't seen it until now.

The next day, at the school library, I checked out a book of U.S. maps and found Rock Springs. With my ruler, I measured the distance—nearly 800 miles. A pang of disappointment blossomed in my chest. It was too far away.

For the next several weeks, I thought of every conceivable way we could get to Rock Springs, Wyoming. But regardless of how foolproof my plan was, one thing tripped me up each time. I didn't know if Daddy wanted to see us.

I would have to talk to him, but I didn't know how, and I didn't know who I could ask. What I did know was that sometimes a check included a phone number. So, for the next month, I checked the mail every day after school. Sometimes I was too late, and Momma had already collected the mail. After a full month of no mail from my dad, I knew I had missed it. But I was determined to find a way.

I kept the original envelope tucked carefully in the center of my math textbook, and since a textbook was always found under my arm or lying open in my lap, it made this the perfect hiding spot. I pulled it out once more and hid in the bathroom with the door locked. I examined the envelope for clues. Searching for something, anything, to help me find my dad.

The little red stamp had a date. I think I had heard it called the postmark date before. Didn't that have something to do with when it was sent? For the next three weeks, I waited for what felt like an eternity, and I'd yet to tell Lucy about my plan. I didn't want to give her false hope. I needed to be sure this was going to work.

On the day I believed the envelope would arrive, I called the school and pretended to be Momma. A sleepy voice came from my mouth as I spoke with the school secretary.

"Hello, this is Amy Walker. Helen Birch's mother. She's sick."

"Oh, poor girl," the secretary said.

"Can you excuse her?"

I had perfect attendance until now, but this was worth it.

I spent that school day hiding in a small space between our triplex building and the side fence. I kept my eye on Mickey's arms, counting down the minutes until the time in which I thought the mail would arrive. My body ached from sitting in the same position for so long. When the white and blue postal truck pulled up to our mailbox and deposited our mail, I leaped from my hiding place and sprinted to the mailboxes at the edge of the yard.

This part was risky. If Momma looked out her bedroom window, she'd catch me. I planned to quickly sort through the mail when I got to the box, but I felt exposed standing out in the open. Instead, I took it all back to my hiding spot.

As I sifted through the mail, envelopes and ads fell into the dirt and weeds. One after another, I looked at each piece, searching for the golden ticket, but I had no such luck. Disappointed, I considered giving up. Eventually, I decided to try one more time, but if the envelope didn't come, I'd have to find another way.

On the second day, after crouching in the narrow space outside our triplex for hours, I was rewarded with a crisp white envelope with Daddy's name and address inscribed in the top left corner. I wanted to run inside, open the envelope, find a phone number, and call Daddy. But Momma was home, so I returned to my hiding spot to plan my next steps.

After school the following day, I tried to open the envelope with steam before Lucy was home and when Momma was asleep. The heavy pot on the stove hissed and bubbled as I held the envelope over the boiling water. My heart raced as the steam rose and curled around the edges of the white paper. I knew I had to be quick. I couldn't risk getting caught.

The envelope grew damp and wrinkled in my fingers, the glue stubbornly refusing to loosen its grip. I fought the urge to scream in frustration. This was harder than I believed it would be. Just as I was about to give up, I noticed something. The envelope had turned translucent, the writing beneath it visible like a ghostly imprint. My eyes widened as I read the words that appeared before me.

Daddy's full name, address, and phone number.

"Yes!" I yelled, immediately clamping my hand over my mouth. My ears strained to listen for sounds of Momma stirring in her bedroom.

When the coast was clear, I wrote the number on notebook paper, folded it, and stuffed it in my math textbook next to the original envelope. The urge to call was strong, but I made myself wait. I needed to plan what I would say.

I struggled to concentrate the next day at school, my mind racing in anticipation. In the middle school locker room, girls chatted like clucking ducks as the metal lockers slammed open and closed.

UNTITLED FOR NOW

I hid in the bathroom stall, far from the eyes of the other girls whose high ponytails matched the pitch of their shrill valley girl voices. Their crisp white sneakers squeaked on the locker room floor, and while they stood out there gossiping and spraying clouds of sweet-pea body mist to cover the stench of puberty, I tried to get my heart under control. Pink and beige tiles lined the walls, and I locked my eyes on a single chipped tile as I pulled my shirt over my head.

I only had to make it through this last hour, and then I could go home and dial the number I had worked so hard to procure. I picked my clothes up from the floor and took a deep breath before joining the gaggle of pubescent girls for P.E.

My anxiety continued to build until it was unmanageable. When I got home, my hands trembled as I dialed the number. I recognized his voice immediately, but his greeting surprised me.

"Amy, I sent the check," his gruff voice snapped.

"What?" I said, confused.

"I sent the check! I don't control the mail."

"Daddy..." My voice wavered, and there was a long pause before he spoke.

"Helen? Does your mom know you're calling me?"

I had planned this moment so perfectly. I knew exactly what I would say to convince Dad he should come for us.

But instead of my perfectly contrived monologue, I froze, and in one breath, I said, "I'm sorry. I'm sorry I called. This was stupid. I'm sorry."

"Helen, slow down. Where is your mom?"

"I don't know. I'm sorry."

"Hold on just a minute. Don't hang up. What's going on?"

Later that night, I listened with my ear to the bedroom door as Momma talked to Daddy on the phone.

"Sam, you haven't seen these girls in six years, and suddenly, you want them to visit you in Wyoming?"

I could only imagine his response.

"A month?" Momma said, surprised. "It's not my fault you live in Wyoming." She paused. "And I assume you'll withhold child support that month? Right? The bills don't stop just because you want to see your kids."

When we heard the phone click back on the receiver, Lucy and I scrambled away from the door and jumped onto my bed. I'd filled Lucy in on what I had done. She was upset that I didn't include her but forgave me quickly. She was always quick to forgive me, which I didn't deserve but appreciated.

Momma came into our bedroom and shut the door behind her. Her bewildered expression made her look insane. She wore the same pair of jeans and black hoodie every day, and her hair was a frizzy mess that once resembled a bun on the top of her head.

I waited for her to yell, but in a flat tone, she simply said, "Your father is picking you up on the first day of summer vacation. You'll go to Wyoming with him for one month. Make sure you're ready."

With that, she turned around and left. My mouth fell open, and I looked at Lucy. We couldn't believe it worked. Lucy broke our collective shock with a smile, and soon we stood grinning at each other. Although the reprieve from Momma would only be temporary, I couldn't help but hope for permanence.

Chapter 14

The closer we came to Rock Springs, the more muted the landscape became. The low mountain range framed the flat earth off in the distance, and an occasional butte or rocky feature was the only geographical point of interest among the miles of hardy sagebrush, juniper, and prickly pear cacti. People and towns were a rare commodity and grew farther apart the longer we drove.

Daddy didn't talk a lot and appeared to lose interest as Lucy and I babbled on. I didn't know him like I thought I had. It had been too long, and too much had happened. The passage of time and the weight of life created an unbridgeable chasm between us. So instead of talking, we listened to classic rock, tapping our hands to the music to expend our nervous energy.

We arrived at a sprawling trailer court just as twilight set upon us and parked in front of a modest, single-wide trailer. Inside, the house was clean and simply furnished, reflecting my father's solitary existence. The trailer comprised two bedrooms. Daddy slept in the room at the far end of the elongated rectangular space, while the other bedroom was in the hallway before the bathroom, overflowing with construction supplies and tools. Daddy was a handyman.

"I didn't have time to clear out the second room for you, so you can sleep here," he said, gesturing to the sofa and avoiding eye contact.

He lifted the cushions and pulled on a lever inside, revealing a bed. Unable to form words, I just stared, begging him to notice me. I needed him to see me, to acknowledge my presence, but he wouldn't. My heart fluttered hollowly in my chest. After over twelve hours of silence in the car, why did I expect more? Still, I mentally begged for a glimmer of warmth.

I'm here, Daddy. It's me. Please see me. I'm right here.

Daddy didn't look at us until he was done making the bed. He seemed lost for words, so he only said, "Goodnight, girls," before heading to his room.

The next day, at the break of dawn, Daddy entered the living room, where he laced his work boots and stuffed his pockets with his wallet, keys, and a multitool.

"Stay put until I get back," he muttered, leaving for work. Unsure whether we were allowed to venture out, Lucy and I stayed inside the trailer and lost ourselves in books and television shows until he returned that evening.

I tried desperately to connect with my dad in the days that followed. I told him things about me and even asked him questions about himself, but he never listened when I spoke and only gave clipped answers.

He still resembled the man in the photograph I had stared at each day since we left North Carolina six years before. Although, his hair had thinned, and wrinkles had formed around his eyes. He no longer sported a thick mustache. Instead, a thin goatee framed his mouth. I yearned to know him, but he seemed adamant about keeping his distance.

After a week of being cooped up within the trailer's four walls, we were all going stir-crazy. Lucy and I longed for the desert we had left behind. Surprisingly, I missed Momma more than I thought I would. This feeling of homesickness caught me off guard, and I needed to break free from our mundane routine.

"We should take a walk," I told Lucy one morning.

She looked up from her book and gave me a face that expressed uneasiness at the idea.

"Dad said to stay inside."

"Dad isn't here."

She relented, and we left the confines of the trailer. Unlike the blistering heat of the desert, the plains of Rock Springs were tepid. It had yet to rise beyond 90 degrees, and the summer air was comfortable. I found myself wishing for palm trees rather than sagebrush. Groups of people gathered at the backs of trucks, and rows of girls sat on tailgates talking to boys. There was already an established ecosystem in the trailer court, and we were not a part of it.

On our walk, one girl called to us. She had fire-red hair, and her foundation was two shades too dark for her face. She wore bedazzled low-rise jeans and a top that showed her midriff.

"Hey, you're new," she said, eyeing us with curiosity.

I was suddenly self-conscious.

I hesitated for a moment before responding. "Yeah, we're visiting our dad for a few weeks. I'm Helen, and this is my sister, Lucy." I gestured toward Lucy, standing beside me.

"Cool. I'm Sierra. Come hang out whenever."

I shuffled my feet and shoved my hands in my pockets.

"Cool."

As we walked away, Lucy said, "What was that?" She mocked me. "Cool."

"Stop! It wouldn't hurt to make some friends." I crossed my arms.

"I guess. If you're into that sort of thing. But can you make friends with someone who doesn't look like that?"

"You're too quick to judge."

However, Lucy's intuition was spot on—Sierra was not a good friend. Despite this, I continued to leave the house each day to hang out with her, and the more time we spent together, the more infatuated I became. Something was intoxicating about how she would dole out small parcels of affection, leaving me yearning for more, like some consolation prize I could never fully claim. She would leave me feeling included and rejected all at once. Sierra ignored Lucy, who was immune to her rejection. There was no fun in taunting someone who didn't care.

Sierra flirted with the boys who lived in the trailer park, all of whom were several years older than her. She would treat them with the same level of mixed attachment that she treated me, and they ate it up. It was pathetic. I was pathetic. Between my dad and Sierra, I had a thing for rejection.

Along with being immune to Sierra's judgment, Lucy was also wary of her.

"I don't know why you think you have to impress her. She's a brat," Lucy said to me.

"What's wrong with wanting to be her friend?"

"I just don't think she is a friend …"

Lucy and I could not agree on this, and soon, Lucy stopped coming with me to hang out with Sierra. Although Dad never gave us permission to leave the house when he was gone, he didn't seem to mind if I wasn't there when he got home. I found it easier to be out with Sierra than to try any harder with my dad. I would rather Sierra reject me than him.

Three weeks into our visit, my dad came home from work early. Sierra and I were in the bathroom applying thick layers of makeup we shoplifted from a nearby drugstore. It was so stupid to steal something we didn't need, and my heart raced the whole time, but I desperately wanted to impress Sierra.

Dad knocked on the bathroom door.

"Helen, family meeting. Livingroom. Sierra, go home."

I rolled my eyes for show as Sierra packed up the stolen makeup and left.

"Have fun," she teased, walking out of the house.

In the living room, Dad sat on the couch, his hands held together in front of him.

"I don't know how to tell you this," Dad began.

Lucy and I waited as he sighed deeply before speaking again.

"You will not be going back to California. At least not right now."

"Really? Why?" Lucy asked. She bit her lip and smiled. She was more hopeful than concerned.

Dad gazed at the ceiling. He was at a loss for words as he scratched at his goatee.

"Your mom ... um ... got into some trouble. If I take you back, you'll go into foster care."

"How long do we get to stay?" If I was being honest with myself, I was also hopeful despite our dad's emotional distance. I missed the desert, but not enough to go back. "According to the social worker I spoke with this morning, it could be a while."

Dad was unsure of what to do.

Lucy let out a rush of air and leaned back. "Doesn't surprise me."

"I knew things were bad. But this bad? I wasn't expecting this." Dad shook his head, his frustration palpable.

"Are you mad?" I asked. My first instinct was always to assume someone was mad, but why would he be? He was our dad. He should be happy we can stay longer.

"No. I'm not mad. I wasn't planning on having you live here full-time. I'm not equipped for this."

There it was. He didn't want us. The rejection hurt. I don't know why he bothered to have us visit. What was the point of this? Suddenly, I was angry. For years, he ignored us. He didn't bother to call, and now he has a chance to be a real father, and he's upset about it. I shook my head and pressed my lips together.

"Just take us back. I don't give a shit if we go to a foster home. It's better than being here with you."

"Helen," Lucy called out as I stood to leave.

"Helen," Dad said, "that is not happening. You have to understand. I haven't seen you since you were seven and Lucy was five. I don't know how to do this."

"And whose fault is that?"

Before he could answer, I walked out the door and headed to Sierra's house. The screen door slammed shut behind me, and it took all I had not to break down.

Sierra proved to be a good distraction from it all. For the rest of the summer, before 8th grade, Sierra and I made our rounds in the trailer court, hanging out with friends, flirting with boys, and testing every boundary imaginable. Overpowered by a need to be liked and accepted, I had all but nearly forgotten Lucy.

My dad struggled against me, and I fought tooth and nail right back.

"Helen, you're grounded," he said after Sierra, and I were caught smoking cigarettes in Sierra's backyard by her mother.

"Good luck with that," I replied.

By the time school began, I had fully integrated into Sierra's crowd. Like Sierra, I began to shape my eyebrows into such thin lines a camera flash would nearly all but wipe them out. Sierra and I stood side by side, dosing each other in body glitter and sprays until we coughed uncontrollably from the fumes. We held a lighter's flame in the school bathroom until the eyeliner pigment became soft. Collectively pulling on our lids, we darkened our waterlines.

For the first time, I was accepted. I belonged. Well, sort of.

Sierra liked to create drama. For no reason other than her amusement, she spread a rumor in which I called a group of girls at the school bitches and sluts. I was currently on the outs. I hated these games.

That day after school, I received prank call after prank call on my dad's home phone.

I complained to Lucy, and she gave me a look that said, *told you so*.

Frustrated, I grabbed my book bag and left the house. Even with the warm weather, a rare occurrence in Wyoming during October, the trailer park was eerily quiet. A large oak tree growing on the park's outskirts offered a place to sit out of view. I didn't want anyone to find me. Pulling out a copy of *Of Mice and Men* I borrowed from the school library, I took refuge at the base of the tree.

In the distance, leaves crackled under the foot of someone walking in my direction. A tall, lanky boy with soft, warm eyes and a strong square jawline stood before me. I recognized him as one of the boys who often hung out at a house on the other side of the trailer park.

"Hey," I said curiously.

The boy shifted his weight from one foot to the other, hands in his pockets. He looked uncomfortable.

"Uh, sorry to bother you. I just saw you were alone over here, and I, uh."

His nervousness was cute.

"And?" I nudged him to finish his thought.

"Well, I wanted to know if I could sit with you."

Oh, my goodness. Sit with me? That's all?

Nodding, I moved my bag, which sat atop a patch of grass.

When he was settled, he let out an exaggerated sigh and smiled up at me.

"What?" I said, amused.

"Nothing." His smile widened. "I'm Eric."

With confidence, I pushed my hand out and introduced myself, "I'm Helen."

His hand was just as warm and soft as his eyes. He looked at his lap, smiled again, this time to himself, and admitted, "I know."

A quiet boy. Eric never raised his voice beyond a volume barely loud enough to be heard. Sweet and gentle.

Eric quickly replaced Sierra. I no longer pined for Sierra's attention because I found what I needed with Eric. He cared for me. Unlike Sierra, Eric's love was unconditional and not given out in small doses at his whim but fully and all the time.

I didn't want my dad to screw it up, so I kept our love a secret. Especially since he was a sophomore in high school, and I was only in the eighth grade.

It wasn't until months later that my dad discovered I was seeing him. Eric often picked me up from school so I wouldn't have to ride the bus. Dad was never home, so he never knew. Until one day, we were caught making out in Eric's car in Dad's driveway.

Dad was enraged. He threw his hands up as he paced our living room floor. "I know teenage boys. I was a teenage boy. He only has one thing on his mind."

"You don't know anything about him!" I said, incredulously.

Dad tried to stop me from seeing Eric, but his efforts were wasted. I was going to do what I wanted, and my dad would not stop me.

For nearly a year, I defied my father at every turn, and Eric was always there to catch me. Eventually, Dad gave up.

CHAPTER 15

Present Day

I wake slowly, careful not to open my eyes in case the memories I dreamed try to escape. I decipher, categorize, and comprehend the various pieces of my life. A life I have lived. It's nothing groundbreaking, but it is almost as if I'm peeling back the protective layers just enough to see a new line in the portrait of my life.

A bar where old men sit and drink away their afternoons. The first time I saw a palm tree. Lucy—barefoot, her feet pounding into the desert sand.

I try to create a timeline and form a connection between these things, but the humming in my ears makes it difficult to think straight. All the memories feel like snapshots floating in time and space. Moments of clarity sit in a nebulous atmosphere. None of them precede or follow another.

The only new memory that feels solid is Lucy. I remember my sister, a wild child full of energy and light. She was fearless but careful. She was small but so vibrant. She existed beyond reality in the wonder of her imagination. Her memory makes my heart swell, but worry creeps in.

Where is she now? Does she know I am here? And if she does, why hasn't she come? Why hasn't anyone come?

After my session with Jacqueline, faint bursts of memories popped into my head, but instead of relief, I felt isolated. Loneliness makes a home within my chest, expanding and hardening until it becomes a large rock, heavy and painful. The rock takes up so much space I have no room for air, and it floods my system until it spills from my eyes.

I don't want to be alone. But I am. I am scared of what I might remember, but I also don't want to be forgotten. As I move throughout the day, the rock grows larger and heavier with every step, every motion, every breath. It expands from my chest into my stomach, making me queasy and dizzy. I sit with this rock at breakfast. I sit with this rock as I wait to receive my medication. I sit with this rock in the shower, letting the water's force plaster my hair to my face. I am dull and languid by the time I make it to group therapy, where we sit in folding chairs arranged into a circle. I may fall apart.

I try to listen to the words of others, but my rock deafens the noise, and I only make out fragments of what they say. Trying to think of something other than the overwhelming loneliness in my chest, I count the chairs. One, two, three, four, and then fourteen. There are fourteen chairs in this circle. I once sat in a circle just like this. I remember it now. Children of varying sizes sit in chairs—some are restless, kicking their legs or squirming in their seats, while others listen attentively.

I try to share with the group. I want to share my loneliness, but the rock has grown so much that I struggle to form words. At the nurses' station, I ask to talk to someone who can help me. Help me understand why I am so alone.

"Ma'am, I am sorry, but I don't have anyone to call," a nurse says.

"Lucy Birch? Can you help me get in touch with a Lucy Birch?"

"Do you have her phone number?"

I shake my head.

"I'm sorry, ma'am. Without her contact information, I can't help you."

No one can help me.

A memory of me sitting on the floor rushes in. It lands hard in my mind. Someone trashed the house. Furniture tipped over, papers scattered across the floor, and kids' toys blanketed the ground. In my memory, I screamed until my throat was raw. There is an intense likeness to how I feel at this moment.

I seek clarity, but it doesn't come. My mind feels like a canvas hurriedly painted over with white paint. Under the white, another painting exists. That painting has detailed line work and contains every color imaginable. It's my existence illustrated—my memory. But I only faintly see the painting underneath, where the white paint is thinner and less opaque. I try to bring those spots into focus, concentrating on the meaning behind the trashed living room.

In the second group session, I find my voice. I start with a memory of Lucy. But soon, everything I know to be true tumbles out like water from a breached dam. Tripping over my words, I cannot get my limited memories out fast enough. I keep talking because talking feels like a chisel to the rock in my chest. The rock crumbles a little more with each word, becoming smaller with each strike. I verbalize my loneliness and my fear of isolation. More than my fear of isolation, I wrestle with the fear of learning more.

The mental acrobatics I have done all day wear on me, and I'm asleep before lights out.

My eyes fly open and are met by an endless sea of darkness. I can barely make out the outlines of my surroundings. I can't remember where I am.

Remember, remember, remember.

I take a deep breath, pulling it through my nose, filling my lungs. Parting my lips slightly, a steady stream of air escapes as I slowly exhale. I must have been dreaming. I sift back through the images in my head. Lucy and I sitting in the backseat of a blue sedan. My grandpa, an old fat man, cooking dinner in the kitchen. Aunt Joy painting a tiny chair made from an egg carton. A small white casket lowering into the ground. It's like a montage of brief clips.

The newest clip that sticks out includes a boy named Tyler. He sits in the crook of a tree branch. One of the many trees that line the end of our street creates a barrier before the desert. He swipes the hair out of his eyes, and his brows knit together at the sound of Uncle Pete's voice. My heart races, and we look through the branches to see my uncle in the street, one hand held to his mouth to amplify Tyler's name.

I choose not to push the boundary of the memory any further. Instead, I play with the fringes of other memories, lifting ever so slightly to reveal more of what lay underneath. I don't dare rip at the paper that obscures the full memory from view, but instead, I allow myself to enjoy the parts that feel good.

I return to the memory of Aunt Joy, who painted furniture for our homemade dollhouse. Her tongue stuck out over her top lip as she concentrated. Then I see her on the ground outside. Her belly is large and round. She is pregnant. She moans, and I run. A baby is born—our new cousin. His name is Nathan.

"Nathan," I whisper aloud, testing the name on my tongue. The sound of a bed creaking and sheets shifting reminds me I am not alone.

"Who?" says a voice from the darkness, but it doesn't sound like my roommate. I freeze, trying to discern who is in the other bed.

"Hello?" the voice says.

"I'm sorry. Who are you?" I think back to the day before, searching for the missing context. The room was empty when I came to bed.

"I'm your new roomie, Ashley. Helen, right? That's what the nurse said. Just got here a couple of hours ago. You were asleep when I came in."

"Oh."

"Who's Nathan? Is he your boyfriend, husband, secret lover?"

I'm struck by her forwardness. The room is too dark to see her, so I only have her words and tone to base any judgments. It's probably fine to tell her.

"My cousin," I finally reply.

"Huh. Interesting." She moves on the bed, and I try to make out her shape.

"Why?" I press, curious why she finds my cousin interesting.

Ashley chuckles. "Because if I call out a man's name in the middle of the night, it's definitely not going to be my cousin's."

Ashley's chuckle turns into nonstop giggling, and it is infectious. I don't understand what comes over me, but I can't stop once I start. We are both completely overtaken, laughing big belly laughs. Light floods the room, and Ashley and I stop laughing. I cover my face with my arm, trying to block the invading light.

Squinting over my arm, I see a middle-aged woman peering through eyeglasses, the frames as transparent as the lenses.

"I'm glad you all are having fun here, but the other patients are sleeping. Please, keep it down and try to get some sleep, all right?"

Ashley and I both nod. I can see her now. Ashley is a young Asian woman, likely only in her early twenties. The door shuts, and it's dark again. It takes immense control to stifle another uncontrollable fit of laughter.

When we both calm down, I lie on my back and stare into the dark, listening to Ashley breathe. Over time, it slows to a steady rhythm. Part of me longed for the silence afforded to me by my last roommate, but maybe I was wrong. Maybe I need liveliness.

I think back to my dream and try to lift the surrounding edges again, but they have since blurred. Instead, I inspect the remaining images until I fall into a deep sleep.

The next morning, I wake up to a song. I vaguely recognize it, but Ashley's awful singing voice makes it difficult to place. I tell her so, and she throws her pillow at me. Another moment of connection. I hold it in my chest and let it soothe my worries.

At breakfast, we sit together, and she tells me how she ended up here.

"My dad made me come here."

"He can do that?" I ask.

"I cut."

"What?"

"Cut." Ashley twists her arms, showing glossy white scars trailing from the inside of her elbow to her right wrist. A thick white bandage covers her left wrist.

I shake my head, unsettled by the brazenness with which she revealed her scars. "That is a lot of scars. Why do you do it?"

Ashley stuffs her toast in her mouth and talks with bits of white bread floating around her tongue. "Because it makes me feel better."

"How does it make you feel better?"

She shrugs. "I don't know, but I know it works. My therapist says that cutting has something to do with positive and negative reinforcements and that cutting provides both for me. It's hard to focus on being sad when you're bleeding. Sometimes when the physical pain subsides, it takes the other types of pain with it. Does that make sense?"

It makes little sense to me. The thought of cutting into my skin makes my stomach turn, and I decide I'm done with my oatmeal.

"No, but that's okay. So, your dad forced you to be admitted?" I wondered how that works. I am being held here against my will, so she must be too.

"Sort of. He threatened to cut me off if I didn't get help. Ironic right? Cut me off?" She roars wildly, and although it should not be funny, it is, and I chuckle at the joke.

Ashley begins to unwrap her bandage, but I do not want to know what exists underneath. Before I can protest, the dressing falls away, and there is a fresh cut in the beginning stages of healing. This time, Ashley's laugh breaks. "I guess I cut too far."

The moment is uncomfortable, but I force myself to stay present.

"So, what's your story?" Ashley asks.

My brow furrows, and my eyes fall to the table. "It's kind of untitled. I don't remember anything."

Ashley perks at this. "Really?"

"Mostly, but it's coming back—in flashes."

"So, you're only untitled for now." She grins at me. "What's it like?"

"What's what like?"

"Losing your memory?"

Ashley puts down her cup and leans in.

"It's kind of like a Polaroid camera. Each time I get a flash, my brain fills in the gaps around it. I only remember my childhood at this point. I know my name, my age, and things I shouldn't know, like how a computer works, but I don't remember most of the last thirty years of my life. It's bizarre."

"I'd say so. So, how do they fix it?"

"I don't know. Memories come to me in pieces, or something I see might remind me of something I once knew. I don't really want to remember, though. I'm afraid of whatever I forgot. You know?"

"No, not really." Ashley turns her attention to re-wrapping her wrist. Her black hair covers a portion of her face as she concentrates.

Uncomfortable with the state of her wrists, I focus my eyes upward and study her profile. Ashley is a petite girl with a heart-shaped face. Her chin comes to a perfect point in juxtaposition to her soft cheeks and short rounded nose. All her features are beautifully balanced.

I don't know why I thought Ashley would understand why I don't want to remember. I don't understand why she cuts.

"Oh," I say.

"No offense," she continues, "but, the past is always bound to catch up with you."

CHAPTER 16

Before Helen Lost Her Memory

Dad, Lucy, and I drove several miles out of town to a small trailer house. It sat at the end of a gravel road on a dirt lot far off the highway. One of five trailer houses, they were all positioned in different directions. There was no real sense of where one yard stopped, and the other began. It was almost as if someone threw a handful of houses into the air, and they stayed where they landed.

This trailer was the only one among the scattered houses with all its windows still intact and void of old automobiles or other large pieces of metal and debris in the yard.

The inside of the trailer was scarcely furnished with an old green sofa decorated with small pink flowers and a round dining room table, just large enough for three mismatched chairs. Endless wood paneling darkened the space, but this was our new home. This was where we would live with Momma.

It had been over a year since we left California, and somehow, I thought leaving that place meant I had gotten out. But no, Momma followed. I couldn't blame my dad for moving her out here. I'd given him hell. He deserved it, but still. My actions had consequences, and I would be wise to learn that.

I had not talked to Momma since we left her. She called, but I was angry, too angry to speak. Too angry to lie. I wanted to move on and hated being forced to look back.

Dad showed us around the trailer. It had two bedrooms—one for Momma and one for us girls. Our bedroom was furnished simply like the rest of the house. Two twin beds on either side of a bedside table. No dresser. The pressboard closet door had a hole, likely from someone putting their fist through it. Images of Matt putting his fist through drywall came to mind, and I made a mental note to cover it.

Lucy claimed her bed, the one to the left.

"What do you think?" I asked.

She shrugged, and I knew she felt just as torn as I did. "It's fine."

Lucy had been fierce and headstrong for as long as I could remember, but her response told me she had given up. I was angry about the change, but even more, I felt scared. I didn't know if I could survive Momma one more time.

Only a few days later, Momma arrived on a Greyhound bus. Just her and a duffle bag. She looked weathered, her skin blotchy and burned, her hair bleached by the sun. She was missing at least two more teeth, and dried blood darkened her chapped lips. Her eyes were wet with tears as she opened her arms wide like a seagull, ready for flight. I turned away and climbed back into the car, not ready to embrace her.

For weeks, I lived in parallel to Momma and Lucy. Lucy had already let the wall she built to protect herself crumble. Conversely, I added a few more bricks to mine each day, allowing it to rise higher and higher so no one could peek over.

One Saturday afternoon, shortly after my freshman year of high school started, I lay in bed waiting for Eric to arrive. When Eric's car pulled up to the house, I jumped up, fastened my watch on my wrist, grabbed my bag, slipped on my shoes, and headed for the front door.

"Where are you going?" Momma asked.

I ignored her.

"Helen, stop where you are right now!" Momma yelled.

I ignored her again, and she moved toward me, pulling at my arm as I tried to exit the house.

"I understand you are angry, but I am still your mother."

"No, a mother wouldn't have done what you did. Therefore, you are not my mother."

She let go, and I walked out, brimming with undeniable self-righteousness.

Eric and I were planning to go to dinner, but I asked if we could drive until we found a spot away from prying eyes. We pulled onto a dirt patch on a road far out of town. I straddled his lap in the backseat, starving for his touch. Our kissing became frantic and hurried, and I bit his lip as he pulled away.

"Ow, that hurts." He held his hand to his mouth, pressing two fingers lightly on his bottom lip.

Tenderly, I apologized with a light kiss, which deepened quickly. My hunger increased. I reached for the hem of my shirt and pulled it over my head. He pulled back to gaze at my exposed chest and cautiously put his hand over one of my breasts. His touch was soft and apprehensive. I appreciated this, but I didn't want soft. He kissed my neck as his hands worked, trailing kisses from just below my ear to my nipple. I moved in a circular motion on his lap, groaning with pleasure, hoping the sound would push him to act with more confidence. Frustrated by his slow pace, I reached for his belt, but he stopped me.

"Not here." His warm eyes showed concern. I flipped to the seat beside him and hurriedly pulled my shirt back over my head. The rejection was painful—like a dagger straight to my chest. *Why didn't he want me?*

"Why? Am I not good enough? Are you too good for me?" I asked. An accusation colored my tone.

"No. I just want it to be right. I think we should wait."

Eric brushed the hair from my face. Still kind, still gentle, and still in love with me. I folded into him and rested my head on his chest. His heart beat quickly, and I listened closely, waiting for it to slow to a regular, steady rhythm.

"I'm sorry." I sighed. "Sometimes I feel you don't love me."

I knew it wasn't true, but I needed him to tell me how loved I was.

"You can't mean that. You know I love you."

"Then why don't you want to have sex with me?"

Other girls were being pressured to have sex all the time, but this boy, my boy, still wasn't ready.

"I do, but I told you, I think it's important to wait. I want our first time to be when we are both ready."

I was ready. He wasn't.

By the time we pulled up to my house, it was dark. I kissed Eric long and hard, trying to prolong the time before I had to go inside. He sat back, catching on to my game, so after a final peck on the lips, I went inside.

Momma was on the sofa waiting for me. She held a cigarette in one hand while the other rested on a leg that jiggled as she bounced it incessantly. She must have been sitting here for hours, as the ashtray next to her showed evidence of that.

"Helen, can we talk?"

"No," I said and walked to my bedroom.

"Matt is on his way here."

I whipped back around. "What? I thought he was still in prison. When did he get out?"

"He will be here tomorrow."

"No!" I shook my head vehemently. "No! Momma, listen. I'm sorry. Don't bring Matt here. Please, Momma. Please." My contention turned to begging, and I hated it. If I thought I couldn't survive Momma before, I definitely couldn't survive her with Matt here.

"I can't do this by myself, Helen. Look at us. I'm not even capable of getting my teenage daughter under control. I need him."

She didn't care about us. She never cared.

I didn't know what else to say, but I reached for anything that could help.

"Dad won't let you," I warned.

"Your father has made his choices. He doesn't get to dictate mine."

I ran toward my room and threw myself on my bed. I grabbed my pillow and screamed into it until my throat burned and my voice became hoarse.

Lucy sat on her bed, sketching in a notebook. "What's happening?" she asked.

"Matt." It was the only word I could get out.

She didn't press for more, fully understanding what would happen, and instead crawled into bed with me.

"I don't want him here either," she whispered into my hair. Lucy had always been there for me, and I consistently failed her. I was supposed to take care of her, and here she was, taking care of me.

I sat up and held her face in my hands. "I'm going to get us out of here. I don't know how yet, but I will. I won't leave you behind this time."

Matt's return extinguished any hope I had left for a relationship with my dad. I called him that night, desperate to stop the inevitable.

"I'm sorry, Helen. I don't know what you want me to do," he said.

He wasn't even going to try.

Matt arrived clean and sober. He was still charming and, on the surface, seemed nice. But old habits die hard, and little time passed before Momma and Matt were using again. As much as I hated the drug use, it was nothing compared to sitting on my bed with Lucy and listening to Momma beg Matt to stop hurting her.

I'd lost my way before. I had prioritized acceptance over what I needed, what Lucy needed. I was done messing around. It was time to get serious.

Chapter 17

At the intersection of Interstate 80 and Highway 191, Rock Springs was a transient town that catered to roughnecks and coal miners. People were different in this place. Severe winter conditions and back-breaking jobs hardened people. The wind always blew, and there were more trucks and guns than people.

I knew that if I was to make a better life for myself and Lucy, we had to leave Rock Springs behind. My plan was simple. Do well in school, get a job, and pray. I believed that with hard work and determination, I could graduate high school, attend college alongside Eric, and build the life Lucy and I deserved.

I began working at a local diner during my freshman year, and by the time I was a sophomore, the small restaurant had become a second home. Each week, I stashed away cash, becoming less dependent on the whims of Momma and Matt's care. But it wasn't easy.

We lost heat in our house shortly after my sixteenth birthday and the New Year.

"Ah!" Lucy yelped as her feet kicked up from the linoleum floor in the kitchen.

I stood at the sink, running water and testing the temperature.

"I think our heater broke," she said, shivering.

I threw my head back and groaned. I didn't know how to fix a furnace, which meant I needed to wake Matt. Hopefully, he was in a good mood today.

I knocked at Momma and Matt's door and cracked it open. Matt snored, but Momma woke up.

"Hey," she said.

"Um. Mom, the heater isn't working. Can you wake Matt?"

Several minutes later, Matt came out of their room, shivering. He had changed since the days when he would strut around our cul-de-sac in California, acting like the neighborhood pretty boy. Time had taken its toll, leaving behind a protruding beer belly despite his rampant drug use. His face bore the weight of life in the form of deeply set wrinkles.

"Damn, it's cold," he said, pushing the greasy blonde hair out of his face.

I gestured to the hallway closet where the furnace was located. "Can you fix it?"

He opened the closet door and lowered himself before a large gray cylinder of metal covered in years of accumulated dust. Leaning against the interior wood paneling in the hallway, I prayed for a simple fix as he tinkered around. Several minutes later, he grunted as he lifted himself from the floor.

"It's not broken. We're out of propane."

"Okay?"

He scratched his head. "Sorry. It's going to have to wait. We just spent the last of our money on rent. Let's hope our pipes don't freeze. Should only be a couple of weeks. Dress in layers."

His solution was layers. I stole a glance at Lucy, and she rolled her eyes. *I'll just have to do it myself.*

I wouldn't wait until Momma and Matt had the money to fill the tank. Matt had a job at a local junkyard but was unreliable, as were his paychecks.

The following day, I walked into the diner. The click-clack and scraping of silverware and excited conversations mingled in the air. I inhaled the smell of breakfast—fried eggs, burnt toast, and sausage and slowly let out the air, forcing myself to think about the task at hand. I needed to make $140. I was working a double, so maybe it was possible.

"Hey Helen, can you take the back?" my coworker, Bethany, called out. "Lisa called in sick today, so we need to split her section."

More tables equaled more money. She had answered my prayers. Bethany whipped around the corner of the restaurant's bar, a perfectly balanced stack of plates lining her left arm. Quickly, I threw on my apron and tied it in the front so our patrons couldn't pull at the string when I walked by. My Mickey Mouse watch read 6:58 a.m.

By 8:00 a.m., the diner was so packed we could barely keep up. We weaved in and out around the room, grabbing empty plates and refilling cups of coffee. We called out orders to the cooks as we clipped yellow carbon copies to the metal spinning wheel at the kitchen window.

"Chick fry over easy and a short stack!"

Every second counted on the floor of the diner. In small pockets of contentment, we tallied our checks and took turns standing at the register, counting back change.

When the breakfast rush slowed, we sat at a booth in the corner near the busser cart to eat or smoke before checking on the last of our tables and doing some much-needed cleanup.

I worked straight through the day, jumping from one mealtime rush to the next until we shut off our light and turned the sign around at 8:00 p.m., letting those who may be on the lookout for late-night food know we were closed.

Sitting at a table, we dug crumpled bills from our apron pockets and sorted the various denominations, counting out our take-home-pay. I prayed as I counted. It would cost over $200 to fill our tank, which would last us more than a month. I already had sixty dollars. One, two, three … twenty, thirty, forty. Ninety-five dollars. I could fill it halfway, but they charged a thirty-five-dollar service fee each time. It would be better if I could fill it all the way.

"Shit. It was busy, but people were all in a rotten mood today. I should have made way more than this," one of the waitresses said, and the rest of us agreed. Carefully stacking the bills, I folded them over and shoved them into my pocket for safekeeping.

In the diner bathroom, I smacked tears away from my face. I was so tired of crying all the damn time. My chest felt tight, and I sat on the toilet, trying to regain control. Maybe I should call my dad and ask him for the money. I wrestled with the idea. I rarely talked to him anymore. I wouldn't call him. It was better that way.

"Helen, are you going to finish your side work or sit in the bathroom all night?" asked Bethany from the other side of the door.

"Coming! Sorry!"

At the sink, I splashed some water on my face and stared at myself in the mirror. Y*ou will find a way.*

Out on the floor, I wiped the tables. As I did, I called to Bethany. "You working tomorrow?"

"Yep, I come in for the after-church rush," she said, rolling her eyes. The eye roll was to be expected. Church people were rude, didn't tip well, and complained a lot.

"Is there any way I can take your shift? I'll swap you for literally any shift you want. I could use the money."

Bethany agreed, and I breathed a sigh of relief. *I can do this.*

After work, Eric and I made loops on Main Street, cruising as most teens did on Saturday nights. But, unlike others who bumped music with their windows down, competing for airspace, it remained utterly silent in Eric's car. Eric had just told me he was not returning to school after the winter break and wanted to work full-time for his dad's plumbing business.

"You only have one semester left," I said.

"I don't see the point."

This was not how it was supposed to go. Why would he quit now? He was supposed to graduate and then work to save money. That way, when I graduated, we could take Lucy and leave. He agreed to this. We were supposed to go to college together. That was the plan.

"What about our plan?" I asked, afraid to look at him.

"It's your plan, Helen," he sighed.

The disappointment settled heavily in my chest, rendering me speechless and unable to argue further.

At home, Momma and Matt were asleep. Matt's snores made the house tremble. I wondered if they had just turned in for the night or had been asleep all day. The accumulated disappointments of the day weighed on me. I wanted my life to be different, but it seemed no matter how hard I tried, it wouldn't be.

In our room, Lucy sat perched on her bed, swathed in layers of blankets that cocooned her from head to toe. She left only her hands out so she could draw in her notebook, and I watched as a dragon came to life on the page before her. Lucy was talented in so many ways. Over the years, her chaotic energy took the form of limitless creativity. On the outside, she was calm, but inside, her mind wandered through imaginary lands full of mystical creatures, castles, and heroic quests.

"Have they left their bedroom at all today?" I asked as I emptied my pockets before untying my apron.

Lucy looked at me and shook her head. "No," she said, knowing what I was really asking—did Matt go to work today?

Frustrated by everything outside my control, I engaged in the nightly ritual that often helped calm my nerves. Under my bed was an old lunchbox I purchased from a yard sale in town. The metal lunchbox reminded me of our grandpa's house. The sides were painted avocado green, the same color as Grandpa's bathroom fixtures, and the face had a flower power design that reminded me of a crocheted blanket that decorated the top of Grandpa's recliner.

I sank to my knees and pulled the lunchbox into my lap, unlatching the metal clasps and lifting the lid. Inside were sixty dollars, an old photo of my dad, a third of a postcard, and an assortment of college brochures pilfered from the counselor's office. Some were already so worn from the constant folding and unfolding. Fanning the brochures out across the floor, I stared at them. Beautiful brick buildings with pristine landscaping, students hard at work, colorful flags, and cartoonish mascots decorated the covers. Usually, the brochures filled me with hope, but today, anxiety swelled inside my chest. I wanted to rip up the brochures. Rip up my plan. Throw it away. Forget about it entirely. However, I forced myself to put the brochures back in the lunchbox and close the lid. I promised myself I would find a way.

I didn't call Eric for a ride to work the following day. I couldn't rely on him anymore, and it was better I figure shit out by myself. So, even though I knew it would eat into my cash, I called a taxi. We hadn't had a car in months. Momma sold the car Dad bought her when she moved here, probably for drugs, and since then, random cars would occasionally show up at our house, none mechanically sound.

I waited outside for the taxi to arrive, standing among bags of trash that never made it to the dumpster, car parts from the junkyard, and other odd bits that littered the landscape outside our trailer. When a shiny 1976 Cadillac Seville pulled up, I felt embarrassed as it looked utterly out of place against the backdrop of chaos. Climbing into the passenger seat, I couldn't help but admire the shine of the conditioned leather and black plastic dash.

As soon as I closed the door, I scurried to open it again, unsure whether I should move to the back, but the taxi driver's voice stopped me. "No need to move to the back, ma'am. Feel free to sit there if that's where you're comfortable."

The man in the driver's seat was in his early sixties. He wore a short-sleeved, blue plaid shirt with opal-colored, western-style buttons, Levi Jeans, and wide-framed glasses. He had combed his hair neatly up and over, and the smell of his piney pomade mixed nicely with spearmint gum and Old Spice cologne.

"Where are you going this morning?" he asked. His nasally voice suggested he was from Texas.

"Work. I mean the diner on main street," I replied, staring out the window.

"You got it, ma'am." With a firm grip, he shifted the car into drive and pulled away from the wreckage that was my front yard. "You're a bit young for ma'am, so why don't you tell me your name?"

"Helen."

"My name is Billy Ray Howard. My friends call me Bill, but you're welcome to call me whichever you please," he said with a warm smile.

"My friends call me Helen, so I guess that is what you can call me. Nice to meet you."

Billy Ray was a talker. By the time we had finished the trek down the dirt road and onto the highway, he had told me his entire life story. He had two sons, a daughter, a wife, and four grandchildren. He described each of them in such perfect detail that a vivid picture of each person scrolled through my mind. Billy Ray's candidness and friendly nature made it easy to share parts of myself with him. Our conversation flowed with remarkable ease, resembling a seamless game of ping-pong. Before I knew it, we were at the diner, and I was so glad I had taken the taxi. As the car came to a complete stop, I reached into my wallet to pay my fare.

Billy Ray held his hand up to stop me. "No need. The first one is on the house. What time shall I pick you up later?"

Flustered by his statement, I struggled with the zipper on my wallet. "Oh no. I can pay. How much is it?"

The left corner of his mouth stretched up. "No need. Just let me know what time to be back."

His generosity felt unnatural. "Are you sure?" I asked.

"I'm certain."

"Okay, I will be done at 8:30 tonight," I said, reaching for the door handle.

"See you then." He tipped his head and shifted the car back into drive.

I stood on the sidewalk, watching as he drove away. Shock stripped me of my manners, and it wasn't until I was inside the diner that I realized I had never said thank you.

CHAPTER 18

His smile was alarmingly charming, and I think he knew it.

"Are you doing anything tonight?" he asked. Everyone at the table—two girls and another guy—stared at me, waiting for my answer.

"Uh, I work until 9:00, so probably nothing."

Why did I lie? I have plans with Eric—my boyfriend.

"Want to come to a party?" His smile widened, making his left eye crinkle slightly in the corner. My heart fell into my stomach.

I fidgeted with the pens clipped to my apron pocket.

"I don't know anything about a party."

He chuckled. His laugh was utterly disarming. My knees felt weak.

"I am telling you about the party. You should come." He looked at me, and I felt like I might faint.

"Okay." I looked down at my feet and back up quickly.

What am I doing? Am I flirting? Oh, this is so gross. What is wrong with me?

He wrote the address on a napkin and slid it over to me. I tucked it in my apron and spun on my heels, trying to keep my face neutral until I turned around. Once I made it a few feet from the table, I heard the girls giggling uncontrollably and remembered how to breathe.

Bethany was on the other side of the diner, watching me. I opened my mouth and widened my eyes, screaming soundlessly.

When I made it over to her, she teased, "He's cute."

"I know, and he wants me to go to a party."

"You should," she said. "You're sixteen. When was the last time you went to a party?"

"Never," I admitted.

"You're supposed to go to parties, not pull double shifts and skip sleep to study."

"It's just I ..."

"One night of fun will not be the end of the world. Tell you what. I'll do both of our side work so you can leave early and get ready. You can't wear that to your first high school party." She eyed my clothes.

I looked at my bleach-stained shirt covered in dried mashed potatoes from leaning over a table to clean it, a table on which a toddler had smooshed the soft potatoes along the length of the edge.

"But what about Eric? Should I have him come with me?"

"Do you want him to go with you?" She raised her eyebrows as she asked the question.

I had to admit. I didn't. I wanted to flirt with that guy. "What do I tell him?"

She waved her hand through the air. "Oh girl, I will not get in the middle of that." She had listened too patiently as I complained about Eric and how our lives were no longer going in the same direction. I was sure she was sick of it.

When the restaurant closed, I called Eric and canceled our plans, promising we would talk soon, but not tonight. "I don't feel well. I just need to go home and get some sleep. Brittany must have given me whatever she came to school with this week."

The pang of guilt that came with lying blossomed, but I quickly released it and called Billy Ray.

The old taxi driver had been my most trusted confidant for the last several months. Sometimes when he dropped me off at home, we would sit in his car and talk for hours about all sorts of things until he got another call. These were conversations filled with dreams, ambitions, and echoes of a life I wanted but felt was out of reach. I told him how I yearned for a better life, and he provided counsel in response. He wasn't like anyone else I'd met before. He didn't expect anything from me.

Billy Ray drove me home and waited outside while I changed my clothes and added a fresh coat of mascara.

"Where are you going?" Lucy asked.

"A party."

"Does mom know?"

"No, and don't tell her? If she asks, just say I'm spending the night at a friend's house, but you don't remember which one."

Was going to this party a good idea? I felt torn between my responsibilities and the need to be a normal teenage girl sometimes.

When I climbed back into Billy Ray's car, I handed him the napkin with the address, and he drove me to the house without asking what I was up to.

As I got out of the car, Billy Ray said, "Hey. Looks like a fun party. Do me a favor and call me when it's over. I don't care if it's 3:00 a.m. Your ride home is on the house. Got it?"

I nodded.

"Just promise you'll call me before getting in a vehicle with someone else. Okay?"

I could see the concern on Billy Ray's face. He wanted me to be safe. He cared about me. I felt bad that he did. I didn't want to inconvenience him, but I was also grateful for him. Half the time, Billy Ray wouldn't let me pay. He said our conversation was enough of a payment for the ride. He was a good person with no agenda and looked out for me—something no one else seemed to do.

Inside the party, I walked around, looking for the boy who invited me. I could ask around, but I didn't know his name. Feeling utterly out of place, I sat on the sofa and pretended to belong, bobbing my head to the music, my hands tucked between my thighs, waiting. All throughout the house, people laughed and talked and danced. Everyone seemed to know one another, and I was the only one left without a genuine connection. The only wallflower.

I eventually had enough and stood to leave, regretting my decision to come in the first place. I didn't belong here. But, as I looked for a house phone to call Billy Ray, I saw him—and that brilliant smile. He looked straight at me.

His name was Jude. I liked how his name felt on my tongue when I said it aloud. *Jude*. He grabbed my hand and led me to the kitchen. His fingers were long and lanky. He was tall with soft, wavy brown hair and that disarming smile. A red solo cup filled with vodka and lemonade sloshed as he transferred it to my hand. I sipped the drink. It was disgusting, but I drank it anyway, letting the cold liquid warm my insides.

Party guests passed a joint around, and I froze when it came my way. I was going to be laughed out of this party. I considered taking it. Maybe I didn't have to inhale.

I decided to say no. I'd rather be laughed at. Jude held the joint between his thumb and forefinger, pursing his lips as he took a slow drag. His mouth created a little O while he held the smoke in his lungs, letting it seep into his body. He blew it out slowly, and it was hypnotizing.

"Want to go outside? It's loud in here," he said as he passed the joint to the next person.

I smiled and nodded.

Outside, we leaned against a car. His body pressed into mine, and he bent to reach my lips. His hot, wet kiss engulfed me. It was cold outside, but the vodka and his touch kept me warm. His hips, angular and sharp, dug into me the more we kissed. He picked me up and placed me on the hood of the car. I wrapped my legs around him. I liked it.

When he asked if I wanted to go somewhere we could be alone, my mind flashed to Billy Ray. I'd promised him I wouldn't get in a car with anyone else, but Jude's gravitational pull was too strong. Taking my hand, he led me to a dark green Jeep. He fiddled with the dials inside, promising it would warm up in no time. We drove to the end of town, and I watched the lights scatter into steaks across the dark sky. Eventually, those lights faded as we traveled down an unpaved road and into darkness. It was like the roads Eric and I would find. Roads where we would sit in his backseat, pushing boundaries without ever crossing the line. A sense of guilt crept in. I was so familiar with guilt that I almost craved it.

We parked, and for a while, we talked. I liked how he talked more than his smile. He was articulate. He lived with his aunt and attended the local community college where he was completing his general education requirements for a degree in English Literature.

"You sure are prepossessing," he said, tucking a loose strand of hair behind my ear.

"What does that mean?" I asked.

"Attractive," he whispered, and I felt stupid for not knowing that.

His smile faded, and I wished for it to come back. He moved toward me deliberately, and his eyes narrowed on my face. His fingers ran up the base of my neck, through my hair, and stopped at the back of my head. With a force I was unprepared for, he stole my breath and kissed me—hard and eager. I knew what I was doing was wrong, but I didn't want it to stop. I wanted him to want me.

"We can move to the back." He signaled to the empty space in the back, where the seats folded down.

Wrapped together in the back of Jude's Jeep, we explored each other's bodies. He licked and nipped the skin between my ear and shoulder, and I returned the favor by running my hands across his back, massaging the skin under my fingers. His hands slipped into my shirt, and he released the clasp on my bra in one swift motion. Pushing my shirt up, he covered one small breast with his long, lanky fingers and bent to bring the other into his mouth. I tilted my head back, caught up in the euphoria.

Jude was hard against me, and I couldn't breathe. I sucked in some air but needed more. Again and again, I tried to catch my breath until he stopped. Hyperventilating, I started to cry, and he pulled away, but I didn't want him to. I sat up, still unable to control my breath, and he pushed himself up beside me, rubbing my back.

"Are you okay?" he asked. His brows pulled inward, and his mouth turned down at the corners.

"I don't know," I mumbled. I couldn't think straight. I didn't know what was going on with this body of mine.

"It's okay. We can go," he said.

"No! I don't want to go." I shook my head.

Jude then pulled me into him, and we lay together in silence. After a while, he said he was going to take me home, but I pulled his face back to mine, and just like before, he kissed me. Jude sat up and took off his shirt, his pale skin glowing in the moonlight. I stared up, frozen, as he worked to free himself from his pants. His erection was visible through his loose cotton boxers. He again rested beside me, and we continued to kiss, our hips moving together in a circular motion. I sensed his fingers on the button of my jeans, and I let him undo it. He slipped his fingers between my skin and the waistband of my underwear.

"Are you sure?" he asked.

I kissed him hard and pulled away, leaving the trace of a "yes" on his lips. He tugged at my jeans, and when I was free, he pulled off his boxers. Kneeling between my exposed thighs, he looked down at me. He moved into me, but I stopped him.

"Shouldn't we use a condom?" I asked.

"Are you on birth control?" I frowned and shook my head. I wouldn't even know where to get birth control.

"It will be fine. I'll pull out," he promised.

I nodded before fully comprehending his solution, and suddenly he was inside me. I let out an unexpected cry. He groaned in response, excited by the noise. It stung, and I bit my lip, attempting to stifle the pain. It was over quickly, and he pulled away, leaving me with a white milky substance on my inner thigh.

After we dressed, we relaxed against each other.

"Does it always hurt?" I asked.

He looked at me, alarmed. "This was your first time?"

"Sort of." I looked away, humiliated. My face grew hot, and I thought I might hyperventilate again, but Jude pulled me tight to him and placed a kiss on the top of my head.

"Only the first time."

A while later, Jude drove me back to the party so Billy Ray wouldn't worry. It was just after midnight when Billy Ray picked me up, and as we drove home, he must have sensed something was wrong because he asked me if I was okay and had fun.

I smiled softly and whispered, "Yeah, I'm just tired." And even though that was the truth, I couldn't shake the feeling of remorse for what I had done. I had cheated on Eric, and the guilt ate at me.

As we drove, I tried to rationalize my behavior, telling myself that Eric and I were on different paths, and our love was no longer enough to sustain us. But deep down, I knew what I had done was wrong, and the only option was to tell Eric the truth.

The next day, Eric and I drove to a local park where we planned to eat lunch. As we unwrapped our sub sandwiches while sitting in his car, he said, "Hey, I know things haven't been great between us."

Okay, here was my chance to say, "*Yea, Eric, things haven't been great, and I'm a cheating whore.*" But I didn't. I couldn't.

"I've thought a lot about the future and what you want for the both of us. I know you see in me things I don't see in myself. So, I guess what I'm trying to say is that I'm going back to school because I know it's important to you. I talked to Mr. Wells today, and he said I could go to school half days and use the hours at my dad's shop as work release credits."

His eyes, which had rested upon the field of dead grass ahead of us, traveled to my face. My heart shattered. I couldn't break his heart, too. He loved me, and I messed it all up. He was choosing me, and I felt appalled by how I failed to choose him. The thought gutted me, and I shivered.

"You cold?"

"Yea. I'm cold," I whispered, moving closer to him.

Eric leaned toward me and held a hand to my cheek before placing a gentle, loving kiss on my lips. Maybe I could pretend like nothing ever happened. I could just move on and not look back. It was only one mistake. It was nothing.

Eric returned to school, and I tried to push what happened with Jude out of my mind. I wanted to erase it all, banishing the memories and the associated emotions, but I was too weak. All it took was for Jude to show up at the diner a week after the house party. It ignited the familiar yet destructive pull within me, and once again, I found myself with Jude in the back of his Jeep on a county road in the middle of nowhere.

I was a disgusting waste of a human being.

CHAPTER 19

I jolted awake. Cold sweat drenched my body, and the clammy sensation was repulsive. The queasiness in my stomach triggered an involuntary response, causing my mouth to water. Despite the darkness still enveloping the sky, it felt like I had been asleep for an eternity, leaving me disoriented and bewildered. The queasiness intensified, and I sprinted from my bed to our bathroom. In a rush, the contents of my stomach unloaded into the toilet. Again, my gut wrenched, expelling the rest.

Lucy followed me into the bathroom. "You okay?"

"I think I'm sick," I said, groaning. I doubled over again, dry heaving into the dirty toilet bowl. My face came too close to the brown copper stain that sat where the water's edge stopped. I spat slimy bits of lettuce from last night's dinner into the bowl, the taste putrid and unappealing.

"No, duh." Lucy handed me a warm damp washcloth, and I wiped my face, thankful for her.

"Do you want me to get you some saltines?" she asked.

I waved the washcloth toward the bedroom. "Go back to bed. I'll be fine."

In the confines of the bathroom, the convulsions continued. Small amounts of yellowish-green liquid left me until all I had left was air. I fell asleep on the cold bathroom floor, waking up hours later as Lucy stepped around me, getting ready for school.

"How do you feel?" Her voice wavered with concern.

I moaned, pushing up on my hands. I was terrified that I would be sick again if I moved too fast. But to my surprise, I was no longer queasy. Instead, my stomach rumbled.

"I'm hungry."

Sitting in bed, I gratefully accepted the bowl of instant oatmeal Lucy had prepared. With each bite, I felt a little better, and by the time I finished, I felt fine—just tired. Little did I know the fatigue and the unwelcome recurrence of vomiting spells would persist. Every morning, before the break of daylight, I woke suddenly and bolted out of bed like a racehorse startled by a cannon. After not making it twice, I learned to keep a trashcan nearby. As I heaved in the early morning, Lucy held my hair, delivered cups of ice water, and cleaned the vomit from my cheeks. She was too good to me.

School was brutal. Exhausted, I kept falling asleep in class, and my teachers would have to wake me. The other students would watch as I wiped away the small puddle of drool left behind on my desk. Normally, I'd be mortified, but I was too exhausted to care.

The nausea was only an additional layer that complicated my already complicated life. After I realized I couldn't simply push Jude or the memories away, I decided to break up with Eric. But each time the opportunity confronted me, I failed.

With Eric back at school, he could tell things were off between us, but he didn't push it. Eric never pushed me to do anything. He only took care of me.

On the third day of vomiting spells, Eric met me at school with a large thermos of savory soup his mom had made—another thoughtful gesture to make me feel like a terrible person. Thankfully, after seven days of unrelenting morning nausea, I woke feeling okay. The vomiting had ceased, and I was optimistic that whatever bug plagued me had finally worked its way out of my system. Wellness felt like freedom, and I celebrated with a large bowl of frosted cornflakes before school, relishing each sweet and crunchy bite. The absence of sickness filled me with such elation I felt as though I was gliding as I walked through the halls of my high school.

In my third hour of English, I listened to my classmates deliver oral book reports. Then it was my turn. Mrs. Johnson called on me. "Helen, you're up."

I stood and took a deep breath, preparing to deliver a presentation on the book, *Of Mice and Men*. I read it for the first time years ago, but it was a favorite, and I hadn't felt well enough to read anything new.

I approached the front of the room and turned to see a classroom full of expectant faces staring back at me. Suddenly, the entire room wobbled like the inside of a busy bouncy house. I blinked hard to orient myself, but a wave of nausea crashed through me, and my mouth watered. Not now. Oh, please, not now.

"Helen, are you okay?" a boy in the second row asked the moment before I ran to the trashcan. Unfortunately, on my way there, I lost my footing and came crashing down between two desks. The class gasped as pain shot through my left knee, and I wretched onto the dark blue carpet. The cornflakes from that morning's breakfast sat in a half-digested heap on the floor.

I lay in the nurse's office as she checked my temperature and asked me about my symptoms. She tried to call Momma, but no one answered. Of course not.

"I've been sick for a week, but it's weird."

"Weird?" the nurse asked as she pressed lightly on my stomach.

"It always starts in the middle of the night, and I feel better just before school. But, today, I didn't get sick until the third hour," I said.

"Have your parents taken you to the doctor?" she asked.

I almost laughed. Take me to the doctor? That would require them to give a fuck, and it would require me to be home long enough for them to notice.

"No, they've been busy."

Tapping her pen on a clipboard, she took a seat. "Helen, I'm going to ask you something. But I don't want you to take this the wrong way."

"Okay." I braced myself.

She hesitated before delivering her next question. "It sounds like you might have symptoms of pregnancy. Is there any way you could be pregnant?"

As soon as she asked, the entire universe tilted.

Could I be pregnant? I flashed back to the moment Jude asked if I was on birth control—the moment before he was inside me. But he had pulled out. Right? I saw it. He pulled out.

I left the nurse's office in a daze. *Pregnant.* There was no way. I turned the corner to find my locker and saw Eric standing next to it. It was time to tell him what I had done.

Chapter 20

A dry-erase marker scrawled out words, bringing the whiteboard to life. The word abortion was louder than the rest. I turned it over in my head, examining it, reaching for the times I had heard the word spoken aloud.

Abortion.

It reminded me of the rumors I'd heard of a junior who had three abortions. A number likely inflated to sensationalize the story. "She is such a slut," the kids would say while exchanging whispers in the hallway. The girl had walked by, aware of the rumors, her head hung low in shame. I wish I had reached out to her, linked my arm through hers, leaned in, and whispered, "It's going to be okay."

"Today, we are going to discuss pregnancy and the options available to women who may not want to be pregnant," said Mrs. Casteel.

In my freshman year, Mrs. Casteel also taught my health class. We had learned abstinence first—if you don't have sex, you can't get pregnant. Smart. But in this class, child development, we would learn what happens if we failed by having sex.

Ironic. That is the word you used to describe such a coincidence, right? Or at least that is how Alanis Morissette used it in that one song. Ironic because this was today's lesson, and only the day before had the nurse at the free clinic confirmed I was pregnant. Since that moment, I'd existed in a daze. Unable to process how this pregnancy would impact my life.

Mrs. Casteel delivered handouts to our desks and instructed us to read them out loud. My classmate read the story of a woman who had an abortion. "Grief overcame me after. The pain was almost too much to bear. I regretted my decision."

In graphic detail, we learned about the process of an abortion. A baby, a heartbeat, a life ended. My classmates called it murder.

The next article was a story about adoption. It provided us with a happy ending.

"Giving my baby boy to loving parents with the means to care for him was the best decision I could have made. I know now, my baby will have a life I could never give him alone," read another student.

Message received—abortion was not the answer. Adoption was. I poured over the information in our packets, looking for instructions. Step-by-step directions on how to give a baby away. None existed.

Paralyzed by the lack of clarity, I could not face the reality of my situation, praying it would go away all on its own. I couldn't fathom all the outcomes and could not speak the truth aloud.

A week later, I was relieved when we moved on from the unit on pregnancy and birth. It was behind me. At least, that was what I told myself until Mrs. Casteel pulled out two robotic babies, one with a blue cap and one with a pink cap.

We were to learn how to care for a baby, and the first step was to take the baby home. Each student had a scheduled day. The girls giggled, and the boys groaned. The babies came with two diapers, a bottle, and a pacifier. Each item had a small magnet that, when placed on the baby, would signal its needs were being met. Caring for the baby was simple. The baby cries, and you soothe it by changing, rocking, feeding, or using the pacifier. React quickly or lose points for neglect if too much time passes. Mrs. Casteel showed us how to hold the baby to support its head.

"Letting the head fall could be fatal. If the baby's head falls, you will lose points," Mrs. Casteel told us.

We all took turns holding the babies and practicing supporting the neck and head. We then took turns learning how to rock the baby and soothe it.

It seemed easy enough.

At the end of the lesson, Mrs. Casteel passed a schedule around. I was slated to take the baby home the next day. My hand shot in the air.

"Yes, Helen?" Mrs. Casteel said.

"I have to work tomorrow. Can I have a different day?"

Mrs. Casteel rolled her eyes. "Just because you have other commitments doesn't mean you can ignore the responsibility of a baby. In fact, you all have commitments outside of school, so many of you will have to answer this question. What would you do if you had a baby and had to work, go to practice, or do anything where you couldn't care for a baby?"

A girl raised her hand.

"Yes, Jessica?" Mrs. Casteel asked.

"You get a babysitter. Duh," she said with a sneer, and the class laughed.

After school, I handed the robot baby to Alison, a girl in my class. She was nice enough to offer to babysit for me.

She slung the small cross-body diaper bag over her shoulder and reached for the baby carrier and baby.

"It will be good practice for when it is my turn."

After work, I picked the baby up from her house. She named the baby for me—Daisy, after the little daisy flowers on her onesie. It was a stupid name, but I didn't tell her that.

"Daisy cried three times, but it was no problem at all," she said, cooing at the robot baby. *She knows it's a fake baby, right? It can't hear her.* Again, I didn't say so and instead thanked her as I walked back to where Billy Ray sat waiting in the taxi.

At home, I made the sofa for the night. I didn't want to wake Lucy when the baby cried. Just as I got comfortable, the baby started, but I was quick to place the bottle in its mouth. It made a swallowing noise while I held the bottle to its lips, and I closed my eyes while Daisy ate.

My eyes flew open at the sound of the baby crying again. I searched for a clock. It was just past midnight. I tried the bottle again, but it wouldn't stop. Digging through the diaper bag, I pulled out the pacifier and placed it in the baby's mouth. It continued crying. I reached into the bag again, feeling around, but there was nothing left.

The bag was empty.

Lights flickered on, and Momma stared at me as I frantically threw stuff around the living room, searching for the lost diaper. Each minute, the crying got louder and more desperate. I grabbed the baby from its carrier and tried rocking it gently, swaying back and forth as I made a shh sound, forgetting it couldn't hear me. I was no better than Alison.

Matt and Lucy came into the room, and I couldn't keep my emerging tears at bay. I didn't know how to do this. I couldn't do this. I looked at them, hopelessness written all over my face.

"What is that?" Momma said, grimacing at the noise.

"It's an assignment for school," I yelled over the crying. "I think it needs a diaper change, but I can't find the diaper!"

Matt and Lucy looked for the diaper. Lucy was on her knees, peering under the furniture. Matt turned over the couch cushions. Momma reached for the baby, confident in her ability to mother. As I handed it to her, the baby's head fell, and it cried even louder.

How much louder could it get?

"Momma! You can't let the baby's head fall."

"I know how to care for a baby, Helen. I raised the two of you."

If that is what you call it.

Several minutes passed as we looked for the diaper, finally concluding it wasn't here. It must have been at Alison's house.

I called Alison, tapping my foot as I waited for her to pick up. No answer. It was after midnight. I hung up and dialed Billy Ray.

Please answer, please answer, please answer.

"Hey kid, everything all right?"

Relief settled in at the sound of his voice.

"Billy, I need a ride," I said, wiping snot from my nose.

He didn't ask where or why. He only said, "Hold tight. Be there in a jiffy."

"He's coming," I said, ending the call. The baby was louder, and Momma rocked it fast and with significant force.

"Momma, you can't rock it so hard!"

"I know how to rock a baby!" she hissed.

Matt came forward to help, but Momma swung the baby in the opposite direction, deflecting his advance. He looked irritated, and I waited for him to blow, but he didn't. I gave up and went outside. The chilly air bit at the skin on my face, wet from overwhelmed tears.

"I'm so sorry," I said to Billy Ray when I jumped into his passenger seat.

"There's no reason to apologize, kid. You call me anytime. I mean it."

When we arrived at Alison's house, I knocked on her door. It was freezing outside, so I bounced to stay warm. No one answered, so I knocked again.

"You sure they're home?" Billy Ray yelled from a cracked window. I shrugged my shoulders and turned back to the door, knocking again.

Finally, Alison's mom answered the door, looking less than pleased. She clasped her robe around her and, with no concern for the circumstances of my visit, demanded, "What in god's name?"

"I'm the girl who Alison babysat for earlier. I think I left the diaper here, and I can't get the baby to stop crying without it."

Without a word, she shut the door, leaving me wondering if she would come back. A few minutes passed before she and Alison both appeared at the door. Alison handed the diaper over.

"Sorry," she said. Alison's face was pink with embarrassment.

"No, I'm sorry. I really am."

Before I could thank her, the door shut in my face.

We could hear the baby's cries from outside as we pulled up to my house. Inside, Momma was rocking the baby more vigorously. I ran for the baby, taking it from Momma. I was careful not to let the head drop again as I laid it on the sofa. My hands trembled as I tried to change the diaper. I fumbled, unable to make sense of how it went on. I was crying again, and the tears obstructed my vision. Lucy placed her hand on mine and grabbed the diaper from me. In one quick motion, she turned the baby over and placed the magnet in the diaper on the baby's back. The silence that followed was glorious.

The next day in class, Mrs. Casteel scanned my baby while we filled in a worksheet.

"Helen, can I speak to you in the hall?" She placed the baby on her desk, and I followed her out of the classroom.

In the hall, Mrs. Casteel stood with her arms crossed. "Your baby has twelve cases of shaken baby syndrome, fifty-seven head drops, and was neglected for more than an hour last night."

"It isn't my fault." I tried to explain, but she didn't let me finish.

"This assignment is 50 percent of your grade. I'm sorry, but you will not pass my class."

I felt stricken by disbelief. "But wait, I have a 4.0. I've never failed a class before. So there has to be something I can do. I can write a paper or take the baby home again."

School was the only way out. What would Lucy and I do now? I kept screwing everything up.

"I'm sorry, Helen, but my decision is final. If this was a real baby, it would be dead. I hope you understand the severity of that. This was not an assignment to be taken lightly."

Mrs. Casteel walked back into her classroom, and I let my legs give way, my body crumbling to the floor. The hallway was vacant, except for me. I thought about the baby I was pregnant with. I thought about my baby cousin, who I had already failed—Nathan. If I couldn't take care of a fake baby, there was no way I could take care of a real one.

UNTITLED FOR NOW

I couldn't ignore my circumstances anymore. I had to tell someone. I needed help.

CHAPTER 21

Present Day

Jacqueline sits across from me in her office. Her face is warm and comforting, but her eyes remain icy and knowing. Eyes that can see through me to the years I have lived since our last session two days before.

Ashley's words replayed— the past is always bound to catch up with you. So many memories from my childhood have resurfaced, and from what I can tell, running is my best option.

"You have regained some of your memories? That is wonderful, Helen."

I bite at my thumbnail. "I don't think it is worth celebrating yet. I only remember bits of my life and nothing beyond my childhood. I can't tell if they are memories or dreams."

She adjusts herself in her seat. I have learned that Jacqueline does this when she is about to deliver less-than-desirable news. People have their tells. "Unfortunately, it might be difficult to know the difference for a while. If a memory comes to you while you are awake, it will likely be more solid. You may remember when I said that hypnotherapy is one strategy we could use."

I nod.

"Although effective, it is easy for someone like me to plant false memories in your head. I am careful not to suggest false information, but it is still possible. It is likely the same for your dreams. Dreams contain references from all the stimuli you experience. Therefore, you could blend experiences from more recent memories into your childhood memories."

"So, there is no way to be certain?" I sigh. This whole mess is so frustrating. Didn't she say she specializes in this? Why is everything so unclear?

"Memory is subjective to a degree. Even without memory loss, no one's memory is perfect. However, once you remember enough to know why you attempted suicide, we will introduce you to an outpatient care program."

The reminder of my suicide brings me back to Ashley and the cuts on her arm.

"How did I do it?"

Jacqueline seems to be pulled away from a train of thought. "Do what?"

"How did I try to kill myself?"

Somehow, I think knowing this might help. Maybe my attempt is related to a longtime vice like Ashley.

"You swallowed a copious amount of over-the-counter and prescription pills all at once," she says without emotion. "It was a lot of pills."

Gold star for effort. Too bad my execution wasn't quite up to snuff.

Jacqueline disrupts my thoughts. "In an outpatient program, you can continue to work on your memory, and you will have access to people and artifacts to help you substantiate what you recall."

"Wouldn't this go much quicker if I had all those things now?"

"Actually, Helen, I am glad you brought that up. I do have the items that you came to the hospital with. I thought we could look at them together."

Jacqueline stands and walks to a box next to her desk. "We could not locate a cell phone. Cell phones are like portable phones that have loads of information in them. They have your contacts, socials, pictures, etc."

"I remember what a cell phone is," I say, sneering. "I lost my memory but not my common sense."

"Sorry about that. Every case is unique." Jacqueline lifts the box and sets it on the desk. She pulls out several items. A pair of black slacks, a blazer, a sage green blouse, earrings, and a watch. Under the watch's crystal face is Mickey Mouse. His hands don't move. The watch appears to be broken.

I run my fingers over each of my possessions. Picking up the blouse and admiring the keyhole detail in the front, I think of a question. "Couldn't someone just go get more of my things? I presume I got to the hospital by ambulance? So, the authorities should know where I live."

"You did not arrive by ambulance. A young woman brought you in, but we do have a record of your address. It was on the hospital paperwork.

However, we don't make it common practice to go into people's homes and take items."

A young woman? Who was she? My sister? Surely if it was Lucy, she would have visited.

I examine each item more closely. The clothing is high quality, and some of it is custom-tailored. Upon closer inspection, I see that the watch is cracked, and the leather strap is worn around the edges. It seems out of place next to the clothing. I reach for it lay it on my wrist, and fasten the buckle. The buckle looks new. A memory comes into focus.

I am trying to move forward but am being pushed back. He won't let me leave. I hurry to the car, and my watch falls to the ground. The buckle has been broken for a long time. I turn around, but he is there, coming toward me, and I see his heavy work boot press into the face of the watch. It cracks.

"My watch! My watch," I scream, sinking to the ground.

He kneels on the ground and cradles my head in his hands. He is sorry. He didn't mean to. All he wanted was to talk. He runs his hand over my belly, swollen with pregnancy. I come out of the flashback.

"I'm a mom," I whisper. I look at Jacqueline and say louder, "I'm a mom."

I search through the few snapshots of my memories, rapidly trying to find something that tells me more, but nothing is there. Only flashes of recent memories and clues come to mind. Stretch marks along my stomach. A scar across my abdomen. How? How did my mind run past those details? I am a mother.

My pulse quickens, and I feel the need to run. My child is out there, and I am in here.

"You are," Jacqueline confirms.

She knew. Of course, she knew. This feels more like a game than therapy, and I'm tired of playing it. My breathing becomes labored as my frustration builds.

"You seem distressed," Jacqueline says.

"What else should I be? You knew I was a mother. You knew I had a child. Why wouldn't you tell me that?" My voice continues to rise in volume.

"I think we should end for the day. You need to rest."

"No! I need to know what happened. Where's my child? Where is she?" I'm standing. My arms are stretched out at my sides. Jacqueline doesn't flinch.

"You need to rest."

I don't want to rest, but I know losing my shit won't get me anywhere, so unwillingly, I leave Jacqueline's office knowing I am a mother.

Later in my room, I lay stiff as a board on my back, trying to categorize my memories. Each memory is a glowing dot floating nonsensically in my head. I try, but I can't make sense of the dots. Some glow brighter than others, and all have varying levels of closeness. I want to reach for my child's face but can't. It is not there.

Frustrated, I remove my slipper and throw it as hard as possible at the wall. In the room next to me, someone screams. Guilty of causing distress, I yell, "Sorry!"

This is so fucking impossible.

The door flies open.

"Guess who got a diagnosis today?" Ashley shouts as she runs and jumps onto her bed.

"You act like it's a rite of passage," I reply.

"It kind of is," she says, removing her slippers and socks.

"Well, don't keep me on the edge of my seat."

Ashley is a good distraction. I am grateful for her until she says, "Cancer."

That is not funny. Cancer is not a joke, but I choose not to say so. She can see the distaste on my face.

"Just kidding! Gosh. I have borderline personality disorder."

"Is that a good thing? Having your diagnosis?"

She pauses for a minute, thinking. "I guess it is irrelevant," she decides, nodding to herself for assurance.

Irrelevant is right. What is a diagnosis other than some crude classification of our present symptoms? Symptoms with a cause. Humans aren't born broken. We become broken.

"How are you holding up? You had therapy today, right?" she asks, grabbing her long black hair and pulling it over her right shoulder. She coils the strands around each other.

"I don't know. I feel like I'm going insane," I sigh.

"Lucky for you, I am insane."

Ashley doesn't seem insane to me. Quite the contrary. Her bigger-than-life personality is something I am envious of. She is a shiny, beautiful soul.

"I have a child, but I can't remember them. How do you forget you have a child? I don't even know their name, how old they are, or what they look like. I only know they exist. Even more, I tried to kill myself. And now what? Is my child all alone? It's all because of me."

I feel bad for dumping this on her, but I don't know what else to do. Tears spill around my worries, and Ashley comes over and wraps her arms around my shoulders.

"I'm sure they are not alone. You wouldn't do something like that."

I place my hand on hers. "Thanks, but I can't be sure."

Later that night, I wake in a cold sweat, my shirt sticking to my skin, drenched from perspiration. I hear someone screaming in the hallway as people shout directions at each other. A sliver of light lies across my bed, and I notice my blanket on the floor. I must have kicked it off in my sleep. Ashley stands at the crack in the door, watching, and I can hear whispers of patients acting as bystanders to the scene in the hall. Some gasp while others laugh.

"What's going on?" I ask Ashley, reaching for my blanket.

"A patient hung themselves from the television in the rec room," she says, staring into the hall.

"What?"

"They used the mount to do it." Ashley's speech is quick and frantic. "Suzy, that woman who talked about how she believed God was talking through her when she was manic. Remember her? She found him and wants to get him down, but they won't let her."

How is this possible? This place thought of everything. How could they miss a mount on the wall?

"How do you know all this?"

"Because I was with her when she found him."

My heart drops at the image of someone hanging from the back of a television.

"Oh, my God. I'm so sorry," I tell her as she shuts the door, and the darkness engulfs us again.

"That's how my mom did it, you know? I was the one to find her as well," Ashley confesses.

The gravity of her confession causes me to sway where I stand. What a terrible thing to find your mom dead. It feels like the ultimate betrayal.

Although I can't see Ashley, I imagine her down-turned lips and misty eyes. But when she opens the door again to peer out into the hallway, I'm surprised to see her standing with her shoulders back and her jaw clenched.

Chapter 22

Before Helen Lost Her Memory

Jude picked me up after work, and we drove out to the middle of nowhere like we always did. We hadn't spent time together outside his Jeep since the first night at the party. He said he liked it better that way. He got me all to himself, but sometimes I wished for something different. I knew nothing about Jude's life except that he went to college in the town over and lived with his aunt.

I'd broken up with Eric but was too much of a coward when the time came to tell him the real reason. So, I lied.

"You want to break up?" Eric had asked.

"Yes. I just don't love you anymore."

The look on his face haunted me. But I was free, which meant Jude and I could be together.

When we pulled off to the side of the road, Jude wasted no time reaching for me. His hands quickly unclasped my bra, pushing it from my chest as he trailed kisses down from the tip of my ear. Grabbing my hand, he thrust it into his groin, his hardness telling me he was ready. I rubbed him over his jeans awkwardly, unsure if the hesitant back-and-forth motion felt good. But he groaned, letting me know he wanted me to continue. He pulled away from me and ritualistically climbed to the back.

Two blankets and a pillow sat on the folded seats, and he hastily made a bed, stretching one of the blankets out and fluffing the pillow. He was soon stark naked and lying on his side, his head held by one hand while the other patted the space beside him.

I started to climb back.

"Hey, wait, will you grab a condom? They're in the glove compartment," he asked.

He had been careful to use a condom ever since that first time. I wanted to tell him it was unnecessary, but the words were stuck like cotton balls in my throat. So instead, I nodded and complied with his request.

As I settled next to him, he moved a strand of hair from my face and gazed into my eyes. Maybe, just maybe, he would be happy when I told him. I imagined his response—a mixture of shock and joy as his hand found my stomach, realizing, for the first time, he was going to be a father.

Then, interrupting my daydream, Jude kissed me, and I kissed him back, impassioned by my imagination. We moved through the motions of making love slowly and deliberately, and for the first time, something happened within me that stole my breath. The sensation coursed through me so fully that I felt limp and heavy when it dissipated. He rolled off me and pulled the second blanket over us, warming our bodies, which were left cold once we separated.

"I love you," I said, and he smiled at me. I waited for him to say it back, but he didn't, and panic crawled under my skin.

"Do you love me?" I asked tentatively.

"I think you're amazing, and I enjoy spending time with you." He was still grinning.

I tasted bile in my mouth. "So, you don't love me?" I yanked the blanket off him and pulled it over myself as I sat up to find my clothes. The trepidation settled in, and I needed to get out of the damn car. He grabbed my wrist.

"Helen, stop," he urged.

I pulled it away as tears rimmed the edges of my eyes. I turned away from him, unwilling to let him see me cry.

"What is going on, Helen? I thought we were having fun?"

I can't believe this. He thought this was fun? Being sixteen and pregnant is not fun.

I turned back to him, and with as much venom as I could muster, I yelled, "Fun? Having fun? What the fuck, Jude? I thought this was more than that. When were you going to tell me it wasn't?"

He seemed bewildered by my accusation. "I don't understand. We only ever hook up."

"Isn't that just great?" I shouted. "I'm pregnant and in love, and you're just having fun."

Jude's face turned several shades paler. "What?"

"I thought you loved me," I whispered.

"Not that part."

I knew exactly what he meant, but I wouldn't give him the satisfaction of brushing past the fact that he thought this was all some game.

He shook his head in disbelief. "You can't be pregnant."

My eyes bulged in response. *I can't be pregnant? I guess he knows better than I do.*

"We always use a condom," he clarified.

"We didn't the first time, Jude! Did you really pull out? Because I am pregnant. Very pregnant. I have been sick for a month, but you wouldn't know that because you never ask me about my day or what was going on in my life. Instead, you talk incessantly about the stupid books you are reading and how college is life-altering. You sound pretentious and out of touch. You go to a community college, for crying out loud!"

With each word, I came to realize he was right. This wasn't anything deeper than sex. I had no clue what I was doing. All I knew was I was hurting and wanted him to hurt as much as I did. I wanted him to know what it felt like to be rejected.

He was silent while I finished dressing. His lack of reaction amplified my frustration, and I snapped.

"Are you going to take me home or just sit there?"

Before turning the key to start the ignition, he turned to me, his eyes pleading, and I thought maybe he would tell me it would be okay. But instead, he said, "I'm sorry, Helen. Let's forget about this tonight and talk about it tomorrow."

But tomorrow never came. For a week, I waited for his call or for him to stop by the diner, but he never did. Finally, unable to wait any longer, I used the diner's phone to call his house. His aunt answered.

"Is Jude there?" I took a deep breath and concentrated on disguising my anxiety.

"Um, no. I'm sorry."

"When will he be back?"

"Not for a while, I would guess. He went back home … to his dad's house." Her tone told me that she was reluctant to offer more information, but I pushed on anyway.

"Where is that, and for how long?"

"Who is this?"

"A friend from school. We are working on a project together," I lied.

"I'm so sorry, but he's gone home permanently. His dad lives in Minneapolis."

"Minneapolis?"

"Yes. Minneapolis, Minnesota. Look, I'm real sorry. I'm sure this is inconvenient, but he's not coming back, so you might want to get a new partner for your project."

As I ended the call, I was still trying to wrap my head around what just happened. He was gone. He left me. I was alone.

I found Bethany in the back of the diner refilling the ranch bucket and asked her if she could watch my tables for a few minutes. I needed a break.

"Is everything okay?" she asked, but I couldn't answer her question.

I ran through the back door and into the alleyway behind the diner. Uncontrollable sobs coursed through me as I leaned against the dumpster. I was so damn stupid. My body jerked with each sob, and tears clouded my vision. I screamed into the night air and kicked the dumpster repeatedly until my leg was sore. Time passed, but I wasn't aware of how much.

A car rolled slowly through the alley, and I closed my eyes, shielding them from the glare of the headlights. The car stopped, and Billy Ray's voice beckoned.

"Hey kid, you need a ride?"

"No, I'm still working, but maybe later?" My voice was hoarse from screaming.

"That would be fine, too, but Bethany called me. Said you might need a ride home."

I looked back at the diner, confused, until I remembered the back door slamming after my first sob. She saw me break down.

Turning back to Billy Ray, I said, "That might be a good idea, actually, but can you wait just a minute? I need to get my things."

He tipped his head, letting me know he was happy to wait.

Inside the diner, Bethany was busy taking care of double the tables, mine and hers, so I waited near the kitchen and away from customers' eyes until she could speak.

When she came around the corner, she was holding my bag. "Hey girl, we all have bad nights. Just go home. It's not that busy tonight. I'll give you your tips tomorrow. Okay?"

"I'm so sorry," I said, as my eyes stung against the threat of fresh tears.

"No need to apologize. Go home and rest. I'll see you tomorrow."

Traffic lights and headlights blurred past as Billy Ray drove me home. The way the lights stretched wide into distorted, starburst shapes reminded me of the night I met Jude. I felt disgusted with myself for being so naïve and foolish.

"Awfully quiet tonight, kid," said Billy Ray.

"Sorry."

"No need to be sorry. I'm just not used to it. We usually talk the entire way home, and you have yet to say two words tonight."

I turned to him, and he stole a quick glance at me before returning his eyes to the road.

"Can I tell you something?" I asked.

"Yes, ma'am."

Time to rip the Band-Aid off.

"I'm pregnant," I said. The words spoken aloud to Billy Ray felt different in my mouth than when I said them to Jude.

"That is quite the pickle now, isn't it?"

I was relieved and couldn't help but chuckle. It sure was a pickle. "I guess. It isn't exactly ideal," I said. "I don't know what I'm going to do."

"What do you want to do?" he asked, not a trace of judgment in his voice.

"I'm not sure. I know I don't want to end the pregnancy."

He snuck another quick glance toward me.

"But I also don't know how to give a baby up for adoption."

"I see," he said, bobbing his head in understanding. "What does Eric say?"

I paused before answering. I had to decide what I wanted to share.

"Eric isn't the father," I finally said.

"Huh. So, what does the father say?"

I wasn't sure how to explain that he left us, and as much as I wanted to, I couldn't blame him. I guess I wasn't worth sticking around for. But maybe it was a good thing. I learned a long time ago you can't count on dads.

After a long pause, I said, "There is no father. He wants nothing to do with me, so as far as I'm concerned, he doesn't exist."

Billy Ray nodded again. "How do you feel?" he asked.

I took a deep breath, trying to hold back the tears that threatened my eyes. "I feel like I ruined my life, and I'll never make it out now."

"Make it out?" He glanced over at me, his eyebrows raised.

"All I wanted was to get out from under my family and do better, but I messed it up. I'm destined to be just like my mother." I admitted this fear to him and myself.

Billy Ray stayed silent for the rest of the car ride until we arrived at my house. We sat for a moment, listening to the quiet hum of the engine before he turned to me.

"Helen, I know it feels like your life is over, and you've messed it all up. But let me tell you. As a man who has lived a full life and raised three children, this is not the end for you. It is only the beginning. If I have learned anything about you over the last several months, it is that there is nothing that can stop you. You are an incredible young lady, and this miracle is going to make you even greater. I promise you, Helen. This is not the end."

In bed that night, I fixated on the ceiling fan above. It hung, broken and unmoving as wisps of dust bunnies dangled over the sides of the blades, dancing lightly in the breeze that came through the faulty seal on our bedroom window. I didn't know if Billy Ray was right, but I sure hoped so. I would try to be as great as he thought I was.

Chapter 23

Cold jelly was released onto my exposed skin, and a woman with sandy blonde hair pulled back from her face placed a wand on my stomach.

"So, I'm going to apply some pressure. Just let me know if you're uncomfortable, okay?"

She moved the wand, spreading the slick goop on my stomach. An image appeared on the monitor. I saw various shades of gray and indistinguishable shapes.

Momma stood beside me, resting her hand on my arm. I knew it was a gesture of comfort, but as much as I needed her here, I wished she wouldn't touch me.

"Have you ever had an ultrasound before?" the woman asked.

I shook my head.

"So essentially, what we are doing is using this transducer," she gestured to the wand, "to emit high-frequency sound waves which produces an image of the inside of your body. It's completely safe and will help us get a good look at your baby. Do you hear that? It's your baby's heartbeat," she said, her face warming at the sound.

Momma teared up as her eyes locked on the ultrasound monitor.

"That's my grandbaby," Momma whispered, gently squeezing my arm. I felt scared to look at the screen. Already, I had this overwhelming connection to the life growing inside me, but it still didn't seem real.

Momma had been excited from the moment I told her I was pregnant. She said a baby was always a blessing. Her support of my pregnancy further complicated our relationship. I needed her love, but I was leery of it.

Surprisingly, Matt was also supportive, and I didn't know what to do with all their excitement over my baby.

They had asked about the father, and just as I told Billy Ray, I remained adamant that there wasn't one. Momma didn't press and only said it was probably for the best. She was right. It was for the best.

"Oh, look there," the ultrasound technician said. "Your baby is sucking their thumb."

I couldn't help myself. I had to look, and there it was—a perfect little black-and-white silhouette of a baby. My baby. With some encouragement from Momma, I chose to raise this child, but I still wasn't sure I could do it.

"The heartbeat is at 148, which is normal and healthy. And based on these measurements, it looks like you are about seventeen weeks along. Do you want to know the gender?"

Momma blurted out, "Yes!"

The technician looked at me, and I nodded in agreement.

"Congratulations. It looks like you are having a girl."

My heart stopped. I was going to be a mother. I'd known that simple truth all this time, but it was different now. I was going to have a daughter.

Upon leaving the hospital, I realized, in all the excitement, I had left my bag in the ultrasound room. I told Momma I would catch up with her and retraced my steps. Coming around the corner, I heard the voice of the woman who did the ultrasound. I stopped just outside the door, listening to her talk.

"That poor girl. She is just another baby raising a baby, and it doesn't look like she will have much help from her mother."

"That's so hard," another voice said.

"You should've seen it. Her mom was so high she ticked the entire appointment. If you ask me, that baby will be lucky if it finds its way into the foster care system."

I didn't want to hear the rest of the conversation, so I came around the corner. The technician's eyes widened as she saw me, aware I had caught her. The woman she was talking to tried to cover up the conversation and said, "Oh yeah, my niece needs a lot of help."

Yes, I was stupid enough to get knocked up, but not that stupid.

"I left my bag," I said, a scowl on my face.

The technician did not make eye contact with me as she led me back to the room. I grabbed my bag, and the woman shifted her weight from side to side. After I picked it up, I turned to her. My face was hot with rage.

"My baby is going to be just fine because I am going to make certain of it. I know I'm young, but I have been through more than most people, and I'm going to be a fantastic mother."

I walked out with self-righteous confidence coursing through my veins and made a promise to my baby girl. "It's me and you," I whispered while holding my stomach. "We're going to be all right."

Being told I couldn't do it only fueled my desire to prove them all wrong.

At work that night, frustrated by the technician, I complained to Bethany.

"Can you believe her? Who says such a thing? She doesn't know me."

Bethany took a long drag of her cigarette while I rolled sets of silverware across from her. The restaurant was dead except for one table of regulars in the non-smoking section.

"I mean, she has a point," she said as she tapped her cigarette on the edge of the crystal ashtray. Her response struck me.

"How can you say that? You think my baby would be better off in foster care?" I asked.

"No, Helen, but you have to admit. You don't have a lot of support. You want to move out of your mom's house, but how do you plan on going to school, working, and caring for a baby by yourself? Something's got to give."

"I've been saving this whole time. Every single dollar." My chest vibrated with uncertainty as I spoke.

"I know you think that's enough, but it isn't. You will not make it on a part-time waitress income."

At home, I kneeled before my bed and found my green and flowered metal lunchbox. I pulled my tips out of my apron and counted each dollar. Then, I wrote thirty-nine dollars on the notebook paper that kept the ledger.

"Do you have enough yet?" Lucy asked, not looking up from her book.

"Not even close, but we still got time," I said, rising from the floor.

I turned toward her and revealed something that had been on my mind since my conversation with Bethany.

"I've decided to drop out of school. I can't do it all, and I think moving out of here is more important. School doesn't pay the bills."

I sat on the bed across from her, pulling a foot into my lap to massage the bottom. They hurt more than the day before.

"Do you think you'll be able to take me with you when you go?" she asked.

She looked at me, waiting for an answer.

"Absolutely." I wasn't leaving her behind again.

Lucy changed the topic. "I was thinking. You should name your baby after one of the sisters in this book." She held up a well-loved copy of *Little Women*. The same copy I received for Christmas years ago from Grandpa. "You always loved it so much."

I smiled broadly, happy to talk about something lighter. "Oh yeah? Which one? Meg? Amy? Beth?"

Before I could finish listing the sisters, Lucy said, "You know which one."

"Jo?"

"Yeah." Lucy put the book down and pulled her blanket into her lap. "I can't help but imagine she'll be like Jo—creative and daring. I like to think she will be brave too."

I placed a hand on my stomach, a habit I had recently started.

"Is she kicking?" Lucy asked.

"Not yet. I still have some time before that happens."

Lucy sat on my bed and placed her hand on top of mine. "It's pretty cool you are growing a human."

"You don't think I'm too young?"

"Of course, I think you are too young, but does it matter?"

"Maybe not."

Three months later, after working many doubles, I saved enough money to rent a small apartment or trailer house. Billy Ray said he would help me figure out the lease. I was optimistic, believing I could bring Lucy along if Momma allowed it. Winter was approaching, and my baby would be here soon. It was time to go.

Over the last few months, Momma became increasingly more involved in our lives. It was almost as if she sensed we were leaving her again and was trying to change our minds about wanting to go. But no matter how much Momma tried, I knew better than to let her get to me. We were getting out.

On a Sunday morning, I woke to the smell of bacon and pancakes coming from the kitchen. Assuming it was Lucy, I hoisted myself out of bed to see if she needed help. I was surprised to find Momma at the stove flipping a pancake while bacon sizzled in the frying pan next to it. Lucy sat on the sofa, and I looked around for Matt.

"What's going on?" I asked, unsettled by the disruption of the status quo.

"Good morning, darling. We've got a big day ahead of us," Momma said.

"What do you mean?"

The shift in behavior was unsettling. Momma had been supportive throughout my pregnancy, seeing it as a way for her to shine, but pancakes? This was too much.

"We're going to go look at a house right after breakfast. Matt went out to get more pancake mix. Don't pancakes sound good?"

"A house? Since when did you decide you wanted a house? Can we even afford a house?" I tried to process the information but had more questions than answers.

"Don't be silly, baby. This trailer is far too small for another person, especially a baby."

I made eye contact with Lucy, who looked as puzzled as I was.

"I don't need you to get a house, Momma. I'm moving out," I said.

Momma stopped cooking and turned to address me. "I know that is what you think you're doing, but you can't raise a baby on your own. You're gonna need help. Plus, you're still a minor and don't have my permission."

Anxiety rose like lava from a volcano about to erupt. She couldn't be serious. I'd made it very clear I wasn't going to stay here.

"I'm not moving anywhere with you. I won't do it."

"Don't you use that tone with me, Helen Joy."

"Don't use my middle name! I am not a child," I hissed.

"Well, you sure are acting like one."

"Fuck you!" I yelled.

Momma stopped cooking and waved the spatula in my face. "You will not talk to me like that as long as you are under my roof!"

"Your roof? I want nothing more than to get out from under this damn roof. You're worthless. You know the only reason we have this roof, heat, and food is because of me, right? Or are you too high to realize I've been the one carrying us?" I turned and stormed back to my room before she could respond. I had to get out. They were delusional if they thought I was going to stick around.

I dropped to the ground, falling harder than I intended as pain shot through my knees. The pain only exacerbated my frustration. Reaching underneath my bed, I found my lunchbox. I was not waiting another day. I couldn't. I undid the metal clasps, flung it open, and found it empty except for my ledger and the no-longer-relevant college brochures. I fell back, horrified. Where did it go? I thought back to last night. I hadn't opened the box because I'd spent my tips on groceries.

Scrambling to my feet, which was more difficult to do each day, I rushed into the kitchen. The lunchbox was in my hand. I threw it at Momma's feet.

"Where the fuck is my money?"

"God dammit, Helen. I'm trying to do something nice for you, and this is how you thank me? You throw a lunchbox at me?"

"Doing something nice for me? What are you talking about? You stole my fucking money."

My thoughts came in too fast to process. Why would she do this to me?

"Why do you think I took the money, Helen? Why? Riddle me that?"

"I don't know. Because you're a leech who just takes and takes?"

"I wanted to surprise you. Please, just see the house. I did this for you. I already put the deposit down. I just wanted to help you." She was crying.

Her form seemed to shrink with every word. This was something she had learned to do over the years. And it worked.

"I love you, darling. I love you so much. Please look at the house, and if you hate it, I'll get your money back. I promise."

The rage left my body, and remorse took over. The familiar war inside me continued to betray me, oscillating between disgust and love for my mother. Love won.

"I'm sorry, Momma," I whispered.

She moved toward me, wrapping her arms around me. "It's okay. You're under a lot of stress. It's okay. I got you. I got both of you."

CHAPTER 24

Billy Ray pulled into the hospital parking lot and turned back with an encouraging smile. "You got this, kid."

I reached into my bag to pull out the fare, but he raised his hand.

"Ah, don't you worry about that today. You can get me next time."

I lowered my head, aware arguing with him was fruitless, and waited for Momma to exit the front passenger seat before I opened my door.

On this day, I would become a mother.

Although winter was here, the snow and ice had yet to appear. Despite the lack of precipitation, the world was frostbitten. The cold clung to every surface. Tiny white crystals were the only sign of the freezing temperatures. The bitter air tried to possess my fingers, so I crossed my arms and buried my hands.

My body ached with the added weight of a placenta, amniotic fluid, and a baby. It had become increasingly difficult to do anything physical, including walking. I pumped my legs to hasten my pace and keep up with Momma's longer stride.

I was terrified and determined. I wasn't sure I could do this. What if I failed her? Until now, I had convinced myself I could do this, but was I kidding myself? All I knew was I wanted to be better than my mother.

I made my way to the front desk to check in for my induction. I was due five days ago, and if it were up to me, I would wait as long as possible. I needed more time, but my doctor said she needed to come out.

After checking in, I sat in the waiting area. Momma sat next to me, and before I could object, she put her arm around my shoulders to embrace me.

I cringed. This was our dynamic. She'd show affection, and I'd recoil. But then, I'd feel bad for being so cold and would fake warmth to help ease my conscience. I tried to push past how uncomfortable Momma's touch made me, but it was hard when I could tell she was high. It was clear by her dilated pupils and how her hand twitched every few seconds. I wished she could just stop.

In the waiting area, I watched a woman and a young man walk into the hospital. It was Eric. We hadn't spoken since I broke it off. I rationalized keeping my distance was better, but I felt immense shame for what I had done. Eric's eyes landed on me as he and his mom approached the front desk where I had stood only minutes before. His eyes found my face but quickly traveled to my large stomach. I looked down, unable to make eye contact. Of all days, this had to be the one we ran into each other. I quickly grabbed my bag and pretended to rummage for something.

"Is that Eric?" Momma said, and I shushed her.

"Don't," I pleaded.

Understanding, she leaned into me and whispered, "Are you okay, darling?"

I flinched as her hot, sour breath wafted over me. "I'm fine," I mumbled, my skin crawling with unease.

Eric and his mom sat in the waiting area, facing the opposite direction, and I prayed for him not to turn around. Finally, my name was called, and I breathed a sigh of relief.

Inside the labor and delivery unit, a nurse brought me into a birthing suite. The room was a standard hospital room—clean, sterile, and medical. The nurse examined me as I glanced around the room. I knew she thought I couldn't do this, that I was too young. Too ill-equipped. She didn't have to say anything. I just knew.

When she left, I went into the bathroom to put on the gown she had left behind. The cotton hospital gown didn't cover my butt, and I felt exposed. My breath was shaky, and my hands trembled as I peered at myself in the bathroom mirror. *Get a grip, Helen.*

In the room, Momma and I waited. Her constant clicking and the strange jerking motion of her hand made me want to crawl out of my skin. A second nurse came into the room, and my muscles tensed. The inevitable judgment would be much harder to endure while nearly naked. She introduced herself as Gail. Tall and lanky, with shaggy brown shoulder-length hair, she smelled of lavender and offered a gentle smile. I relaxed. Her eyes focused on me as she hooked up various medical instruments and sensors. She moved gracefully and with immense efficiency, not missing a beat. Soon my discomfort melted away.

Over the next hour, my doctor and several nurses came in and out of my room to explain procedures, administer induction medications, and take my vitals. I ignored Momma's persistent questions and outbursts of speech.

"I was a teen mom, too, you know?" Momma said to one of my nurses with displaced pride.

The nurse chuckled uneasily and replied, "Oh, so it runs in the family?"

When the contractions started, they were dull but throbbing. The pain was not severe yet, but it felt like slight pressure working through my pelvis. I imagined my cervix widening with each occurrence. The pain was good. It meant the medicine was working. The contractions were a gift. Gail offered medication to ease the pain, but I refused. I wanted to feel each one as they grew stronger and closer, crashing around me. Enduring this pain meant I could endure anything.

The progression of my labor was slow, so I opted to walk around the hospital to speed up the process.

"I'll come with you," Momma said, getting up to help me.

"No, I got it. I'd like to be by myself."

Momma's face told me I'd hurt her feelings, but I didn't let guilt change my mind this time. In the hallway, generic framed prints lined the walls, and I wondered who chose these pieces. They were awful and boring. I stared at a landscape as a contraction rolled through me. I focused on every brush stroke, imagining the flick of the artist's wrist until it was over.

Within a few hours, the contractions became more regular, and the pressure in my pelvis worsened. Gail explained she must check to see how dilated my cervix was.

"I'm going to use my fingers to feel inside you. I promise I'll be gentle," she said.

Any modesty I tried to maintain was for naught. Stirrups held my legs up and far apart, and with a long slender hand concealed by a latex glove, she sunk her fingers into me. When she pulled away, I released my breath.

"Four centimeters," she said.

I didn't know what that meant, but I felt too embarrassed to ask.

Many hours later, I was still in labor. I no longer embraced the contractions. I resented them. Exhaustion had taken my willpower. My nurses fawned over how polite and kind I was while in such pain, and despite wanting to yell and scream, I stayed quiet and kind because I liked that they liked me. During my last check, I was at nine centimeters. I had since figured out what it meant.

The goal was ten. I had been at nine for eight long hours and would not progress any further. They had come in to talk about the possibility of a C-section, and I had told them absolutely not. My baby was still doing fine, and I could do this on my own. I didn't want help.

Walking or sitting in the bathtub was no longer allowed, and I lay strapped to monitors, hugging my pillow tight to my chest during each contraction. The second time the doctor came in to talk about a C-section, I was too tired to be stubborn.

In the operating room, my nurse explained the process of anesthesia. Bending my back to elongate my spine, I leaned forward into the nurse.

"Relax," she said, rubbing my arms.

Relax so they could stick a large needle in my back. Easier said than done.

But I did it, and within minutes, the bottom half of my body was entirely numb.

Momma appeared beside me, now dressed in blue scrubs and a matching disposable cap. She held one of my hands, which was strapped down to prevent me from moving during surgery. Sleep crawled over me, and I fought to stay awake. I had been in labor for so long and was exhausted. Occasionally, a tug or a pull on my stomach would bring me back to consciousness, but not for more than a second before I drifted out again. And then, the sound of a baby's cry traveled through the room.

"Congratulations. You have a healthy baby girl."

I could hear her cries, but I couldn't see her. I turned my head from side to side, looking for her. Momma was gone, too. My chest constricted with worry.

"Where is my baby?" I cried, but they ignored me. I wasn't loud enough.

"Where is my baby?" I repeated louder this time.

"We will have her right over to you after a few quick tests," someone said.

And just as they promised, she was there, cradled in the arms of a nurse. With one hand, the nurse unfastened one of the straps that held my hand in place and positioned the baby so I could hold her to my chest. She was covered in a white cast, and traces of blood remained in the creases of her skin. She was perfect.

I didn't know it would feel this way. I didn't know that the love that filled my chest could be this powerful. Before now, I wanted to be a good mom in spite of mine. I wanted to prove everyone wrong. To be different. But at that moment, meeting my daughter for the first time, I wanted to be a good mom simply because I loved her.

UNTITLED FOR NOW

"Do you have a name yet?" the nurse asked.
I thought of Lucy. "Josephine, but I'll call her Josie."

CHAPTER 25

I knew being a mom would be hard, but sometimes it felt impossible.

Sleepless nights, colic, and double shifts at the diner marked my existence now. When Josie was brand new, my breasts were so engorged and heavy that it made feeding her difficult. Hungry, her little face would skim across my flesh, but she couldn't latch. Eventually, she became too upset to eat, and we'd both end up crying. Her because she was starving and me because I felt as though I had failed her. Together, we lived in a helpless state with no end in sight.

Lucy would come to help on the hardest days, drawn by my sobs, which echoed through the house. The moment Josie was in her aunt's arms, the crying would stop. I should've been grateful for the help. I should have thanked Lucy, but I let my inadequacy fuel unjustified anger. I wanted to be good enough. I wanted to do it on my own, but I couldn't.

"She won't stop!" I said through tears one night.

Lucy lifted Josie from my lap and cradled her close to her chest, making shushing sounds against Josie's head.

"She hates me."

Lucy's face was serene and calm as she said, "She doesn't hate you. She knows you're stressed and can feel how overwhelmed you are. The only reason she stopped crying when I picked her up was because I was not upset. It's not about loving you. She loves you, Helen."

As much as I appreciated the sentiment, it didn't make me feel like less of a failure.

Eventually, it became easier. Practice made progress, and by the time Josie was four months old, I had settled into motherhood. Each morning, after we were ready, I put her in her stroller, and we walked to the child development center, a nonprofit daycare located in the middle of town. Lucy then assumed care for Josie after school and watched her until I came home from work. We were making it work.

Momma and Matt loved Josie, but I was careful not to let them get too close. Although I let Momma babysit a handful of times out of desperation, I tried to minimize my reliance on her. She said she was sober, but I struggled to trust her.

Sometimes guilt relating to my lack of trust would seep in, especially when Momma and Matt were supportive and helpful. Small acts of kindness, like washing Josie's bottles or offering to change a diaper, made me question the justification for my apprehension.

The house we moved to had three bedrooms and two bathrooms. The second bathroom was in Momma and Matt's room. I had to pee one day, but Lucy was already in our bathroom. I quietly snuck past Momma, who was asleep in her bed, to use her bathroom while Matt was working at this little junkyard across town.

In the bathroom, the toilet paper roll was empty. I opened the cupboard under the sink, hoping to find a roll, but something caught my eye. A small plastic bag filled with about a tablespoon of white powder lay at the edge of the bottom of the vanity. I reached for it, and my heartbeat intensified as I grasped the bit of plastic.

Josie was six months old and so close to crawling. Sometimes when the other bathroom was occupied, and she was awake, I would bring her in here and set her on the floor while I used the toilet. An image of Josie fisting this bag and putting it in her mouth flooded in, and I saw red.

I marched into Momma's room with electricity coursing through my veins.

"Momma!" I yelled. I punched her square in the jaw without giving her a chance to wake up. The moment my fist connected, an unfamiliar monster surged forth from within, propelling me to unleash a relentless flurry of punches. My rage intensified with each strike. Meanwhile, Momma, confused and defenseless, raised her arms in a feeble attempt to shield her face from the sudden assault.

"Helen, stop! Helen, stop! Ow! You're hurting me!" Finally, alert enough to defend herself, she grabbed my arms and pushed me away from her.

"You lied to me! You fucking lied to me! You're still using!" I screamed in her face as spittle flew from my mouth.

"No, I'm not!"

I took a step back and released myself from Momma's grasp. From my pocket, I revealed the little baggie of white substance. Holding it between two fingers, I waited for Momma to explain.

"That's not mine!" She scrambled into a sitting position.

"Then why was it on your bathroom floor?"

"I don't know."

"You know, it's fine that you are a piece of shit, mother, but I will not let you ruin my daughter's life like you have mine. I will not."

Momma didn't say a word. Her head only shook from side to side as I spoke. Her disheveled hair and alarmed eyes made her look wild and crazed. I turned around to leave. I had nothing else to say to that woman.

From behind me, Momma yelled, "Can we just talk, Helen? Please? Please, just talk to me."

"You get clean, and I'll think about talking to you."

Unfortunately, talk was cheap, and as much as I wanted to pack our bags and find a way out, we had nowhere to go.

So, I did what I needed to do. I worked and got my GED, and I started saving money again. This time I'd get out, and Lucy would come with me. We would make it work.

But saving money was harder when you had a baby to provide for. I picked up every shift offered to me, but unlike before, I had to ask myself if it was worth the sacrifice of leaving Josie each time. I mourned the fact that her daycare workers and Lucy saw her more than her mother did.

One night, when the restaurant was too slow to keep both servers on, I agreed to be the server who stayed. I could have gone home to Josie, but ten dollars was ten dollars and another step closer to freedom.

With only one hour until closing, a large family of twelve came in. A wave of relief hit me, and I thanked God. Unfortunately, I gave thanks a moment too soon. That table was more demanding than the after-church crowd, and they kept me running. The delivery of a soda refill would prompt a request for a side of ranch, and the delivery of ranch prompted requests for all new silverware because the hard water spots on the butter knives grossed them out. It was Wyoming. The water was hard.

I must have walked between our prep area and their table thirty times before their food was out. The group's matriarch, a woman with platinum blonde hair and copious amounts of eyeliner, declined when I offered to refill her drink. Yet minutes later, she held her glass up and shook the ice while calling to me, "Yoo hoo! Are we supposed to get our own refills?"

I wanted to drop their drinks into their laps, but I smiled broadly and doled out pleasantries like Tic Tacs while peppering them with kindness. "Of course, sir. Absolutely, ma'am. My pleasure."

When they left, I felt like I had waited ten tables. Then, eager to see the tip I had earned, I glanced at their credit card receipt. A zero with a slash sat above the tip line. Surely, they left cash. I bussed the table. I was certain it would be under a plate or cup. People did that all the time.

Two wet dollar bills lay folded under a perspiring cup. They hung limp, pinched between my thumb and forefinger. Two dollars? Fuck.

Tears threatened my eyes as I threw the remains of their dinner on the bus cart. Dishes crashed into a bin, and my hands trembled. In the kitchen, I unloaded the bus cart for the dishwasher just as my boss walked around the corner.

"We have a customer," he said.

My temper boiled over, and I groaned, dropping the bin before walking back toward the dining room. Immediately, the guilt from my outburst trickled into the fissures of my brain.

Sitting in a booth was a guy. His hands rested on the table, fingers woven together.

I forced myself to smile, channeling my stress into false confidence. "It's your lucky day. You get my undivided attention tonight. Unless another lucky customer walks in before closing."

"Let's hope that doesn't happen," he said as the left corner of his mouth rose, revealing perfect pearly whites.

"You're in for a real treat." I cocked my head to the side and smirked.

I always marveled at how I could be this confident, cool girl when I waited tables. Over the years, I had tested various renditions of my personality, and this one was a fan favorite among customers. It was so at odds with who I really was.

"What can I get you to drink?"

After I took his order, I yelled into the kitchen, giving them instructions for his food and my dinner. It was slow enough to knock out my side work while I waited for our orders. I couldn't help but be curious about the guy eating by himself and stared at him while I refilled salt and pepper shakers.

He had straight brown hair and was overdue for a haircut. His short fingernails were rimmed with black, and his fingers were stained gray. He wasn't exactly attractive but had a nice enough smile. Two rows of perfect teeth sat inside his mouth. He must have had braces. He caught me looking, and I called out, "Need a refill?"

"Nah, I'm good," he said.

I blushed, embarrassed that he caught me, and returned to sanitizing the prep area. When my orders were up, I slid a bottle of ketchup and mustard into my apron pocket and delivered his food.

Standing before the table, I hooked my thumbs into the belt loops on my jeans.

"Anything else I can get for you?"

"How about your number?" He smiled.

"Sorry," I replied. "I'm fresh out, but maybe next time."

I walked away. Flattery was nice, but I didn't have time for boys. I slid into my own booth, facing him. He watched me as I unrolled my silverware and dunked a straw into my drink. I tried to keep my eyes diverted as I prepared to eat but found his gaze exhilarating. Then, out of some strange pull toward exhibitionism, I met his eyes and took a massive bite of my sandwich.

He must have viewed my display as a challenge because he took a larger bite of his burger.

I couldn't stop myself. We were now competing over who could take the biggest bite. My jaw extended far beyond what was comfortable as I took another enormous mouthful. The amount was too much for my mouth, and I couldn't chew it. He laughed. The laughter was contagious, and I caught it. I thought I might choke as I brought a napkin to my mouth to cover my exposed, half-chewed food. I lost, and he used that moment of humility to extend an offer.

"How about instead of eating over there, you eat over here? I could use the company."

I eyed him suspiciously. I didn't have any excuse to not sit with him. "Are you going to ask me for my number again?"

"Not if you don't want me to."

I might regret it, but I reasoned it couldn't hurt.

At his table, conversation rose and filled the dining room. His name was Andrew. He grew up here in Rock Springs and worked at a local tire shop only a few blocks from the diner, which explained the gray and black stains on his fingers. Only a few years older than me, his parents homeschooled him, and they still lived together on a large ranch.

An hour into our conversation, my boss called from the back, "You leaving yet? Did you lock up?"

Oh shit! I had lost track of time. It was long after closing, and I had yet to lock the door and flip the sign. Realizing the time, I popped up from the booth.

"I'm leaving," I called out, rushing to flip the sign and cash Andrew out. "Give me one minute. I'll get your ticket."

After I handed Andrew his change, I walked him to the front door so I could lock it behind him. As I opened the door, Andrew shifted his weight from one foot to the other.

"I enjoyed talking to you. Could we do this again sometime?"

"I don't think so, but thanks." I felt bad for being so rude to him after he had been so nice to me, so I amended my statement, "I also enjoyed our conversation."

He pulled a bill out of his pants pocket and shoved it in the front pocket of my apron. "I forgot to tip you."

"Thanks for remembering. Have a good night."

I shut the door behind him and engaged the lock.

As we left through the back, my boss said, "Looks like you have a new boyfriend?"

"Nope. No boyfriends for me, boss."

CHAPTER 26

The low rolling hills and buttes peppered with sagebrush flashed by as Andrew, Josie, and I drove to his parents' ranch. I checked my reflection in the sun visor mirror for the fourth time since we had left my house.

"Stop worrying. They're going to love you," Andrew told me.

I couldn't help but be anxious. I had asked him a thousand questions, trying to discern what kind of people his parents were, but he would only tell me they were great. Great was not enough for me to know how I should behave. Sure, I knew their names were Betty and Rich, and I knew what they did for work, but that was not enough.

Although it was a brisk fall day and the heater in Andrew's car only half worked, I sweated profusely. Lifting my left arm, I found a perfectly round wet spot at my armpit. *Oh, fantastic.*

Andrew and I had only been dating for a couple of weeks but had known each other for four months. It started innocently. He would come into the diner to eat after work and always requested I take his table. Then, the next thing I knew, he was giving me rides home, taking me to the grocery store, and helping me assemble furniture. At first, I told him we could only be friends. But the first time I saw him with Josie changed everything. He had a way with her that no one else did. Her face would light up every time he walked into a room. He lifted her above his head and blew raspberries on her stomach, eliciting bubbly giggles that rang through the air.

The first time he kissed me, he told me he loved me. I said it back out of some self-manufactured obligation, but he was a good guy, and I could do a lot worse. I deserved a nice guy from a nice family, but at the same time, it made me nervous. What would Andrew's parents think of me—a teen mom, a high school dropout, a nobody?

I got out of the car, and Andrew rushed back to unbuckle Josie from her car seat.

While he was busy, Andrew's mom, Betty, came out of the house. She was a small woman with a muscular frame. Andrew said she taught pilates part-time in between taking care of the ranch. It showed. She came toward the car and all but rushed me.

"I am so glad you could make it! Andrew has told me so much about you!" She embraced me and then pulled back to look at me. "Andrew was right. You're stunning."

I blushed at her compliment. "So are you?" Nervous, my voice rose on the last syllable, making what was supposed to be a statement a question instead.

She laughed. "Well, I used to be quite the looker when I was your age, but I do my best to maintain some youthfulness for the sake of Rich." She nodded toward the house. "Come on, let's get you inside. It's cold out here."

The inside of the house was pristine. This was the house Andrew grew up in. The house he still lived in. Glossy wood detailed the cream-colored walls, and the furniture looked clean, new, and plush.

Andrew handed Josie to me. "I'm going to find my dad."

He held a thumb over his shoulder, signaling where he thought he could find his father.

"He's probably still in the shop. I told him to come in about thirty minutes ago, but you know your father. He won't stop until his work is done," Betty called after Andrew.

Betty glided around her kitchen. She was in her element.

"Do you like asparagus?" Betty asked me.

I'd never had asparagus, but I couldn't admit it, so I told her I liked it.

"Great, we'll have some with the steaks tonight. Also, I have some baked potatoes in the oven, and the grill is heating up on the back deck. It's not exactly grilling season, but steak is never as good on the stove. Don't you agree?"

I nod, even though I wouldn't know. We didn't eat steak at my house. I was way out of my league here.

"I was going to bake an apple pie, but I saw these brownies at that grocery store." Betty lifted a plastic container of brownies. "I thought they'd be delicious with some ice cream. I promise I will bake something next time you come over."

Next time.

She talked so much that I was safe giving minimal responses while still feeling like we were carrying on a full conversation. I followed Betty's instructions and helped prepare dinner while Josie munched on pieces of banana in a highchair.

"I just contemplated getting rid of this highchair and some other baby stuff I have, but I thought to myself, Betty, you never know. You might need it. And I did!"

I smiled politely.

Betty watched as Josie brought a fistful of mushy yellow banana to her mouth.

"You know, I always fed Andrew a little something before dinner, too. That way, he was busy while I cooked and full enough at supper time that I could enjoy my meal."

When it was time to put the steaks on, Betty found Andrew and Rich in their family room in the finished basement, watching a football game.

"These steaks will not grill themselves gentlemen, and Rich, you haven't said hi to our guest," Betty called from the top of the stairs.

Rich emerged and walked into the kitchen. He picked up a sheet tray of steaks and turned to me. I couldn't help but notice how much Andrew resembled him.

"Sorry about that, Helen. I thought I would let you ladies get to know each other. Plus, I already feel like I know you. You have been a hot topic at dinner as of late."

I blushed and looked at Andrew, who was also blushing.

When dinner was ready, we sat at their large dining room table. Betty arranged the food on matching serving ware in the center of the table, and our plates were each decorated with little tents made from red fabric napkins. One carafe held iced tea and another held water.

Everyone filled their plates, and not wanting to make a fool out of myself, I went last. As I lifted my fork, I saw Andrew, Betty, and Rich all holding hands.

"We always say grace. Would you like to join us?" Rich said.

I put down my fork and reached for Andrew's and Betty's hands. They bowed their heads, and I followed suit. Grace flowed from Rich's lips, and I studied each word, trying to commit it to memory in case they ever asked me to say it myself. It wasn't like I had never prayed before. I'd been to church. Usually, it was only when Momma needed help with the light bill or rent, but I had been. Billy Ray went to church and invited me a few times too.

After we were done saying grace, Betty asked, "Andrew says you like to read?"

"I do," I said through a mouthful of potato.

"So do I! There's a book I am reading called *Wild at Heart*. I'll let you borrow it if you'd like."

"Thank you. That would be nice."

"It's a Christian book, and it is really interesting. It has helped me understand my husband and son a lot better."

"Oh, yeah?"

Rich piped in, "It's about how men have a natural inclination toward battle and how we often struggle with our identities when we become fathers. It's really interesting because if you think about it, boys will gravitate toward items needed in battle from a young age."

I was still stuck on the identity crisis brought about by fatherhood. Was that the problem with dads?

"What do you like to read?" Rich asked.

I exchanged a glance with Andrew. My brain was blank. I didn't know why I was so nervous. Andrew recognized it and began to speak for me.

"She enjoys the classics. *Lord of the Flies, Frankenstein, Of Mice and Men.* You know, the boring stuff."

I tittered at that last part. "The boring stuff! Wasn't it just last week you cried at the end of …"

"Shhh!" Andrew held a finger to his lips.

"Don't shhh me! We watched *Of Mice and Men*, and you cried!"

Rich held his hand to his chest and feigned an incredulous gasp.

Andrew grinned, and Betty laughed as Josie squealed in her seat. Somehow, dinner was so much more comfortable now.

After dinner, Rich pulled out a deck of playing cards, and for the first time, I played rummy. Then, when Josie rubbed her eyes, it was time to go.

"You'll come to church with us on Sunday, won't you?" Betty said as we put our coats on and headed toward the car.

"Sure," I said.

My life changed drastically after that first dinner with Andrew's parents. I found myself at church every Sunday morning and at family dinners at the ranch every Thursday evening. On Wednesdays, I went to an all-women's Bible study. Betty took me shopping and spoiled Josie with new outfits and toys. She taught me to cook and how to grocery shop for a family. She shared cleaning tips and philosophies on parenting. I spent almost as much time with Betty as I did with Andrew. And boy, did Betty adore Josie.

We celebrated Josie's first birthday at Betty and Rich's ranch. My family was there, but Momma, Matt, and even Lucy looked out of place among Andrew's family and church friends.

My life was suddenly so full it was brimming over the edge. It felt like this was who I was meant to be.

When the familiar exhaustion came, I asked God why. Andrew didn't like to wear condoms. He said they hurt, but I wasn't worried because I was on birth control. I missed a few days here and there but didn't think much of it. I should have known it must be taken every day.

I was terrified the night I told Andrew. I prayed that this time it would be different. That he might stick around. And he did. Even more, he was happy. Andrew rested his hand on my flat stomach and said, "I'm going to be a dad."

I had wanted out. Out of the life I was born into. And while this was not the original route I imagined, it must have been God's will. It was as if my path was being laid at my feet, and although I was the one walking, I had no real agency over the direction. God had a plan for me.

CHAPTER 27

When we announced our pregnancy to Betty and Rich, Andrew also proposed. He couldn't afford much, but with his parents' help, he bought a modest white gold ring with a tanzanite stone.

Shortly after the proposal, Andrew got a job at a local power plant and encouraged me to quit my job.

"You deserve a break, and I make enough money now. I can give you one," he said during family dinner.

"As much of a break as taking care of two children under two can be," Betty added with a raised eyebrow.

So, I quit my job, and Andrew and I found ourselves a small three-bedroom home for rent. The house was older but nicer than most places I had lived. It felt like I had lucked into some alternate universe. It was a fairytale.

"I like you barefoot and pregnant." Andrew winked as he sat at our small kitchen table, watching me cook dinner. I couldn't help but smile.

Everything was happening as it should. The only thing missing was Lucy.

When I turned eighteen, I told Andrew I wanted Lucy to move in with us. I was finally old enough to be her guardian, and I thought all I needed to do was to convince Momma to let Lucy go.

It wasn't the first time I had expressed this to Andrew, but it was always something in the future. It was never possible until now. I asked if Lucy could move in on New Year's Day and my eighteenth birthday. This request led to our first fight.

"No. Lucy is not moving in with us." Andrew shook his head at the thought.

"But why?" I asked. The fact he instantly said no without even considering it surprised me. I leaned back in my chair at the kitchen table and crossed my arms.

"We're not going to ruin a good thing."

My frustration grew, as did my tone of voice. "I don't understand. How does that ruin things?"

"I told you I don't want her here! This is *my* house. Why do you feel entitled to have someone else move into it?"

Was he implying this wasn't my house? Entitled? He loved Lucy, and she would be an immense help. She wouldn't ruin anything!

With an exaggerated huff, I stood from my seat at the kitchen table. "She's my sister!"

He stood up, too, matching my energy. "I'm aware. She also has parents. Your parents. She doesn't belong in my house."

"This is my house too!"

But was it? Was this my house? I felt trapped and out of control, and I began to cry.

Andrew shook his hands at me, irritated. "Why are you crying!?"

But I was too overwhelmed and struggled to get the words out. I tried to gesture with my hands that I couldn't speak, but it didn't help. The more I cried, the angrier Andrew became.

"Stop fucking crying!" He punctuated his statement by driving his fist into the kitchen wall.

My fight or flight kicked in, and I knew I needed to get out. It was time to go. I found Josie in her playpen and hoisted her onto my hip. I grabbed the keys from the table and started for the door, but Andrew was quick.

"Helen. You can't just leave every time things get hard. You need to stay and talk to me," he said through clenched teeth. He was scaring me.

I positioned my body so Josie was on the opposite side of Andrew and pushed past him. At the car, I quickly buckled Josie into her seat and got into the car. I didn't know how to drive yet. I was learning but not confident enough to drive with Josie, so I looked around, lost and unsure what to do.

The light caught an object on the concrete walkway. It was my watch. A watch I had worn nearly every day since my tenth birthday. I couldn't leave it. I hesitated, torn between locking myself in the car and retrieving the watch as Andrew came out of the house.

I had just gotten out of the car when I heard the delicate crack as Andrew's boot pressed into the watch's face. Devastation hit me like a bag of rocks, and I cried out, sinking to my knees. My body folded in on itself until I sat sobbing in the gravel driveway. My resolve had dissolved at the sound of fractured glass.

Andrew appeared in front of me, pulling me to his chest. He ran a hand over my hair. The watch he crushed rested in his other hand. An apology. I felt completely overwhelmed. So much happened so fast. The hole in the kitchen wall, me trying to flee, my watch. And now I leaned into Andrew, soaking in his care as he apologized for losing his temper. I was confused.

In the days following our fight, he doted on me. His affection amplified, and the more he gave, the more I needed it.

It took some time for me to understand why Andrew didn't want Lucy to move in. I was going to be his wife, and it was important to him we had time to ourselves. Disrupting our life with another person was selfish.

A couple of weeks after our fight, I went to see Lucy. It seemed like ever since Andrew and I moved in together, I barely saw her.

"How's the wedding planning going?" Lucy asked.

"Good. Betty is doing most of it."

"It will be here soon," she said as she cut out squares of colorful construction paper and glued them to a piece of scavenged cardboard. She was creating an intricate board game covered with monsters and nymphs.

I smiled, impressed by her ingenuity.

"Yea." I pulled my bottom lip into my mouth and contemplated my next words.

"Hey Lucy, I talked to Andrew about you moving in."

She perked up and put her scissors down.

"Oh yeah? What did he say?"

I let out a sigh, and Lucy's shoulders squared at my hesitation.

"It's okay, Helen. I understand."

"No, you don't. Andrew wants to concentrate on our marriage, and he feels we need time with just the two of us after the wedding. That's all. Maybe in a little while, you know?"

Lucy looked at her lap before looking at me.

"I know you're worried about me being here with Momma and Matt, but I promise, it's not so bad. They're doing better. Honestly, most of the time, I forget I live in a house with two other people."

Lucy never wanted to be a burden. She tempered her headstrong nature to put others at ease. I knew this about her, which made this all so much more difficult.

"Lucy." I knew what she was doing. It wasn't okay. I was supposed to get her out, too. She was counting on me.

She shook her head, choosing a piece of green paper from the stack. "No, really. I don't need you to rescue me."

Her words stung a little. I had become so accustomed to believing she needed me, but maybe it was me who needed her.

"Are you sure?" I whispered.

"Yeah. I'm sure."

Guilt steadily ate at my insides after leaving my old house and Lucy that day. This was the path that God wanted for me, but why was Lucy not included? Maybe if I gave Andrew some time, he would change his mind.

Our wedding day was beautiful. Lovely people sat in pretty pews decorated with tulle bows and orchids, offering reassuring smiles. Although I was clearly seven months pregnant, these people, mostly church friends, were all so kind. I didn't deserve such grace. My family: Josie, Lucy, Billy Ray, Dad, Momma, and Matt, were all there to support me during this monumental occasion. Maybe one day, I may mend some of the brokenness that troubled our family.

As I approached the altar, Andrew mouthed the words, "You are beautiful."

A blend of conflicting emotions coursed through me as I stood before my soon-to-be husband. I knew I loved him, and he loved me, but a subtle unease gnawed at my insides.

CHAPTER 28

Laying on the sofa, sleep tendrils wrapped around each of my limbs, and I calculated whether I could sleep. Josie was down for a nap, dinner was in the slow cooker, and the dishes could wait. I gave myself permission to sleep.

I dreamt of laughter—the joyful kind. I bounced a smiling infant on my knee, and Andrew sat beside me on the couch. He smiled at me, his face warm and loving, and I looked back at our baby, surprised to find I was not holding her anymore. She was sitting without support and toppled backward as I lunged forward, terrified.

"You're fucking sleeping?" Andrew yelled.

I blinked hard, trying to make my eyes adjust to the light faster. The top half of my body was hovering above the sofa cushions. Andrew wrapped his hand tightly in my shirt and lifted me from where I lay. I tried to pull away, but he tightened his grasp. His nostrils flared, and his brows pushed together, creating a deep V.

"This is what you do while I bust my ass at work all day?" he sneered.

"Let go of me!" I yelled.

Andrew released my shirt, and I fell back onto the couch. My mind raced. What time was it? Was Josie okay? Did I not hear her wake up?

I scrambled off the couch, disoriented.

"Where do you think you are going? I'm not done talking to you." He grabbed my biceps, and I jerked away from him.

"Stop! I need to check on Josie!" I turned away but felt his hands heavy on my shoulders.

"How many times do I have to tell you that you can't just walk away?"

Suddenly, I was being propelled back. It happened so fast, but also time slowed.

I shifted my weight, hoping to protect my pregnant belly as the room slid before my eyes. The focus on my stomach caused me to lose my balance, and I hit the coffee table hard. Pain erupted from my right forearm, but I was confused. The side of my torso hit the coffee table, not my arm.

Then I saw it. A broken glass cup that sat on the table—one of the dishes I said could wait. The jagged glass glinted in the light, forming little mountains capped with my blood, the same blood that trickled from a gash on my forearm.

The pain from landing on the table was secondary and pulsated through me. I held my breath for a second before I cried out.

Andrew's nostrils were no longer flared, and his brows were now lifted in concern. His anger disappeared as quickly as it had come on.

"I'm so sorry. I'm so sorry," he said. "I didn't mean for that to happen."

Shocked, I only watched him. He reached to examine my arm. His movements were rushed and shaky as he tried to stop blood flow. When my brain finally made the connection between Andrew and what happened, I pulled my arm away from him.

"Get away from me!" I scrambled backward, kicking my feet out.

He made another attempt to touch me, and I clambered back further." Get away from me!"

Josie's cries traveled into the living room. She was awake. I looked toward the hallway where her bedroom was located, afraid to move.

"Helen, I'm so sorry. I didn't mean to hurt you."

I stared at him, conflicted, and looked at my arm. I couldn't wrap my head around what had happened. Why was he so mad that I was asleep?

"I was just sleeping," I said, still puzzled.

Andrew only nodded, and Josie's cries grew louder. I pulled myself up from the floor, and Andrew grabbed my arm to help. I didn't pull away from him this time. He wasn't going to hurt me.

"Go clean up your arm. I got Josie," he said before walking away.

I stood at the kitchen sink, rinsing my arm as drops of blood speckled the dirty dishes. I applied pressure to the wound, and although I knew I should be angry, I only felt embarrassed. I couldn't work out what had happened and didn't know what I was supposed to do next. How could I let this happen?

Andrew came out with Josie on his hip. Her face, red from crying, was now bright and smiling. He tickled her side, and she giggled. I pushed my feelings down. I needed to hold it together—for Josie.

Later that night, Andrew expressed his remorse. He'd had a bad day and called before he left work. When I didn't answer, he got worried. He didn't mean to hurt me. It wouldn't have happened if I had stayed and talked to him. I couldn't reconcile my thoughts, and it was easier to believe him than not.

The day our baby, Raina, was born, I dispelled all remnants of fear and anger. It was irrational to hold on to such feelings. Andrew's elation knew no bounds when he cradled our newborn daughter, Raina, in his arms for the first time. He openly wept, and seeing him so touched by the life we created together made it easy to reason that the incident in which I cut my arm was just an accident.

The happiness we collectively felt in the hospital was at odds with how we would fare after arriving home. Nothing prepared me for the wave of depression, anxiety, and helplessness I felt with my second child. My mind slowly crept toward a darkness unlike any I'd known before. I wanted to be present, to enjoy motherhood, but instead, I cried. Raina was such an easy baby, unlike her sister Josie. She could be easily soothed and remained consistently content. While I was at odds with my inner turmoil, Raina was at peace, blissfully unaware of what was happening around her. She was my little ladybug.

The more depressed I became, the angrier Andrew got. My tears infuriated him, which further exacerbated my depression. We fought constantly. Most of the fights were stupid. I overspent at the store, burned dinner, or told someone something I shouldn't have. During these fights, he would tell me I was stupid, ungrateful, and entitled. It was true. God had blessed me, and I was ruining it.

We were stuck in this cycle of tears, anger, remorse, and love. Over time, I depended on the familiar pattern but wanted so badly for it to end. I felt myself withdrawing from everyone outside of Andrew's circle. I was too ashamed to admit I was wrong.

On one of my few good days, I cleaned the house while Raina slept in her swing and Josie played quietly. I had asked Andrew to take out the trash earlier that day, but two bags still sat next to the kitchen trash can.

"Hey, I need to mop. Can you take out the trash?"

"If you're going to nag me, you can do it yourself," he said as he sat on the sofa playing video games.

I threw my arms up and marched back to the kitchen. "Fine! I do everything else around here."

"What did you say?" he yelled from the living room.

I ignored him and hoisted the two bags of trash from the floor. As I walked past where Andrew sat, he stood and followed me. I thought he was going to take the trash from me, and I would not let him. I would do it myself. However, he didn't reach for the bags. Instead, he thrust a hand into my hair and grabbed a fistful. Trapped, I had no choice but to follow him as he walked me to the back door. My gaze bounced around the house as I looked for an escape. But it wasn't necessary.

Andrew flung the door open and whispered in my ear, "If you want to act like a bitch, you can live like one." He threw me out of the house and onto the ground.

I sat there, unable to move as I willed my heart to slow. I was in shock.

A moment later, he returned with the bag I had dropped during the assault. Andrew dug his fingers into the plastic, ripping it apart before unloading the waste on top of me. The worst part was that I let him do it. I was pathetic. Maybe I deserved to be treated like trash.

The next day, Andrew pretended as if nothing had happened. He was charming, and because I was constantly hungry for affection and wary of anger, I pretended, too.

"I love you," he said, kissing me on the cheek as I washed dishes.

"I love you too," I said.

"You mean it?" I knew his question came from a place of guilt for what he did, but I chose to alleviate his remorse rather than irritate it.

"I do." And I wasn't lying. I did love him, but something had to change.

A few weeks later, while Andrew was at work, Betty sat in my home and held Raina in her arms. Betty always seemed to have the answers. She knew exactly what to do and when to do it. I wanted to confide in her and tell her about my struggles.

"I knew I would love being a grandmother, but I couldn't have imagined I would love it this much," she said to me.

I was busy folding laundry while we sat and visited. I stopped to study her. I wrestled with what I was about to say.

I took a deep breath. "Can I ask you something?"

"Sure." She made kissy faces at Raina as I spoke.

"Did you and Rich fight a lot after Andrew was born?"

"Oh goodness, how could we? We were so happy to be blessed with our boy."

I stared down at my hands, ashamed.

Betty shifted where she sat with Raina and glanced at Josie, who was playing with blocks on the floor.

"It's none of my business, but Andrew tells me things. He's always been a momma's boy. It's difficult for him to see you like this. You don't even brush your hair anymore. If you just tried a little harder."

Try a little harder. I held her words in my mind.

"You know, what always helps me when I'm going through something? Talking to our pastor. If you haven't already, I recommend it."

I considered her advice but was too ashamed to confide in anyone else. So, I told myself I would try a little harder, and I did. But the damage was done. Andrew slowly became more complacent in our relationship and his responsibility to our family.

When Raina was about three months old, I woke up one morning, and Andrew was still in bed. The alarm clock read 7:22 a.m. He was late for work.

"Wake up, Andrew! You're late!" I said, shaking him.

He grunted and rolled over.

"I'm not going."

"Did you call in today?" I asked, confused.

"No, and I'm not going to."

He couldn't miss work. We depended on him. "That is not funny, Andrew. We have bills to pay. We need this job."

He turned around to look at me. "No, you need this job. You fucking gold digger."

I left the room, afraid I might start a fight if I stayed any longer. I would ask for help one more time. I couldn't do this alone.

At the church, bookshelves lined the walls of Pastor Tony's office, and books that couldn't fit lay in piles on his desk. His office smelled like old leather and pencil shavings. I sat across from him, nervous about detailing the inner workings of my marriage. So, I took a deep breath and tried to emotionally distance myself from what I was about to say.

"Andrew gets angry a lot."

Pastor Tony nodded, and when I didn't continue, he said, "And?"

Distance yourself, Helen.

I didn't want to cry or appear hysterical. I needed him to hear me. I swallowed and continued. "He gets mad and sometimes breaks things or punches the walls. I've tried, but when he gets mad, I start crying, which makes things worse. He quit his job too. Says he'll find a new one, but we were barely making it already. I just don't know what to do."

Pastor Tony pressed his lips together and stared at me for a solid minute before he responded.

"I'm glad you came to me, Helen."

I was relieved at those words.

He cleared his throat. "Imagine how Andrew must feel. He's a good man. But he's young, and he's taken on a huge responsibility in a short amount of time."

"I know, but what am I supposed to do?"

"Does Andrew hit you?"

I flashed back to our fights. Never once had he hit me. I could tell Pastor Tony about the things that happened, but that wasn't his question.

"No."

"Good. A man shouldn't hit a woman, ever. Have you read Ephesians?"

I shook my head. I didn't dare admit that I struggled to read my Bible at home.

A large Bible lay open on Pastor Tony's desk. He carefully flipped through the thin pages until he found what he was looking for. He read aloud in the same voice he used during church service.

"Ephesians 5:21-28 says, 'Submit to one another out of reverence for Christ. Wives, submit yourselves to your own husbands as you do to the Lord. For the husband is the head of the wife as Christ is the head of the church, his body, of which he is the Savior. Now as the church submits to Christ, wives should submit to their husbands in everything. Husbands, love your wives, just as Christ loved the church.'"

He looked up at me, judging me.

"Do you know what that means?"

I replayed the words in my head, terrified of getting the answer wrong. "It means we are supposed to love and serve each other?"

"Yes, but most importantly, you are to trust your husband. He is the head of your household, and in return, he will love you. Stop fighting against him. Help him."

Help him. I was supposed to help him. I would try. I left the church and went straight to the local workforce center to find a job.

CHAPTER 29

I was at work only days before Christmas when I made the call.

"Hey, honey, what's up?" Andrew said.

"Did you go to the doctor yet?" I asked.

"Um, no. I haven't had time."

Raina hadn't been feeling well for several days. A constant stream of acidic diarrhea exasperated a pretty nasty diaper rash. My pediatrician, who had a soft spot for my kids, was consistently there to ease my worry. I called the office that morning. The nurse said to stop by, and they would give us a stool sample kit.

"I'm sure it's only a stomach bug, but it doesn't hurt to check," she had said.

Andrew had one job. Pick up the kit, but he had yet to do so.

"What have you been doing all day? I would go myself, but I can't."

A deep sigh came from the receiver.

"Well ..." He hesitated. "The kids are asleep."

The anxiety that bubbled up in moments like these made my skin crawl with irritability. I had no choice but to go back to work, and Andrew treated being at home with the kids more like babysitting than actual parenting.

"Then wake them." I rolled my eyes, trying to keep my frustration at bay.

The waning volume of the television in the background told me he was moving through the house.

"I don't know if we should go anywhere. Raina's acting kind of funny," Andrew said.

"Funny?"

"Her breathing is labored, and she isn't waking up."

My heart quickened with worry. "What do you mean?"

"I don't know. You'd have to be here."

"Take her to the hospital. Right now! I'll meet you there." I was practically yelling.

"But Josie's still sleeping."

"I don't care. Wake her up! Look, I'm leaving work right now. I'll meet you at the hospital."

"I can pick you up," he said.

Why was he concerned with me? Didn't he understand the severity of the situation? Our daughter was acting funny. That's what he said, wasn't it?

"Don't worry about me! Go to the hospital," I shouted as my manager glared at me from across the room.

I hung up and approached her, trying to explain the situation quickly and begging to be let go. I was afraid of losing my job. I was still new, but instead of reprimanding me, she offered me a ride. As we approached the hospital, I saw Andrew back out of the pediatrician's parking lot across the street from the emergency room. *What the hell is he doing?*

We followed him into the hospital parking lot. I jumped from my manager's vehicle as Andrew pulled into a parking spot. I raced for the back seat, but Andrew cut me off before I could get to the car. He nonchalantly reached in to retrieve Raina. *Why the fuck is he going so slow?*

My body was shaking, and I crossed my arms, trying to steady myself. It was a calm winter day, and although there was no snow, the cold turned each exhale into puffs of white. When he finally emerged from the back seat, holding Raina in his arms, I fell in step with him as we walked to the emergency room entrance.

"Why were you at the doctor's office? I told you to come here," I said, berating him. I needed to stop.

"I thought that's what you wanted," he replied.

"What did they say?"

"They said she looks fine, but we could come here to get her checked out."

Something didn't feel right. Andrew was unhurried as he walked. I mentally begged him to move faster but it was as if the world was in slow motion. I clenched my jaw, trying to stifle my aggravation.

In the hospital, I looked at Raina, really looked at her. Her eyes were closed, but she wasn't asleep. Whimpers came from the back of her throat, but her face remained expressionless. She seemed to be stuck in a nightmare. Alarm bells rang through my mind, but I couldn't identify the exact threat.

A mere moment passed before the hospital staff noticed our presence and rushed us into the emergency room. They were expecting us. They knew something was wrong.

Slow motion became hyper speed as nurses wasted no time pulling Raina from her car seat and laying her on a hospital bed. I watched, perplexed and devastated, as they cut off her clothes, shined a flashlight in her eyes, and fastened various instruments to take her vitals. The medical staff yelled instructions to one another. I didn't know if they could hear my constant barrage of information over the noise, but I kept yelling anyway. Maybe something I would say would be a clue to the underlying cause.

"She's five months old today! She's had diarrhea! She has a mild heart murmur! She ate bananas for the first time yesterday! What is wrong with my baby? Can you help her?"

Andrew stood silent and wide-eyed as I yelled information and questions into the air. So often, I hadn't known how to help my babies, but this time was different. This time, the consequences of my ignorance felt greater.

The doctor noticed me and asked, "Has she recently fallen or hit her head?"

I looked at Andrew. But he didn't answer. We plunged into silence.

Say something! I stared at him, assuming the worst. Maybe he left her on the couch unsupervised. Maybe he hit her head on a door as he was carrying her to her room. He did something. *Tell me what happened.*

I broke the silence and said, "I don't know. I have been at work all day."

I turned to Andrew, pleading with my eyes.

Answer the damn question.

His face drained of color. He appeared to be paralyzed by fear. He was terrified.

Finally, he shook his head. "I'm so sorry," he whispered.

My eyes moved back to the doctor, hoping for a follow-up question. Another explanation I could grab onto.

But he didn't ask any more questions and instead said, "We need a CT scan."

I followed as they carted Raina away, but the nurses stopped me. I momentarily struggled against the hospital staff, but Andrew grabbed my arms and pulled me back. I fell into him and prayed. "Please, God, please let my baby be okay. Please, God, please."

"She'll be okay. She has to be okay," he said, rubbing my back. He provided no comfort as questions crept up around the edges of the turmoil.

I pulled away and turned toward him. "Why were you going so slow?"

"What?"

"When you got out of the car, you were moving so slow. You never walk that slow."

Andrew always walked ahead of me and was unbothered when I had to run to catch up to him. We'd argued about it many times.

"I don't know what you are talking about." He tried to brush me off.

"And why did you go to the doctor first? I told you to go right to the hospital."

"I didn't think it was an emergency."

Not an emergency? Raina's whimpers replayed in my head. *It was clearly an emergency.*

He shook his head and planted his face in his hands. "I'm sorry. I wasn't thinking."

Conflicted, I sat in a chair to collect my thoughts. The back of my head hit the wall behind me, and my mind flashed to Josie.

"Where's Josie?"

Andrew sunk into the chair next to me and placed a hand on my thigh. "She's with Lucy."

My shoulders dropped. I needed to get my emotions under control.

"Helen?"

I ignored him as I tried to process the information in front of me.

"Helen, could you look at me? Please?"

I met his eyes. They were wild with fear.

"I did what I thought was best. We are here now. Okay?" His warm hand brushed over my fingers. I melted.

"I'm sorry," I said. We sat there frozen and silent ... waiting.

Sometime later, the doctor came in and asked to speak with me privately in the hall.

"When was the last time you saw your daughter?" he asked.

"This morning before I went to work."

"What time was that?"

"About 7:40 a.m. Why?" I didn't understand his line of questioning.

"And what was she like? Was she fussy? Irritable?"

"No. The opposite. She was happy. She's always happy in the morning. Even though she's been sick, she was still happy."

I remembered that morning. The house was quiet except for Raina's soft coos and gurgles as I tickled her feet and bopped her nose. She kicked her legs back and forth, fixated on my face as I spoke softly to her.

"Well ..." he paused, and my stomach dropped. "She is showing signs of a brain hemorrhage. She is unresponsive, and her eyes are both dilated. Her CT shows a significant amount of bleeding."

My stomach lurched, and I swallowed to keep the bile down. "What does that mean? How did this happen?"

"You mentioned that she's had diarrhea?"

I nodded.

"Dehydration can cause an aneurysm."

I should've called the doctor sooner. I should have ... I should have done so many things differently. But something nagged at me, and I couldn't stop wondering.

"Why did you ask to talk to me privately?"

The doctor cleared his throat and appeared uncomfortable but delivered the rest with a coolness that made it feel unreal. "Although it is possible this is the product of a ruptured aneurysm, it is unlikely. It is more likely that her bleeding is caused by a head injury."

Which one was it? An injury or dehydration?

"My husband said she didn't fall or hit her head today." I struggled to make sense of the information, remembering that Andrew didn't actually say anything. He only shook his head and apologized.

"That is why I wanted to speak with you privately. This type of brain bleed often indicates child abuse."

The room spun, and I had to hold the wall next to me to stay upright.

"I can't say definitively," the doctor continued, "but because of the situation, we are required to report it."

"Report it?" my voice caught in my throat.

"The police and social services will be here soon to talk to you."

I forced myself to focus. I needed to be there for Raina. "Fine. They can talk to me, but where is my baby? Can I see her?"

The doctor had been so matter-a-fact up to this point, but now his entire face sank. "Unfortunately, no. She is being prepped to be flown to the children's hospital in Denver."

"Can I go with her?" I begged as fresh tears emerged and flowed down my face. I held my breath, praying.

He exhaled. "No. I can't allow you to see her until social services and the police clear you. She'll be gone before you're done with the interviews."

I nodded my understanding, but the reality was I understood nothing. Everything around me blurred, and his voice grew muffled. I didn't even notice when he left to go speak with Andrew.

For the next several hours, I answered questions in a small conference room.

"Can you tell me if you noticed anything unusual about your child before you left for work today?"

"No. Nothing unusual. Everything was fine. She was fine."

"Does your husband have a history of abuse?"

"He gets angry with me sometimes, but never with the kids."

Never.

I felt as if I was deep at sea. The floor bobbed and moved underneath me, and I struggled to keep my balance as I tipped from side to side. I don't know how I held it together. I just did.

Our families arrived at the hospital at some point—Rich, Betty, Momma, and Matt. Dad was out of town but said he would meet us in Denver. After my last interview, I found Andrew talking to his mom.

"I'm scared, Mom. They're looking at me. They think I did this." His voice was shaky, and his eyes darted back and forth.

When Betty saw me out of her peripheral, they stopped talking.

"How you holding up?" Betty said.

I shrugged. I only wanted to be with Raina.

The quiet winter day had turned into a blizzard as we left the hospital. Snow came down with an unforgiving force, making it hard to see beyond thirty feet. A storm warning came through, and we would have to hurry if we wanted to beat the storm.

Andrew wanted to stop and talk, but there wasn't time. I couldn't. We quickly made our rounds in town, stocking up on tire chains and fuel. My house was our final stop, but as we pulled up, we found the police already there. They wanted to come inside.

"Do you have a warrant?" Rich asked.

"They don't need one," I said. "Please, just make it quick. We need to get on the road."

I pushed through to go inside. Andrew grabbed my arm and pulled me aside.

"They have no right to look through our house," he said.

"We have nothing to hide, Andrew. None of this will matter once they figure out what is wrong with Raina."

The police came in with flashlights, walked through our house, and opened doors. I was ashamed of the mess. Dishes were piled high in the sink, and mountains of laundry were in the living room. A trash bag that never made it outside sat on the kitchen floor, and the carpets desperately needed vacuuming.

"I'm sorry it's so messy. I can't seem to keep up."

The police didn't respond, obviously unaffected by my apology, but I could feel their judgment.

Josie was in bed. Lucy said she'd been fussy, but I wasn't surprised. She was connected to her sister like I was connected to Lucy. The police opened Josie's door, and light from the hallway illuminated her tiny body, curled up peacefully in bed. She was sleeping deeply. Her face was slightly flushed, and her blonde curls were damp.

I didn't want to leave Josie here, but a plan had already been formed. Bethany, my friend from the diner, would stay the night with Lucy and Josie.

While the police finished their search, I packed a bag. Christmas was only three days away, so I packed the gifts for Raina that I had yet to wrap, along with a couple of fresh changes of clothes. I didn't want her to miss out on her first Christmas.

We all piled in Rich and Betty's large SUV, which could withstand the icy conditions and fit Andrew, me, and our parents. After about an hour of silence, Matt and Rich started chatting about things unrelated to our reality. I didn't understand how they could be so flippant.

Andrew nestled close to me in the back seat.

"I'm so sorry," he said. "It's going to be okay." His hands massaged the muscles in my shoulders.

"It might not be," I said.

That moment was the first in which I vocalized what plagued me most. The idea that she might not make it out alive.

"What if she doesn't? What if she dies?" I whispered, the possibility soaking through my skin with each word and coiling into my heart.

"Why would you say that?" he said.

I didn't respond. He was right. I shouldn't have said such a thing.

The snowstorm was relentless, and we crawled along the highways. Frustrated that the weather, of all things, was keeping me from my daughter, I forced my eyes closed. If I slept, maybe time would stop taunting me. I drifted into a fitful sleep, only partially conscious of the world around me.

Chapter 30

When the vehicle came to a stop, my eyes flew open. We had arrived, or so I thought. But we hadn't. The SUV and at least a dozen other vehicles on the road were at a standstill. Only a mirage of headlights and brake lights shone through the blowing snow.

"What's happening?" I asked.

"The pass is closed. We have to find another way or wait out the storm," Rich said.

I sat up. "Find another way!" I begged.

"Maybe we should get a hotel and try in the morning," Andrew offered.

Everyone looked at each other to gauge if that was an acceptable course of action. The clock read 2:00 a.m., and they were tired. I didn't care. Finding a hotel was unacceptable, and I was repulsed at the suggestion.

"I can't sit in a hotel while my daughter is fighting for her life in a hospital. I'll walk if I have to." I knew it was an absurd threat, but I would try.

"Don't be ridiculous," Andrew said.

"I'm being ridiculous?"

Betty interjected, "Nobody is walking. We will find a way. We won't stop."

I mumbled a thank you and folded into myself.

It took nearly twelve hours, double the time it should have, but we made it. During the drive, I forced myself to sleep as much as possible. By sleeping, I could force time to move faster than when I was awake. My leg juddered uncontrollably as we pulled into the hospital's parking garage. *Five more minutes. Five more minutes.*

Momma's cell phone rang.

"Hello?" she said. Then her face contorted.

"Why?" Momma yelled into the receiver.

I held my breath, waiting. I could only assume the other shoe had dropped.

When she ended the call, I looked at her expectedly. She turned to Andrew and wagged her finger in his face.

"You son of a bitch! You did this."

"What?" I said, distressed. Andrew's face was stoney except for his lashes that batted with force each time he blinked. We all stared at Momma and Andrew, perplexed by the interaction.

"That was Bethany. She tried you first, Helen," Momma said, not taking her eyes from Andrew. He didn't speak, but his brows furrowed. Perspiration appeared between the lines on his forehead.

I reached around to find my cell phone.

"Social services are taking Josie," Momma said.

"What! Why?" I exclaimed. My heart began its marathon, and my stomach flipped.

"They said we will understand when we talk to the doctor."

Still rolling through the parking garage, I couldn't wait any longer. Something was wrong. Social services would not have taken custody of my two-year-old, Josie, without cause. I flung myself between the second row of bucket seats and pulled at the door handle, only to find it locked.

I was erratic. I screamed, "Please let me out! Let me out!" Rich hit the brakes.

I pulled and pushed the door handle until I was outside the SUV, and my feet were on the ground. I didn't think. There was no time for it. I only ran. My legs carried me as fast as they could toward the hospital building. I couldn't stop, and I didn't dare look behind me. I had to get to my daughter.

In the hospital, my momentum nearly threw me over the counter. "I'm here to see Raina Miller," I said. The words spilling from my mouth were barely recognizable.

She was in the Pediatric Intensive Care Unit. I spun around, ready to run again, but the woman who answered my question tried to stop me. I wouldn't let her. At the elevators, my finger slammed the button for the fourth floor. Waiting for the damn thing, I tried to catch my breath. My body buzzed with adrenaline.

Inside the elevator, I watched Andrew run toward the closing doors. He flung himself through the gap, causing the doors to reopen, and pushed a name tag on my chest. The image of Momma's finger in his face flashed before me. I needed answers.

I stuck the name tag to my shirt while we made the ascent. The moment the doors opened, I catapulted onto the fourth floor. Spinning, I looked for a sign to point me in the right direction. A staff member asked to help me, and I struggled to slow my breathing. Through strangled tears and much louder than I intended, I said, "My daughter. I'm here to see my daughter."

A nurse escorted us to Raina's room. She was asleep on a hospital bed that looked far too large compared to her tiny body. Tubes and tape were affixed to her, and I watched her chest rise and fall. She was alive. I watched her closely, savoring each time her chest expanded and deflated. I slowly approached her bedside and placed a hand on her foot. I expected to feel her warmth, but there was none. Her toes were small, swollen, and cold. Their purple hue reminded me of little grapes.

I wrapped my hands around her feet, trying desperately to warm them up, but they could not absorb the heat. A nurse stood by, watching me.

"Why is she so cold?" I asked, dreading the answer.

"Dr. Jones will be in to talk to you," the nurse said as I crouched at Raina's bedside, kissing her delicate fingers.

Andrew kneeled beside me, and with one hand on my back and the other placed just over the top of her small helpless body, he bowed his head. His body shook with immense sorrow, and I wanted to cry with him, but I had no tears left. All I had was hope, so I bowed with Andrew and prayed.

The doctor interrupted our prayers. We moved to the bright blue upholstered chairs at the edge of the room. Andrew's hand squeezed my thigh, bracing me for what would come next. The doctor detailed her injuries. A hemorrhage. A brain bleed.

"We assessed her brain activity at 9:00 a.m. We tested her response to pain and her brain stem reflexes. Unfortunately, she did not respond."

She was on life support. Tubes and IV fluids were her life force, and without those, she could not survive. At 9:00 p.m., the hospital would assess her again. That was the protocol.

I felt empty as I listened to the doctors. It was as if I had left my body and watched the exchange from an impossible perceptive. I saw a young woman wringing her hands together with vacant eyes. Her husband engaged in the conversation, caressed the top of his wife's thigh. The doctor delivered a message that would forever destroy these people. How was this our life?

"Is it possible she will recover?" Andrew asked.

"There is very little chance of recovery." The doctor paused before delivering his next line. I saw his worry etched into the lines around his eyes and mouth. "Your daughter's injuries align with blunt force trauma to the head. This is conclusively a case of child abuse."

That news instantly propelled me back into my body. I jerked forward before standing up. Andrew stood too.

Child abuse.

My child was abused.

I remembered him pulling out of the pediatrician's parking lot and his slow walk into the emergency room. His fear was so different from mine. His words, "They think I did this," and all the apologies.

He did this.

"What did you do?" My voice became a deep growl. "Andrew! Answer me!"

He backed up, his hands signaling retreat. Crazed, I grabbed a tissue box from a table and threw it at him. He turned to deflect the blow.

"I didn't hurt them," he said, backing away from me. His eyes looked the same as they did that day when he stared at my bloodied forearm. He was terrified.

"Get out! Get out! Get away from my daughter! Get away from her," I yelled, waving my arms.

"I'm sorry," he said before leaving the room.

The doctor spoke again, but I couldn't hear him. The only noise I heard came from the breathing tube and monitors attached to Raina. I went back to her and climbed into her bed, careful not to disturb the machines that kept her alive. He was sorry. He was always sorry.

I prayed again, harder than I had ever prayed before. Harder than the time I prayed for God to make me a better wife, or the time I prayed for a way out of my Momma's house, or for Momma to get clean, or to soothe Andrew's anger. This time I wasn't only asking for God's help. I was bargaining with him. I would do anything. Anything God wanted if it meant I could keep my baby.

I lost track of all time. I had no idea how long I had laid in the hospital bed with Raina before my parents were in the room with me. Momma put her arms around me on the bed, and we cried together. I lifted myself out of Raina's bed, allowing my sobs to travel from the bottom of my stomach to my throat. They made me sick with nausea, but they wouldn't stop. I wanted my body to hurt as much as my heart did.

Andrew stood outside her room, barely out of view, talking with his parents. They shot glances my way, and I could tell they were upset. I wanted to reach out to Betty and Rich and tell them to come in. Tell them I knew they loved her, but with Andrew there, I couldn't.

So, I told Momma to let them know. When she did, they shook their heads. They were a family, and leaving their son was not an option. That was their choice. I wasn't letting him near my baby.

I sat at her bedside for the next ten hours and watched the ventilator push air into her lungs. I sang to Raina, secretly wishing the sound of my voice could mend her brain.

Ladybug with wings so bright,
Dancing on petals in the soft moonlight.
Tiny specks of black on red,
It is now time for bed.

Ladybug fly through the night.
Gently drift on a breeze, happy and light.
Rest your wings and close your eyes.
Under the stars where magic lies.

Ladybug with spots so sweet,
I love you more with every heartbeat.
In enchanted meadows, you'll dance and play,
Until dawn brings us a brand-new day.

People came in and out of the room, including my dad, but I paid them little attention. When 9:00 p.m. approached, the doctor and nurses arrived for the second assessment. I sat by, watching closely. They tested her refluxes one at a time. They shined a light in her eyes, tried to make her gag, and squirted water in her ear. I prayed for something to happen each time they moved onto a new reflex, but she exhibited no signs of brain activity. The doctor pronounced her dead.

All the hope I had stockpiled for this moment evaporated, and I was empty. If only I had prayed harder.

Dad came into the room and sat beside me at Raina's bedside. He was silent for a long while, and for the first time, I was happy for his silence. I felt the light pressure of his hand on mine, and it caught me by surprise. I looked up at him for answers.

"I never really got to know her. Or Josie. Or you. I hate that I wasn't there. I just didn't know how to be. I'm so sorry, Helen."

Sorry sounded much different coming from my dad than it did from Andrew. They both felt poisoned by guilt, but self-preservation colored Andrew's sorry, while my Dad's sorry was selfless. We sat silently for a few more minutes when Matt poked his head into the room.

"I hate to ask, but Andrew begged me to."

I rolled my eyes, already annoyed at the sound of his name.

"He wants to see his daughter."

I wanted to say no, but I also understood that I couldn't protect her anymore. The police had yet to charge him, and Raina was his daughter. So, I gave him thirty minutes and put my dad in charge while I had something to eat for the first time that day.

The next morning, I said goodbye to my daughter. She was still on life support to preserve her body until they harvested the parts of her that would save someone else. Standing before her, I tried one more time to warm her little feet, but it was futile, and the inability to do this one small thing crashed around me.

"I'm so sorry I didn't protect you. I'm so sorry," I whispered. "This was not supposed to be your life. It's my fault. I'm so sorry." I wept over her until I couldn't think of anything else to say or do. She was gone. I had failed. I had wanted to be better than my mother, but I was worse. Somehow, in my desire to give them everything they deserved, I managed to do the opposite.

We made the journey home to Rock Springs in Dad's car. In the brief time we were at the hospital, the weather had cleared, and the roads were clean. Only piles of snow pushed to the side of the highways provided proof of the storm.

Social services called on our drive home and informed me I would have a single hour the next day, Christmas morning, to spend with Josie. An hour wasn't enough, but it kept me going. It gave me something to look forward to.

At home, I walked through the doors of my house and instantly noticed how quiet it was. Someone had tried to clean up. Most likely, my friend Bethany. She had washed and put away the dishes, picked up and vacuumed the floors, and taken the trash to the curb.

Walking around the house, my anger boiled up and out. She shouldn't have cleaned. I wanted the mess back. I wanted my house to look exactly as it did when giggles, coos, and soft cries filled these walls. I wanted to hold on to those moments forever—to always remember.

CHAPTER 31

Present Day

The staff scurry through the halls, and patients cry out into the night. A team of EMTs emerge into the hallway, carrying bags of medical supplies and wheeling a stretcher. Distress permeates the hospital, and we wait to witness potential shifts in the atmosphere.

I stand by Ashley, wanting to reach out and touch her, wanting to console her after what she told me, but I don't. I can't imagine her pain. What would it be like to find your mother dead because of suicide? The guilt and grief that must come from such a horrific experience is unthinkable. How does she continue to laugh in a world where such dark things happen?

I can't help but wonder if I did the same to my child. I push the idea away. I can't deal with it.

Ashley and I don't budge from the space behind the door. I think she wants to say goodbye to the young man. A man so determined, he found a way around the bubble wrap so he wouldn't have to live with the rock inside his chest.

After nearly an hour, the sound of wheels approaches us, louder than before. It is time to say goodbye. Although a white sheet disguises the body on the gurney, we know he is there—the young man who lost his internal battle.

The memory hits me upside the head so fast I become dizzy. A baby. A baby on a hospital bed is being carted away. In this memory, I stand and watch. I could not save her. Because of that, she is gone forever. It was my job to protect this baby, my baby, and I failed. My heart implodes, and I know I will never be the same.

I feel the air knock out of me as I plunge into a new memory. I see her again. My baby. This time she's in a casket. She is tucked in as if put to sleep in a darling bassinet. A soft pink blanket and a stuffed bear adorn her sleeping figure. Her dress is so pretty. Her name is Raina.

In the room with the casket, chatter echoes off the walls and assaults my ears. People's voices amplify a headache I suffered for days. I let my eyes travel to my daughter's face. Raina's face appears distorted. I'm terrified. The guilt swallows me whole. I cry out, and everything goes black.

Ashley turns to me. "Are you okay?"

I am crying, and my chest expands and falls rapidly. I can't seem to quiet the chatter that remains like a stain on my mind. I remember. I am not a mother. At least not anymore. I lost my baby, and it was my fault.

I shake my head violently. "No. I'm not okay."

The following day, I'm lethargic and move through the hospital sedated and dull. Visions of what I had done kept me from sleeping. I want to forget again. Turn back time. Erase my thoughts. I couldn't bear to verbalize what I recalled, so I lay in bed, shivering into the night. When Ashley asked me if I wanted to talk about it, I could only say, "Please, no." It was selfish given Ashley's heartache, but I couldn't engage even though I wanted to.

After lunch, a nurse calls my name. It is time for my session with Jacqueline. I don't want to go, but I have no choice. I am in a place without choice, without agency. The only control I have is over what I allow myself to remember.

"So, you don't want to remember?" Jacqueline asks.

I assume a position of self-assurance. Back straight, chin forward, jaw clenched.

"I think I'm better off living my life without remembering."

Jacqueline taps her pen on her leg and takes her time to respond. She is choosing her words carefully. "I understand. This isn't easy work." She chews on her bottom lip. "Why don't we do this? You can tell me what you remember, and we can work through that first. Then we can talk about the next steps."

I fill my lungs, willing myself not to comply.

"I don't want to tell you what I remember, and I don't want to talk about the next steps."

Jacqueline sets her pen and notebook on a side table and leans forward. She is wearing a beige dress with a square neckline. I wonder if she ever wears color.

"We have to choose a path forward, and it will be a lot easier for me to provide guidance on which path to take if we work on processing what we already know. Is that okay with you?"

I press my lips together and shake my head.

"I don't understand, Helen. You demanded answers the last time we spoke, and now you refuse to try."

"I'm not a mother," I say.

"You're not?" Jacqueline tilts her chin and squints her eyes.

"No. I'm not." I dig the remainder of my thumbnail into my palm, finding solace in the pain.

"But you are a mother."

My voice becomes elevated. "No, I am not!"

"Yes, you are," she says. Her tone is condescending, and I want to dig my fingers into those stupid blue eyes. I'm bursting with frustration. "My child is dead. She is dead. All right? And it's my fault. I'm tired of your games. Just leave me the fuck alone!"

"Okay, Helen." She is talking to me as if I am standing on the roof's ledge, about to jump. "I need you to start at the beginning. I can't help unless you talk to me."

I'm starting to whine. "I don't want to talk to you!"

Jacqueline glosses over my last statement. "How did she die?" Jacqueline asks.

I tell her before I remind myself that I don't want to discuss it. "I don't know, but it was my fault. I'm a terrible person. The worst." Tears spring from my eyes, and I can't control them. I can't control anything, including what I remember.

"If you don't know how she died, how do you know it was your fault?" Her blue eyes fill with compassion, and I feel bad for wanting to claw them out only a moment earlier.

"Because I remember how I felt in those moments. In those memories, I hated myself. I felt she would still be alive if I had been a better mother." With each word, my voice rises, becoming more strained and high-pitched. "It was my fault. No wonder I wanted to die. I deserve to die." I look at her. The pain in my face is reflecting back at me through her eyes. My breathing is heavy and shallow, and Jacqueline gives me a moment to collect myself again.

"I understand why you're upset, but we don't know which memories we can trust yet. You can't know what truly happened until we uncover more."

"But I don't want to uncover anymore. There has to be another way. An option where I don't have to remember."

"There isn't. Your hesitation is valid. This must be so painful. But let's say you are responsible for your daughter's death, which I know you are not. Don't you think it would be a dishonor to your daughter to forget her? To push her from your memory? Shouldn't she be remembered?"

I'm shaking. My head feels chaotic, like a storm. I think I'm having a heart attack. I grab at my chest, trying to slow my racing heart.

Jacqueline doesn't react to my physiological response and charges forward. "Honestly, I am surprised that so much has returned to you. It's telling. Subconsciously, there is something you need to know about yourself."

I shake my head in response. No, I don't. She doesn't understand. I do not want to remember.

Jacqueline continues. "Helen, the problem is that you attempted suicide. Outside these walls is a life you were living, and if we discharge you tomorrow, where will you end up? There is no reason for you to stay here if you are not willing to do the work to retrieve the memories you have lost, but where would that leave you?"

I pull my legs onto the chair and hug them tightly. "I am sure I could figure it out."

"What if you leave here, and something happens, and everything you have mentally locked away comes flooding back at once? Do you feel equipped to handle it?"

I don't want to answer because she's right.

"Helen?" Her eyes drill into me, so I look away.

"No," I mumble. "But I can't handle the flashes of memories. They're too much."

"That is to be expected, Helen. It is why you are here. So, we can help you, and you can leave here, hopefully, with your memories intact and enough tools in your toolbox to heal."

My chest feels tight, and it's hard to breathe. My fingertips are numb. I can't do this. My chest constricts further, and it's harder to breathe.

"I can't do this," I say.

At the end of our session, Jacqueline prescribes me something additional for anxiety. It will make me groggy but may help reduce the flashbacks.

"We can take it slower, but we still need to do the work, Helen."

I nod slowly.

At dinner, I pick at my food. The gravy is too salty, and the mashed potatoes are too thin.

"This seat taken?" Ashley asks, sitting before I have time to respond. "How'd it go with your shrink today?"

"Fine," I say, spearing a green bean only to throw my fork on my tray.

"You okay?" Ashley's eyes reach for mine.

"I guess. She gave me something else to help with anxiety. Another pill. It's supposed to stifle the memories too."

Ashley spoons a large bite of Salisbury steak into her mouth. "I'm guessing you don't like what you remember?"

I sit straight up and push my tray away, unable to take another bite.

"No. I'm a shitty person."

"I got news for you. We are all a little shitty sometimes," Ashley says, laughing, her steak visibly swimming inside her gaping mouth.

Deflecting, I ask, "How were things with your shrink?"

"I don't see him until tomorrow, but I'm looking forward to it." She rolls her eyes into the back of her head and mimes holding a rope, all while dropping her neck to the side and sticking her tongue out. "I thought I was suicidal before. That guy brings me to a whole new level." She wants me to laugh, but I don't. I don't know how she jokes about these things with what she has been through. "You should come with me to art therapy today," she continues. "It is probably the only thing here worth doing."

I don't want to go, but the alternative is to be alone with my thoughts, and my thoughts include my memories. So, I follow Ashley to the rec room, which is set up for our art therapy session. Ashley and I sit before little birdhouses made of balsa wood.

"Oh, we get to do something besides color today! This is exciting." Ashley squeals. She leans in and whispers, "You know, this place isn't cheap. You would think they could spring for some decent crafts more often. My dad says this is one of the best in the country, but coloring? Really?"

Best in the country? That's news to me. We paint our birdhouses in silence as I contemplate how I ended up here. I'm about done when I decide to ask Ashley a question.

"You told me about your mom last night. Is that why you cut?"

"I was cutting before she died. I hid it from her. She believed I wore long sleeves every day because I was modest. I even had her buy me one of those long-sleeved swimsuits and told her the other styles made me uncomfortable." Ashley continues to concentrate on painting while she speaks. "But one day, I was getting out of the shower, and I had forgotten to lock the door. She came in to take back her hairbrush for the millionth time and found me wrapped in my towel, and my scars were visible. She cried." Ashley's face drops a millimeter at the memory.

"Your mom doesn't sound like someone who would kill themselves. I mean, I don't really know her, but I just get that feeling."

Ashley looks up from her project only for a moment.

"You're right. She wasn't depressed all the time. Nothing like that. Actually, she was fierce. A force to be reckoned with and the strongest woman I've ever known. No one knew she struggled. She didn't tell anyone. We didn't know until it was too late."

I wonder what kind of person I was. Did people know I was depressed? Or did I just break one day?

"My daughter died," I tell Ashley.

She looks at me but doesn't react. Her gaze simply meets my eyes to let me know she is listening.

"And I think it might have been my fault, but I don't know for sure. I feel like it must have been. I can't explain it, but I have all this guilt. I feel responsible."

Ashley nods her head. She understands me. "It probably isn't your fault. For a long time, I blamed myself for my mom's suicide. I'm adopted, and I struggled with that growing up. For a long time, I believed she left me because I couldn't live up to her expectations. Maybe she would have wanted to live if I were a better daughter. If I were more grateful. To be honest, I still sometimes blame myself. I have yet to wrap my head around why she would leave me."

"It's not your fault," I say.

"Precisely." A smiling Ashley holds up her birdhouse. On the back, she painted a noose. I shake my head at her.

"It's funny, right?" she muses.

"I guess it depends on your sense of humor."

CHAPTER 32

Before Helen Lost Her Memory

I struggled with the un-comfortability of others' sadness. I felt responsible for it, like it was mine to relieve.

As the sky darkened on Christmas Eve, my house filled with new sounds. Grandpa and Aunt Joy had made the journey from California to say goodbye to the little girl they never had the chance to meet. It had been so long since I'd seen them, and it was so easy to forget people who once meant the world to you when you lived at the center of chaos.

"Hey, Rugrat," Grandpa said as he walked through my front door.

He held his arms out, and just like when I was a little girl, I found myself cradled in them. His chest shook against mine, and I hated that this old man was hurting, and I couldn't stop it. I remembered the aftermath of Nathan's death. Losing him shattered this family. Maybe the loss of Raina would bring us back together.

When we separated, I spotted Aunt Joy standing behind him. We locked eyes. She knew. She knew exactly what I was going through. Momma had said they were coming before we left the hospital, but I didn't know how much I needed to see my aunt until that moment.

It had been a long time, but over the years, Momma would deliver brief updates on their lives. She didn't talk to them often, just enough to ask Grandpa for money when she needed it. Aunt Joy was released from prison following her guilty plea for the death of her son several years back. While she was in jail, she received her degree through a correspondence program, and within three years of getting out, she graduated and became a family therapist specializing in addiction. She somehow took the worst pain imaginable and turned it into something good. I couldn't fathom how.

Others trickled into the house that evening, including Lucy, Billy Ray, Momma, and Matt. I was half-engaged as they visited. They retold stories from our days in the desert, and together, we found moments of laughter amid our shared heartbreak.

"Remember that time Aunt Joy put Momma's head through the screen door?" Lucy asked.

Grandpa shook his head and responded, "Oh boy! That was an eventful wedding."

"A wedding?" Billy Ray said. His brows raised, and the wrinkles on his forehead deepened.

Aunt Joy squinted her eyes and scrunched her nose. "Yeah, a wedding."

She and Momma recounted the story, but their version was a bit different from the one I remembered.

"Addiction is a crazy thing." Aunt Joy turned, addressing Lucy and me. "Girls, you remember I went to jail right before the wedding, right?"

We nodded.

"Well, my dumbass went to jail because I was transporting drugs for your Uncle Pete."

"Really?" Lucy said.

"The cops started snooping, and I got picked up. I was sure Pete's skanky girlfriend was the snitch, so I called her from prison and threatened to kill her." Aunt Joy smiled at the memory. "I was even more certain when I found out they were getting married. You know they only got married, so she would never have to testify against him, right?"

"Was she the snitch?" Lucy asked.

"No!" Momma exclaimed. "They caught Joy's ass on a traffic cam!"

Everyone laughed except for Billy Ray. I don't think he was used to these types of stories.

"That's why I crashed the wedding and attempted to beat the shit out of her. I'm telling you—addiction is wild shit. You'll believe things and do things you'd never do in your right mind." Aunt Joy shook her head. "I am so happy that life is behind me."

"How are Uncle Pete and Tyler?" Lucy asked.

"Tyler's good. He's working and living on his own. Your uncle? He's still a dick," Aunt Joy said, and everyone roared uncontrollably.

I didn't laugh and instead thought of my cousin, Tyler. He was another person I had let down. I'd promised that things would be different for us, and maybe they finally were for him, but it was no thanks to me. I left him and never thought about how it may have impacted him until right at this moment.

The group continued to laugh and reminisce about the past, but I couldn't sit still any longer. Without a word, I went to my room to wrap Josie's Christmas presents.

I froze in the doorway, staring at the bed Andrew and I shared. Another reminder of all the ways I had failed. About halfway through wrapping presents, there was a light knock at the door. I didn't look up, but the creak of the hinges signaled they had come in. Aunt Joy sat on the bed, picking up a Christmas bow and running her fingers along the smooth ribbon. She didn't speak but waited instead. Finally, I asked her the question that had been on my mind since the moment we locked eyes.

"How did you do it? How did you keep going?"

"You just do." She put the bow down and planted her hands in her lap. "For me, the only thing that kept me going was knowing I would go to prison. It sounds strange, I know. But I wanted them to punish me. I deserved it."

What do I deserve?

As if reading my mind, she said, "But you're much different. What happened to Raina isn't your fault. Not even a little bit."

I couldn't see the difference. "But you didn't murder Nathan. Someone else did. It wasn't your fault, either."

"It's not the same. Andrew was your husband. You should be able to leave your babies with your husband. The men who killed Nathan were dangerous, and I knew it. But I was so fucked up I allowed them into my home, where my child lived. That should never have happened."

I allowed Andrew to be alone with my children, even though I knew he struggled with anger. It was the same thing. It had only been a day, and the urge to punish myself for my stupidity was overwhelming. I wanted to claw at my skin, to mar and bruise myself. I deserved to feel pain.

"But Andrew was angry a lot," I admitted.

"And how is that your fault? You didn't do this."

I wavered between feelings of responsibility and victimhood, unable to settle entirely in either space. I needed to hear that it wasn't my fault. I wanted to believe it, but I also wanted to be punished.

Tears sprung to my eyes, and my lips trembled. "I don't know, but it is."

Rising from my bed, Aunt Joy enveloped me in a tight embrace. I could feel Aunt Joy holding the burden of my grief, if only for a moment, so I could finally breathe again.

The next morning, Christmas Day, the social worker brought Josie to the door. I wrapped her in my arms, breathing in her sweet smell. Although it had only been a few days, it felt like a lifetime since I last held her in my arms.

Still crazed by grief, I whispered frantically, "I love you. I love you. Oh, baby, I love you so much."

Unconcerned with my affection, she pulled away from me when she noticed the presents under the tree. At barely two years old, I was lucky to keep her focus for more than a minute. The presents glinted under the lights on the tree and were much more interesting than her mom or our family, who all sat nearby on the sofa and loveseat. Her face was still pink with cold from outside, and someone had combed her blonde curls neatly into two perfect little pigtails on top of her head. They were taking good care of her.

I loved every inch of her. The way her brown eyes sparkled in the light. The softness of her skin. The smell of baby shampoo in her hair. Her small and slightly raspy voice. Her presence kindled an ember of joy I didn't know I had left.

"For sissy or me?" she asked. Her question squelched the glowing ember.

"They are for you, sweet girl. Santa Clause came while you were away. Should we open them?"

My eyes stung, but I held back the tears. I wouldn't let myself cry. Not in front of Josie. Josie toddled over to the tree we had decorated only a week ago. I remembered my past life as the blue and white bulbs glowed.

My family sat while the social worker stood watching our interactions. I was so focused on Josie that I nearly forgot we weren't alone. Josie put her hand on the largest gift. I pulled it into the middle of the floor, and she ripped away the paper. It was one of those dolls that wet their diapers. She squealed in delight, and the ember reignited. I pushed the doll across the carpet to the other side of the living room and grabbed another gift for Josie, but Josie ran after the doll. She shrieked, frustrated with me. She wanted to take it out of the box and play with it. Laughter sounded from others around the room.

"We can open it after you unwrap all your presents," I said.

She was not having it and stomped her feet in protest.

"Josie, we do not throw fits …" I hesitated, remembering the social worker. Was I allowed to tell her that? "How about I get it out of the box while you open another one? Can we do that?"

She stomped her feet again, and I could feel the social worker's eyes on me. Giving up, I opened the box.

Josie and I sat on the living room floor for the full hour and played with each of her new toys. Then, too quickly, the social worker notified us our time was up.

"Can't you stay a bit longer? Just one more hour? Please?" I asked.

"I have my own family to see. It is Christmas," she said in a flat, even tone.

"But when can I see her again?" My voice sounded desperate.

"I don't know yet. You'll get a call from the department."

"But when will that be?"

"I don't know. We have other cases besides this one." My heart quickened, and my thoughts scattered.

"But I did nothing wrong. I don't understand why I have a case at all." Although I felt responsible for Raina's death, I also couldn't fathom life without Josie. I was her mom. She needed me.

"Your daughter is dead. I shouldn't need to explain why you have a case."

Her words stung like alcohol on an exposed wound. I wanted to beg, to tell this woman that I learned my lesson. I wanted to promise that I would never let anyone hurt Josie, but I kept my mouth shut.

The social worker reached for Josie's hand, letting her know it was time to go, but Josie pulled away and darted over to me. I enveloped her, but knowing I was not winning the social worker's favor this way, I led Josie back to her.

Squatting down to meet her eyes, I said, "Hey Josie, I need you to be a good girl and go with …" I looked over at the woman, realizing I had yet to catch her name.

The woman, understanding, said, "Jennifer."

"You need to go with Jennifer, sweetheart, and I promise I'm going to see you as soon as I can. All right?"

However, before Josie could agree, the social worker reached for her hand again, causing Josie to react. My little girl just didn't understand what was happening and threw herself on the floor. I looked around at Momma, Matt, Aunt Joy, Grandpa, and Lucy, who all sat like deer in headlights. They didn't know how to help me.

Josie screamed and fought the social worker until Jennifer finally lifted her and carried her away. Josie's limbs flew in all directions, and her face reddened as she howled. Once again, I was powerless. I could not help my child.

CHAPTER 33

Jennifer was calculating and untrusting. At least, that is what I gathered from how she regarded me on Christmas morning and knowing this set my anxiety off. I didn't do well in situations where I had to prove myself. I tended to overcompensate, over-explain, and overdo, which in turn, made others more critical. So, the first time I met with Jennifer and an older man with salt and pepper hair at the department of social services, I was brimming with nervous energy. They sat behind a desk, and I occupied a chair in front of them. The office was silent.

Were they expecting me to speak? Was I supposed to plead my case? I had spent hours creating conversations in my head that had yet to happen. In my hours alone, I verbalized these thoughts, practicing them so I could speak without my emotions taking hold, without crying.

I decided to start.

"Listen, I was at work on the day in question. I did not abuse my daughter. Andrew did, and I have already taken the necessary steps to ensure he'll never see Josie again."

They sat like statues as I spoke.

"I packed all his things, and the police escorted him to my house to pick them up. I plan to file for divorce as soon as I figure out how. I don't see any reason why my child should be held from me by the department."

All the words tumbled out rapidly. I was sure I hadn't blinked or breathed since I started speaking.

The man looked at Jennifer and raised his eyebrows. What was he thinking? Was he considering it? I became prematurely excited and fidgeted at the anticipation. Their eyes took note of my restless hands before responding.

"I'm sorry, Mrs. Miller," said the man.

"Please don't call me by that name. My name is Helen Birch."

I wanted to distance myself from Andrew as much as possible.

"Okay, Ms. Birch. The department's goal is always reunification, but in this case, there is an ongoing investigation, and there are still things we don't know."

I nodded my head. I didn't want to appear insolent, but they had to know I didn't do this. "Have you talked to the police? They said I'm not a suspect."

"Not a suspect at this time. And even if you are cleared of potential charges, it is common for women in your situation to reunite with their husbands."

"Ex-husband," I corrected.

"You are not divorced yet," Jennifer said.

"But you must know I plan on getting divorced, right?" I felt myself losing control, so I forced myself to stop speaking. The walls of the small office were closing in.

"We can't answer that question, but maybe you can answer some of ours. By the end of this meeting, we would like to have a parenting plan in place."

Jennifer sat with a pen and a notepad as she asked the first question.

"Is Andrew Josie's father?"

"No." Oh shit. I should have known they would ask.

"Who is?" she continued.

"I don't know," I lied. I wasn't about to have Jude complicate an impossible situation. No one knew who Josie's dad was. I had long kept that a secret. I would rather pretend I didn't know than admit he left me when he found out I was pregnant.

"You don't know?" She didn't look at me, but the man stared hard.

"No."

She moved on, and they zeroed in on Andrew's temper. The more questions they asked, the more apparent it became that they believed I should have known. Question after question cut me down, and I couldn't help but feel defensive.

The man reached for a manilla file folder, which had been on the desk since I arrived. Opening it, he grabbed several prints and stared at them.

"Did you spank your daughter?" His voice was calm and cool.

I was baffled by his question. Raina was only five months old. You don't spank a baby. "No. Who spanks a baby?"

He realized I misunderstood and clarified. "Josie. Did you ever spank Josie?"

"Sometimes. I mean, not a lot. Just a little tap on the butt if she was doing something she wasn't supposed to do," I said. Maybe that was the wrong answer. So, I tried to clarify. "Like if she was throwing a fit, touching something that could hurt her, or doing something she knew she wasn't supposed to do, I'd give her a small pat on the butt. But that's all."

"Do little pats cause this?" The man laid three photos of Josie before me. She was in a doctor's office. Her bare butt was exposed. Bruises covered the tops of her little thighs and cheeks.

I brought my hands to my mouth and gasped, bile rushing up my throat. Did she have these bruises yesterday? How did I not know?

"Who did that to my daughter?" A storm brewed inside my chest.

No one answered.

"Where did she get those bruises?" I yelled. I had lost control. "Answer me!"

There was another moment of silence before the woman spoke. "Her foster mother brought her in the day she was placed."

"So, it could have happened at the foster home?" I struggled to comprehend the situation.

"We don't believe so. Wouldn't you agree it is much more likely she suffered the abuse before being placed?"

"My sister. Lucy can tell you if they were there. She took care of Josie that day. The day that …" I couldn't finish my sentence.

"We will interview your sister, but for now, tell us about the last time you spanked Josie."

I think back to Josie smashing eggs into the carpet, one-half of an eggshell sitting on her head. She was laughing, so pleased with herself, but I felt stressed. I yelled at her and popped her on the butt. Oh gosh, I really was a terrible mother.

"It was a few weeks ago."

I told them the story, but they didn't care.

"Did you know your husband was abusing your child?"

"I told you. I went to work. I wasn't there."

"How did you not notice bruises on your daughter's behind?"

"I didn't notice them because they weren't there when I saw her butt the night before. Then everything happened with Raina, and I didn't go home and examine Josie before I left. My other daughter was in critical condition." My voice was loud and strained, and I couldn't bring it to a normal level.

"We have to ask these questions, Ms. Birch. It's our job. One last thing. We received a report from a Karen Casteel. Do you know her?" said Jennifer.

My brows stitched together.

"You may know her as Mrs. Casteel?"

Recognition must have flooded my face because Jennifer continued.

"She reports you were in her child development class and that you failed the class because you abused the baby you took home for an assignment. Can you tell us a little more about that?"

Oh my god. How? How is this my life?

"Yes. That's true, but it wasn't my fault."

"Of course, it wasn't."

Jennifer's tone, colored by indignation, told me she didn't believe a word I said.

She continued, "It doesn't impact our investigation, but it was reported, so I thought I'd mention it."

Maybe it doesn't impact their investigation, but it definitely raised concerns. Not only for them but for me too. The robot baby. My baby cousin, Nathan. Had the universe warned me, and I was just too stupid to pay attention? Our family was cursed to endure heartache and had no other option.

Done with their questions, they delivered a pre-drafted parenting plan.

"You will receive only one hour of supervised visitation per week. You are to complete a psychological evaluation to ensure you are capable of caring for Josie. You will go to grief therapy with one of our grief therapists and will sign a waiver, allowing us to speak to your therapist about your progress. You will also attend parenting classes. You will make and attend an appointment for family planning. You will maintain a clean living environment fit for a child. You will maintain employment. And you will attend child therapy sessions with your daughter. Understood?"

"Yes," I said. If that was what it took, then that was what I would do.

Billy Ray was waiting outside when I emerged from the department building. He turned to me in the car and said, "You all right, kid?"

"I'm fine," I said, leaning back in the seat.

"You don't gotta lie to me. Really, you all right?"

I sighed deeply.

"No, but I'm going to have to be."

I kept my eyes locked on his windshield, afraid I would lose all control if I looked at him. All those signs had been right in front of me, and I missed every single one.

"Eventually, you'll be all right. But for now, it's okay not to be."

It wasn't about me. It was about Josie. My mind spun. I mentally flipped through each of the requirements set forth by social services. How would I do it all? I only had so many hours in a day and didn't have a car. My chest filled with stress, but I pushed it back down. I would do whatever it took to get her back. I needed a car. I turned to Billy Ray.

"I do need something," I said.

"Okay?"

"A car. I need your help to find and buy a car."

CHAPTER 34

I danced on the fine line between sanity and madness. The pain, hate, and anger that boiled inside me were too much, and it took incredible restraint not to scream to deafen the voices in my head. I wanted to feel it all but worried it might break me.

I should have known.

After I came home from social services, the first thing I did was call Lucy. From the moment I saw the photos of Josie, I felt an ever-growing agitation that Lucy had not mentioned the bruises to me. Unless the bruises weren't there? But if they were, and she didn't bother to say anything … I had to steel my nerves before calling her.

I dialed their house, and Momma answered.

"Hey, Momma, can I talk to Lucy?"

She heard the slight tremor in my voice and asked, "Is everything okay?"

"No, it's not fucking okay. Nothing is okay."

"I know you're upset, but please, Helen, think of someone other than yourself for one minute. I lost my granddaughter, too. You don't need to act so ugly. I haven't done anything but support you."

I had to hold my breath to prevent myself from screaming into the receiver. The last thing I needed was to start a fight, so I lowered my voice and tried again. "I'm sorry. I'm not okay. Can I please talk to Lucy?"

"Fine." I heard her put the phone down and waited until Lucy's voice came through the speaker.

"Hey. What's up?" she said.

Boiling over at Momma allowed my anxiety to reduce to a simmer. "The day … I'm sorry … Umm … the day we took Raina to the hospital, and you watched Josie …" I didn't want to ask her this, but I had to.

"Yea?"

I pushed on. "The day we took Raina to the hospital, did you see bruises on Josie's butt? Like when you changed her diaper. Was there anything there?"

The pause before she answered was unbearable. "They weren't bruises. They were welts. Big red ones," she said.

"Why didn't you say anything?"

"I don't know. Everything was crazy. You were a mess. The police were here. I didn't know what to do."

"But since then?" I was confused. So much had happened, and I felt like I was losing control.

She sighed into the phone. "Helen, you're still a mess."

She was right. I was a mess, but I didn't know how to fix it.

Despite my outburst on the phone, Momma came with me the next day to the funeral home to make arrangements. I stared across the table at a man in his early thirties who was already going bald. He smiled a sad smile, the kind of smile a person used to make you feel comfortable and supported. Yet, I felt none of those things.

Momma was high. I could tell. Her knee bounced as we talked to the funeral director. I channeled my hatred toward her, blaming the drug use. I needed to hate someone other than myself. The hatred felt like a monster living within me. I'd met this monster before, but only in fleeting moments. Now, it stayed with me, taking permanent residence in my chest.

The funeral director looked toward me. I was supposed to decide. I was supposed to have the answers. I was supposed to know what casket to bury my baby girl in, which poems to read, and which songs to sing, but I didn't know anything. All I knew was she was gone. I didn't want this to be my truth. Fuck Momma, fuck this funeral director, and fuck Andrew for doing this to us. Fuck! I was stuck in a spiral of hate and grief, so much so that the time between making the funeral arrangements and the funeral was a blur.

On the day of Raina's funeral, I lay in bed and considered never leaving. But what would people say if I missed my daughter's funeral? I would be a pariah. Pariahs don't get their children back. I needed to fight for Josie. I was all she had and was determined not to fail again.

I swung my legs off the bed, and my feet hit the ground. I had to will myself to stand and put on the dress Aunt Joy bought me for the funeral. After slipping the ill-fitting, frumpy black dress on, I padded down the hall to my bathroom. The bathroom mirror revealed puffy eyes and dry, cracked lips. I had never looked better, I thought. A knock at the front door let me know my time was up.

"Hello?" Grandpa yelled into the house.

"In here."

He came to the bathroom, where I stood, looking like a disheveled mess. "How much longer, Rugrat?"

"I'm ready," I said.

His eyes narrowed as he assessed me. "I'll give you five more minutes. Use it to do something with that hair."

I struggled to put in the effort as the steady headache I had battled for days clouded my attempts. I gave up and used a clip to pull the top of my hair back. I washed my face and applied a thin coat of mascara to the top lashes. I knew better than to put any on the bottom.

Outside, two cars waited to head to the church for the service. I had invited Andrew's parents but never received word of whether they planned to come. They hadn't spoken to me since the hospital.

At the church, we gathered in a small room for close family. Inside the room was Raina's casket. It was white and pink. I knew I chose it, but I didn't remember doing so.

"Would you like to see her?" the funeral director asked.

"See her?"

"Yes. Do you want to see her?" he repeated.

My first thought was no, but then I worried that I might regret not seeing her one last time.

"Yes, please," I said.

The funeral director approached her casket and opened the top. I slowly stepped forward and peered inside. A stuffed bear Billy Ray gave her the day she was born and the blanket I crocheted for her while I was pregnant were visible within. She was wearing her Christmas dress. It was light gray and pink with embroidered white snowflakes. She also wore a bonnet that once belonged to me—an artifact my dad had held onto for all these years. I had yet to let my eyes move to her face, but I pushed myself to do so.

I screamed and backed away. Her face looked swollen and distorted. It didn't look like her. People rushed to my side, and I cried into the chest of someone who smelled like sweat and musky perfume.

By the time the service was ready to begin, my screams had reduced to sobs. As grievers came in to give their condolences, my sobs turned to vacant, watery stares. Physically, I was there, but emotionally, I wasn't. Paying attention to the service was difficult, and as much as I tried to concentrate, my mind wandered. By the end, I couldn't recall anything that had happened. The eulogy, the songs, the poems—they all blended together.

In the days following the funeral, everyone went back to their respective lives. They moved through their days as before and somehow expected me to do the same. But I didn't know what to do with myself once everyone left. The loneliness was like nothing I had experienced before. It felt like a massive rock in the center of my chest.

Walking through my house, I searched for a purpose, finding nothing but sad memories. My living room was the room where Andrew pushed me and left a scar on my arm as a constant reminder. It was the same room where I'd fall asleep on the sofa, cuddling Raina in my arms, her sweet little face tilted toward mine. The same room where Josie and I spun in circles, dancing and laughing. I couldn't do it anymore.

I didn't know what I was doing. I couldn't think straight. I threw anything I could get my hands on, ripping the mirror off the wall and smashing it to the ground. I ran to the chair in the corner and tossed it across the room. I knocked down every item not fixed to the wall and tossed every pile of paper I saw into the air. They fluttered down, and I caught as many as I could, ripping them to pieces.

When I couldn't find anything else to destroy, I ran my fingers along my scalp and pulled at my hair. Clumps came out in my hands. The pain felt good. Sitting in the center of the floor, among the ruins of my living room, I screamed until my voice was only a strangled whisper.

CHAPTER 35

I sat across from the child therapist and Josie's foster mom, Patricia, while Josie played with an assortment of wooden blocks on a colorful carpet between us.

Patricia complained about my negligence.

"She hasn't given me anything for this baby. No clothes, no diapers, nothing. She came in only pajamas. Didn't even have shoes on."

"I'm sorry," I said.

I never thought for a moment about those things. I never considered asking my sister or Bethany if they packed a bag for her.

Patricia ignored my apology. "This child has experienced significant trauma. She reenacts it, you know?"

My eyes darted from Josie to Patricia's face.

Before I could ask how, the therapist did.

"When you say reenact, can you describe what that looks like?"

"Well, I don't want to be crass, and the child is right here, but it's apparent she heard these words before, so I guess hearing them once more won't hurt." Patricia chewed on her bottom lip, deciding how to deliver her message. "When Josie came back on Christmas, she brought a doll with her. At first, she called the doll sissy, which I thought was so sweet but also sad." Patricia glanced at the therapist, measuring his level of sympathy before continuing. "That evening, while we were watching a movie in our family room, Josie slammed that baby doll on the ground. As she did, she yelled *shut the fuck up, shut the fuck up,* over and over again. It was terrifying. We had to get the rest of the children out of the room to protect them." Patricia looked at me with an insurmountable amount of disgust.

"It is not uncommon for children who experience abuse to illustrate the abuse in the form of play," said the therapist.

I stared at Josie, sitting on the floor, playing like a normal toddler. She looked so calm and sweet. I couldn't imagine her doing what the foster mom described, but she must have. I felt devastated she experienced this violence at such a young age.

After the therapy session, Patricia stopped me outside. "You know. You can come to my house and see Josie outside the scheduled visitation if you want. I can't imagine only seeing my child one hour a week."

"Really?" I hesitated. This woman hated me, but here she was, offering me kindness.

"Are you busy on Thursday morning?"

"No. I'm not," I lied. I had to work but couldn't pass on a chance to see my daughter.

"Great. I'll give you my cell phone number. Text me, and I will send you my address and the best time to come over Thursday morning."

On Thursday, I arrived at her home. It was big and fancy compared to my little house. I had to take two trips from the car to carry all the stuff I had brought for Josie. I pushed the button for her doorbell, and it let off a sweet melody inside their home.

Patricia came to the door and was surprised to see three cases of Pampers—I bought the name brand this time—and two cardboard boxes full of clothes, shoes, and other necessities. When I walked in, I was struck by how beautiful her house was inside, too. Everything matched. Deep maroons, soft beiges, and rich browns complimented her jungle theme, including artsy cheetah and zebra-printed statement pieces. The house was so clean I couldn't believe any kids lived there. Where did they play?

Patricia walked me over to a small breakfast nook, something I had only seen in movies. She made two cups of coffee and handed me a coaster with my cup. These people had money.

"Where are the kids?" I asked, looking around.

"Oh, the older ones are all at school. The toddlers, Josie and my son Isaac are watching Blue's Clues in the playroom, and the baby is asleep."

"How many kids live here?"

"Eight." Patricia laughed at the surprise on my face.

"Oh wow, how many of them are yours?"

She shifted in her seat. "I don't have any biological children, but I still consider myself a mom. Even to Josie," she said, smiling sweetly.

I couldn't tell if that was supposed to be comforting or a warning.

"Are they all in foster care?"

"Oh no. I have successfully adopted five of them."

I couldn't read her. Something felt ominous, yet she was being so kind to me. She risked her standing with the department just so I could see my child.

"Can I see Josie?" I asked.

"In time." She sipped on her coffee, leaving her bright pink lipstick on the mug's rim. I didn't want to push my luck, so I followed her lead and sipped my coffee.

"You know, despite what you might think. Foster parents rarely know much about the children placed with us. I've, of course, heard rumors, but I really wanted to hear it from you."

One thing I had learned in the brief time since Raina died was that people were always curious about this sort of thing.

"I think having a little bit more context will help me better care for Josie," she continued.

I wasn't in the mood, but I would play nearly any game if it meant seeing Josie. So, I told her the story.

Patricia nodded eagerly, making a big show of it. She'd make a gasp here or a small moan there as I recounted what happened and tried not to remember how it all felt. I wanted to remain distant from it.

"Wow. That is so incredibly heartbreaking," she said.

"Yea," I agreed, but I didn't elaborate. I gave her what she asked for.

"So, what is your plan?" she asked.

"My plan?"

"Do you plan to divorce your husband? I'm sure you wonder if he really could have done it. I mean, they haven't made an arrest yet, have they?"

It was the first time someone besides Andrew's parents had said anything indicating he might be innocent.

"No. They're still working to gather evidence. They need the autopsy report and still have several interviews to complete. They said it might take some time."

"Are you working with them?"

Thus far, the police were only helpful. I called probably more often than I should, and they never turned me away. They answered my questions and assured me they were working as fast as possible. I appreciated them.

"They have been really helpful. Much more than my caseworker." I shouldn't have said that. I was slipping.

"What do you mean?" Patricia leaned in.

"I'm just trying to get my daughter back. I want her at home with me."

"I understand that. You know she is such a joy to have. She's really a good girl. It shows that you have done a great job raising her."

After nearly an hour of questions, she went to fetch Josie.

Patricia walked back into the kitchen with Josie on her hip, and upon seeing me, Josie wiggled her body, trying to escape Patricia's hold. Patricia fought against Josie for a moment too long before letting her down. Josie ran to me, and my heart filled with warmth as she leaped into my arms.

But less than two minutes later, Patricia said, "Well, we have some errands to run, so unfortunately, we will have to say goodbye to Mommy. Josie, can you say goodbye?"

Already? The whole reason I came over was to see Josie, but I didn't complain. If I did, I might not get another chance. I brushed my hand over Josie's hair, smoothing it lightly, and kissed the soft skin on her cheek. "It's okay, baby. Momma has to go, but I'll see you soon. Okay?"

Josie cried, but Patricia didn't prolong the visit. She picked Josie up with one arm and, with the other, pointed to the front door. "I am sure you can let yourself out."

Josie's fit continued, and Patricia looked at her sympathetically and said, "Maybe this wasn't such a good idea."

I was hurt, but I didn't let it show. I held it together until I was home, and only then did I let the cracks show.

I couldn't feel sorry for myself anymore. If I wanted Josie back, I would have to be perfect. I could no longer waver between anger, distress, and hopelessness. My self-hatred may have served me, but it was not serving Josie.

So, over the next month, I threw myself into my work. I got a second job so I could provide for my daughter better. I went to grief therapy, parenting classes, and a psychological evaluation. Eventually, I got more time with Josie. But more time meant more requirements.

You will set up and report a list of age-appropriate activities to be completed during unsupervised visitation.

You will set up and report age-appropriate rules, rewards, and punishments for the child and use them consistently.

After each visit, you will report how the time was spent. The report should be broken into fifteen-minute increments.

You will not have any person not approved by the department in the presence of Josie.

You will not have individuals at your home after 9:00 p.m.

You will allow scheduled and unscheduled home visits by the department.

Some requirements stung. Not because I didn't want to meet them, but because I always had. But I never argued. I never cried. I never got upset. I just did it.

Patricia's intentions soon came into focus. Rock Springs was a small town. People talked, and I soon learned Patricia pleaded her case for why Josie should remain in her care permanently. A teacher at the child development center, which Josie recently started attending again, stopped me in the grocery store one day.

"How you holding up?" the teacher said.

Placing a case of ramen in my cart, I said, "The best I can. The only thing that seems to keep me going is Josie."

The teacher looked around conspiratorially. "Listen, I shouldn't say anything, but I have to. Did you know Patricia is trying to adopt Josie?"

My eyes widened.

"She comes into the center and talks about you a lot. Says that she feels sorry for Josie and that the system is broken. She asked us to be interviewed again by the department and told us it would be helpful if we could exaggerate. She said it would help protect Josie."

The visit to Patricia's house came into focus, and I had no reason to believe Josie's teacher was lying. I didn't feel like I could trust our social worker, Jennifer, so I kept what I had learned to myself. My only recourse was to do everything I was told and to do it perfectly. I had to get Josie back. I just had to.

CHAPTER 36

A crying baby pulled me into consciousness. Raina's shrieks grew louder as I lay in bed. I groaned, unwilling to open my eyes. *Dammit.* I was so tired. I imagined Andrew on the couch playing video games while Raina cried. Furious at the imagined version of Andrew, I rolled off the bed to remedy the situation. In the hallway, I walked toward the living room. Her crying was ear-splitting, but the hallway lengthened as I walked. The end grew further with each step. My walk turned to a jog and then a sprint. When I finally reached the end, I was out of breath, and the crying had stopped. Andrew stood before me, his eyes full of pain, holding Raina in his arms. I wasn't fast enough. I didn't save her.

I emerged from the nightmare, tears spilling down my face. Sweat soaked my nightshirt, and I gulped a large lungful of air. Dread permeated my being as I jumped out of bed and ran to the living room to find it dark and empty. I stood listening to the quiet.

It was only a dream. It was only a dream. I repeated this to myself, but it didn't ease my trembling legs and hands.

The nightmares came so often that I was afraid to sleep. With permission from social services, Lucy stayed with me, and the nights she was at my house, the nightmares didn't come. I selfishly asked her to stay as often as she could.

"You know, we can make this permanent," Lucy said one morning as I drove her to school.

"What?"

"I can live with you. That way, when you get Josie back, you have some help." She paused for a moment. "It would help me, too."

I didn't know why I hadn't thought of that sooner. I had been so caught up in my grief and trying to get Josie back.

"I'll talk to Momma tonight," I said.

"No need," Lucy said.

"Why?" I asked, taking my eyes off the road just long enough to study her face.

Her voice was firm. "I already talked to her, and as long as you are okay with it, I'm free to go."

It was the best news I had received in a long time.

"Okay, but you'll need a room and a bed."

"Don't you have three bedrooms?" Lucy asked.

I did, but they were all spoken for. There was my room, Josie's room, and then there was Raina's nursery. My chest tightened, and Lucy, knowing my worry, put her hand on my shoulder.

"I can stay in your room for now," Lucy said.

That evening, I took Lucy to pack. I parked the car and followed Lucy to the door. Momma sat on the front porch smoking. A blanket hid all but her face and a hand. Smoke curled around her, and she shivered with cold.

"Hey," I said.

"Hey." She took a long drag and looked out to the street. The neighborhood was quiet. The only movement was a light rustling of branches in the breeze.

"I guess you need her more than I do," Momma said. Lines around her lips appeared as she took another drag of her cigarette.

"We need each other, Momma. You know that, right?"

"Oh, I know. But, you don't need or want me, and I can't say I blame you."

The truth made my heart ache for Momma. I still loved her.

"I love you, Momma."

"I know you do." She stood and solemnly went inside, leaving me alone on the porch. I wasn't going to chase after her or apologize for things I had not done. Not anymore. She'd have to learn to lick her wounds. I needed to take care of myself because that was the only way I could care for Josie.

Lucy and I quickly fell into a routine. Wednesdays and Saturdays were Josie's days. The anticipation of seeing her for a few hours on those evenings kept me going. I would track our time in fifteen-minute increments on a piece of notebook paper, documenting every detail. Each time I turned in my logs, I prayed for news about Josie's case, but there was never any. I was getting impatient. I needed to try and expedite the process.

"You don't have an appointment," Jennifer said to me when I walked into her office on a Monday morning in March.

"I'm sorry. I didn't know I needed one," I said, crossing my arms — a protective stance.

"And this couldn't wait until tonight's visitation?" Jennifer's mouth twisted with displeasure.

"No." I shook my head, reconsidering my decision to come here. I was nervous, but I couldn't wait any longer. It had been three months. Three months and the only progress I had made was unsupervised visitation two nights a week.

Jennifer pushed away from her desk and looked at me expectedly. She held out her hands, gesturing for me to sit. "Since you are already here."

This woman hated me. I knew she did, but I so desperately wanted her to like me. This woman had immense power over me, and as much as I tried not to be, I was afraid of her and what she could do and withhold.

"Well. I ... I've completed my parenting plan and wanted to know how much longer it will be. When will I get my daughter back? I mean, full-time."

Her eyes drilled into me, and I wanted to make myself small and invisible, but I knew I had to be big and brave. Josie needed me to be brave.

"Do you really believe that's in Josie's best interest?" she asked. It felt like a trick question, but I charged ahead.

"Yes, I do. She should be with me. I am her mother."

"It's interesting you say that because the foster family is interested in adoption, should you become a suspect in your daughter's case."

My airway constricted, reducing the oxygen to my brain and suppressing my ability to process information.

"What?" I whispered. Even though I already knew this, it was devastating to hear. I knew Patricia wanted to adopt Josie, but how could she believe I was a suspect? How many times had Detective Garcia, the officer assigned to our case, vouched for me? He repeatedly told them that I was not a suspect although they hadn't formally charged Andrew.

"Look, I know how that may sound, but we can't be certain Josie is safe with you."

What did these people want from me? They saw me as the villain no matter how hard I tried.

I took a deep breath, trying to steady myself. I couldn't overreact.

With measured words and an even tone, I said, "You know I didn't do anything to hurt my children."

"That's what you tell us, and I am sure your husband says the same thing."

"Ex-husband," I clarified.

She disregarded my statement.

"Let's say you're not guilty. We at the department feel like you haven't grieved. Regardless of who's at fault, losing a child is heartbreaking, and you don't seem affected by it. That concerns us."

I'm damned, regardless. I had tried to present myself as calm and rational, but instead, I cut myself off at the nose. They wanted to see a grieving mother, and I was. However, with all the requirements, the counseling, and the psychological evaluation, I had believed they wanted something else entirely.

I didn't argue with Jennifer. I couldn't. I had to appear calm. I knew my monster would emerge once I started, and I would never see my daughter again.

Several weeks later, the ringer on my cell brought me to consciousness. It was 2:00 a.m. I reached to see who it was. Betty, Andrew's mom. Something must have happened. Did they finally arrest him? Curiosity took over, and I accepted the call. I froze when I heard his voice on the other end.

"Helen? Helen? I know you're there. Please, Helen. Please talk to me. Helen, I miss you. Helen?" he said. The monster inside me emerged and dove out of my mouth.

"You piece of shit! You have some nerve."

Lucy woke and looked at me wildly. She mouthed his name, and I nodded. I should have hung up, but something kept me on the phone. It was the pull toward the unresolved.

"Helen, please calm down. I just want to talk. Will you just talk to me? Please. I can explain."

And there it was, the promise of an explanation. Raina's death, Josie's injuries. None of it made sense, and on nights I couldn't sleep, I lay awake asking myself how something like this happened.

"Look, my parents hired a lawyer, and I'm not supposed to talk to you, but I need to, Helen. I need you to know what happened." My monster retreated into the crevasses in which it lived. Her potency was weakened by curiosity.

"What do you mean?" I asked, wondering if there was something we missed or a plausible reason we had not considered.

"Tomorrow night at 10:00 p.m. Meet me at the end of the dirt road leading to my parent's house. I'll explain everything."

The phone went silent, and I grappled with calling him back but thought it better not to. The next day, I went straight to the police station.

"He wants to meet," I told Detective Garcia.

"Do you *want* to meet with him?"

"No. I just … He said he could explain what happened. I need to know."

I had thought of every possible explanation. Maybe there was something I missed while drowning in grief. What if he wasn't guilty? What if I was wrong? It wasn't likely, given Josie's bruises, but I had to know.

"We could send you in with a wire." Detective Garcia turned over a sheet of paper and wrote on the back. "Say you meet him here." He drew a small circle in the center of the page. "You can park at the edge of the dirt road just off the highway, and we can put a patrol car here and here, so no one would know." He drew the road, the highway, and two circles representing the patrol cars. "With a wire, we'll be able to listen and record your conversation. That way, if anything happens, we'll be close by."

"But why would you do that?" I asked.

"We are still wrapping up the investigation, but it would move a lot faster if we had a confession. I don't know what he will tell you, but if he confesses, we want it on tape."

"How do I get him to confess?"

"It sounds like he already wants to tell you what happened, but you might have to act a little to coax it out of him. We'll have to see how it goes."

A few hours later, a female officer taped a black box the size of a deck of cards and a wire to my torso. After it was fitted and tested under my oversized sweater, Detective Garcia prepped me to meet Andrew.

"We will be nearby listening the entire time. If you feel you are in danger for any reason, I want you to say *I'm sleepy*."

"I'm sleepy?" I repeated.

"Say that phrase, and we'll be there immediately. You have nothing to worry about."

I wasn't worried Andrew would hurt me. He was desperate for a lifeline, and I was means to his end.

I dimmed my headlights as I approached the edge of the dirt road. My car rolled to a stop, and I switched off the ignition. A loud thumping came from my chest. Surely Andrew would be able to hear my heart pounding. I tried to calm myself but jumped at the rap of his knuckles on the passenger window. I pressed the unlock button, and he got in.

"Can we drive?" he asked.

"No," I said, shaking my head. "I don't want to."

"Okay," he grabbed my hand and brought it to his mouth without permission. His soft lips caressed my knuckles, and I had to resist pulling my hand away. The sweetness he showed me reminded me of how he acted all those times after he lost his temper.

"I've missed you so much," Andrew said, and sadness echoed throughout the car.

"I've missed you too," I lied. Saying those words made my stomach twist.

"Can I kiss you?" he asked.

"I'd rather you didn't." I teared up, completely overwhelmed by the situation.

"That's okay. We can just talk." He sat back. In his hand was a stack of printed pages. "How's Josie?"

I didn't want to answer. I didn't want him to say her name, but I had no choice. "She's okay. She's in foster care. I don't know if you knew that."

"I did." He shook his head as if trying to rid himself of all thoughts. "I'm so sorry, Helen. I know this has been hell."

Hell was exactly what this was.

We sat in silence for a moment. Just on the other side of the road was an antelope grazing in the brush. I told myself that when the antelope left, I would push myself to ask for the answers he had promised. But I didn't need to.

"I brought you this," he said, handing me the papers.

"What is it?" I took them in my hand. It was several articles printed from the Internet. The pages were littered with medical terms and sparsely highlighted yellow.

"I've been doing research," he continued. "There's all this information about how vaccinations can cause brain bleeds. If you read, you'll see. I think Raina got the vaccines they talk about in this paper. Actually, I know she did."

My stomach sank. This was his explanation? I really thought he would come in here with something more believable.

"A vaccination? All children go for vaccinations. If they were dangerous, doctors wouldn't give them to children." Disbelief colored my tone.

"I'm serious, Helen. There are tons more where this came from. I emailed this doctor in Virginia, and he said he will help me."

"Help you? Help you with what?"

"With the case."

He was already preparing his defense. I couldn't decide if that made him guilty or if it was simply a product of how others treated him in the wake of Raina's death.

"Oh," I said, unable to form more complete thoughts.

"I needed you to see this. I need you on my side, Helen. You're my whole world, and I'm scared. I'm scared I'm going to prison."

Of course, he felt scared. Vaccinations didn't cause this. I needed more. I needed him to confess. Leaning over to him, I brushed my lips against his, and he opened, hungry for affection. I felt I might be sick when the wetness of his tongue touched mine. I pulled back.

"I know. It must be so hard," I said, trying to sound compassionate. I needed him to believe I was on his side. "But I can't be there for you as long as you're a suspect. They have Josie. I can't risk it."

"I get that." He looked away as though contemplating some other possible future.

"Andrew," I took his hand and peered into his face, thinking of how much I had once loved him. It was the only way. "You don't have to lie to me. You know, I would understand. I always understand."

Andrew smiled at me and brushed my cheek with his free hand. "You're the only one who has ever understood me. You accepted me for who I am," he said. His statement validated all the ways in which I enabled him and his behavior, and even though he didn't mean it that way, it hurt.

"I do, Andrew. I understand you and accept you." I drew in a breath and delivered a message I was sure would haunt me forever. "Remember the time we watched the movie based on the book *Of Mice and Men*?" I asked him.

"Yeah. Why?"

"Remember Lennie. He was so sweet and gentle, just like you. Of course, you are much smarter than Lennie, but you remind me of him. Sometimes, I think of myself as the George to your Lennie because I love you and am so devoted to you."

Andrew looked at his lap as I talked.

"Remember how Lennie didn't know his strength and accidentally killed Curley's wife? He didn't mean to. He really didn't. My heart hurt so badly for Lennie when that happened."

"Yeah," mumbled Andrew.

I continued, "Our daughter was so little and so fragile. I know you didn't mean to do it. I know you loved her, and my heart hurts for you as it did for Lennie."

"It wasn't my fault," he said, caressing my hand.

"I know. But I can't help you if I don't know what happened."

He only shook his head and continued to slide his fingers over the back of my hand. I wanted to jerk it away. I wanted to hurt him and force him to tell me what happened, but I remained in character. I forced eye contact with Andrew and waited. His lips turned down, and he shook his head again. He wasn't going to budge.

When it was over, I was certain of what Andrew had done. I had watched him lose control and then, afraid of the consequences, become loving and gentle once again. The most predictable part of our marriage was how he showered me with love in the aftermath of the violence.

He was guilty.

CHAPTER 37

Present Day

"Ms. Ashley, did you get consent from Ms. Helen before you started drawing that?" I roll over in bed.

My favorite nurse, the one who giggles at the end of her sentences, is changing Ashley's bandage. It is after lunch, and although they frown upon us skipping group therapy and hiding in our room, the new medication made me drowsy. Ashley was adamant that I needed her to escort me to our room, and she must have stayed.

"What are you drawing?" I ask.

The nurse's eyes dart from me back to Ashley. Something played at her lips, telling me it was amusing.

Ashley lifts her notebook, which appears to be a drawing of a woman sleeping, but the woman is not on a bed. Instead, she rests on a row of big block letters stacked on each other. The letters spell the phrase: "Forgetting is Surviving."

"Is that me?"

"You got me. My therapist suggested I draw instead of cut, so I am drawing my roommate because she is the most interesting thing in this hellscape."

She reminds me of Lucy, who spent most of her days inside our home, lost in the graphite of her pencil and the smooth texture of paper.

"It's not so bad," the nurse said, chuckling.

"You're just saying that because you work here. You get to leave. We're stuck." Ashley turns her attention back to the drawing as the nurse attempts to re-wrap her arm.

"I'm glad you moved on from nooses," I say.

The nurse looks up at this and shakes her head. "Oh boy. I don't know what I'm going to do with you girls."

Girls. The nurse was much older than us but being called a girl felt odd. I didn't say anything, though. After dealing with patients all day, our nurse had earned the license to call us whatever she liked.

Ashley shuts her sketchbook and slides her pencil into the wire spine. "You know what? You're right. I prefer a more morbid model. Let's go to the rec room to see who I can find."

When the nurse is done, Ashley and I make our way to the rec room. As we pass the cafeteria, I notice it is visitation time. People flood into the area to meet with patients. I get a cup of water from the beverage cart before the room becomes too full.

As I reach for a cup, a hand falls on my arm. "Oh, my goodness. Helen, is that you?" I hear a voice say. "I thought you were in Bora Bora."

I pull my arm away from a mousy woman whom I don't recognize. Then, bewildered, I wait for her to say more.

"I thought it was some kind of eat, pray, love shit."

Ashley comes up beside me and grabs hold of my hand. She could sense that I needed her, recognizing this must be a person I can't remember. The woman doesn't pick up on my confusion and keeps talking.

"Is Chelsea covering for you? I mean, she must be, given she was the one who told us you booked a last-minute vacation." The woman doesn't notice I have yet to say a word and continues talking. "Wait," she looks around as if she just had an epiphany. "You're a patient?" She is now tickled with herself. "Oh, my goodness. Do Mark and Elaine know? The office has been so weird since you left."

The cotton in my windpipe makes speaking feel impossible. I don't know what to say. I don't remember what happened. I feel Ashley's hand squeeze mine, and I know what she is saying. *Say the word, and I'll take care of it.*

"I never thought I would see you in a place like this," the woman continues.

She is a small woman. Her pinched features and dull brown and gray hair make her look like a rat. I try to place her face. I should know it, but my mind is blank.

"I mean, I'm here, but I'm only visiting my brother." She holds up her hands to communicate her innocence. What is she innocent of? Not being crazy? "I'm sure you understand. I love him, but he's a little cuckoo if you know what I mean." She circles her ear with a finger. This whole interaction rubs me the wrong way. When Ashley makes light of being crazy, it feels fun and relatable, but when this lady does it, it makes me want to punch her in the face. And yet, she keeps talking. "He went off his meds again. Happens at least once a year." She rolls her eyes, and her voice bares her contempt for the mentally ill.

Finally, she realizes she is talking to a person, not a door. "Helen? Are you okay? You look like you might be ill."

"Who are you?" I croak, my head swimming with questions.

The mousey woman's face contorts. "Oh, you can't be serious," she scoffs. I continue to stare. "Oh, my god. Are you serious? You really don't know who I am?"

I shake my head. "I don't remember anyone. I lost my memory."

"Lisa. My name is Lisa."

I shake my head, still unaware of who this woman is.

"Oh gosh, what about Josie?" The woman puts her hand to her mouth.

"Who?"

"Your daughter." She juts her head forward as she says this.

She must have me mixed up with someone else. "My daughter's name was Raina," I say. I may not remember much, but I remember that.

"Raina? Her name is Josie. Are you messing with me? Our girls grew up together. Of course, Josie always tried to keep up with Madison, but I can't blame her."

I look back at Ashley, hoping she can give me answers to the questions shooting off like fireworks in my mind.

"I have a daughter?" I ask.

Ashley's brow furrows.

"God, yes," says the woman. "Does she not know you're here?"

My stomach lurches.

"Helen, you look ill. Where are you going? Helen?" I hear the mousy woman yelling as I turn and stomp toward the nurse's station. The hospital falls silent. My confusion and rage are felt by those around me.

My voice is a growl. "I want to talk to Jacqueline now!"

"I'm sorry, but she is not a regular doctor here," a nurse says.

I grab the ledge of the counter and push my body over it. "I don't care. Get her here now!"

"Ma'am, we are going to need you to calm down." The nurse holds out her hands.

"I am not calming down until I see Jaqueline!" I swipe at a clipboard, a jar of pens, and a stack of papers on the counter, throwing them all to the ground.

Still on the counter is a tissue box. I grab it and throw it. A memory flashes before me. I am in a hospital room, and the doctor says my daughter has no brain activity. She was abused. I am screaming. Andrew, my husband, backs up. His hands are in the air. He is retreating. "I didn't hurt them," he says.

Then I see Andrew, his hands in my hair, pulling at it. He throws me outside. "If you want to act like a bitch, you can live like one," he says.

I slam my body into Uncle Pete. Josie asks me where her dad is, and I lie. Matt smacks Momma across the face after she calls him an asshole. Josie cries after skinning her knee on the sidewalk. Andrew holds me and whispers, "I'm so sorry," in my ear. The rush of images overwhelms me. I feel trapped and out of control.

The next thing I know, I'm screaming on the ground. Kicking my feet out from under me. The nurses try to approach me, but I throw out a limb each time they come close.

"Get away from me! Get away from me!" I scream.

Eventually, someone uses a bear hug to restrain me from behind me. It is the nurse who always giggles at the end of her sentences. She's the first person I connected to in this place, and the smell of her soap and the familiarity of her touch puts me at ease. I feel the pressure of the hug, and my body goes limp.

"I'm sorry," I mumble. "I'm sorry. I'm so sorry."

The nurses escort me away. The mousey woman stares with her mouth agape.

The hospital staff give me another sedative and put me in a rounded room with a bed. Although I feel the pull of sleep, I fight it. In my room, I try desperately to sort through the images, but there are so many. They seem to be stuck together, and it's like I must peel the water-damaged pictures apart. I am now certain of one thing. I have two daughters.

I try to imagine her now. The daughter I still have. But I only see her as a small child. I can't see beyond that. I try to envision what she looks like today, but it's hopeless.

How could I forget her?

I remember my statement on the intake form Jacqueline shared with me the first time I met her.

I am my mother.

Variations of Momma's face come into view. I sit on the toilet while she gently coats her lashes with mascara in front of the bathroom mirror. Then she is sad. Tears stream down her face as she begs Matt to stop. I beg him, too, but I cannot say it aloud. She sits behind me, her hands twist in her lap, and she sniffles repeatedly. I'm disgusted. Admiration to desperate sympathy to disgust. That was the trajectory of our relationship.

Does my daughter find me disgusting?

The next morning, immediately after vitals, a nurse takes me to meet Jacqueline. She's sitting in her normal chair, concentrating on the stack of printed pages in front of her. She uses her pen to keep her place on the page and doesn't look up as she says, "I hear you created quite the scene yesterday."

I'm ashamed, but I won't let her know that. I sit in the yellow chair and bring my knees up to my chest.

"I was hoping you could wait until our scheduled session because I needed to confer with some colleagues. But, Helen, in our last session, it became painfully aware that the parts of your memory your brain let in were so fragmented that remembering without help might bring more harm than good." Jaqueline puts her pen and papers on the table beside her, and I can see a picture of me in the top corner of a page. I lower my legs and lean in to look.

"I take full responsibility for how painful this has been. I was worried I could influence your memories if I shared too much, but I have decided it might be for the best to share what I know."

I should be relieved, but I am seething. How could she think it was best to have all those memories rush in the way they did? If she just told me, I could have processed the information without reliving my pain.

"I'm tired," I say.

"I imagine you are," Jacqueline replies.

"No, I am tired of your games. I don't want to play them. So, either tell me what you know, or I'm leaving. I will find a way out of here."

"Helen, I'm not playing a game. I am trying to provide you with care, but you're right. I won't hold anything from you anymore. In exchange, I need you to trust me."

"I don't trust you."

Jacqueline nods and pulls her bottom lip into her mouth momentarily before detailing all she knows.

CHAPTER 38

Before Helen Lost Her Memory

On the first day of April, Andrew was arrested in his parents' home on suspicion of first-degree murder, child abuse resulting in death, and child abuse. The autopsy report was the nail in his coffin. Bleeding in both retinas, an acute subdural hematoma, bruising on her jaw and head, blood in the spinal column, severe flexion and extension of the neck, bruises the shape and size of fingerprints on Raina's front and back where she was held during multiple traumatic events.

Our church—not my church anymore—all supported Andrew and his family in their time of need. The pastor, the man who counseled me in my marriage, spoke out against Andrew's arrest. The news even quoted our dear pastor:

"He's a good kid, and he comes from good people. The church and his family are here to support him. He's innocent until proven guilty."

It was insane to me that even with all the evidence, his church still deemed him a "good kid." Meanwhile, I received dirty looks from the people I used to worship with each Sunday.

I believed I would breathe again once the police finally arrested Andrew. I hoped the monster inside me, growing more powerful each day, would simply disappear. But instead, this monster had become all-consuming, and I could no longer push it down. I had lost the battle, and the monster was now in control. I waited precisely one week after the arrest to confront Jennifer, my social worker. With Andrew arrested, I could see no reason for them to keep Josie from me.

"Did you see he was arrested?" I asked Jennifer when she dropped Josie off for visitation.

"Yes. I saw that." She was impassive.

"Doesn't that mean Josie comes back home?" I said as I stripped my daughter of her jacket and shoes in my living room.

"This isn't the appropriate time to talk about that," Jennifer said before leaving my house.

So, I waited, giving them the benefit of the doubt. It must be a lot of paperwork to place a child with their mother again. But after hearing nothing for an entire week, I'd had enough. I went to Jennifer's office.

"No appointment again?" she noted when I walked in.

I cocked a smile and shook my head in response. I didn't need to garner any courage for what I was about to say. The monster claimed dominance. I stayed standing.

"It has been seven days. Seven days since his arrest. What the fuck do I have to do to get my daughter back? Or are you going to play your sadistic fucking games with me until she is eighteen years old?"

Jennifer looked as if I slapped her across the face, and honestly, I wished I had. She was a sick fucking bitch to string me along when she knew full well my daughter belonged with me. Some game they played. She and Patricia. No wonder that woman was able to adopt five children so easily.

My body emitted radioactive raves of rage. I waited for her to give me another excuse.

Tell me I haven't grieved enough. I fucking dare you.

But then she said, "We can complete the process for reunification tomorrow."

I let out a rush of air. Tomorrow? Maybe my anger was what she had been waiting for. She wanted me to get mad. I couldn't understand why, but I was glad it worked.

Patricia came to social services the next day with Josie and a box of her things.

"I am going to miss you so much, my Josie Bear," she cooed in Josie's ear. "I just love her," Patricia said, finally looking up at me. She held onto Josie's little body as Josie struggled to wiggle out. Patricia cried big crocodile tears, and I wanted to laugh in her face.

"Maybe Josie can visit? I know her sisters and brothers are going to miss her so much!"

Josie ran from Patricia's embrace and into mine. I lifted Josie onto my hip and glared at Patricia and her tears. I wanted to tell her what I thought of her, but I simply turned and walked away.

That night, Josie, Lucy, and I all snuggled in my bed and watched a movie on an old bubble television. It felt like home.

In the months that followed, I worked multiple jobs while Lucy focused on school and helping me with Josie in the afternoons. We struggled. It wasn't easy, but it was peaceful.

Billy Ray would come by occasionally, stick a twenty-dollar bill in my hand and say, "You can use this more than I can." And with a tip of his head, he would leave. He never minded that I was too busy for him. He was only happy I was pushing forward in life. I wasn't going to stop until we thrived.

The court case, in which Andrew faced life in prison, dragged on. Andrew's family, church, and attorney arrived at each court date and made a mockery of what happened to my children. The outpouring of support from Andrew's church and family was all his defense attorney needed to convince the judge to grant him reasonable bail.

They requested extension after extension, working to prolong the inevitable. At the preliminary trial, I was not allowed to listen to the testimony provided. However, my dad, who had been around more since Raina's death, was always willing to sit in and give me a play-by-play. We hadn't committed to mending our broken relationship but sitting together in the rubble was progress. Maybe one day we'd work at it.

The defense brought forth expert witnesses. One doctor testified that the medical evidence was used to make a rush judgment. She told the court that my baby was never right from birth. Andrew's attorney asserted Raina was a sickly child, but being sick and being sickly are two different things. She wasn't sickly.

I learned that Betty and Rich were forced to sell much of their property to pay for Andrew's defense, and when the money from their land ran dry, the church helped raise additional funds. However, the church could not sustain the exorbitant cost of expert witnesses and a high-priced defense attorney.

In late July, over a year and a half since my daughter's death and just before Lucy would leave for college, Andrew entered an Alford plea in return for a sixteen-year sentence with the option to get out in six on good behavior. Although he would go to jail, an Alford plea was a slap to the face.

Under such a plea, Andrew accepted responsibility for the crime while also claiming innocence. He would never admit to what he had done.

On the day of his sentencing, I addressed the court.

In the courthouse, the judge called in the defendant, and my ex-husband walked to a table before the judge. He looked different. He had gained significant weight and wore eyeglasses. He looked harmless, but he wasn't fooling me.

My family was there with me—Lucy, Billy Ray, Dad, Momma, and Matt. When I was called before the court, I reminded myself that the statement was to the court, not to Andrew.

As I walked to the wooden podium, I felt like my legs might collapse. I stoked the fire within and pushed that energy through my limbs. Standing at the podium, I looked down at my notes, reminding myself of what I came here to say. My gaze traveled to the crowd, and I found Andrew's family sitting in the second row. The family I believed had been mine as much as his.

I cleared my throat to speak. When I began, the sound of my voice bounced off the courtroom room walls and caught me off-guard. I took a deep breath and started over.

"I don't hate Andrew. I pity him. I know what it feels like to grieve Raina, my daughter. My heart aches when I remember I will never hold her again. I shudder each time I hear the phantom squeals of joy coming from the part of my house in which she used to sleep, only to realize they are a figment of my imagination. It destroys me when I think of how I will never know her favorite color, favorite meal, or favorite type of music. I'll never know her passions. I'll never watch her grow and develop into a young woman. My memories of her will always be confined to five short months of life. To miss her and to grieve her the way I do is torture. If I were to light myself on fire, I am certain it would hurt less than losing her."

My hands shook on top of the podium, but the rest of my body appeared solid to the crowd. I took a deep breath and continued.

"Although Andrew will not admit what he has done. He has to live with that truth for the rest of his life. He has to live knowing that he murdered his daughter. My daughter. I can't begin to imagine how that must feel, but I know it must be excruciating, and for that, I pity him."

When my gaze lifted back to the room, I didn't make eye contact with Andrew but instead found my dad's eyes. They were wet. For the first time, he saw me, and I quickly turned my eyes away. I didn't want to be seen.

After Andrew's sentencing, my dad found me outside the courthouse, sitting on a bench. I was still trying to calm my racing heart, which had been erratic since that morning.

"Can I sit?" he asked.

I scooted slightly to one side and gestured at the empty spot.

He sat and let out a rush of air. "I promised myself I would never tell you this. I thought it would only hurt you," he said.

My brows knit together in response. "Tell me what?"

He cleared his throat. "Do you remember your secret garden?"

"Yeah." The memory always made me smile.

"I need you to understand why I wasn't there for you. I'm not making excuses. I should have been there, but maybe this will help you understand."

I felt confused by how such a happy memory made him so solemn.

"When you were little." He paused, lost at sea, as he thought about his next words. "You and I would spend hours outside picking flowers and digging in the dirt. You loved it so much. It was really just a lot with a bunch of overgrown weeds, but to you, it was your secret garden."

"I remember," I said.

He continued, "One day, I was at home watching TV when there was a knock at my door. You and Lucy were with your mom." He hesitated and looked at his hands.

I didn't understand why this was so hard for him to share, but I waited.

"Anyway, it was social services. Your mom had reported she was concerned. She thought that the secret garden was some type of sick euphemism for something inappropriate, so she reported sexual abuse."

"Why would Momma do that?" I whispered. My relationship with my mom was already shaky, but this obliterated any possibility of a relationship in the future.

Dad brought his hands together, pressing his palms against one another. "I still don't know. Frankly, I think she wanted out of North Carolina, and I was standing in the way of her being back with her family. After that, I felt scared. Scared to hug you, scared to be alone with you, and too scared to fight for you. I didn't want to be seen that way, and I know it isn't an excuse, but it's the truth."

A wave of conflicting emotions washed over me. I ached to forgive him, but how could I? If he wasn't such a coward, if he fought for me as I fought for Josie, my life and Lucy's would have been so different. I knew what it was like for people to look at you like you were the person responsible for your child's harm. It didn't stop me, but it stopped him.

CHAPTER 39

Two weeks after Andrew's sentencing, Lucy left for college. She had worked hard and funneled her passion for art into pursuing everything I once believed myself capable of. Proud was an understatement. She had done it. She put in the work, and she would make it out. Her campus was five hours away at the Denver School of Arts, and Billy Ray had agreed to take her. I couldn't go. I had to work, so we said our goodbyes as Billy Ray watched from his car.

"Please, take this. It's not much, but I've been saving it for you." I tucked a hundred-dollar bill into her hand.

"Helen, no. I'll be okay. Dad gave me some money to hold me over until I get my grant and scholarship money."

I hadn't told her what Dad had told me. She might still have a chance at a relationship with him, and although Momma ruined my chances, it didn't feel right to do that to her.

She tried to push the money back at me. She had grown into such a beautiful woman. Over the years, she had learned to tame and define her curly brown hair. Her freckles complimented her amber eyes, and her smile was genuine and warm.

"Just take it, Lucy. Please. Buy yourself a lava lamp or whatever kids decorate their dorm rooms with."

She laughed and hugged me. My chest shuddered as I tried to suppress the tears. I didn't want to cry. I wanted this moment to be happy. Lucy pulled away from our embrace, and we locked hands, smiles decorating our faces. We didn't need words.

She turned to get in the car.

"Wait, one more thing," I said to her, reaching into my bag. I pulled out my copy of *Little Women*, the same copy I received on Christmas when we lived with Grandpa. Sticking out from the pages was my third of the palm tree postcard and an old photo of our dad.

"I want to give these to you. Please, take them. Let them give you hope when you need it."

She reached for the book, turned it over in her hand, and opened it to look inside. The hardcover was beaten up, and the pages were starting to lift from the spine. The edges of the photo and postcard were worn and rounded.

She took out the piece of postcard and held it out to me. "I can't take this. It's yours."

"I want you to have it," I said. "As long as you have it, I will feel like I am with you."

She pressed her lips together, tucked the piece of torn postcard along with the photo of our dad into the book, closed it, and held it tight to her chest.

"Just do good things, Lucy. Do good things." I held in the tears pooling in my eyes. I knew she would do incredible things. With her talent, compassion, and no patience for bullshit, she was going to be okay. Unable to spend more time saying goodbye, I turned to head back to the house.

"I love you, Helen," she called out to me.

My voice cracked as I shouted back, "I love you too, Lucy. I'm so proud of you."

I went inside and into Josie's room and crawled into bed beside her. It was only me and her now, and that was all right. We had all we needed. It was time to go. Lucy was at college, and I had no reason to stay here in Rock Springs. After I learned the truth from my dad, I swore I'd never speak to him or Momma again.

And given that I couldn't entirely trust Grandpa and Aunt Joy to keep where I was going a secret, I also had to cut ties with them. It would be better this way. Billy Ray was still here, and although he would be fine without me, I wasn't entirely sure I would be okay without him. I sure as hell was going to try. Getting a fresh start and becoming a new person would feel good.

Billy Ray helped me make the arrangements to leave. He taught me how to book a flight and provided endless information about Charlotte, North Carolina—the place Josie and I would move to. On the morning of our flight, Josie ran in a figure-eight path, her arms out to her sides, blowing raspberries into the air. At three and a half, she had endless energy.

"Are you an airplane?" Billy Ray asked.

"Airplane!" Josie screamed as Billy Ray picked her up and held her horizontally so she could fly.

I brought out our suitcases. I'd sold my car and all our other possessions, albeit it wasn't much. All we had left were in these two suitcases, both gifted to us by Billy Ray. I packed and stored boxes of Raina's belongings in Billy Ray's garage. He promised he would find a way to ship them to me when I landed on my feet. I only kept her blanket and a small album of photos with me.

Billy Ray drove me to Casper, Wyoming, where I would catch my flight. The late summer air was crisp and dry, blanketing the various shades of brown and gray that made up the landscape. For miles, we saw only sagebrush and dirt. This place, Rock Springs, which I had called home for seven years, would soon be a distant memory. I would never come back. We were starting over. Josie would experience no more suffering. I would make certain of that. Only a single hesitation lingered. I didn't want to leave Raina behind. Yet, this was easier. Reminders of my loss agitated the raw wound within my heart. I wasn't sure my heart would ever heal, but leaving might stop the bleeding.

"You sure you're going to be all right, kid?" Billy asked, tapping his fingers on the steering wheel to his favorite Elvis song.

"I think so."

I had found a small one-bedroom apartment to rent in Charlotte on Craigslist. It wasn't much, but it would do. I had enough money for three months of rent, utilities, and food. After that, I would have to find childcare, get a job, and buy a car. I had done those things before and knew I could do them again. Sometimes I worried I was only running away from the things that caused me pain, but how could I be when I was running toward a better life? I didn't have much, but I did have hope.

At the airport, Billy Ray lifted my suitcases from the trunk while I unbuckled Josie's booster seat from the back. Standing on the curb, I instructed Josie to hold the suitcase like it was my hand. When I was sure she understood, I turned to say goodbye to Billy Ray.

He had never hugged me before, as we'd always shaken hands. I was completely unprepared when he wrapped his arms tight around me, but I melted into his embrace. He had bestowed so much wisdom and understanding over the years. I was really going to miss him.

"I love you, kid." He pulled back from me and placed a hand on my shoulders. "You're going to be just fine."

I knew he was right.

When we were done with our goodbyes, I turned toward the airport, but Billy Ray stopped me before I could walk away. "Helen?"

I turned. "Did I forget something?" I looked around, mentally inventorying my and Josie's possessions.

"No, kid. I was wondering … why North Carolina?"

I smiled, thinking about my answer. "Because it's the only place I've been truly happy, and maybe if I go back, I can find that happiness again."

"Sounds like a plan," he said.

I smiled big and said, "Goodbye, Billy Ray."

With the tip of his head, he walked around his car and got in the driver's seat.

Inside the airport, I checked the time out of habit. My Mickey Mouse watch, long broken, was simply a reminder of where I come from.

Chapter 40

The classifieds lay open on our kitchen counter. The paper was stained with grease from my fingers. A McDonalds' breakfast sandwich sat next to the newspaper, half-eaten. Using a black marker, I circled any job postings I was qualified for.

First thing each day, Josie and I would leave our apartment to buy the newspaper and enough food for the day. Then, after breakfast, I'd push her in an umbrella stroller door to door as I looked for a job. I dressed in my nicest clothes, the same ones I wore every day, and we set out. The first stop we would make that day was at a local community college only a few blocks away. The ad said they were looking for a full-time custodian for twelve dollars an hour. It was good money.

Charlotte was unlike any place I'd ever lived. My memories of North Carolina were faint, but Hubert, the town we had lived in, was small and rural. Charlotte was the home of busy streets and tall buildings made from glass and steel. I wished I had a car because then I could take us beyond the city, allowing Josie to see miles of trees set against blue skies. One day, we would find a place to dig our toes into the dirt and make flower crowns from dandelion weeds.

I stood before the brick building that held the college, remembering the years in which I fanned college brochures out on my bed, wishing for a better life. Large white columns, reminiscent of colonial architecture, surrounded the building, and trees covered it in shade. It was beautiful. This life was not perfect, but it was better.

Inside the college, I found a woman stationed at the front desk. I approached her, smiling, and asked about the custodial job. Her eyebrows shot up at my question, and when she spoke, I was taken aback by her thick southern accent. It was laced with enough sugar to make a gallon of sweet tea.

"Oh, dear. I know the ad came out today, but to be honest, we've been hiring for a while, and they made an offer yesterday. There's still a chance they won't accept it, but it's unlikely. People want the health insurance that comes with the job."

I was disappointed, but I tried not to let it show. "Are you hiring for any other positions?"

"Not right now, but listen, you fill out an application anyway. Then, if another position opens up, I can make sure they call you."

This woman must have been a mother. I could tell from the way she sympathized with me. She couldn't help but look at Josie in her stroller as she talked.

"Thank you," I said. "I've been looking for a job all week, but no one wants to hire a single mom and a high school dropout. Too big of a liability if you know what I mean." I chuckled and shrugged my shoulders.

She handed me an application and a pen.

While I was busy writing, Josie sang a song about where the watermelon grows.

"Ain't she the sweetest," the woman said.

"She's a good girl."

I could feel the woman's eyes on me, studying me as I filled out the application. I tried to hurry. I didn't want to take too much of her time.

"Have you thought about going to school?"

I chuckled and looked up. "I can't afford that, but maybe one day."

Josie was done with her song and began to whine in her seat, so I unbuckled her from the stroller and handed her a small wooden puzzle from my bag to keep her entertained while I finished.

I went back to filling out the application, and the woman continued.

"You could get paid to go to school here."

I looked at her, curious. "Paid?"

I helped Lucy fill out her financial aid, but she had gotten so many scholarships I assumed it cost a lot of money.

"You're a single mother, right? There are these things called Pell Grants. If you qualify, which I'm sure you do, it'll pay for your classes and books, and you'll probably have enough left over to help subsidize your cost of livin'.

Of course, you'll still have to get a job, but we have work-study positions open all the time. It's minimum wage but a job all the same."

"Didn't the semester already start?" It was late August, and I assumed classes started several weeks ago based on when Lucy left.

"Sure did, but today's the last day to add/drop courses. So, if you're willin' to put in the work, you can still attend."

I stared at her, trying to determine if she was someone I could trust.

"Look, it's real easy. Hand me that application." She reached out her hand.

"But I'm not done."

"I know. Change of plans. You mentioned you dropped out of high school. You got a GED?"

"Yeah."

She snatched the application from under my hand and pointed to a row of computers nearby. "See them computers over there. Go sit down, and I'll be right over to show you what to do. What's your little girl's name?"

Josie spoke up, "Josie."

"Aren't you precious? I'm Sheila. How old are you, darlin'?"

Josie held up three fingers, and Sheila's face lit up in response. "And smart too! Now, come on over here, Josie. You can sit in my chair. I keep some crayons and colorin' books in my desk for my grandkids when they visit. Do you like graham crackers? I have some of those, too."

I sat at the computer and waited. I had no clue what I was doing.

"Okay." She looked over my shoulder and adjusted her glasses. Her perfume was strong but pleasant. "You see that icon? Click it."

I fumbled with the mouse for a moment too long, causing my anxiety to soar before I even got started.

"That's our website. Now, you're goin' to click the button that says apply. I'll be over there with Josie. You're lucky you came in so early. It's usually fairly quiet until about 10:00 a.m."

When I was done with the application, Sheila asked, "How far away is your house?"

"About a ten-minute walk."

"Perfect. Do you have a copy of your tax return from last year?" Sheila was pushy, but maybe I needed to be pushed.

I nodded.

"Go get it and come back. I go to lunch at noon, so try to make sure you're back by 11:00 a.m."

I made it back to the college less than thirty minutes later. I practically ran the whole way, afraid I would miss my shot if I took too long. This opportunity felt like something important.

A line of students stood at Sheila's desk, and I was suddenly overcome with fear.

What am I doing here? I don't belong in college.

I went to leave, but before I could, I heard her southern drawl more exaggerated than before.

"Don't you dare go anywhere. Wait right there. It'll only be a few more minutes."

All the students turned to look at me, and I was instantly mortified.

Josie called out "Hi!" to everyone who turned our way.

Sheila walked me over to the computers when it was my turn. This time, only one remained unoccupied.

Another student walked to the desk, and she called out, "You're going to have to hold your horses, missy. I gotta get this one goin' on her financial aid."

When I finished the financial aid application, Sheila directed me to the registrar's office.

"Tell her I sent you and not to give you any grief. She gives you grief, you tell me. Okay?"

The registrar didn't give me grief but gave me enough of a side eye for me to know she was annoyed. Josie sat on my lap and twisted two pieces of my hair together while the registrar looked over my paperwork.

"What's your major?"

"My major? Uh. I don't know. What can I pick from?"

"Associate of Arts, it is. Do you have your Accuplacer scores?"

"My what scores?" I hadn't been to class yet, and I already felt dumber than a doorknob.

She sighed deeply. She was a large woman with short brown hair and a permanent scowl. "You're going to need to take English and math. You'll need Accuplacer scores, so I can determine placement, but it's a little too late for that."

She stared at her computer screen as I waited for her to tell me it was too late and I needed to leave.

"Astronomy or geology?" she asked.

"Uh … geology?"

She handed me a piece of paper with my schedule written out in chicken scratch.

"Your schedule is not ideal, but that's what happens when you wait until the last day to enroll. You get what's left. Your first class is tonight at 6:00 p.m. It is on the third floor of the Elizabeth Building."

I almost told her I couldn't. I didn't have anyone to watch Josie, but instead, I thanked her and hurried out of her office.

At home, I paced the living room while Josie napped. I didn't know what to do. What if I brought her with me? Would they let me in? What if I didn't go, and it messed up any chance of ever going to college again?

When 5:30 p.m. rolled around, I decided to risk it. I would take her to class and see what happened. I was the first one there and took a seat in the empty classroom. Josie ate the peanut butter and jelly sandwich I packed as my foot tapped the ground. I tried to steady my racing heart when the professor walked in. I waited to be chastised.

"Good evening. I'm Jeff Spears. Sheila told me you might bring your daughter. It's fine with me as long as she isn't a disruption." Jeff walked over to Josie and bent down to her level. "I heard you're a good girl. Can you be quiet and listen while your mommy learns?" he asked.

Josie stared at him with her big brown eyes.

"I'm going to take that as a yes," Jeff said as he went back to the front of the classroom and unpacked his messenger bag.

Students piled into the classroom, and I soon realized I was unprepared. I had my schedule, but all the classes were abbreviated, and I didn't know what the three-letter codes meant. Therefore, it wasn't until Jeff handed out the syllabi that I knew I was in World Religions. I also didn't have a textbook yet. The girl next to me, Elaine, slid her book between us on the table.

"You can share with me," she said.

I was grateful for her kindness.

Josie was perfect the whole time, but I flinched every time she made a sound. Only when class ended could I relax again. I'd made it.

Every day, I walked to campus with Josie and studied in the common area near Sheila's desk. Sheila helped me find childcare, apply for food stamps and Medicaid, and get a job helping her at the front desk. She also helped me study when it wasn't too busy.

Soon, everyone that worked at the college knew Josie and me. Josie was a favorite. She made her rounds each morning, visiting the faculty. She knew that Kathy, the math instructor, kept candy in her top left desk drawer. Dave, the earth sciences instructor, taught Josie the names and properties of the various rock samples he kept in his office. And occasionally, he would gift Josie a stone to add to her collection. The psychology instructor, Lisa, let Josie help water her plants.

Elaine, the girl who shared her textbook with me, soon became my best friend. She was a tall girl who loved people. Her bigger-than-life personality was only out-matched by her height. She was a magnet and attracted everyone to her. She made friends easily, which is how I met Mark.

Unlike Elaine, Mark was a computer science major who was as serious and analytical as they came, but he somehow completed our group. All three of us met at my place for study dates and movie nights. The college became our family, and on graduation day, Josie sat with Sheila as I made my way to the stage to give the commencement speech. Everyone knew Helen and Josie, but no one *really* knew me. I kept my past and my grief to myself. My speech was the closest I ever came to revealing myself.

"I don't like to tell my story because it is sad. So, I won't, but I will say I am proof that even the saddest stories can have a happy ending. I know if you are willing to put in the work, as my friend Sheila once told me, you can make your happy ending come true, too."

That year, Josie's preschool class took photos of the kids with a sign that denoted what they wanted to be when they grew up. Josie's sign said, *A graduated person.* It wrecked me in the best way.

Chapter 41

I never understood why Momma avoided questions until Josie was old enough to ask her own. But I didn't want to be like Momma. I didn't want to avoid Josie's questions, so I became a liar instead.

During Josie's second-grade year, I registered her for Girl Scouts. I beamed with pride as I enrolled her in the quintessential activity. The mere act of Josie becoming a scout seemed to embody the normalcy we longed for. Each badge I ironed onto her small brown vest symbolized hope. We were building the life we deserved.

Josie adored Girl Scouts. So, when I arrived one afternoon to collect her after a troop meeting and found a glum-faced girl reluctantly shuffling toward the car, my heart teemed with concern.

"What's up, buttercup?" I said to Josie, who climbed into the backseat, her face drawn into a pitiful pout.

"Nothing," she mumbled.

"Doesn't look like nothing." I narrowed my eyes and peered at her in the rearview mirror.

She pulled a half sheet of paper from a purple pocket folder and jutted her arm out. I reached for it and brought the paper to my face to read what made her so gloomy.

The heading read *You're Invited to the Annual Daddy Daughter Dance*.

A stabbing sensation speared my heart, and the air in the car suddenly felt stale and hot. It made breathing difficult, and I blinked hard to get my thoughts straight. Twisting around, I smiled softly at Josie while holding up the invitation.

"This is why you are upset?"

"I don't have a dad, so I can't go." She fought to hold back tears.

My smile broadened even though I was screaming inside. "Yes, you can. I'll go with you."

"You are not a dad." She crossed her arms.

"Lots of kids only have a mommy. I am sure several of your friends will be there with their moms or grandpas."

"No," she shook her head. "I already asked. Everyone is going with their dad."

I bit my lip and squeezed my eyes shut before opening them wide. I took a deep breath, trying to muster as much excitement as I could.

"Okay then! We will have our own dance! We will play any music we like, choose the snacks, and, best of all—be in charge of the decorations."

The top of Josie's lip rose, and her irises slid to the left. She was not impressed.

"And …" I continued, desperately trying to think of something that would turn this around. "I will take off work tomorrow so we can spend the whole day shopping for the perfect dress and shoes."

She perked up. "And a crown?"

"Yes! And a crown! Now, let's go home. We can start planning our dance while we eat dinner."

Josie uncrossed her arms, and the phantom of a smile graced her lips.

A few weeks later, twinkling lights hung from our ceiling fan and trailed along the walls of our modest living room. Josie wore a fancy pink dress with ample amounts of tulle and glitter. Exuberantly, she pranced and pirouetted through our apartment. We created a makeshift dance floor by pushing our furniture to one side of the room and hanging a disco ball from the ceiling fan. We sipped on red punch between songs and ate off-brand wafer cookies arranged to look fancy on a plastic plate.

My heart pounded, and sweat dampened my skin after we danced three times consecutively to *Shut Up and Dance* by Walk the Moon. Josie, finally out of steam, collapsed with me onto the floor. We lay side by side, catching our breath between intermittent giggles. Josie swiped at the hair that had fallen from her half-ponytail, and her crown sat abandoned on the floor nearby. She looked at me and said, "Mom, where is my dad?"

The familiar sting I felt in the car weeks before resurfaced. I didn't want to tell her who her dad was any more than I wanted to tell her about our life in Wyoming. Telling her would only lead to heartbreak, and it was my job to protect her. Unable to avoid this question, I lied.

I sat up and crossed my legs, signaling for Josie to do the same. I reached out and encompassed her tiny hands in mine.

"Your dad died a long time ago. He never even got to meet you." I said this with such conviction that I would have believed it had I not known the truth.

Her eyes grew large. "He died?"

I couldn't decide if I was being kind or doing her an injustice with this lie, but the truth seemed worse.

"How?"

"In a car accident. I'm so sorry. I should have told you sooner, but I wanted to wait until you were older."

She didn't cry, but I could see that behind her somber expression, she was trying to determine how to react. Selfishly, I reached for a way out of the conversation.

"Ice cream?"

She smiled her toothless smile, and we left the dance floor to fill our bellies with mint chip.

Unfortunately, Josie always thirsted for more, and over time, the lie grew so much that I felt like I was losing control. Although I swore never to return to Wyoming, I did once to attend Billy Ray's funeral. He had passed away in his sleep. Josie was only nine, and I had not spent a night away from her since she was in foster care. I couldn't leave her with anyone, but I needed to say goodbye to Billy Ray. So, we flew to Wyoming. At the funeral, Josie and I sat in the back of a church and watched his family mourn their loss. Although I felt the familiar pangs of grief that I had long buried within myself, this loss was different. Billy Ray lived a full and happy life. He did well in this world, and because of him, I would too. Although the loss of such a great man was sad, it was also okay.

After the funeral, Josie and I took a short walk around the cemetery. When we came to Raina's grave, I placed a modest arrangement of red daisies on top. They reminded me of ladybugs, and ladybugs reminded me of Raina. Raina didn't have a headstone, only a plastic marker that the cemetery provided. She deserved a headstone, but that would mean facing my hurt, and I still didn't feel equipped for such a thing.

"Mom, who is this?" Josie asked as we held hands and stood before her sister's grave.

"I don't know, baby," I lied again. "I just thought she had a pretty name and could use some flowers."

I wrestled with telling Josie the truth for years. At first, I thought—when she was older. But as time passed, I realized telling her about her sister would lead to questions I was unprepared to answer. I kept telling myself I was protecting her.

We only stayed in Rock Springs long enough to pay our respects. Then we drove to Denver to see Lucy. I hadn't seen her since the day she left for college. Lucy landed a job running an art program for at-risk youth. She found fulfillment in her work as well as a small community of Dungeons and Dragons enthusiasts.

"You are so big!" Lucy said to Josie as we climbed out of the rental car.

"I've always been like this," Josie said, smiling broadly. She ran to give Lucy a hug.

Lucy laughed. It was hard to believe it had been six years since I last saw her. Everything and nothing had changed.

In Lucy's kitchen, she sliced a bell pepper for dinner as we talked. Josie was in the other room, watching cartoons. Lucy lived alone, and when I asked her about dating, she scoffed at the idea. I guessed that witnessing relationships like mine and Momma's had ruined the idea of love for her. Regardless, she seemed happy.

"Did you see Tyler got married?" Lucy asked.

Lucy was my only connection to our family.

"He did? That's great!"

Lucy placed the knife on the cutting board and gave me a hard stare. I hated when she looked at me as if she was the big sister. "I don't blame you for pushing everyone away, but they miss you."

"Who? Mom?"

She let out a chuckle. "God, no. You know I don't talk to her. Everyone else. Tyler, Aunt Joy, Grandpa, Dad."

The truth was, I missed them too. But if I let them back in, I worried my life would somehow go back to the way it was before. I'd fought so hard to get out, and the only reason I'd made it this far was because I separated myself from who I once was.

"They ask about you," Lucy said.

Alarmed, I asked, "What do you tell them?"

"Nothing. I only tell them that you're doing well. That's it."

My shoulders relaxed, and I let out a small puff of air.

Lucy went back to slicing the bell pepper. "You know, Tyler would never say anything if you didn't want him to. You should reach out to him."

I wrestled with the idea. My hesitancy around Tyler was not tied to fear like it was with the others. Instead, I was consumed by the guilt that came with knowing I made him a promise and never kept it. But eventually, I gave in. When we got back to North Carolina, I found Tyler on social media. I created a fake profile and followed up on my friend request with a message.

Helen: Hey, Tyler. It's Helen. I know it's been a long time. I'm sorry. Lucy said I should reach out. I hope that's okay. I miss you.

He responded only minutes later.

Tyler: I'm really glad you did. I've missed you too. How are you?

From that point on, Tyler and I stayed in touch. I set strict boundaries to protect Josie, and he never pushed. But as Josie got older, her questions continued.

Where did you meet my dad? Why don't I have grandparents? Did my dad have any sisters or brothers? Did you and my dad get married? Do you think you'll ever get married? Where was I born? Why did we move to North Carolina?

I could only answer her questions with half-truths, afraid that if I told her more, she would one day go looking for answers.

Over the years, I continued to go to school online while working full-time. By the time I was twenty-six, I had obtained two more degrees above my Associate's. These degrees and the relationships I'd built led to a position as an academic advisor at the community college. The same one that helped save my life.

One day, while on my lunch break, I listened across the campus courtyard as a college student cried desperately into her phone.

"I'm sorry, Jason," she said. "Please don't. Please, Jason. I'm sorry."

I didn't know what the situation was, but the plea in her voice sounded so familiar. I felt as though I were looking through clouded glass for the rest of my day. I couldn't get that girl's voice and her plea for forgiveness out of my head. I wished there was a way I could pop up on her phone anonymously and tell her everything I knew. I thought about that girl all day and scolded myself for being so weak. She needed someone, and I was too afraid to help. Then, it came to me. Maybe with help from my friends, I could pop up on her phone.

I called Mark. He wrote code for a living, but I wondered if he could build an app. On the phone, I bit the bullet and gave him a reason to help me.

"I'm about to tell you something about myself that no one else knows," I said.

"Okay?" He sounded preoccupied, but I continued on.

"Eight years ago, I was married." I took a deep breath. "That man abused me, beat Josie, and murdered my second child."

"What? Hold on. Let me go outside."

From there, I detailed my past, and Mark listened.

"Oh god, Helen. I had no idea."

"Of course, you didn't. I don't advertise it, but I need your help. Do you know how to build an app?"

"Of course, I do. Why?"

Mark, Elaine, and I sat at my kitchen table the next Saturday, and I filled Elaine in on my life and the plan. She tried to hug me when I told her about how I lost Raina, but I held my hands out to stop her.

"Don't. Don't feel sorry for me. Just help me."

Together, we sketched out what it would look like to have an app that connected people to real relationship counselors in minutes. An app that gave tips on healthy communication and educated the user on the signs of abuse. An app that provided resources and guidance if someone was ever in a dangerous situation.

When Mark showed us the first workable demo of the app, I knew we would change the world for the better.

A year later, Andrew got out of prison. My anxiety amplified, and I held the truth and Josie even closer to my chest. I reinforced the locks on our doors and kept a close eye on the whereabouts of Josie at all times. I didn't believe Andrew would come looking for me, but I would not risk it.

I managed my fear by finding solace in work. When I was busy building my company, Ever Before, my insurmountable anxiety temporarily disappeared. Eventually, Mark finished the app. Between Mark's genius, my passion, and Elaine's people skills, we believed we were on the brink of something great.

"We just hit 10,000 users!" Elaine said as she entered the coffee shop, joining Mark and me for our weekly Friday morning meeting. We were only a couple of years into operating our business.

"That's amazing!" Mark replied, and we gave ourselves a little round of applause.

"It's not quit your job money yet, but at this rate," said Elaine as she sat down.

Mark stuffed half a croissant in his mouth and spoke between chewing. "Helen, if you had told me this app might make us rich, I wouldn't have believed you."

"We are not doing this to get rich!" I laughed.

"Maybe not you." Elaine rolled her eyes and stole the half-eaten pastry from Mark's hand.

"Hey! Get your own!" he said, grabbing it back.

By the time Josie was in middle school, our app had finally taken off. Over the years, our subscriber numbers soared, and we hired a team of remote staff to manage what we had built. Eventually, we rented a large office building and filled the space with people dedicated to our mission. Each morning, with a smile plastered on my face, I made my rounds and thanked every person at Ever Before for their contributions. Faces would light up with each interaction. It wasn't until I made it back to my office that the smile I wore melted from my face. This life, this company, was all too good to be true, and as I looked around at what I built, I couldn't help but worry that the success I stood on would eventually crumble.

Chapter 42

The keys clicked in response to the swift movement of my fingers. Email was the bane of my existence. The *BING* that sounded when an email came in was the opposite of music to my ears. While chirping birds welcomed an early spring morning, I was inside at my kitchen table, trying my damnedest to clean out my inbox before I flew out to California. It had been twenty-three years since I was last there. For so long, I avoided places marked by heartache, but enough time had passed that being recognized was incredibly unlikely.

The stairs creaked under footsteps. Josie was a hurricane, storming in and out of spaces and rushing from here to there. She was always in a hurry to go somewhere. A college student, Josie was busy. Even more, finals week was just around the corner. She filled her days with classes and study groups.

Josie entered the kitchen and pulled the refrigerator door open, throwing a protein shake and a container of strawberries in her bag before spinning on her heels and heading toward the front door. Her shaggy, dyed black hair moved with her.

"No good morning, no hi, no see you later? What's up with you?" I asked, teasing her.

"You're busy." She slipped her tennis shoes on by the door.

"I'm not too busy to say hi," I remarked.

"I'm late," she yelled back, and the front door slammed, eclipsing the end of her sentence.

Her departure caused dread to flood my gut. Something was off. This wasn't normal. Call it mother's intuition. The only explanations I could come up with were pregnancy or drugs, but both seemed unlikely. She was a good kid and always had been. She was a hell of a lot better than I was. I grabbed my phone and debated what to do. My fingers rolled over my screen and found Chelsea, my assistant's number.

When she answered, I said, "Good morning!"

"Good morning, Ms. Birch. Are you excited for your trip today?"

"Actually, Chelsea, change of plans. Something came up with Josie, and I am going to have to postpone. Can you push my flight to tomorrow morning? Talks don't start until tomorrow afternoon, anyway."

It was unlike me to push off work, but Josie was a priority. I had harped on our team for years about the importance of work/life balance but rarely took my own advice except for when it came to my daughter.

Still considered a startup, Ever Before already employed over a hundred people and had record-breaking downloads. We were currently negotiating a massive deal with the largest dating app company in the world, Live4Love. Although they might be larger, they needed us. Recent negative press related to selling user data had them in hot water. The partnership would provide Live4Love's users with complimentary access to our app.

"Absolutely, Ms. Birch. I'll email you a revised itinerary."

"Can you also send Mark and Elaine a message with my new arrival time?"

They were already in California, but I could trust them to take care of things until I got there. Mark was the brains behind the technology, and Elaine was the face of our company. I provided the passion. Some called it workaholism, but passion sounded better.

"You got it," Chelsea said.

I didn't know what I would do without Chelsea. She was the best assistant I could have asked for. Kind, courteous, quick, and frankly, I couldn't manage my work without her. Mark and Elaine would have to handle the executives from Live4Love. I wasn't much for wining and dining our partners and investors, which they knew, so it wouldn't be a surprise that I changed my itinerary. Mark and Elaine knew me better than anyone else. Not only did we build a company together, but we also built a life. I watched Mark get married and have five little girls. He desperately wanted a boy, but his wife finally said no more. Although Mark was a serious man with an insane amount of intelligence, he was a softie around his children. He was meant to be a dad.

Mark and I placed bets on whether Elaine would ever get married, a secret we would both carry to our graves. But she surprised us both last year

UNTITLED FOR NOW

when someone swept her off her feet. I had always liked the idea of Elaine and I being two single ladies against the world, but Ed, her husband, was her perfect match. After she met Ed, she tried to set me up, but I wasn't interested.

The night of her bachelorette party, Elaine was so drunk I didn't know if she would make it down the aisle the next day. Her eyes crossed, and her words slurred. We sat in the bar bathroom as she spoke unintelligently about the purpose of life, only moments had she emptied the contents of her stomach into a toilet.

"Helen, I've known you for a long time," she mumbled.

"Yes, you have." I offered her a bemused smile and shook my head lightly.

"Don't you think? I mean. Hmmm?"

"Yes?" I laughed at her inability to form a coherent thought.

"You never date. Ever." She placed a heavy hand on my thigh.

"No, I guess not," I said.

"You deserve love!" She shot her arm into the air to declare it.

"I have plenty of love," I told her.

"But what about sex?" she whined. Her false lashes had come unglued at the corners, making her wildly inebriated state so much more comical.

I laughed harder. "You don't need a man to have sex." I winked and plucked remnants of her dinner out of her hair.

"I guess," she said before laying her head on my lap and closing her eyes.

I had all the love I needed.

My phone vibrated and brought me back to the present. It was Elaine.

Elaine: Of course, you would ditch me! It's fine, though. I will survive—laugh, cry emoji.

Me: You always do—wink face emoji.

I backed out of my text with Elaine and scrolled to find Josie's name.

Me: Any chance you could meet at Mom and Pops for dinner? I changed my flight so we could have dinner.

Josie: I have plans. Study group.

Me: You can't miss one study group for your mom?

Josie: I have a chem test tomorrow.

Me: I'll help you study at dinner.

Josie: Fine. What time?

Me: Yay! See you at 6!

Mom and Pops was just what it sounded like—a little country restaurant with the best chicken pie in North Carolina. Josie's favorite. When I arrived,

Josie was already there. Lost in thought, she twisted and ripped a napkin into tiny shreds.

I bent to kiss the top of her head before taking my seat across from her. "I'm so glad you could come!"

Her smile was strained. Josie could never hide what she was thinking. One of the most expressive humans I'd ever known, she wore her heart on her sleeve and her face. She was an artsy theater kid who wore thick black winged liner and had about four too many facial piercings. I told her when she was eighteen, she could pierce whatever she wanted, and she did.

"So, what's going on with you?" I asked after the waitress brought us two sweet teas.

"Not much," she said.

"That can't be true. You're never home. How are your classes going?"

"They're fine." She folded her straw wrapper accordion style until a small square sprung to life as she released her pinch on the paper. She was anxious.

I asked about every facet of her life for the next twenty minutes. I went so far as to ask her if she was watching anything binge worthy. But each time, she replied with short responses followed by dead air. Josie would rather stab at her chicken pie than talk to me.

Finally, I sucked in a deep breath and let it all out at once. I was simply going to go for it.

"Why are you avoiding me?"

Her eyes widened, and her posture stiffened, but then she hung her head and stared into her mutilated chicken pie. "I don't know what you're talking about," she whispered.

"Yes, you do." I tilted my chin and gave her my best mom stare—at least, that is what Josie has always called it.

"I don't want to talk about it," she said.

"Too bad. There is obviously something wrong, and I can't fix it unless I know what it is."

I reached for her hand. "You can tell me anything. I promise. I'll understand, and even if I don't, I'll try."

Her fork fell to the table and clanged against her plate. She refused to make eye contact. "I'm not worried about you understanding. I'm worried about you lying."

My stomach plummeted as the webs of my fictional past clung to my lungs. "Try me," I said, my tone colored by the challenge.

"No." Josie shook her head, stalling as she took a sip of her water.

"Really? You are not going to give me a chance to explain whatever you think I'm lying about?"

After letting out a long, low sigh, she said, "Why don't we start with the fact that my dad is not dead? Or maybe we can talk about how you used to be Helen Miller? Or maybe the fact you had another daughter? Why don't we start there?"

"I … I …" I stuttered, at a loss for words. It wasn't a strand of the web she found. It was the whole damn thing. Josie's mention of her sister sliced through me.

Josie grabbed her purse and jumped from the booth. It took me a moment to process what happened, but the moment I did, I threw two twenty-dollar bills onto the table and ran after her.

"Josie, Josie, Josie!" I was frantic by the third iteration of her name.

She flung herself around with such force her pleated black skirt lifted into the air.

"What?" she growled back. She certainly was my daughter.

"How did you even … How did …?"

"How did I find out that your entire life, my entire life is a lie? I can't believe you would think I'm this stupid."

"I don't think you're stupid! I only …"

She cut me off. "Me and my friends did one of those DNA tests. Did you know I have a brother?"

My mouth dropped open.

"Yeah, Mom. I have a half-brother, who I never got a chance to know because of you. Once I found that out, it wasn't hard to find the rest. You've always been so private, and now I know why. It all makes sense."

A sense of panic and desperation I hadn't felt in more than fifteen years settled in.

"Josie, I can explain." Tears spilled from my eyes.

But once Josie started talking, she couldn't stop.

"You know what the worst part is? Do you?"

I shook my head.

"I have no idea who you are. I've learned more from a DNA test and a Google search than I ever learned from you. All these years, my entire life, you lied to me. I don't know you." She pinched her lips tight to keep them from trembling. I could see how much I hurt her. I felt myself losing control and fought desperately to regain my composure with little success. I fought to find the words that would fix this.

"But you do know me," I finally muttered, but she was already gone.

Chapter 43

I pulled into our driveway, surprised to be home. The drive was missing from my short-term memory. I turned off the ignition and rested my forehead against the steering wheel. The sensation of the cool leather relieved a bit of the pressure building from within. When it was no longer effective, I sat up and pounded my fists against the steering wheel until the honk of my horn startled me.

Inside my house, I paced and dialed Josie's number for the fourth time. It went straight to voicemail. A dull throb crept behind my eyes, and I pinched the bridge of my nose. I would give her a few days to cool off. Surely, she would come around and allow me to explain that it was my job to keep her safe, and I couldn't shatter her heart the way Raina's death shattered mine. I was only doing my job.

By the time the clock read 10:00 p.m., I was in bed, but I couldn't sleep. Finally, I gave in to the anxious energy and got out of bed. For the next several hours, I emptied the fridge of expired food, shampooed the carpets, scrubbed sticky residue from the exhaust hood above the range, and packed a suitcase for my trip to California.

At 5:00 a.m., I stood at the edge of my driveway as a taxi driver loaded my suitcase into his trunk. The early morning air was cool and felt good against my burning skin.

"Are you coming? Ma'am, are you going to get in the car? Hello!"

I looked up to see the driver already in the car. Another chunk of time missing. He beckoned for my attention through the open passenger side window, but my gaze skittered around. Temporarily confused, I quickly found my footing.

"Sorry. I was lost in thought," I muttered before climbing into the back seat.

Dawn was beginning to lighten the sky as we made our way to the airport, bringing forth a warmth as the earth prepared for a new day. I focused on the variations of pink and purple that decorated the sky as the driver chatted endlessly. The dull throb behind my eye had transformed into a raging migraine. I pushed past the pain, trying to mentally unwind my tangled mess. From Charlotte to Los Angeles, I created imaginary conversations, rehearsing all the words I would say to Josie. However, the more I explained, the louder her words rang through my mind. *Mom, I don't know you.*

After landing, I found myself standing in baggage claim, despite not checking a bag. Thankfully, Mark was waiting for me nearby.

Get your head straight.

I fell into step with Mark as we navigated the airport. Mark had been in California with Elaine for the last several days, and his meetings centered mainly around the technology and what it would take to integrate our services.

"We don't have time for you to freshen up," he said.

"I wasn't planning on it."

He gave me a side eye, so I checked my appearance in the sliding glass doors of the airport as we exited. What looked back at me was startling. I saw a woman sloppily dressed in business casual. Her buttons were all misaligned, and her hair was a frizzy and tangled mess. Dark circles rested under her eyes, creating a haunted look. She was not a C-suite executive capable of brokering a big deal.

In the car, Mark said, "Look, I wasn't going to say anything, but I have a feeling that Live4Love has changed their intentions."

"Okay?" I said, re-buttoning my blouse.

"At this time, and it is only speculation coming from some of their software engineers, but there's a rumor that the execs are interested in an acquisition, not a partnership."

"Let's hope a rumor is all it is because we are not selling."

"I mean, depending on the offer …," Mark said as we approached Live4Love's headquarters.

"We are not selling," I repeated, more firmly this time. I couldn't believe Mark would even entertain such a thought.

Thirty minutes later, Mark and I entered a large conference room and found Elaine already seated at the long table.

"Hey, chica! You look like shit."

"Thanks," I said with a wry smile.

"Rough night?" Elaine asked.

"You have no idea," I said with a deep sigh. "Josie and I got into a fight."

Before Elaine could ask, fifteen execs and other staff entered the room. The number of people startled me. It was only supposed to be their board of directors. I flipped through a legal pad I brought, looking for the page where I wrote down each of their names. I had only met them a few times over Zoom. Members from Human Resources, Legal, and Partner Relations passed by me, and I stood in front of my seat while they introduced themselves. Once they had all filed in, we took our seats.

We made small talk, and Elaine shared how she had taken several of their team members to karaoke the night before. They all politely laughed as a few recounted the events.

I tried to stay present in the conversation, but it took significant effort. I was grateful when it was time to start the meeting.

"Let's get down to brass tacks," said the CEO of Live4Love.

The woman to his right, legal, slid three manilla file folders over to me, Mark, and Elaine.

"Just a standard NDA. I hope you understand."

"Haven't we already signed one?" I asked.

"This is a revised version based on the conversations we will have today," she said without blinking an eye. I thought back to the rumors Mark shared with me but shook my head, dismissing my unease. I signed the document and looked up to find Mark and Elaine sitting alert. Their backs were straight, and they held their hands in their lap. Something felt off.

The CEO of Live4Love began the conversation. "To be honest, we were already excited to partner with Ever Before, but after speaking with Mark and Elaine, it has become increasingly apparent that your company has the potential for even greater success. We have spent years trying to develop the technology that Mark and his small team of developers have created in only a few short years."

It was true. Our technology was impressive. Our app not only provided the ability to chat with a counselor in real time, but it also used an algorithm that provided suggestions for content and could pair users with counselors. It was wildly advanced.

"We would like to buy you out."

I looked to Mark and Elaine for an explanation, but they were already peering inside a second set of file folders passed to each of us.

I opened mine, but before I could digest what was before me, Elaine shouted, "Holy shit!"

Trying to catch up, I glanced at the figure printed in front of me, and my mouth dropped. I had never seen so many zeros. Turning to my partners, I watched as they exchanged excited glances.

I stared down at the number again and then shut the file. "We are not selling," I said.

The execs from Live4Love did not respond. They knew that the best way to win was to stay silent.

"But Helen," Elaine said. "This is a lot of money. We could retire."

"I don't want to retire," I said, ignoring Elaine. I stayed stoic and made unwavering eye contact with the Live4Love team.

Finally, the CEO spoke up. "And you won't have to. If you read the terms, we are willing to maintain fifty percent of your workforce. We would gladly make room for you. You would no longer be an owner, but you'd be a leader here at Live4Love." He gestured with his hands at the expansive building in which the conference room was located.

"Absolutely not. If you only keep fifty percent of our workforce, that means over fifty people will lose their jobs."

We had grown our team to over a hundred people over the years, and those people were my family.

"Yes, but we will help you develop an attractive severance package," said the man who earlier introduced himself as the Chief Human Resource Officer.

"No. I came here to talk about a partnership—not selling my company."

The room was silent.

"Why don't you sleep on it? Take some time. Tour our facilities. Talk to our teams. I'm sure you will be more than impressed with what we have built here."

"But why? Why do you want my company?" I asked.

Mark finally spoke up. "It isn't only your company, Helen."

I felt blindsided. It was now apparent that Mark and Elaine were in on this. How could they?

I snapped. "Why does it feel like while I was in Charlotte, keeping things afloat, you and Elaine were here brokering a secret deal?"

Elaine looked down. Mark only made that comment in the car to feel me out and warm me up to the idea.

"We are not selling." I rose from my seat and headed out the door. Righteous indignation fueled every step, and after more than twenty-four hours awake, I needed it. I was near the exit when Elaine caught up with me and grabbed my arm.

"What the hell? What was that Helen? I want to retire. Doesn't it sound nice? Retirement before forty?"

I pulled my arm away and stepped outside. Elaine continued to follow me.

"No, it doesn't sound nice," I hissed, spinning to face her. "This company is all I have. I don't want to see it ripped apart by those jackasses." At the sidewalk's edge, I raised my arm to call a taxi.

"Where are you going?"

"Home. I need to get back to Josie."

When the taxi pulled up, I climbed inside and glared at Elaine. I wanted her to know exactly how I felt about her deception.

I wouldn't sell. I was not about to let a string of zeros compromise the company we built. Mark and Elaine should have been ashamed of themselves.

On the flight home, my head pounded, and the monster inside roared with rage. How could they? And now, a deal that meant a lot for our company was probably off the table. I ran my fingers through my hair, my agitation building, and my elbow hit the hand of the passenger next to me. Whisky and coke sloshed out of his cup and onto my shirt and face.

"Fuck!" I yelled, shaking my wet hands in front of me.

"Holy shit! That drink was like ten dollars."

"I'll give you ten dollars if you shut up," I hissed.

The man with the empty cup glared at me. "What is wrong with you?"

A lot. A lot is wrong with me.

A flight attendant came over to help clean the mess, and after I was mostly dry, I fished a credit card out of my wallet and handed it to her.

"Anything this guy wants, put it on this."

I arrived in Charlotte after midnight, and it seemed like the universe was still out to get me. My carry-on got stuck in the overhead bin, and it took the combined efforts of two flight attendants and one sympathetic passenger to free it. All the while, a restless group, desperate to catch their connecting flight, griped behind us. Then I unwittingly climbed into the wrong taxi, which was only apparent after a bewildering detour twenty minutes out of the way. By the time I arrived home, I was so irritable I couldn't think straight, and after punching the wrong code into my security system three times, the blaring alarm sent me over the edge. Overwhelmed, I sunk to the floor, succumbing to a surge of uncontrollable sobs while the alarm's piercing sound cut through the air like a serrated blade.

After the police left, I ascended to my bedroom, feeling the weight of exhaustion. Having been awake for over forty consecutive hours, my fatigue felt bone deep. The familiar energy Josie brought into our home was missing, and I felt the urge to open her bedroom door and wrap myself in her blankets.

I sighed and turned the doorknob, allowing a sliver of anticipation to mingle with my weariness, but what I saw was devastating. I was met with a nearly empty room. I would have thought someone had robbed us if it weren't for the fact that the rest of the house was intact. The only things left in her room were artifacts she had long outgrown and an envelope placed on her bare mattress. As I approached her bed, I recognized my name written in Josie's sloppy handwriting, but it didn't say Mom. It said *Helen*.

CHAPTER 44

Present Day

I sit in Jacqueline's office, waiting for her to tell me what she knows. I need her to fill in the large craters between the memories that recently surfaced. The office seems to hold its breath, crawling with unspoken truths.

"This information is public. All you have to do is google it." Jacqueline spoke matter-of-factly. Her fingers deftly pick up a stack of papers and shuffle through them purposefully.

"As you already know, your name is Helen Joy Birch, and you were born on January 1, 1987. You gave birth to your oldest daughter, Josephine Lucille Birch, when you were sixteen. At that time, you lived in Rock Springs, Wyoming. Your life before her birth is a mystery. Unfortunately, I can't tell you much about it."

I do the mental math. "So, my daughter is nineteen? She's an adult?" The realization of time passing and the swift transition from child to adult causes a complex blend of questions and emotions to flood my head.

"Yes. It appears she is a full-time student at the University of North Carolina School of Arts. In a local newspaper article, it says she played a major role in the fall production of Lucy Prebble's Enron. A significant achievement, given she was only a freshman."

I don't remember any of this, but my heart fills with pride.

"Does she know I'm here?"

"That I don't know, and we can't tell her without your permission. But, if you want, I can try to help you reach her."

I think about it, but something tells me not to. That I should keep this from her.

"But what about my other daughter? The one who died?" I ask.

Jacqueline looks at me and holds me in her soft blue eyes for a moment. She is assessing her delivery but doesn't need to. I have already experienced the flood of grief that came with remembering her life and my loss.

"Raina Olivia Miller died at five months old on December 23, 2005. Your ex-husband, Andrew Miller, was charged with her murder. He pled guilty in 2007. He was sentenced to sixteen years but was released after six years due to good behavior."

"And where is he now?"

I flashback to a moment when Andrew had his hands in my hair. I hear the word bitch in my ear.

"He's dead. He died of a heart attack only two years after being released."

The rush of information is difficult to process.

"Now, you don't have a social media presence," Jacqueline continues, "which is interesting given your position."

"My position?"

"Yes. You co-founded an extraordinarily successful online relationship counseling app. I have colleagues who recommend your app to their clients."

"An app?" The jump from a grieving mother to a successful entrepreneur doesn't make sense. Maybe she is mixing me up with someone else? Could it be someone with the same name?

"It's called Ever Before. You have this catchy little slogan that goes something like, 'Your happily ever after begins with Ever Before.' Usually, when someone is part of a successful startup, they prioritize their personal brand as much as their company's brand. You seem to have left that all to your cofounders."

"Cofounders?"

"Mark Van Warren and Elaine Pierce. These two people seem to be in the spotlight. There are countless articles about your company's growth, but they rarely mention you. I was fortunate to find this article."

She hands me the printed article with my photo. The title reads, *Who is Helen Birch? The cofounder of Ever Before stays hidden from the spotlight.*

"It's one of those one-off websites covering obscure news. It reads more like a gossip column and doesn't provide anything but speculation, but it does mention your deceased daughter."

"Are you sure this is me?" I ask, even though it is clearly my face in this photograph.

"Yes, I am sure."

I'd been certain that if she told me what she knew, it would all come into focus. But I still only have flashes of memories, and none are complete or coherent. My head spins and throbs as I process the information. I need to get out of here. I need to find my daughter. I can't put this puzzle together while confined within a hospital. Maybe if I say I remember, she will let me leave. I know enough. I can bullshit the rest.

I widen my eyes and drop my jaw to appear as if I am experiencing a revelation. "I remember everything. I remember why I attempted suicide, my daughter Josie, and the company I built, Ever After."

"Ever Before," Jacqueline corrects me.

"That's what I meant. Of course, it's still a little fuzzy, but I remember it all."

Jacqueline studies me. She is skeptical.

"Great!" she says. She examines me a moment more before moving on. "Now, we do the hard part. We work through the trauma that got you here in the first place."

My stomach sinks. This was not supposed to happen. "Fine! I don't remember, but I want to leave."

"I've told you why that is not a good idea," she warns.

Biting my lip, I weigh my options. "It's just all so overwhelming. I don't think I can do this anymore. It's too much."

"I understand that this is uncomfortable, but healing always is, and based on the little bit I know about you, I know you can do this."

I gaze around the office, trying to avoid the inevitable, but I know I can't. I swallow the lump in my throat and look directly into Jacqueline's eyes.

"Okay. I'll try."

CHAPTER 45

Before Helen Lost Her Memory

Josie's letter taunted me through the night. I could hear her words. Words imagined. Angry words that would end me. So, I resisted the urge to read them. Instead, in the morning, I called and texted her, but she wouldn't answer. So, I called her best friend, Madison, who was the daughter of Lisa, one of our employees. Lisa was a gossip. She was Elaine's hire. Not mine.

Madison picked up on the first ring. I didn't want to embarrass Josie, but I needed to know she was okay.

"Hey, Ms. Birch."

"Hi Madison, how are things? How's your mom? I haven't seen her in a while now that she works on the other side of the building." My voice was peppy and bright. It was an act.

"She's good! Everything is going fine," Madison said.

"Oh, well, good! Have you heard from Josie? We got in a bit of a tiff, and she won't answer my calls," I said downplaying our fight.

Madison's long pause told me she knew what tiff I was referencing. "Uh. Yeah. She is staying with Bridget. They had an extra room, so Josie moved in."

"But, she's okay?" I asked.

"Yeah, totally. She's great."

"Thanks, Madison. Also, could we keep this between us? I don't want your mom asking me questions at work or anything."

"Oh yeah, I won't tell her. If I did, everyone would know."

I hung up the phone, and my hand dropped heavily to my side. Josie was okay. That was all that mattered.

Although I managed to get a few hours of sleep the night before, I was still so exhausted that my hands shook as I dressed for work. I was going to go in and pretend nothing had happened. Maybe Elaine and Mark would, too. Maybe they would see it as forgiveness, and we could go about business as usual.

At the office, Chelsea greeted me. "Coffee?" she asked, blissfully unaware of the turmoil inside me.

My shoulders dropped with relief. Something easy. I would need copious amounts of caffeine to get through the day. "Yes, please."

I worked in my office for several hours. All my meetings were in the afternoon since Elaine and Mark wouldn't be returning until mid-morning.

Just before lunch, Chelsea popped her head into my office. "Ms. Birch, Mark called. He wants you to meet him in his office."

What a power play. His office. I could play this game too. "Tell Mark I'm grabbing lunch first, and then I will be by."

I smiled and headed to the café across the street to clear my mind. *Serves him right.*

In the café, I stared out the large glass windows at my booth. A mother and her daughter, probably five or six years old, sat on a bench outside, enjoying large ice cream cones. I pictured myself and Josie in the pairing and longed for the days when she was little. She was my world, and I had been hers ... up until now. According to Josie, she didn't know me. I remember thinking the same thing about my mother. I never knew the real her. I only knew her addiction and her tendencies, but I never knew her. And even more so, I never understood her. Was that how Josie felt about me?

I held off on returning to the office to talk to Mark for as long as possible, but eventually, I couldn't avoid it anymore. So, I cleaned up the mess from my lettuce wrap and headed back across the street.

When I walked into Mark's office, Elaine was sitting on the edge of Mark's desk, and Mark was in his office chair. They were talking but stopped the moment I walked in.

"It's like that now?" I crossed my arms.

"What are you talking about, Helen? Gosh, paranoid much?" Elaine laughed off my remark and took a seat in one of the two chairs in front of Mark's desk. I took the other seat.

"After what you two pulled in California, I'm still in shock. Why would you do that to me?"

Marks lips formed a tight line, and his eyebrows came together. "We thought you would be happy. You've worked so hard, and we thought maybe you would be grateful for the opportunity. Also, it would be good for us to get a break, and it would be even better for Jazz. She wants me home more." Mark was referring to his wife.

I needed to check my ego. These were my friends. I was being too harsh. "I get it, but you can't surprise me like that," I said, my tone softening.

Elaine held up her hand. "We know that now."

"Good! I'm glad that's over." I felt so much relief. It was one less thing to stress about.

Mark and Elaine exchanged glances again.

"What? What are you not telling me?"

"Don't be mad, Helen. Ed and I want to travel, and Mark wants to spend more time with the five leeches he created."

"Hey!" Mark said as she winked at him.

"Helen, we own the majority of the company—the majority of the shares. I spoke with our lawyer this morning. You don't have a choice. We are selling."

I raised my arms and pushed my fingers into my hair. "I don't have a choice?"

Elaine's head shook while Mark's gaze shifted downward.

I walked out of Mark's office, unsure of how this could be happening. They were really going to sell, and I couldn't stop them.

I was engulfed by powerlessness. Doubt and confusion gnawed at my thoughts. As I passed each office, I considered the person inside. We were a team. How could Elaine and Mark, my best friends and partners, do this to them?

I returned to my office, and before shutting my door, I called out to Chelsea. "Cancel my meetings. I have a fire to put out." I crumbled to the ground as thoughts about all the things that had gone wrong raced through my mind. I wanted someone to blame but could only blame myself. I lied to Josie, and I put too much trust in Mark and Elaine. I should have known better. I had brought devastation down on myself and others for as long as I could remember. When would I learn?

Utterly exhausted, I closed my eyes, but the tangled web of thoughts wouldn't cease. One thought untangled itself from the rest. I plucked it from the web and examined it closer.

I want to die.

Chapter 46

In the following weeks, a haze of numbness enveloped me, and I found myself mechanically navigating through the demands of regular life. I sent emails, reviewed reports, and attended meetings, all while operating on autopilot. Beneath the surface, anger simmered, but I didn't know what to do with it this time.

It had been two weeks since Josie revealed what she learned and two weeks since my partners decided to sell my company. It had also been two weeks of unrelenting insomnia. I couldn't sleep. At night, the sheets strangled my legs, and my pajamas, wet with sweat, clung to my skin. Josie's face, colored by disappointment and heartbreak, haunted my sporadic dreams.

It had been two weeks since I could eat properly, and consuming food was now an arduous ordeal. Each bite required every ounce of energy I possessed. The food would stick in my throat, gummy and dense, and I'd have to force myself to chew and swallow.

It had been two weeks of my stomach being twisted in knots and my head aching with each breath I took. The constant throb within my skull felt like the encore of an intense rave.

Although my partners' disloyalty was minor compared to the betrayals of my past life, this was harder. I saw no way forward. The monster I carried within roared and abused my insides, and I was sick from the constant beating.

I found myself thinking a lot about Momma. Over the last two weeks, I couldn't help but draw unsettling parallels between her choices and my actions. I was no better than my mother. She denied me answers, but hadn't I done the same to Josie? She chose her addiction over her children, but hadn't I chosen my fear over Josie being part of a family? I needed to talk to Momma. I needed to understand her so I could understand myself, and as much as I didn't want to admit it, I loved her, which meant maybe Josie still loved me. Maybe it wasn't too late.

I had let down so many people in my quest to be different that I somehow fell into the same trap as my mother. And, now today, I would contribute to the impending letdown of more people who deserved better. We were supposed to put together a plan for the acquisition of our company. No one knew what was coming, and in the days leading up to now, when I sat in our team meetings, my mind wandered to the faces of those sitting around the table. Each person believed in our mission and in us, and now their lives were about to be profoundly impacted. I couldn't do it. I didn't want to be a part of it, so I called Chelsea on my drive to work that morning.

"Good morning Ms. Birch. What can I help you with?" Chelsea sounded chipper and happy.

"Hey, Chelsea. Listen, I can't come in today. I'm not feeling well. I think I caught a stomach bug. Will you cancel my meetings?"

"Sure, but what do you want me to do about Mark? He said today's afternoon meeting was important. Can I do something to help?"

"You know Chelsea, actually you can. Tell Mark to eat shit." The weight I carried started to feel lighter.

"Um. Really?"

"Yeah, tell him to open his fat gullet and swallow an ungodly amount of shit," I laughed.

"Are you okay, Ms. Birch?" Chelsea's voice was full of confusion.

"I'm great, Chelsea, just great! Have a good day. I'll see you tomorrow." I could tell that the sudden change in my behavior unsettled her, but it felt good. I ended the call and laughed wildly.

"Eat shit, Mark!" I yelled into the cab of my car.

A moment later, I thought of one more thing and called Chelsea again. "Hey, Chelsea. I need one more favor. Could you find someone for me? I don't know how hard it will be, but could you try?"

"Uh … sure. Who?"

"Amy Michelle Walker."

"Is she a relative?"

"She's my mother. I don't know where she lives or anything else about her life, but could you try to find her phone number?"

"On it."

"Thank you, Chelsea."

Traffic was at a standstill because of an accident up ahead. Three vehicles had collided, smashed to pieces, and a thought entered my mind. I wished it were me. I wished I was dead. I shook my head to dismiss the idea, unsettled that my mind had gone to that dark place again.

As I drew closer to the accident, another image flooded in. My body. Lifeless and lying in the center of the road. The image was tantalizing. It would be a relief to no longer worry or hurt. I was tired. These thoughts weren't normal.

I parked my car, only to realize I was at Josie's school. I didn't remember choosing to come here. These gaps in my memory were occurring more regularly, and it was troubling. I phoned Chelsea and told her I wasn't coming into the office.

"Hello, Ms. Birch. How are you feeling?"

"Feeling?"

"You called to say you were staying home sick. Is there something else I can help you with?"

"I called you?" I asked.

"Yes. An hour ago. You said to move all your meetings and asked me to find some information for you."

My body went cold. When did I talk to her? I couldn't remember. I needed to sleep.

"Chelsea, I've got to go." I hung up before she could say goodbye and looked out over Josie's campus. Unlike the school I attended, this one was more modern and much larger. The library rose before me. Glass and vertical steel rods decorated its façade. I could just go in, find a place to sit and wait, and maybe I'd see her. If I could just talk to her, then I could sleep again. It was the last week of classes, so she was likely here. But knowing it would probably make things worse, I put my car in reverse and backed out of the parking lot.

On the drive home, I was careful to stay alert and aware of my surroundings. The problem was I couldn't get the picture of me lying on the highway out of my head. Maybe I could cause a single accident, like running into a brick building. I wouldn't harm anyone but myself. I searched for brick buildings without realizing I was doing so. The monster was eating me alive.

When I arrived home, I looked around for signs of Josie. No luck. She hadn't been here since the day she took her things. I moved into the kitchen and opened the fridge. I was not hungry, but it was something to do. My fridge was empty aside from a couple of protein shakes and old takeout I had ordered but could not eat. I took out the leftover lo mein and threw the Styrofoam box in the microwave.

Leaning against the counter, I waited. I wanted to fall asleep right there, but no matter how tired I was, I couldn't sleep. I only needed a couple of hours, but it wouldn't come.

I ambled to my bathroom. I'd been popping sleeping pills like Advil, and they put me to sleep but couldn't keep me there. Regardless, I had to try again. I opened my medicine cabinet and reached for the sleeping pills. Shaking two into my hand, I stared at them for a minute before swallowing them dry. I wandered back to the living room and slumped onto the sofa. At least on the sofa, my sheets couldn't strangle me.

A beep from the microwave launched me out of sleep. I looked around wildly, expecting Josie to pop out from around the corner. But the house was quiet. She wasn't coming home. I looked down to find the bottle of sleeping pills in my hand. How long had I been asleep? The clock above the mantel said 11:00 a.m. Surely, I hadn't been asleep for long. I searched my mind for the day's events but came up short. The microwave beeped again.

"Shut up!" I yelled.

I was so tired.

I stumbled to the kitchen and opened the microwave door to find a container of leftover lo mein. I didn't remember putting it in there, so I took it out and threw it away. Although I didn't drink often, and never more than one, I reached into my small liquor cabinet to grab a bottle of vodka. I only kept these spirits on hand for entertaining, even though the only people I entertained were Mark, Elaine, and their families.

"Who will drink my vodka now?" I threw my hands up as if the inanimate objects in the room would answer my question. I took the vodka to the bathroom and peered into my medicine cabinet. I needed to sleep. I was desperate.

I brought the bottle of vodka to my lips and tilted my head back. The vodka burned the back of my throat, and I stifled a gag. I put the bottle in the sink while I rummaged through years of collected medications. One after another, I threw bottles of prescriptions and over-the-counter meds into my sink. Everything and the bathroom sink. Unrestrained laughter erupted from my chest. It was so funny.

Some of these pills were over ten years old, which probably impacted their efficacy. I opened bottle after bottle, swallowing the contents and following it with a big gulp of vodka. I would finally get some sleep.

I topped off my sleep cocktail with a bottle of nighttime cold medicine and returned to the sofa. I liked my sofa. Josie and I had spent hours in a furniture store, laying on sectionals, recliners, and sofas until we found the perfect one. It was the most fun – shopping ... for furniture.

On my coffee table was the letter Josie had written. I picked it up. It was time to read it. I sat back, and the room began to spin. I tried to peel the envelope open, but my vision was fading. Gripping the letter tightly, the room faded to black. It was time to sleep.

An earthquake brought me back to consciousness. My throat burned, and the smell of vomit permeated the air.

"Helen, Helen! Wake up, Helen!" a voice screamed, but it was so far away. I tried to open my eyes to see who it belonged to, but I couldn't. My body convulsed, but nothing happened. Then I shook involuntarily again. I was choking, and stale putrid liquid bubbled up.

Something in my throat made me heave again. What was that? I opened my eyes for a fleeting moment and saw Chelsea. She was crying and screaming, and her hand was in my mouth, choking me. I wanted to fight her. Yell at her. Leave me alone! I need to sleep! I'm tired! But my muscles were weak, and I couldn't speak. My stomach lurched again, but nothing came up. And then it went black.

CHAPTER 47

Present Day

"How do you feel now?" Jacqueline asks.

I think about it. I had just explained to Jacqueline how my perception of my mother had transformed throughout the seasons of our life together. I don't know the last time I talked to my mother, but I know through it all, I loved her.

"Guilty," I say.

I bite at my thumb nail. The nail is so low that the skin where my nail once was is raw and pink.

Jacqueline regards me for a moment.

"Why do you feel guilty?"

"I don't know." I begin to fidget.

Although I have such large gaps in my memory, there are these universal truths, emotions embedded so deep within my psyche I know them to be true. The guilt coats my skin and seeps through, filling my organs.

"Let's focus on that feeling. The feeling of guilt. I want you to hold that feeling in your mind. Find another place or time in which you felt guilty."

I sit with the feeling of guilt. I am careful to sift any other emotions away from the guilt so it is raw and pure. There is no particular moment in which guilt isn't familiar. I can't pinpoint one. I have always felt guilty.

"All the time."

"All the time?" she repeats.

I swallow the saliva in my mouth, although it is not much. My mouth is as dry as the desert. "I have felt guilty every moment of my life—at least every moment I can remember."

"Can you be more specific?"

It's impossible when this tapestry of self-blame is all woven together, but I pick apart the threads, trying to expose them.

"When Momma would cry. When social services came to our home. When Andrew lost his temper. When I left Tyler. When I left Lucy. When I failed to protect Nathan. When Josie went to foster care. When Raina died. I felt guilt for all of those things. It was me. I either did those things or failed to prevent them."

"So, the things you listed. You think they are your fault?"

I look away from Jacqueline, ashamed of all I have done. "Yes. I do."

"It must be nice to be so powerful that everything is your fault." Jacqueline looks at me, unblinking.

My brows come together as I try to understand what she is saying. Powerful? I'm not powerful.

"I must tell you, Helen. How you feel is normal. Anyone who has been through such traumatic events would likely feel the same, but I think it is important to understand guilt because guilt is about remorse. We feel guilt when we are aware we have done something wrong."

My gaze travels back to her face. She sees through me again. Her translucent eyes seem waterier than before.

"Based on what I know and what you have told me, you have done nothing wrong. Sure, you made mistakes. We all make mistakes. We are human, but all those things you listed, you weren't at fault for any of them."

I nod, although I disagree.

"Often when we say guilt, what we really mean is shame. Shame is painful, but it is not guilt. Shame is based on belief, not fact."

"What does it matter? Guilt, shame, it's all the same," I say.

Jacqueline licks her lips and taps her foot on the ground. She is getting impatient. "Helen, can we agree that you were not at fault for any of the things you listed?"

I press my lips together, unwilling to release the blame.

"You did not cause those things to happen. What you feel is shame. Let me ask you a question. If you were in my seat, looking at a woman who has experienced all the things you have, would you blame her? Would you be unkind to her? Would you think she is a bad person?"

I want to say yes because I know that woman is me, but I push myself to imagine a woman who is not me. A woman who has the exact same story. How would I feel about her? But instead of a woman, I see a young girl sitting in front of me. She has frizzy brown hair and freckles on her face.

UNTITLED FOR NOW

She looks like autumn but yearns to be summer. She is me many moons ago.

"She was only a girl. She never deserved any of that," I whisper and tears spill down over my cheeks.

"You're right. She didn't. You didn't."

When our time is up, I head back to my room. Jacqueline says I don't have to do group therapy today if I'm not up for it. She has decided to move her schedule around and will see me again tomorrow.

Ashley is in our room braiding her hair when I enter, and I'm so glad to see her.

"You're okay," Ashley observes.

"Much better than yesterday," I tell her.

"You know, I always say each day is an opportunity to be better than you were the day before."

I raise an eyebrow at her. It doesn't sound like something she would say.

She laughs, knowing. "Okay, my dad says that. Speaking of …" Ashley straightens her legs and flexes her toes. "My dad is going to be here in a couple of hours. I'm going home."

My heart flutters, and I feel a mild panic frothing toward the top. "But why?"

She shrugs her shoulders. "I'm no longer a danger to myself or others, which is mostly true. So, they are transferring me to an outpatient program."

I crawl onto my bed, using the action to gather my thoughts. "But I don't want you to leave."

Ashley's eyebrows shoot up. "Why?" she asks.

"Because you're my friend."

As much as I hate this place, Ashley makes it bearable, and I don't want to go back to how it was without her. My heart pounds a little harder. I can't explain why this is so hard, but I don't want her to leave me.

"I'm sorry," she says, and I realize I'm being ridiculous.

"No, I'm sorry. I was just surprised, but I'm going to miss you."

Ashley takes out her notebook and a pencil and writes something on one of the pages. She rips the paper away from the spiral binding and hands it to me. It's her phone number.

"Call me when you get out," she says.

"Really?"

"Uh, yeah! I need to know the title of your story."

I take a minute, but then I remember. I said it was untitled, and she said for now.

"I remembered quite a bit," I say.

"Is that why you lost your shit? I thought that bitchy lady just freaked you out."

"Well, she did, but I also remembered things." And for the next hour, I tell Ashley what I know to be true and about my session with Jacqueline.

"She's right," Ashley says. "You're not responsible for any of it."

Hearing it twice somehow solidifies it as fact. A light knock at our door, which was already ajar, alerts Ashley that it is time to go meet with her case worker before being discharged. The nurse gives us time to say goodbye, and we hug in the center of our room. I'm sad to see her go, but it's okay. Sometimes people come into your life for a reason. They have a purpose. Once they fulfill it, it's time to move on.

As she walks out the door, she looks back. Her expression is mixed—half sad and half reassuring. Then, something happens. One moment her face is clear before me, but then it glitches, and another face is there. A girl with dyed black hair and large brown eyes stands before me.

Ashley is gone when it all rushes in. I stand affixed to the ground as the memories swim around my head. The crevasses of my mind fill rapidly with a cerebral liquid containing iridescent images of all the things I'd forgotten. Picnics at the park. Josie's curly blonde hair poking out beneath a large, rimmed sun hat too big for her head. Dancing in our small kitchen and eating popcorn in bed. She is on stage performing, and I am so overwhelmed by her talent that I weep. Josie's at her first homecoming dance and her high school graduation. She's rolling her eyes as I beam with pride and ask for just one more picture. Josie and her friends piled into my car on our way to buy spa day supplies and snacks. Singing to the music, I tell myself to always hold space in my heart and mind for this memory.

They come so suddenly that I must hold my breath, fearing they will all evaporate. I see so much joy—joy I didn't know I had.

But then I see it. Josie's disappointment in me. Her hurt. I betrayed her, and she couldn't forgive me. The images of joy vanish instantly. It is my fault. This is not shame. This is guilt.

CHAPTER 48

Present Day

Electrons pulsate through me, and the energy has nowhere to escape causing my hands to shake. Chelsea, my assistant, meets me at the hospital entrance with my social worker, who delivers a plan for outpatient care. Chelsea is the young woman who took me to the emergency room and saved my life.

She says she was worried after I instructed her to tell Mark to eat shit and then forgot I had already called her. I want to laugh and play it off as nothing serious, but I let her tell me what happened.

"I just had this feeling that you weren't okay. I don't know. I felt bad for going to your house unannounced. You're such a private person, but I'm really glad I did."

I'm glad she did too.

In Chelsea's car, I struggle to make conversation. This woman quite literally walked into my home and found me heavily sedated on the edge of death's cliff. She says at one point, she was certain I had stopped breathing. Ashamed that she found me like that, I change the topic and ask about work.

"It's going," she says, shrugging her shoulders and letting out a rush of air. "I don't know exactly what is going on, but I know enough. Enough to know not to trust Mark and Elaine. FYI, they think you booked a last-minute trip to Bora Bora."

We pull into my driveway, and I sigh as she walks me inside.

"Are you sure you don't want me to stay?" she asks. "I can totally stay."

"No, I'm okay. Thank you."

She dawdles, and I know she is afraid to leave me alone.

I grab her hands and hold them in mine. I feel so bad for putting her in this position, but I'm so thankful for her. If I know anything to be true, it is that even with all the ugly, there are still good people in this world.

"I'm going to be okay. I promise. Please don't worry. I can't thank you enough. I wouldn't be here right now if it wasn't for you."

Chelsea gives me a tight smile, and I release her hands. Then she reaches into her purse.

"I'm scared to give this to you. I'm not sure why." She holds out a piece of paper folded in half.

"What is it?"

"You asked me to find someone. Amy Michelle Walker, your mother."

I look inside and see my mother's name, address, and phone number. She is still in Rock Springs.

"Also, you were holding this when I found you."

Chelsea pulls out the letter from Josie. I stare at the letter for a moment too long, scared to take it. My fingers reach out for the soft paper envelope. I can't avoid it anymore.

In the hospital, I felt lost. And although the revelation that I'd hurt Josie nearly sent me back into another downward spiral, the rush of memories from our life together, even amidst all the lies, kept me afloat.

My life was so full of suffering but also so full of happiness. I did it. I built a life far better than anything I could have ever imagined. And even though I am lost right now, I know I would rather be lost somewhere beautiful than arrive at a desolate place.

Once Chelsea is gone, I scan the contents of my house. The last time I was here, I could barely function. I still don't feel capable of much, but I feel better than I did on that day. Jacqueline believes I struggled with dissociation long before I lost my memory. She said to have come as far as I have is inspirational. But she also warned that what others would call resilience is a byproduct of dissociation and my endless need for validation. By allowing myself to become consumed by my work and providing a different type of life for Josie, I remained disconnected from myself. It's a coping strategy, but it's not sustainable.

I think about those rocks in the Betty Ford Rehab Center backpack. I'd been carrying around quite the load for an exceedingly long time. Now, holding Josie's letter in one hand and my mother's information in the other, it is time to unload those rocks. I lift one above the other alternatively. Eenyy, meeny, miny, moe. Momma wins.

I have to hunt for my phone, but I eventually find it dead in the microwave. How it got there, I have no idea. I put it on the charger and sit by, rocking back and forth. I am anxious, but I can do this. When my phone comes to life, I let out a rush of air and pick it up.

I worry I may be sick as I dial Momma's number, but with each ring, my stomach settles, and I convince myself she will not pick up.

"Hello?" a woman says.

"Momma?"

"Helen? Is that you?"

Something inside of me breaks open, and a rush of pent-up anxiety flows free. Wet, hot tears pour from my eyes.

"Oh, Helen! Are you okay? What's wrong?"

I sniffle, and when the words come out, they are froggy and hoarse. "No, Momma. I'm not okay."

Momma and I talk for over an hour. She's clean and has been for nearly ten years.

"I thought if I got clean, you and your sister might come back. But I waited too long to get my shit together," she says.

"Why didn't you try to find us?"

"I was scared that if I did, you would turn me away."

I can't fault her for feeling that way. I probably would have too. I hear the flick of the wheel as Momma ignites a lighter and, a moment later, the long drag of her cigarette.

"Can I be honest with you?" I ask.

"Yeah," she says, her voice croaky.

"I've loved you my whole life, even when I didn't want to. There were a lot of times that I hated myself for loving you. And there were even more times when I felt guilty because I loved you and hated you at the same time."

I hear a long exhale and the creak of a door hinge as I await a response.

"I was a shitty mom. Shit, my mom was a shitty mom. She loved us, sure, but we weren't reason enough to stay alive. For a long time, you weren't reason enough for me to stay clean. I've made a lot of bad decisions in my life, things I am still ashamed of. But, as long as I was high, I didn't have to feel the weight of my shortcomings. You and your sister should have been enough."

For the first time, I understand my mother. For years, I ran from the things that amplified my guilt, things I believed were a product of my shortcomings. I ran away, and Momma got high.

I'm not saying my mom is a good person or a bad person. She is just a person. A human who has and still is hurting, just like me. And in our reckless desperation to make the hurt more bearable, we left a trail of devastation behind us—collateral damage.

I think about her relationship with my dad. How she single-handedly disrupted our innocent relationship because she wanted to move. I need to ask her about it.

"Momma, why did you accuse Dad of being inappropriate when I was little?"

She coughs. "He told you? That asshole,"

I don't know why, but I laugh. "Someone needed to tell me," I say.

"Look, I'm not proud of what I did. My dad did things to me—my biological father. Not your grandpa. And the truth is, I felt trapped in North Carolina. I can't explain it, but if I had to stay there one more day, I would go insane. I know it isn't an excuse, and it probably doesn't make much sense to you, but your dad never did anything. He loved you, and I was selfish."

The sheer absurdity of it all hits me. I swallow a fit of laughter. Momma made certain that my father wouldn't be there for me or Lucy because she felt trapped. It makes no sense, but at the same time, I understand.

"You know I was mad when he told me? Mad that he didn't fight for me like I fought for Josie?"

"I get that."

"I think it's time I forgive him."

"I'm so sorry, Helen."

"It's okay, Momma. I'm also a shitty mom. I hid so much from Josie. I thought I was protecting her, but I was avoiding the things that caused me pain. It was selfish, and now, she won't talk to me. Maybe she'll call me in fifteen years ... if I'm lucky."

"Helen. I don't have a lot of advice to give. In fact, my best piece of advice is to be careful following any of my advice. But if I could offer one piece that I am certain is good. It would be to not wait fifteen years for your daughter to come to you. It's not worth the time lost."

When I'm done talking to Momma, I turn Josie's letter over in my hand. I'm not ready to read it, but I need to.

Opening the letter, I see Josie's words written carefully along the lined notebook paper. I take a deep breath and force myself to absorb the contents.

Dear Helen,

I'm calling you Helen in the hopes that one day, I can call you Mom again. As I write this letter, you feel like a stranger. I've never told you this, but my whole life, it felt like you weren't there even when you were right beside me. I don't know how else to explain it. I knew you loved me, but you remained disconnected.

You always talked about the future—the life we would have one day. I wanted you to be with me in the moment, but you never were. I didn't realize the reason you spent so much time looking ahead was because you feared what was behind you. I know that now, and the more I learn, the more questions I have. But I can't trust you to be honest with me. So, after finals, I'm leaving town to find answers. I know it seems extreme and dramatic, but I need to know you. I'll be back when I find my mom.

Love,

Josie

Her words crash down around me with the force of a ton of bricks, shattering the remains of the illusion I had carefully constructed for years. In my relentless pursuit of a better life, I had inadvertently denied Josie the essential connection she needed. I really was a lot like my mother. Not the same, but the common thread of our curses was undeniable.

I remember what Momma said. It isn't too late to break the curse. Josie is out there looking for me, and she won't find me if I stay put. Momma was right. I shouldn't wait for Josie to come to me.

I begin to formulate a plan. First, I message Lucy and then Tyler. They would have told me if Josie showed up, but I wanted to let them know, just in case. I have no idea where she's going. Momma didn't mention seeing her, so I can only assume she isn't in Rock Springs.

Next, I need to take care of my business. I can now see that selling Ever Before is in my best interest but won't let them blindside my team. I find my laptop, plug it in, and begin to type out my last email.

When I'm done, I call Chelsea.

"Is everything okay?"

"Everything is great. Can you do me a favor? Josie is in California, I think. I hope. Will you book the next available flight for me? I need to go find her." I have no way of knowing for certain that she is there, but I'll travel anywhere if it means being with her again.

"Sure. Is that all?"

"Once you finalize the travel details, can you send them to my personal email? And when you're done, will you transfer me to Mark or Elaine?

Whoever is available. Also, watch your email. You're going to want to see what comes in."

I wait on the phone while Chelsea books the flight.

"Elaine is available," she says. "I'm transferring you now."

I take a deep breath and wait for Elaine to answer.

"Hello?"

"Hey Elaine, it's Helen."

"Oh Helen, how was your trip?" She hesitates mid-question.

"You know I wasn't in Bora Bora. I'm sure that mousey bitch has already told the entire office where I was. But, since you asked, it was delightful. There's nothing like a failed suicide attempt followed by nearly two weeks in a mental hospital with no memory."

"Uh …"

"No need Elaine. I just want to let you know I've reconsidered the proposal, and I'm on board with selling to Live4Love."

"Really? I knew you would come around. You're my best friend, Helen. I don't know what I would do without you."

"Elaine, I'm not done speaking. I will sell, but I will not help with the mess you have on your hands."

"What mess?"

"Oh, you'll see." I end the call and push send on the email I drafted.

Dear colleagues,

For seven years, we have collectively built a company we can be proud of. Ever Before saves lives. I know this to be true because nearly twenty years ago, I was in an abusive relationship that resulted in the death of my youngest daughter. I have never forgiven myself for what happened, and I don't know if I ever will. This is all to say that the work you do is important. Whether you answer the phones, write lines of code, or are one of our counselors, you have been integral in furthering the mission of Ever Before.

That is why I am saddened to share this news with you. As many of you know, we have been in talks with Live4Love about a potential partnership. Amid those talks, Elaine and Mark decided it was best to sell the company. I tried to fight it, but together, they own the majority. When the acquisition happens, half of you will lose your jobs. I'm telling you this because I cannot, in good consciousness, allow them to blindside you like they did me. I'm here for you should you need me.

With love,

Helen J. Birch

Pushing send on an email never felt so good. Breathing a sigh of relief, I go upstairs to pack a bag just as a text message from Lucy comes through.

Lucy: She left four days ago. Made me promise not to tell you. Don't hate me.
Me: I don't hate you. Do you know where she is now?
Lucy: She went to visit Tyler.

Good thing my flight is going in the right direction. I'm curious to see if Tyler texts me back.

When I am done packing, I hurry out of the house and into a taxi. The stillness of the car ride allows time for fear to snake its way into my chest. I grip the tops of my thighs and try to push past it, but it is too fast and engulfs me.

What if Josie learns who her mother really is and wants nothing to do with me? I know Jacqueline and Ashley said it wasn't my fault, but what if Josie thinks it is? What if she hates me when she learns of all the things I failed to prevent? Or all the ways I failed to protect her and her sister?

As the taxi pulls up to departures, I wipe my clammy hands on my pants and force myself out of the car, but the dread follows. Walking through the airport, I struggle with each step but press on. By the time I take my seat on the plane, I am sweating profusely, and my breathing is quick and shallow.

As the last of the passengers trickle onto the plane, I want to jump up and exit. I don't think I can do this. Just as I'm about to stand, an elderly gentleman sits down next to me, blocking the aisle. A familiar scent wafts up to my nose. Spearmint, Old Spice, and piney pomade. The fragrance washes over me, and I breathe it in carefully, hoping he doesn't notice. What are the odds that a man who smells like Billy Ray would sit next to me? I close my eyes, and I can hear my dear friend's voice as clearly as the day we sat in his taxi and I told him I was pregnant with Josie.

I promise you, Helen. This is not the end.

I press a palm to my heart. Its rhythm slows, and a gentle smile plays at my lips.

All right, dear friend. I hear you.

Just as we're about to take off, a message from Tyler comes through.

Tyler: Josie left yesterday. She had a lot of questions, and I know you are going to hate me, but I answered them all. She is now headed down to our old stomping ground.

Me: You and Lucy must be talking. Like I told her, I don't hate you. Thank you for telling me where she went.

Josie needed to hear the truth from people who were not me. But when I find her, I'm going to tell her everything Tyler and Lucy missed. Everything. It was time to face my pain. Tyler only needed to say old stomping ground for me to know exactly where to find her.

It is morning by the time I arrive, and the familiar desert air lingers on my skin. Although the air is warm, goosebumps appear along my arms, and I run my hands along the length of them, trying to reduce the prickly sensation. I park in the gravel driveway of the house that still belongs to my grandpa. The metal flowers with spinning petals still line the driveway, but the house is now painted a soft blue. I hear the crunch of the gravel under my feet as I move toward the house. I knock on the door.

"Who's there?" a loud, gruff voice calls from inside.

"Grandpa?" I wait a moment.

"Are your hands broken?" he yells back.

I shake my head and laugh.

Twisting the doorknob, I anticipate being transported back in time, but when I open the door, I barely recognize the place. The furniture is new and arranged differently than I remember. The photos that always hung on the wall have doubled, and the carpets are now a soft beige rather than dark green. The only familiarity comes from the old Filipino man with salt and pepper hair sitting at the old kitchen table.

"Hey, Rugrat," he says.

"Hey, Grandpa."

"You looking for Josie?"

I bite my bottom lip and nod. Although I'm surer of myself than I was when I boarded the plane, I am still terrified of what she may think of me.

Grandpa leans forward in his seat and places a hand on a knee. "I told her how you loved the desert when you were a kid and how you spent hours in that lot playing pretend and collecting seashells. She walked down there just a bit ago to check it out."

I stand there, unsure of what to say next. I want to apologize for all the years I was gone, for pushing him away with everyone else, but I don't know where to start.

Before I can process these thoughts fully, he says, "It's all right, Rugrat. Go get your girl. I'll be here when you're done."

I tip my head and spin on my heels to go find Josie. As I walk down the familiar street, I can't help but notice that much of the cul-de-sac is the same. The asphalt still crumbles into the dirt along the sides of the road, a familiar swing set sits rusted and falling apart in a yard, and abandoned vehicles take space in empty lots. The houses are still in rough shape, although the poverty-stricken area has worsened since I was here last. Beyond the end of the street, the desert lot still lies undeveloped, and I can see a figure sitting on a dune far in the distance.

I want to run to her, but I force myself to walk. I need to be present in this moment because this moment, right here, is the most important one of my life. So, I take my time and feel everything I have pushed down and disguised for so long. The guilt, the anger, the pain, and tremendous grief course over me with each step.

I'm nervous as I approach the young girl who, for the first time, is beginning to understand where her mom came from. When she looks at me, I wait for words that will inevitably sting, but she doesn't speak. Instead, she pats the ground next to her. The sand is still cool from the night before. In her hand she holds one-third of a postcard with faded palm trees printed on one side. Her hand finds mine, and she steals a glance at me before staring out at the desert landscape. I sit upright, prepared for the blow, but her words surprise me.

"I forgive you," she whispers.

It is not what I expect, but perhaps it is what I deserve.

If she can forgive me, maybe it is time I finally forgive myself.

GET EXCLUSIVE CONTENT FROM DESIREE MOORE

I invite you to become a valued member of my VIP Readers Club. Join today to gain access to exclusive content, exciting updates on new books, and a **FREE Epilogue**. Dive back into the lives of Helen, Josie, and Lucy and witness their next step in healing.

To access the epilogue, simply sign up at my website.

Visit www.desireemoorebooks.com/readersclub to join.

Printed in Great Britain
by Amazon